Lifelong romanc— —
New Zealand. Writing feeds her very real ——
with happy endings and the endorphin rush they
create. You can follow her at jcharroway.com,
facebook.com/jcharroway, instagram.com/jcharroway
and twitter.com/jcharroway.

Cara Lockwood is the *USA TODAY* bestselling author
of more than eighteen books, including *I Do (But
I Don't)*, which was made into a Lifetime Original
movie. She's written the *Bard Academy* series for
young adults, and has had her work translated into
several languages around the world. Born and raised
in Dallas, Cara now lives near Chicago, with her
husband and their five children. Find out more about
her at caralockwood.com, 'friend' her on Facebook,
facebook.com/authorcaralockwood, or follow her on
Twitter, @caralockwood.

If you liked *Forbidden to Want* and *First Class Sin*
why not try

King's Rule by Jackie Ashenden
Playing with Fire by Rebecca Hunter

Discover more at millsandboon.co.uk.

FORBIDDEN TO WANT

JC HARROWAY

FIRST CLASS SIN

CARA LOCKWOOD

MILLS & BOON

First Published in Great Britain 2018
by Mills & Boon, an imprint of HarperCollins*Publishers*
1 London Bridge Street, London, SE1 9GF

Forbidden to Want © JC Harroway

First Class Sin © Cara Lockwood

ISBN: 978-0-263-27372-4

MIX
Paper from
responsible sources
FSC® C007454

This book is produced from independently certified FSC™ paper
to ensure responsible forest management.
For more information visit www.harpercollins.co.uk/green.

Printed and bound in Spain
by CPI, Barcelona

FORBIDDEN TO WANT

JC HARROWAY

MILLS & BOON

To romance readers—you're awesome.

CHAPTER ONE

Kit

THE DECISIVE RAP at the door drags my attention from the dreary, grey view of London in the drizzle and back to my computer screen.

'Just a minute.' I shoot a scowl at the closed door and curse the interruption.

I'm thirty, part-owner of the family business I share with my brothers and head of luxury hospitality. I shouldn't have to vet my own visitors or schedule my own appointments, but my assistant quit last week and I haven't yet worked up the enthusiasm to hire a replacement.

This week will be hard enough without having unexpected extras piled on my plate. No doubt Reid, my efficient eldest brother, has circulated a company-wide memo outlining why my appearance at the office and my regard for polite discourse might be a little more sporadic than usual. The benefit of being the grieving widower, the family fuck-up, is that my usual demeanour provides the perfect antidote to the trivial. Unless it's vital, people tend to steer clear.

'Yes?' I yell.

The Faulkner Group has many staff who could pander to my every administrative whim, but over the last three years I've managed to scare everyone off. Now only the brave venture close to my perpetual scowl for my signature on something my brothers deem important to the smooth running of our six London-based hotels.

Reid strides in, his thousand-pound suit immaculate and the air of authority his senior-sibling status grants him on display as if he wears a sandwich board emblazoned with his title: *Head of the Faulkner Group, oldest of three brothers, here to keep the runt of the litter in line.*

That I'm even physically in the office *this* week should appease the control freak in him, but one look at his expression tells me he expects more.

My back tenses, lifting the hairs above my collar. He's going to be disappointed—we Faulkners are cut from the same cloth.

'Kit, a moment…' It's not a question, a fact that slides sandpaper beneath my skin and rains nails down on my already tingling scalp.

I spin my chair from my view of the city, ready to hear him out with the minimum of interaction and then remind him of tomorrow's date.

He's not alone.

This adds hypodermic needles to the downpour

of nails. If he expects to add social interaction to my to-do list, he'll need to come back next week.

Fucking Reid. He's aware of my triggers. Understands how tightly I run my ship since my life turned to shit. I slide my scowl from my brother. Reid's companion is female.

My body perks up, an unwelcome slug of testosterone to the bloodstream, a half-arsed attempt at interest in the opposite sex. I've trained myself well in recent years. Forced myself to notice other pretty faces, appealing figures and interesting personalities.

She's tall. Striking. Long, dark hair and a tanned, make-up-less face. The outfit covers a lean, athletic body. High, full breasts, a tapered waist and enough generosity through the hips to scream woman—all clad in a T-shirt decorated with some Japanese Kanji symbols and a pair of black skinny jeans.

My libido stirs—she's a beautiful woman. And noticing beautiful women, scratching a mutual itch and moving on, is what I do now. *All* I do. For good, bad or ugly.

Still, if Reid thinks he's replacing my last assistant with this dressed-down beauty, he can think again. I have rules, and professional work attire is rule number one.

I raise my stare from her slender, denim-clad legs. *Who wears jeans to a job interview?* She's made my dismissal easy—I don't need an assistant. And this casually dressed stranger, however compelling, looks completely at odds with the Faulkner Group's workplace dress code.

I drag my body from the chair and straighten to my full six feet three inches to piss Reid off, who stands an inch below me, then slide the glare levelled on my brother to my visitor, dropping the annoyance in deference to her beauty.

'Kit, this is Mia Abbott.' Reid introduces the woman as if I'd been expecting her unconventional company.

My lips stretch with a flicker of greeting. Yes, she's striking, but she's superfluous to my current workplace requirements and, this week, a *definite* unwanted distraction.

Then she smiles.

I double-take.

Mia's wide smile transforms her face like floodlights switching on behind her dark eyes. I hold the air trapped in my chest and reassess the entire Mia Abbott package, my cock stirring despite my current state of mind.

She's mid-twenties, stunning in a way she probably doesn't know it, the sun-kissed, slightly upturned nose dotted with golden freckles. Her earthy dark eyes glow in the wake of that happy-go-lucky smile still hovering on her face, despite my less than welcoming reception, and her mouth… Fuck—full lips, naturally red, a perfect Cupid's bow.

Promising… I reassess my staffing needs despite the constant swirl of self-directed disgust that accompanies any thought of a sexual nature. Why couldn't Reid have introduced Mia next week, or any day after tomorrow?

Still, the timing isn't Mia's fault and perhaps she's not even here for me.

I take Mia Abbott's hand, my grasp firm and a fraction too long for polite convention. Her returning shake presses my fingers together in a strong, warm caress that's neither intimidated nor flirtatious. *Interesting...*

My eyes dart to her left hand...single.

The only flaw Mia seems to possess is her habitual fidgeting, her fingers drumming against her thigh at odds with the wide, confident smile and the assertive handshake. Sadly, she won't be around long enough for me to find *that* irritating. Working for me, if she makes the grade, won't be easy. I keep erratic hours, spend days at a time ignoring my phone and use sex to remedy the unfixable parts of my life. Of course, I'm a gentleman—no woman leaves my bed without her world completely rocked.

'Good to meet you,' she says, her smoky voice sexy and accented.

My eyes return to her full lips as I try to place her variation of English. 'Where are you from? Australia?' I could listen to her talk all day. I slide my palm from hers, disengaging from our formal greeting, and shift an inch closer. I'm rewarded with a warm wave of her scent—some sort of flowery shit, perhaps honeysuckle, and fresh air.

She laughs, an uninhibited throaty chuckle, as if I've said something hilarious. I freeze. It's been a long time since a woman laughed at me. Doesn't she understand the rules of the boss-assistant dynamic of polite deference? Or the less appropriate but honest subtle lick of those luscious lips while her amber-speckled stare dropped to the front of my trousers.

Perhaps she has no interest whatsoever in sleeping with an emotional train wreck and no unrealistic ambitions to fix me.

Well-played, Reid.

'I'm from New Zealand.' She shrugs. 'Trust me, there's a *big* difference.' Despite her semi-mocking smile, her seemingly calm assessment, the fine-boned fingers resume their fidgeting.

Perhaps she's not quite immune to the Faulkner charm after all...

But if she's sticking around, best she understand who's in charge from the get-go. It's *not* Reid, who seems to have come over all slack about the office dress code. I have rules. Rule number two—her rockin' body, her lively, mischievous stare and her pouty lips aside—our connection will work best with a bare minimum of communication. Especially over the next two days.

At the timely reminder of the date, my stomach rolls, sharp and unpleasant, banishing the Mia-directed kick of lust. For the thousandth time this morning I force my mind away from memories and in particular my anniversary. If only I could distract myself with the delectable Mia.

Nope.

Sex is off the table, at least until I've survived tomorrow.

Anyway, my libido was ahead of itself, because exotic Miss Abbott isn't looking at me with the level of interest I've grown to expect from members of the opposite sex. Hell, yes, I'm arrogant, but it's as if I had tattooed *emotionally unavailable widower* on my forehead three years ago in neon ink.

How do women know? I must give off some pheromone that tells them I'm only looking for no-strings sex—the hot, carnal fucking of all their fantasies. On *my* terms.

Of course, once they've experienced the ride, most of them think they can change me, although I'm clear about it from the outset. That they think they'll be the answer to all my problems, start imagining they can put a smile back on my face, *is* the problem.

Reid finally explains his Monday-morning Antipodean companion. 'I'm glad we found you here.' Shadows move behind his eyes, as if he can't decide between relief I'm where I should be and concern that my presence at work might tip me over the edge. He ploughs on. 'Mia will shadow you for three weeks. Can I leave you to give her the tour?'

Wait, three weeks? Shadow?

My shirt peels from my back as my muscles tense. Shelving the charm all three Faulkner brothers once possessed in spades, I question his highhandedness in front of the lady, my patience for his mistake non-existent. 'I'm afraid my brother has been a little premature, Ms Abbott. I'm not currently in the market for a new assistant. Sorry he's wasted both our time this morning.'

Mia's wide eyes flick to Reid, but her full mouth twists as if she and Reid are in on some private joke.

Am I amusing...?

Perhaps she can't decipher the cut-crystal nuances of the Etonian accent that cost my parents a fortune. The hairs on the back of my neck prickle. Who the hell is this woman, rocking up for an interview dressed like a student, only to find her potential future boss laughable? And what the fuck is going on in my brother's head? Refreshing, appealing, sexy—nothing makes up for frank insubordination.

'Oh, I'm not a PA.' Mia speaks, humour igniting the flecks of gold in her irises. Irises she then rolls. 'Wouldn't have the first clue how to organise you. And I'd suffocate in an office job.' Her amused stare scans my space and then settles on me.

So, this is a social visit and despite the cool way she's assessing me with her toffee-apple eyes, perhaps Mia is looking for some holiday fun...

Great! Lay down the rules, check she's on the same page of the casual sex manual and invite her out for a drink on Wednesday.

I ignore the rising heat in my groin—somehow

still a betrayal. My guts twist, pulled in two opposing directions.

I glare at my brother, an ache radiating through my face from teeth which are clamped together. 'Care to explain?' I'm tired of his interference. I'm not a total arsehole—I know it comes from a place of caring. But it's about time both he and my other brother, Drake, and the old man came to terms with the new, unimproved me.

Reid's lips tighten, a sign he's pissed and probably a little embarrassed that we're airing our soiled Y-fronts in front of the enigmatic Ms Abbott. He's like that—do the right thing, keep everyone else on track, boldly navigate the waters, no matter how rocky.

Reid clears his throat. 'Mia is here to make the promotional film.'

I keep my face blank and ignore Mia's tiny cough as she crosses her arms over her waist and looks down at the white carpet underneath her well-worn Converse.

Reid's mouth hardens as he steps closer and dips his voice to a frustrated murmur. 'Look, I know this is a difficult time for you, but we discussed this at the planning meeting last month. You signed off on her appointment.' He slides a tight smile in Mia's direction.

I shoot Reid a hard frown, certain I didn't sign up for whatever the intriguing Mia Abbott is selling, but then, I don't actually read the documents pertaining to the smooth running of our chain of boutique hotels. That was my assistant's job.

My back muscles start to cramp I'm wound so tightly. Whatever has brought Mia around the world, I want no part of it. These days I work best alone. I upset fewer people that way. If I could fuck alone, I'd have no need to interact with others whatsoever.

I slip my hands into my trouser pockets and puff out my chest in my oldest brother's direction—I could still take him and we both know it. 'Promotional film?' I slide an extra layer of bite into my tone. He or Drake can help Mia—she's the last thing I need this week. I snatch another glance in her direction, the selfish-bastard part of me rebelling at passing her company over to either of my single brothers.

She's still smiling as if highly amused by the brotherly face-off playing out for her entertainment. I clamp my jaw closed—I can't decide if I'm pissed off or impressed by her audacity; keen to kick her out on what is probably a glorious arse—my biggest weakness—or kiss the amusement from that wide, generous mouth.

Reid scrubs his hand through his hair and shoots Mia an apologetic look, as if I'm an errant child who hasn't practised scales in time for his piano lesson. 'It's all in the memo. If you hired a new assistant, perhaps you'd find it easier to stay on track.'

My answering grin is laced with antipathy. Reid knows I careered off track three years ago after my wife died, following one measly year of marriage.

And now I've reached an impasse. I work when I want, control what I can and ignore anything else. Having your life literally snatched from your helpless hands will do that to a person.

My brother sighs. 'You know we're revamping the Faulkner Group's website as well as the websites of each hotel. We've brought Mia in to make a promotional video that highlights all the best features our hotels offer, especially the *Off the Guidebook* package.'

The fog clears a fraction. He and Drake need my signature on anything to do with Bounty Events' *Off the Guidebook*. It's my business, offering tailored memory-building experiences for the discerning traveller—one I started after uni—and its links to the Faulkner hotel chain through the once in a lifetime packages we offer our guests ensure a mutually beneficial partnership.

'Well, this is news to me.' I offer Mia an apologetic smile for her wasted trip. I could take her for a consolation drink later in the week...

'You agreed.' Reid scratches a spot just above his left eyebrow—a sign of his mounting frustration. Any minute now he'll drag out the for-fuck's-sake-get-a-grip lecture he delivers at least once a week, one he adopted in his role as self-appointed caretaker to Drake and me after our parents split when I was fifteen.

Without waiting to be asked, Mia moves to the comfy seating area and relaxes into a white leather armchair, where she watches our discussion with bold, fascinated eyes, her fingers tapping a rhythm only she can hear on the chrome arm of the chair.

My hackles rise. I should be annoyed that she's blatantly enjoying this sibling showdown but it's the pulsing blood in my groin that wins the battle, and I have the inconvenient urge to tell Reid to fuck off, then strip her bare and go down on her where she's sitting while she enjoys my view of London. Will she still find me amusing when she's coming on my tongue?

I bite back the surge of testosterone and temper in my next words to Reid out of innate manners for the virtual stranger. 'As you know, this isn't the best week for me—find someone else.'

Besides, business ticks along pretty well. Typical Reid, trying to fix something that's not broken.

Reid's jaw tenses as his stare bores into mine. 'You'll recall the figures I emailed you yesterday.' He's talking about the continuing drop in uptake of the *Off the Guidebook* package, which sets us apart from our main competitors.

He slides a polite smile in Mia's direction. 'Mia's work is award-winning. This is an excellent way to publicise our USPs in what is an increasingly competitive market.'

He doesn't add that I'm the reason sales are down, or that I've lost my drive where growth of my business is concerned. World domination of the luxury travel and recreation marketplace is no longer of interest. He doesn't need to—I've made my peace with the things I can and cannot control, preferring to focus on the former.

Of course, the most satisfying of those easily commanded areas of my life is sex. My eyes dart to the intriguing Mia.

Reid's voice softens a fraction. 'Both Bounty Events and the Faulkner chain will benefit.' Even now he's looking out for my business and reminding me of my responsibilities to the family, the brothers who stand by my side.

Another surge of futility erupts beneath my skin, forcing tension into my hands. I straighten my fingers, although I want to give rein to the fists this new twist inspires. The last thing I need is a distraction as appealing as Mia, and the timing will bite me in the arse.

I lean close, a last-ditch attempt to sway things my way with the minimum of effort. 'We don't need her,' I say under my breath. '*I* don't need her.'

Mia's snort reaches us across the room, a *fuck you* to the subtlety I've tried to maintain for her sake.

She shows her steel. 'I *can* hear you, you know.' Reid and I both turn Mia's way but she looks directly at my brother. 'Temperamental you said, not rude.'

Reid sighs as if slapped in the face with those stained Y-fronts we've aired. So she's been pre-warned about poor widower Kit.

She flicks her attention my way, ebony-hard eyes blazing challenge. 'As of thirty minutes ago,

Mr Faulkner, I'm under contract—all signed and sealed. Unless I fail to deliver the promised product, I expect the balance of my fee on receipt of the final, approved material.' She smiles that dazzling smile, her eyes laced with defiance.

I sigh, turning away from my brother in disgust. If she's here for three weeks to do a job sanctioned by me, one that will get my brothers off my back, I can't even fuck her. 92 messy. Not that she's shown any sign of sharing my physical interest.

My stare settles on the curve of her full mouth, the hint of pink tongue behind straight white teeth… On second thoughts, perhaps I could. Perhaps that's the quickest way to get rid of her. We'll have a good time. She'll realise I'm an arsehole she can't change and want nothing more to do with me.

Reid moves, snapping the soupy tension that coils across the room, connecting this enigmatic woman and me like tentacles.

'Well,' he slaps my shoulder, 'my work here is done.'

I shoot him a look that promises retribution. I must imagine the residual flicker of concern on his face because Reid casts me the smug grin of someone who's not that fond of his teeth. 'Don't forget the theatre tonight—'

'I'm well aware of my professional commitments.'
Although I could do without them today.

Reid nods. 'Give my regards to Mr and Mrs Sanchez.' He strides to Mia, who stands and shakes his hand with another of her knockout smiles. Already there's a warmth to their leave-taking that adds another convoluted twist to my knotted intestines.

Reid's parting shot ends any hope of my day panning out the way I'd planned—getting through, alone, with only my dark thoughts for company.

'Perhaps Mia could accompany you to the theatre tonight?' He tosses a malicious grin over his shoulder, so reminiscent of teenaged Reid, who enjoyed flexing his superior strength over his younger brothers.

Bastard.

He looks to Mia for her nod of approval. 'She doesn't officially start work until tomorrow,' he adds, 'but… I'll leave you two to work out the finer details.' With one last smirk he departs, optimistically closing the door behind him.

If he were any sort of gentleman, he'd have held the door open—the fascinating foreigner currently staring at me as if trying to figure me out won't be staying that long. I turn to the woman I can't fuck or fire, a tight smile on my face.

CHAPTER TWO

Mia

THE MINUTE WE'RE alone the pressure in my lungs builds to screaming point and my pulse thrums stronger. I slowly release the air trapped above my diaphragm through pursed lips to conceal my conflicted urges—either to run from Kit Faulkner or kiss the arrogant smirk from his tempting lips. A wise woman would grab her beloved camera and race back to Heathrow, just to escape the fog of sexual tension and other un-named undercurrents filling his swanky office.

Instead, I lift my chin and return his stare—I never back down from a challenge.

Kit's big, brooding size owns the room—feet planted wide, broad chest on display, hands casually slung in his pockets, his eyes peeling away my layers. Another injection of stubbornness raises my eyebrows in his direction. He can male posture as much as he likes—my cage isn't easily rattled.

The need to prove I'm more than he no doubt sees is easy to ignore. I've never belonged in a box and I'm not about to conform simply because Kit Faulkner is the sexiest man I've ever met.

Whew, I wasn't expecting sparks when I arrived at the Faulkner offices. Shame he's an arsehole.

Ignoring the trickle of excitement raising the hairs on my arms, I settle back, forcing my body to relax into the leather and my mind to remember all the reasons I'm happy being single. My corneas protest, the scalding intensifying until my eyes start to water. Only my competitive nature stops me from getting lost in the stare down. Lost in the centre-of-the-earth-deep navy-blue eyes of his. The annoyance he displays in their inky depths awakens my reckless side, which is never far from the surface.

Let's play, Mr Faulkner.

'So, your day isn't going as planned…?' I cross my legs and swing my foot in time with my heartbeat while I wait for him to fill the stilted atmosphere Reid left behind. Whether his irritation is directed at me—an unexpected stranger forced upon him—or at the handsome, more personable older brother is unclear. But my direct question works. I've definitely poked the bear awake.

His mouth thins—a travesty, because it's full and lush and surrounded by sexy stubble. 'You could say that.' Still no smile, but his teeth scrape his bottom lip as if he's thinking dark thoughts behind those dark eyes, which harbour the unmistakeable flicker of interest.

I evaluate what I know, what's been hinted at and what I've deduced. He's single, hot as and probably highly sexed. And rude. Don't forget rude. I glance at the outer office. That probably explains the missing assistant.

Despite the brief heads-up from the charming Reid—*my brother goes through lots of staff, don't take it personally*—I'm clearly not immune to Kit's conventional, almost cruel, good looks. His hair is a little long and too dishevelled to match the elegant perfection of his older brother, but when teamed with the devil-may-care scruff on his chiselled face and the intense fuck-off vibe in his brooding stare, the look packs a punch like a blowtorch to a cobweb. Because it screams sex. Dark, intense, dangerous sex.

Dangerous because there's a kind of anguish that radiates from behind those eyes in gloomy waves like the sheets of drizzle soaking London today, disarming me to the point that the fleeing-back-to-Heathrow option looks increasingly tempting.

But then, where's the fun in that...?

I smile, showing him I'm not perturbed by his frigid reception 'Well, thanks for this opportunity.' I'm just here to do my job, not to dig into this uptight English dude's psyche. But perhaps I should show more graciousness.

'I'm really looking forward to this commission.' Landing this prestigious contract with the Faulkner

Group will not only fund my next trip to South America, it's also allowed me to visit my brother, who moved to London two years ago to marry the love of his life.

'I think we've established your appointment was nothing to do with me. But perhaps we can make the most of it.' Kit plants himself in the seat opposite, his elbow propped on the chrome armrest and his thumb and forefinger rubbing at his bottom lip as if he's formulating a plan. A plan to deal with me?

I squeeze my thighs together, my imagination like a moth trapped inside a lampshade. Why does he have to make this so…enticing? To stop myself drooling, I look away from his ridiculously hand-some face and focus on London's iconic cityscape behind him.

'Great—it's my first trip to London. I travel a lot but I've never been here.' The buzz of excitement for exploring a new a city runs through my veins.

Perhaps that buzz is the reason Kit Faulkner's stare seems to penetrate my clothes, even my skin, his tortured interest a slither of electricity swooping over to join the persistent throb between my legs.

From looks alone, a quick game with Kit Faulkner is something I'd normally consider. And if that hint of danger in Kit's aura grows any bigger, burns any brighter, I'm doomed.

I uncross my legs while I breathe through the flutter of my pulse in my throat. I won't go there. He's too intense. Too…damaged. Too…consuming.

I don't do relationships, so I have a radar for people only interested in casual. Instinct and the delicious thrumming between my legs tell me I'd walk away from Kit Faulkner's bed not only saddle sore, but thoroughly mind-fucked too.

It's those eyes…

Risk is stamped all over him—not the physical, adrenaline thrill I'm always up for, but the temptation to get sucked into those fathomless pools and the turmoil they conceal. That's not me. Caring that much is the role of a long-term lover or a girlfriend and I've never been either.

I swivel my hips a fraction, pressing the seam of my jeans where I want it to stop me from becoming a cliché and succumbing to the dark, seductive stare thing he has going.

I force a polite, professional smile, willing my body to stand down from this unforeseen attraction to my new client. He's still staring, brooding intensity and heat in his eyes even while he tries to intimidate me with his silent perusal.

My smile stretches. Does he expect me to crumble because he's displayed how inconvenient he finds my presence? My lips twitch, controlled by a sense of perverse devilment.

I lift my eyebrows. 'I *am* free tonight, by the way, and I *love* the theatre.' A lie. I have nothing in my backpack I could wear to the theatre. I'm not the theatre type. I'm outdoorsy, sporty, adventurous—my parents' generation would have labelled me a tomboy. But we don't do labels in our family. Despite being older than most parents, mine are progressive, liberal and non-judgmental. The perfect parents for a couple of kids who don't fit into any mould and who no one else wanted.

Kit works his jaw, ignoring my attempts to steer the conversation back to the job he's paying me handsomely to complete. 'Tell me, Mia…' My name vibrates in his deep English voice. 'Have you seen much of the city? Had time to explore?'

'No. I arrived yesterday, and I'll see enough of London while I work for you. I'm staying with my brother and his husband in Camden until I complete this contract, and then I'll be moving on.'

Keep moving. Keep exploring. Keep free.

A blunt knife burrows between my ribs—old, rusty, predictable.

The prickle of restlessness that travelling normally helps me outrun returns. The irony that my job has brought me here, to a city of millions where one person, somewhere, is related to me by blood, twists my insides.

I breathe through the feeling, reminding myself that travelling the world beats putting down roots. A bird's world view, not an oak tree's.

Kit's fathomless eyes still project a dichotomous vibe that veers from mild hostility to overt interest. Why is he angling to get rid of me? Does he dislike his perfectly amiable brother so much? Or perhaps he's taken an instant dislike to my quirkiness. He needs to pick one emotion and stick to it, though. His indifference I can handle, but his seductive stare, which promises one thing and one thing only, grows harder to resist.

But resist I must.

'Hmm…' he says. 'Well, perhaps I can pay the outstanding balance of your fee. You can leave today. Spend time with your family. See the sights London has to offer.' He smiles then, for the first time, as if my acceptance of his generous but bizarre offer is a foregone conclusion. As if he's used to getting his own way.

I bet he is. Well, some of us aren't easily controlled.

I almost laugh, but I've already sniggered at his attempts to chase me off twice, so I'd best not push my luck. A Faulkner recommendation is worth more than it costs me to ignore Kit's attitude. Intrigue adds to the other unexpected emotions that meeting him has unleashed.

What is he afraid of? What is he hiding?

Energy coils inside. I expected this job to be fun, but Kit's added layer after layer of excitement to the mix until I'm practically trembling from the adrenaline in my bloodstream.

I shake my head slowly, a small smile dancing on my mouth. 'I'm a professional film-maker, Mr Faulkner, with a reputation to uphold, a product to create and deliver. You and your brothers brought me in for a reason.'

No matter how much my libido wants this un-compromising Englishman, I'm no pushover. But he's making this too easy, too much fun. I sit up straighter in the chair, all ready and raring to tackle Kit Faulkner head-on.

'Fuck.' He mutters under his breath, looking away. His fingers massage his brow as if seeking inspiration through telepathy and his jaw muscles bunch. At this rate he'll have no enamel left. I take pity on him, my body's reaction to the unforeseen chemistry between Kit Faulkner and me softening my response.

'Why don't you discuss the project with me, go over the Bounty Events company ethos, provide some creative pointers for the film?'

Instead of trying to sway things your way.

I have the brief Reid emailed to me memorised for today's meeting: the Faulkner chain of small bou-tique hotels is synonymous with high-end luxury; lacking the grandeur of the big London hotels, they offer top-of-the-range luxury, exquisite catering and, if you can afford the services of Kit Faulkner's partner company, Bounty Events, a menu of unique, once-in-a-lifetime experiences, overseen by the ed-ible man still staring at me with impenetrable eyes.

Whatever he hopes to achieve with that look, the resultant effect is the trickle of heat through my blood, the rush usually reserved for when I'm air-borne with my action camera strapped to my head.

'I have a meeting now.' He rises, dismissing me

and makes his way to his uncluttered desk. 'Your arrival this morning was…unscheduled.'

Controlling, arrogant…and grinding my usually laid-back gears. 'Not for me. And not for your brothers.'

He focuses on his laptop as if deaf to my comeback, the epitome of eye candy if you're into the haughty, crisp businessman type. The suit trousers fit him like a bespoke shield of armour, cupping his muscular arse and thick thighs. The shirt, although a little creased where he's sat in his executive leather chair, is expensive enough it could probably walk around this office on its own and he emanates power, wealth, culture, as sure as the outright aloofness he's wafting my way.

My tapping fingers pick up the pace—my worst habit, one that tells me I've been sitting for too long and need to get moving. I press them flat, cross my legs and force myself to enjoy his plush leather armchair, prolonging the showdown.

A battle of wills…?

Well, if you insist, Mr Faulkner.

He must sense his brush-off hasn't achieved the likely intended goal—me scuttling from his office like a frightened mouse. He turns from his laptop screen, looking at me over one broad shoulder.

'So I can't persuade you to take the money and run?'

If this were any other city, if Kit hadn't tried to control this from the outset, I might have been tempted to take his offer. I arch a brow in his direction. 'I'm here to stay until the work is complete.'

With one last sweep of his eyes along the length of my body, a look that dismantles every scrap of my resolve to find him unattractive, Kit turns away.

'If you're determined to complete this project, it will be under my full direction.' He taps some keys on his laptop, once more gifting me a view of his sculpted back and arrogantly broad shoulders.

I smile. The Kit effect fosters my defiance and my curiosity to probe just how deep his control goes. I won't be put into a box, despite my body's instant physical attraction to him.

'I prefer full creative control of my work. We can discuss it further tonight.'

End of conversation.

I stand and he gives me his full attention. His energy leaves me jittery, vibrating, as if I've stepped into his force field and any minute now I'll be reduced to a cloud of excited molecules. It's more of an enticement than a deterrent and I step closer still.

His lip curls. 'Do you own suitable attire for the theatre?' He looks me over, heat back in those eyes, like the blue at the centre of a Bunsen flame. The haughty attitude says one thing, but his baby blues give him away.

I embed my feet in his impractical carpet, hoping the soles of my shoes are grubby from the wet streets outside. 'It's not a jeans kind of affair?' I widen my stare, all innocence, biting the side of my tongue to prevent a smile escaping when he all but rolls his eyes. I'm certain he finds me lacking. Unlike the crisp, sophisticated women I met downstairs, I care little about make-up, manicures or fashion.

'Sadly, no. Is that all you've travelled with?'

I shrug. 'Most of my baggage allowance was taken up with my filming equipment.' I live in clothes hardy enough to weather lying on the ground or climbing over fences, all in pursuit of the perfect shot.

His mouth tightens, and once more I have the crazy urge to kiss him. To push him back into his expensive chair and straddle him while ruining what's left of his overlong hairstyle, just to prove that his body is interested in the woman wearing jeans currently cluttering up his immaculate but sterile workspace.

But I shelve my urges for the thrill of simple physics—opposite and opposing forces.

You push, I push, Mr Faulkner.

His next statement gives me pause, landing another well-aimed blow.

'I'll have something suitable sent over. Be ready by six p.m.' He returns his focus to his laptop, his fingers moving over the keys with speed. Even his hands are sexy.

Damn.

Wait…suitable? Sent over? What the fuck…? This isn't *Pretty Woman*. I won't be playing Julia Roberts to his control-freak Richard Gere.

'I don't need your clothes. We do *have* theatres in New Zealand.' Damn. Now I'll have to waste my afternoon shopping, with jet lag, when I could be hanging out with Will. My fingers dance on my thigh. I press my hand flat. 'It's just a play. Are all Brits as snobby as you?' Will's hubby, Josh, is lovely…

Another snort. 'It's more than a play.' Another hot but assessing look. 'Our clients expect the five-star service they pay for and which we deliver. Anyone can buy the best seats in the house—Faulkner clients want the personal touch. To be schmoozed and personally escorted by me and, if you want this job, by you also. Temporarily.' He licks his bottom lip, contemplating the expression I hope says *unfazed*.

'Personally, I don't care what you wear,' he continues, his eyes sliding over me with enough heat he could be imagining me naked. 'But you *cannot* schmooze two of my most valued clients in jeans. Consider it a uniform, if it upsets you, but if you want the job, that's one of my rules.'

How many rules does he have? And how many can I break? I narrow my eyes while the prickle of a thousand ants covers my skin.

Rules? Uniforms? Schmoozing?

I've spent years growing comfortable with who I am and overcoming where I came from. Tonight, dressed up in some sort of fancy frock so Kit's VIP can flaunt his wealth, won't be the first time I've felt like I don't belong.

But Kit's next words cement my decision.

'Unless Reid has miscalculated…now's the time to back out, Mia.' A small smile tugs at his decadent mouth. My own lips tingle, the urge to kiss him returning in full force. He'd love it if I caved that easily—a big *suck it* to his brother and a way to get rid of the inconvenient woman who doesn't own a cocktail dress with one blow.

'I'm a Kiwi, as New Zealanders are affectionately termed. I'm up to *any* job.'

Including him, his intriguing impenetrable guard and his ridiculous rules.

I offer a saccharine smile. 'I look forward to receiving your couture. I'm a size six shoe and size ten dress.'

Another swipe of his brooding stare scrapes at my nipples. 'I know what size you are.'

Oh, I bet he does. I bet he's used to controlling everything, including the wardrobes of fawning females, before showing them the sheet-clawing night of their lives and then scarpering faster than I could say *Not with this chick, buddy.*

I stand taller, using my height to my advantage. In flats Kit can still peer down at me, but in heels, something I rarely wear, we'd be almost eye to eye. Now, despite the fact that I'm immune to fancy clothes, I have no idea how to put on eyeliner and don't own hair straighteners, my breath hitches as I look forward to tonight, to challenging both his misconceptions and his rigid control.

With one last smirk I can't help but deliver, I offer

him my hand for a curt handshake, turn on my heel
and head for the door. 'See you at six, then.'

My palm tingles as I walk away, still resonating
with his touch, while the hum of an electrical storm
buzzes throughout my nervous system. This job just
became a whole lot more interesting.

And Kit's sheet-clawing ride of a lifetime…tempt-
ing. A chuckle escapes me as I press the button for
the lift. I'm a film-maker after all. Perhaps I'll film
the experience.

CHAPTER THREE

Mia

PRIMPING AND PREENING is so time-consuming—no wonder I don't have the patience for it under normal circumstances. The dresses, plural, arrive at my brother's house from Harvey Nichols within the hour. Multiple extravagant garments draped in swanky bags and wrapped in delicate, monogrammed tissue paper.

I'm half tempted to cut off all the tags and then return them to Kit's office claiming none of them fit. But Kit clearly knows his way around a woman's body, because all but one could have been made specifically for me.

Will and Josh help me select one *uniform* from the exquisite, but over-the-top, creations on offer and then sit me down to watch a YouTube video on how to apply a minimal make-up look. Josh, a chartered accountant, plays make-up artist. A good thing—I'd have probably poked out my own eyeball with the mascara wand.

When I open their front door at the appointed hour, my gait unsteady in the ridiculous heels Kit sent, his tall frame fills the doorstep. Despite the stern lecture I gave myself, his appearance hits me square in the stomach, flooding my hyper-aware system with addictive adrenaline.

Fight or flight? Equally tempting with this sexy sod.

Mouthwatering, smelling divine and wearing the same dishevelled hair, facial scruff and dark stare as earlier, he swoops his eyes over me, a small smile kicking up one corner of his mouth to reveal a single, bracketing dimple.

The pad of my index finger tingles to trace the fine line left by that dimple. The made-for-me dress shrinks two sizes, squeezing my ribcage. That smile, even only a shadow of one…*so not fair*.

'I see you found one that fits?' he says.

The silky fabric may as well be sheer—he looks at me like he's as aware as I am that it's the only barrier between his eyes and my nakedness. His eyebrows flick up. 'Good choice.'

'Whoa… A polite compliment?'

He shakes his head, a ghost of remorse flitting over his face. 'Yes. I was…abrupt earlier. I just don't like surprises, and I wasn't expecting you.'

It's not quite an apology, but I'm still thrown. I focus on the fact the scrummy man cluttering my brother's doorstep has insisted on dressing me up. Why have I allowed such pretentious nonsense? Because I like a challenge? Because I've got something to prove? Some urge to fit into his world, however briefly?

'One would have been sufficient—did you have to send over the entire evening-gown department?' I'm extra-snippy, realising I've done exactly what I said I wouldn't—conform.

Kit shrugs. 'My business, my rules. A uniform, remember.'

I sigh, now regretting the make-up. The uniform crap was difficult to argue, but the face…that was all me.

My belly tightens. Why am I trying to impress this man? Aside from his effortless sex appeal, I usually consider myself immune to everything he represents. But that's clearly the answer—I'm *not* immune to the sexual allure. That dispensed with, I'm guessing the Kit effect would be rendered inert.

He pulls one hand from his trouser pocket, reaching up to grip my elbow. I barely have time to ensure the front door closes behind me before he guides me to the sleek black car idling at the kerb. But those few seconds provide enough time for the heat of his palm to register, to prick at my skin and leave the ghost of a handprint, not quite an itch, not quite a thrill.

I pull my arm from his grip. I can walk unaided. Just about. And now he's touched me, I'm back to square one on the resisting-him scale.

He opens the car door and silently urges me inside, the doorstep smile and its breath-stealing effect now a distant blip. Although I need the timely reminder, neither is relevant.

This is work. Boring work. Absolutely no excitement on offer whatsoever. Definitely no sexual undercurrents.

My temples pounding, already I'm regretting my impulse to accompany him tonight. Already dreading mixing with a packed theatre full of play-loving strangers dressed to the nines. An outsider, out of my comfort zone—why do I always have to push, to prove myself? Why couldn't I have just told Kit where to stick his job, his money and his heated looks and helped Will and Josh shop for baby clothes?

I could have been watching a movie with them right now, having cracked open my favourite Terry's Chocolate Orange—a giant one I bought, duty-free. But that reckless streak in me has me spending the evening with *Grumpy*, while he arse-kisses his wealthy clients.

I take a rational breath, hoping to solve at least one of my problems with a little self-talk. Just because my biological mother lives somewhere in London, doesn't mean I'm likely to run into her in Kit's private theatre box… Not that I'd know her if I literally fell from these outrageous shoes into her lap. And who cares about belonging, fitting in? I have a fantastic, supportive adoptive family and an amazing, globetrotting job.

Pep talk over, I slide the dress flat under my backside in case he wants to return it, uncreased, or pass it on to the next mannequin he tries to intimidate into behaving exactly the way he wants, while Kit rounds the back of the car and slides in beside me. And then we're off.

It's a new experience for me, being chauffeur-driven, but I keep my face neutral, serene, silently enjoying the fizz bubbling up in my chest. I feign uninterest by glancing out of the tinted windows.

'Where are we going? I don't do the Bard.' I turn my undivided attention back to Kit. 'It's a personal *rule* of mine.' I offer a tight smile as my fingers tap wildly against the tiny clutch bag included with the shoes, as if they too need an outlet for being expensively trussed up like a turkey for his pleasure.

Control freak.

'The West End—the Shaftesbury.' His lips twitch. *Actually* twitch. 'The Bard?' He stares, his eyes flicking over my features as if he's seeing me for the first time.

'Yes. Watching Shakespeare is three hours of our lives we can never get back.' I look away, but not before I see him shake his head in…disbelief? Amusement?

Kit slides his arm along the back of the leather seat and angles his body to face me, amused eyes narrowed. My skin tightens in the foreign get-up. I may as well be swimming around under a lens for his invasive inspection—a fish out of water.

He rubs at his bottom lip. 'Not a fan of the theatre?' I shrug.

'What do you like?' His eyes scan my face.

I stare back and his navy eyes burn into mine, latching on to my erogenous zones like heat-seeking missiles and setting off a series of miniature explosions.

'I prefer to be active.' The need to prove myself throbs harder every time he looks down his slightly crooked nose at me and every time I remember I'm in a strange city, closer than I've ever been to the woman who birthed me. But I hold his stare, the rebelliousness helping to counteract the attraction.

'That's why I love my job. What makes me good at it.' I wouldn't be sitting here in his luxury-on-wheels car otherwise. The two older Faulkner brothers I met this morning have a clear vision for their empire and exacting standards for their staff. I shouldn't care, but I want Kit to know that I'm more than the dressed-up doll he's made me with the uniform.

Not that the ridiculous dress he sent over, which barely conceals my braless chest, qualifies. And screw him and his rules. He's rude, obnoxious and acts entitled. 'If you'd just sign off on my ideas for the film you need never see me again. I'll be done filming in a matter of weeks, a fortnight if the British weather plays nice.'

He offers no comeback. The car jolts to the right to avoid some cyclist with a death wish and Kit's thigh glides along mine. It lasts less than a second, but the brief contact is incendiary to my hormones, repeatedly firing my pleasure centres.

Clearly being in London *and* meeting someone who so effectively both winds me up and turns me on is too much for my hormones. I should shag him and get the highly inconvenient urges over with and show him, whether professionally or up close and personally, I'm up to any challenge. Perhaps with the exception of the heels already pinching my toes.

'What do you love about your job?'

Him ignoring my out clause throws me, and I answer honestly. 'Normally I relish the creative aspect of my work, helping clients tell the story they want the world to see, but I suspect this job will present extra…challenges.' Kit-shaped challenges…

A small shake of his head—confident, assured, perceptive. 'Someone with your industry experience, your awards, will have no problem with a short promotional video.'

So, he looked me up. Is he as thrown by meeting me as I am by him, despite myself? Heat pools low in my belly, its sweetness cut by the acidic taste on my tongue.

'Usually my clients are as agreeable as your brothers. Tell me, why are you so rude? Is it just foreigners, or do you try to control everyone?'

For several protracted seconds, I assume he's going to ignore my questions. We face off. His stare sparks flickers of flame. It's not a look of dislike, and it curls my toes in his poncey, overpriced shoes.

'Would it help if I apologise?'

I shrug through my surprise. 'It might.' I smooth

my features into a mask of indifference. 'But in some regards, it's too late. You've already raised the stakes, thrown down an irresistible gauntlet.' I lean in, holding his eye contact, breathing through the burn in my corneas at his proximity and the warm, masculine scent of him, which bathes me like a cloud. 'Adrenaline is addictive.'

The car slows in evening traffic as we butt horns, but I'm barely aware of our surroundings. His sexual magnetism makes my heart thump in my throat. I like sex. Kit is sinfully hot. A plus B could equal a way to dispense with the potent pheromones and reset our working boundaries for this project. My eyes dance over his lips while I mull turning the nagging idea into a reality.

Kit frowns and changes the subject. 'What did my brother tell you about me?' He shoots me a hard look, as if defying me to lie or soften the truth.

I fight a smile and let him have it, right between the eyes. 'That you're difficult to work for, that you go through staff like you change your underwear and that I shouldn't be intimidated by you.'

He stares, frozen and watchful, but it's a look that makes me aware I'm braless beneath this ridiculous wisp of silk.

'Are you?' His index finger and thumb return to that lip. My nipples peak as if craving the same attention. My pulse thrums stronger, roaring in my ears.

Rule one of embracing fear—never admit weakness.

'No.'

He leans closer, as if about to confide a secret while challenge dances in his eyes. I relax every muscle in my body, holding myself perfectly still.

'Despite my *rudeness*?' His smile is brittle, eyes glittering. This game of wills plays tug-of-war with my body—my heart rate spikes every time we make eye contact and the hard kernel of defiance I'm slave to infects my backbone, banishing any leeway I might have scraped together.

I hold the breath in my throat and shake my head. I was right about him—he too enjoys being proved correct, his uncompromising, forthright manner a front. Self-preservation.

I shrug. 'Perhaps it's a front.'

'Perhaps I simply want things the way I want them, Mia.' The conversation has morphed. We're no longer talking about working together. And what do I care how he wants things, as long as he doesn't try to control *me*?

There's something beyond enticing about this man. My body twitches, fighting the urge to lean into him. To see those navy eyes close up. To taste the mouth he habitually toys with.

True to form, he releases another bombshell. 'Did Reid tell you I lost my wife, Laura?'

His brutal statement squeezes my stomach and I suck in a short gasp. A torrent of questions forms in wake of the shock. How? When? Were they married long? Did they have children? It certainly explains his thorny barriers. But I have no interest in breaking those down.

And the perverse in me likes that he tries to jolt me with this intimate, intensely personal detail, likes that he uses what must be his darkest pain to test my mettle. Perhaps a last-ditch attempt to run me off or freak me out.

But it does the opposite, increasing his attractiveness tenfold. Because it seems I was wrong about him.

He *is* safe.

Unattainable. And clearly only interested in casual hook-ups. The likelihood we'll turn the chemistry filling the car into something brief and physical increases.

'No. But thanks for sharing—it helps to put things into perspective.' The sooner we move past the physical, the sooner we can move on from it. The sooner I can get back to being me. 'Look, I'm not intimidated by you. I just want to do my job.'

'No, I see that. You're…different, aren't you? Is it a New Zealand thing?'

I fight my first reaction, rationalising that he probably didn't mean it the way my defensive self-esteem interprets. 'You're forthright and…unconventional. It's not an insult, so you can stop glaring at me.' His index finger traces his bottom lip while he contemplates the conundrum sitting in his expensive car.

'Because I can dish as much as I can take?' I lift my chin. I won't let him see how close to home his observation has struck. I'm a square peg. I reconciled this long ago. But here, in London, so near and yet so far from my biological roots...

I shiver, tingles of unease racing down my bare back. This is why relationships and I aren't meant to be. I'm better alone, free to be myself without expectation or judgment... The tiny part of me clamouring for the validation of belonging stutters like a broken film reel, spliced out of sync.

I let him have the honesty he seems to value. 'You're rude, unprofessional and obnoxious. That *is* an insult.' But even as the words leave my mouth I want his lips on mine, want more than verbal sparring with him, knowing that's all it ever will be— brief, physical, no emotional entanglements. And, while locking horns with Kit makes my blood pound, I'm certain the sex would be an even better distraction.

He laughs, a genuine head-thrown-back bellow that vibrates into my bones. It's short. Not long enough for me to fully appreciate the way pleasure transforms his handsome features, but enough to skyrocket my body temperature when he looks at me with a new layer of heat. 'What shall we do with each other, then, Mia Abbott, as you seem determined to stick around, despite my obvious shortcomings?'

A hundred filthy replies pop into my head. I let him have the forthright and unconventional one he probably expects least. 'Why don't we get this...the sex...over and done with and move on to the job?'

Touché, Mr Straight-Talking...

I must imagine the flicker of excitement I see in his eyes, the one that turns my pulse into a roar of drumbeats, because it's gone in a fraction of a second and his stare hardens, any trace of humour gone. 'You don't imagine I'm relationship material, do you?'

His arrogance shouldn't astound me quite so much. If not for his extreme hotness, his obvious emotional unavailability and the desire to see him as undone as our chemistry renders me, I'd cut my losses and leave him to his floundering business and his boring night out at the theatre.

'You don't imagine I'll fall for your tepid charm offensive, do you? I've never had a relationship and I'm not looking for one now.' I shrug. 'I'm practical. And as blunt as you. You're single, I'm single. Neither one of us is interested in anything beyond sex. Let's get it out of the way and then I can do my job and move on and you can go back to...' I wave my finger in his general direction '...whatever this is.'

He's silent for so long, I'm aware of every muted noise outside the car. The angry blare of a horn, the squeal of breaks, the electronic beep of a pedestrian crossing. Kit's stare scours me like I'm under a giant microscope, and he's cataloguing my nooks and crannies and the freakish antennae sprouting from my head.

But then his tongue swipes his bottom lip and I almost feel it between my legs. From the look in his eyes alone I'm achy and damp.

'I bet you didn't negotiate this into your contract with Reid and Drake.' A small lip-curl hints at what must be a devastating full-blown smile I'll probably never see. 'Wednesday,' he adds with a bitter twist to his mouth, his serious, intense stare pinning me to the leather upholstery.

'What?'

'If you're still interested, I'll fuck you Wednesday,' he says. Like it's a meeting he's slotted into his busy schedule, before the gym and after a conference call.

Today is Monday.

My body can't decide on an emotion, shunting between excitement, outrage and rampant curiosity. 'Why Wednesday?' A control thing? Just because he can pick and choose? Well, fuck that.

A defiant trickle of fire winds its way between the exposed bumps of my vertebrae—I'll tell him Wednesday doesn't work for me, but could I pencil him in for Friday? But my body betrays me, clamouring for the dark, all-consuming sex I'm guessing he delivers; desperate to have done with the distracting deluge of arousal every time I'm in his presence; determined to show him whatever he can dish, I can take.

'Because that's the way I want it.' He leans closer, his navy stare tracing my parted lips and leaving the ghost of a kiss there. 'You should know, I'll be in control. I'll call the shots. If that's not your thing...' Another cocky shrug that fans my body temperature off the scale. He thinks he has tomboy Mia all figured out.

'You should know that's dangerous talk in this day and age. Women are in charge of their own sexuality, Mr Faulkner.' I'm aware I'm the one who brought up sex, and, despite his commanding promise and my rebuttal, my internal muscles clench at the idea of Kit controlling my pleasure. No one's ever bossed me around in the bedroom before, and if I'd been asked prior to meeting the sinfully sexy Kit I'd have sworn on the life of my brother's soon-to-be adopted child I'd tell him he could stick his sexual dominance up his tight, toned English backside.

But his offer comes laced with the hint of danger that whooshes the blood through my head in a rush. And I'm confident I can take him. I wonder how many times he's used the *I'll call the shots* line. I wonder if anyone ever turns the charmer down. I wonder if he used it on the late Mrs Faulkner, a woman whose legacy appears far-reaching, as if Kit literally drags it behind him like Marley's chains.

That we're negotiating sex like a cold, unemotional transaction isn't romantic. But I don't need romance. He's started a chain reaction inside me, luring me towards the recklessness I crave.

Testing where his head is at, I say, 'Or perhaps you're trying to tame the wild girl, eh?'

Perhaps now would be a good time to tell him of my rebellious teens, my reputation as a wildcard...

Kit smiles but it's feline. 'You and your command

of your sexuality brought this up, Ms Abbott. Just because I like things a certain way doesn't mean I don't respect your choices and your right to say no. I'm fully into mutual consent while we explore our mutual pleasure.' His eyes dip to my mouth. 'You can take it or leave it, Mia.' His lips caress the phrase *mutual pleasure* like they're already on my skin, my nipples, my clit.

I press my thighs together, stymieing the burn. My head screams one thing while my hormones stage an intervention.

But he's also given me a bargaining chip. With a rush of exhaled air, I make my decision. I *will* take it, because Kit Faulkner turns me on more than anyone I've ever met. But more so, because I'm up to the challenge. Any challenge. Especially one where the boundaries are so clearly demarcated and the taste of victory already lingers on my tongue.

Kit wears the casual-sex-only vibe like some men wear overpowering cologne. He's safe. I can concede to a few of his sexual demands without risk, but I have a stipulation of my own.

I shrug, while my blood pounds through my belly. 'It's all good—whatever your kink. But I have a condition too.' My breathing accelerates, a chemical cocktail flooding my bloodstream.

He leans in, waiting, his lips parted and his midnight eyes dancing between mine.

I swallow, ensuring my voice will be clear and controlled when it emerges because the parts of me affected by the hormonal maelstrom inside jerk and jitter like chattering teeth. 'You can call the shots sexually, but I want full creative direction over my work—no negotiations. No wasting my time or trying to influence the process, and no interfering.'

I wait, breath held in my throat while I stare him down.

Some sort of battle rages inside him—his nostrils flare, his eye actually twitches and his chest rises and falls, telling me he's used to controlling every aspect of his life, including work. And now I'm burning with curiosity about his dead wife. What happened to her? Has it made Kit the way he is? It would destroy this fiercely controlled man to have such a momentous part of his life turned upside down.

Breath stutters back into my chest in a rush. In that moment I want to reach out to him, to kiss him, more than I want the oxygen that breath delivers to my gasping lungs. He's the last thing I should want—his privileged, conventional lifestyle, his naturally demanding nature, his disregard for social pleasantries are warning bells rattling my skull.

But he's safe.

The fact he's still deeply and desolately in love with his wife is stamped all over him from the creases in the corners of his eyes to the tension he carries around his beautiful mouth and the control he seems desperate to exert on all areas of his life.

My scalp prickles as I wait. I fight the urge to climb into his lap and finish this *now*, today. *Mon-*

day. Just to show him life, free will, is about choices. But losing his wife would have already taught him that harsh lesson and perhaps I simply want to watch him shed the battle-scarred armour, even for a few uninhibited seconds.

Wednesday might as well be next year. He's ramped up my hormones tenfold by making me wait and now my anticipation is stretched taut.

We're still staring, still breathing in unison, still flooding the space with a pheromone mix more potent than the spirits stocked in the car's minibar.

I lick my parched lips. His eyes dance over the trail of my tongue.

I'm frozen, but every nerve in my body urges me to take the leap.

At the last second, his pupils dilate and we lunge in unison.

With a small growl his hands slide into my hair and he cups my face and pulls me onto his kiss. I meet him halfway, my hands gripping his shoulders as wave after wave of relief pounds through me.

He's changed his mind.

We'll dump the boring play, go back to his place and I can start work afresh tomorrow with this... inconvenient distraction nicely tucked away.

Done and dusted. Kit Faulkner put in his place. Back to being Mia.

His kiss is bold, open-eyed, almost defiant, but my body responds—muscles softening and heart rate accelerating, forcing heated blood around my arteries, delivering the hormones that allow me to ignore all the reasons fucking my kind-of boss isn't a good idea.

Firm lips direct my mouth open. His tongue surges inside—sublime, possessive, unapologetic. As good as I'd guessed. I clasp his wrists, clinging on for dear life as I meet his stare, even though my corneas are on fire and my mind screams at me to close my eyes. To block out the carnal, almost cruel intensity in his eyes. As if kissing me today, a Monday, is a dare and he hates every second.

To compensate I kiss him like it's my last second on earth, my mouth a frantic slide on his, my tongue a match for the duel of his, and then I suck on his bottom lip.

He pulls away, his stare savage, breath gusting across my face, and then drags my whole body into his lap, his fingers digging in and a hoarse grunt leaving his throat.

My blood surges, delivering the endorphins to every cell in my body. Perhaps we won't make it back to his place. Perhaps we'll finish this right here in the back of his fancy car before we make it to the Shaftesbury.

I straddle his lap and rise up over him to slant my mouth back over his. I was right about the hair. It's silky and long enough to twist between my fingers. But I don't get to enjoy it for long because he grips my wrists and directs them behind my back with firm, insistent pressure that tells me he's a man of his word. He wants to control this… Well, he can try.

I continue to plunder his mouth as he traps both my hands in one of his, and then his other hand is at my breast, kneading and tweaking and making me moan loudly enough to alert our driver, who sits behind the privacy screen, of what is afoot.

Kit pulls on my wrists, breaking the contact between our frenzied mouths. His stare is almost black with desire, a wildness dancing there that steals my breath and banishes any residual hesitation I have for wanting him.

I do.

Desperately.

Now.

He dips his head and his mouth covers my breast, through the fabric of the silk dress that probably cost him more than my flight around the world.

He's not gentle. His lips clamp my nipple, pulling and tugging while his tongue flicks at the nub. I cry out, the sensation burrowing deep into my belly, sending pulses of fire between my legs.

I knew the second I walked into his office things would be good between us. Just like I intuited his emotional unavailability. Kit oozes distance from every pore. Emotionally, we're as distant as the countries we come from. It doesn't matter. I don't need the trappings.

His free hand skims my thigh as he leans back on the seat, holding me prisoner a short distance away from his mouth, which I want back on me. My breast, my lips, anywhere that helps to slake the burning need he's unleashed so effortlessly.

'Is this what you want?' The bulge at the front of his trousers tells me he wants it too, despite the harshness of his tone. Despite his stupid Wednesday rule.

'Yes.' I've never been more turned on in my life. Perhaps it's the dress and the glamour of Kit's London and limo. Perhaps it's a comedown from the elevated adrenaline I've suffered since my plane touched down in this foreign city, a place I'm tied to through family, both biological and real. Perhaps it's just Kit, as sexy as sin in his tux—impersonal, unreachable, the ultimate in temptation.

With an impatient grunt, he slides his fingers between my legs. His hooded eyes command my stare, which wants to hide from his brooding, detached perusal. But a pulse hammers in his neck, he's steel between my legs and his chest works hard, I suspect to stave off a similar light-headedness to that currently rendering me incoherent.

'Fuck. No underwear?' He probes my slickness, this time with a gentleness I'd have denied he was capable of two minutes ago.

I shake my head, too turned on for speech. In seconds he's primed my clit with his thumb and stretched two fingers inside me so I'm hallucinating stars.

His languid stare latches to mine. A small smile

tugs the corner of his sinful mouth. Mocking me? Daring me? But I'm past caring.

His eyes flick to the wet patch his mouth left on the dress. 'Don't move your hands.' His command is bitten out, grating on my instincts to defy. But we've made a deal and I don't want him to stop what he's doing between my legs, so I concede, crossing my wrists in the small of my back and gripping his thighs with mine for balance in the moving vehicle.

He scoops the strap from my shoulder, exposing my breast, and then resumes his hold on my wrists, as if he doesn't trust me to listen. His mouth covers me, skin to skin this time, but all the while accompanied by his searing eye contact, the high I feel worth my compliance to his need for control.

I whimper. The dual assault is so good I'm seconds from coming and he grins up at me like he knows he's the one to take me there. I plan payback while I ride his hand.

When his teeth scrape my nipple, short grunts of encouragement rumbling up from his chest, I implode. My body jerks forward, crushing him back into the seat, and he releases my wrists to press his palm between my shoulder blades and hold me in place while he wrings the last drops of pleasure from my weakened body.

Wow.

I pant against his shoulder, my hands still clasped in his behind my back. If I turn my head I could kiss his neck, which smells divine—masculine, clean, spicy. I keep still while he slowly releases my hands and slips the strap of my dress up into place. Then he gently slides me from his lap without comment and straightens his own clothing, smoothing his immaculate trousers over his thighs as he glances away to look out of the tinted windows.

When I'm certain about the quality of my voice, I say, 'What about you?' Has he changed his mind? Does he enjoy blue balls? He's still sporting a healthy erection, shifting in the seat as if to get comfortable.

Good luck with that...

I lift my chin, feigning cool indifference at Kit's dismissal, willing my pulse to settle and the flush of my skin to fade. I wait for confirmation or denial. Encouragement or rejection.

He pins me in place with the stare he rounds on me—hot, full of promise and a hint of regret.

'Wednesday.'

CHAPTER FOUR

Kit

I CHECK MY watch and then rap at the blue door behind which I hope to find Mia. There's a light on inside, so someone is up. I roll on the balls of my feet. It's Wednesday and all I've had to chase away the darkness for the last thirty hours is the memory of Mia's sublime bold surrender in the car. A jarring juxtaposition as fascinating as the woman herself...

She fought this thing between us at every step just as fiercely as I did, for her own reasons, even as she took what she wanted from my kiss, from riding my hand between her legs. I couldn't give her more then. But I'm here now, if she still wants the same thing.

My shoulders tense, long seconds ticking in my head, as powerless to the attraction as I was the first time she walked into my office. More so, because now I know she'll not only play by the rules, but she had the wherewithal to secure a few of her own conditions.

Either way, I've had a brief taste of spectacular, and now I'm ravenous.

I couldn't take her home Monday, but I sure as shit went home and used my insomnia to scour the internet for every mention of Mia Abbott. She *is* good at her job. Her social-media accounts, where she posts anything from adventure-travel-type vlogs and corporate promo films to the early and quirky short films she made at uni, have a couple of million followers. She's won a handful of New Zealand short-film awards and, just like the woman herself, her style is unconventional, innovative and fresh. Reid and Drake did well to recruit someone of Mia's calibre. I could argue that this way, me fucking her, we're all getting what we want—me, Mia and the Faulkner Group. But right now I don't give a shit about the family business—otherwise I'd leave her alone. Walk away, no harm done.

My stomach tenses. She's not home…

Perhaps she'll answer and tell me to piss off— she'd have every right. My back muscles join my shoulders and my gut, a sickening wrestle for control of my strung-out body, while I wait on the doorstep in the cold.

When I withdrew from her in the car on Monday, my head was all over the place. Meeting Mia on the eve of what should have been my fourth wedding anniversary left me floundering like a stunned mullet, and I handled it badly. I exhale through pursed lips, squinting through a tiny slit in the drawn curtains as my impatience reaches boiling point.

I knock again, the sinking feeling in my gut as foreign as standing on a doorstep to ask someone out. *Fuck.* What am I doing?

'Coming.' A deep, muffled voice from somewhere inside.

That's not Mia. The last time I saw her at the play, her throaty laugh, her clear excitement for the venue, her wide stare made what could have been an exercise in torture tolerable.

I couldn't even tell you the first name of the clients I spent the night sucking up to, a false grin plastered on my face while they enjoyed the performance from the best box in the house, followed by a VIP backstage experience where they not only met the actors, but also dined with the star of the show at an exclusive restaurant in neighbouring Covent Garden.

Once upon a time I embraced the lifestyle, wore it like an expensive suit. The excess, the exotic travel, off-the-beaten-track adventures and stuff-of-dreams luxury. Now I can barely muster polite conversation for the wealthiest clients who stay in Faulkner hotels and pay through the nose for my services. Thank fuck Mia was there, smoothing the waters in her relaxed, easy-going way.

The door opens to reveal a tall, slightly crumpled man in his early thirties, his hair sticking up in places.

'Yes?' His accent matches Mia's. Is this the

brother she mentioned? They look nothing alike—
he's stocky with a shock of red hair and lacks Mia's
long-limbed grace.

I stick out my hand. 'Kit Faulkner. Is Mia home?'
I stretch my mouth into a non-confrontational smile.
Manners will expedite what I want.

Mia.

Naked.

Me inside her.

'Just a second.' He eyes me with suspicion—*definitely* the brother.

When she comes to the door, she's wide-eyed and
similarly rumpled, as if they'd been snuggled on the
sofa, watching a movie.

And just like that my entire body lightens a fraction, the muscular knots unravelling. My eyes sweep
over her, desperate now to see the whole package
after the tantalising glimpse I had in the car. Now
that I've, once again, pulled my head out of my arse
and survived yet another trigger.

She frowns. 'It's midnight.' She pushes her thick
hair back from her make-up-free face and twists it
as if she wants to tame the wildness. She's pretty
without make-up.

My fingers twitch—I hadn't wanted to rumple
the breathtaking vision of her in the car too much,
but now I want to see her naked, that dark hair kissing her delicate shoulders, the ends teasing her rosy
nipples, the strands falling through my fingers…

'It's…' I check the time again '…four minutes

past.' I drill my stare into hers so she sees I'm deadly serious. 'It's *Wednesday*.'

Reality dawns and she flushes the way she did on Monday as she came around my fingers, her golden skin glowing, highlighting the scattered freckles across her bare shoulders.

At her hesitation, emotion forces steel into my tone. 'Have you changed your mind? It's fine if you have—I'll just see you at Bounty Events tomorrow.' Part of me wants her to tell me to fuck off. I'm an unreasonable bastard. No one sane arrives on someone's doorstep after midnight for sex. At least not without a booty call first.

She looks over her shoulder down the darkened hallway. 'I… I'm staying with my brother.'

I shake my head, showing her I don't want to come in. I have a hotel room near by, all ready to go. I indicate my Aston at the kerb. 'Come with me.' I hold my breath, torn between needing her silent acceptance and expecting her refusal.

Withdrawing without explanation on Monday has surely earned me the door slammed in my face. Perhaps that's the real reason she focussed on the client and barely spoke to me, while I'd reeled from our brief sexual encounter, my gut churning over the looming anniversary.

We both know my body wanted to finish things, but my head got in my way. I won't make the same mistake tonight. Tonight she's mine—if she still wants the same thing. A new level of gut convulsions adds to my restlessness while she wavers. I'm acting unhinged. But all *I* want is what she said *she* wanted two days ago.

Just sex.

She shuffles her feet, reason warring with desire in her eyes. Then she nods. 'I haven't changed my mind. Give me one minute.'

I saunter back to my car, perching myself on the warm bonnet while I wait, some of the tension leaving me now I know she's still on board. It's good to feel something, even uncertainty, after the weeks of numbness leading to yesterday, a day I should celebrate, but which I only dread. Because nothing changes as I relive one of the worst days of my life— like Groundhog Day. Every memory identical, every emotion replayed as if I'm an actor, performing take after take…

I focus on tonight, this thing with Mia, just sex. Something the practical Ms Abbott pointed out that we can get over and done with and move on from. Something eminently controllable. Something that provides me with more than the physical high.

For a few blissful minutes I forget. Forget Laura's pale face as she lay dying in my arms, forget the skin-flaying helplessness of not being able to do anything to save her, forget how I wish it had been me to die in the middle of nowhere—technically she made it to the nearest hospital, but she never regained consciousness and I was told her brain likely died on the side of that volcano in Indonesia.

Mia is back, saving me from another trip down Self-Loathing Alley. She's thrown on a puffer-style jacket and carries a small bag. I don't want to think about what's inside—it looks too small for a change of clothes but could potentially carry a toothbrush.

I open the door for her, my muscles welcoming the return to action. I slip behind the wheel and pull out into the quiet residential street.

'Where are we going?' Her voice is steady. No nerves?

Good. I'm too impatient for distractions, as impatient as Mia was in the car to the theatre. 'A hotel.'

She nods her consent. 'One of yours?'

A snort. 'No. But I've never been there before, if that's what's bothering you.' I change the subject. 'I interrupted your evening.' I'm sorry, but I'm too strung-out to vocalise more than a few words.

She shrugs. 'No problem, we were just done watching a movie.'

I nod, adding another twist to my intestines as I picture the scene of quiet domestic normality. 'Did you enjoy the play?'

She laughs, the throaty sound so unexpected and sultry, I almost rear-end the car in front. 'I did actually. I wasn't expecting to, but it was…fun.'

'Adrenaline-level fun?'

Another laugh. 'Not quite *that* good.'

'So what qualifies for that level for you?' I catch sight of her fidgeting in my peripheral vision and grip the wheel tighter to stop myself reaching out to still those fingers. After our consent talk, I'm not touching her until she asks me to.

'Oh, you know, anything outdoorsy, adventurous—kayaking, mountain biking, kite surfing. And sex, of course.' She shifts in the seat, turning her body to face mine. 'So, why Wednesday?' Her voice holds an edge, but her cool stare settles on me as if she won't take my bullshit evasion this time.

Of course she wouldn't simply accept my non-explanation. She's too smart, too forthright. Qualities I admire. I swallow, my throat tight. My first instinct is to lie. To avoid the emotional black hole. But what difference does it make? We're just fucking. As she said—get it over with and move on. And she'll soon be leaving London. It's almost too perfect a situation, and perhaps the reason I'm so impatient.

Mia is different to any woman I've ever met, as if normal rules don't apply. She's unapologetically herself. She propositioned *me* for sex. And she seems more interested in the work she's here to do than flattering me or trying to burrow under my guard. I can't figure her out. Perhaps that's what has me crawling out of my skin tonight…

'Yesterday was my wedding anniversary.' I force the words out, knowing they'll taste foul but hoping they'll draw a line under this conversation. A sick slug of euphoria warms my ice-cold blood at the ensuing silence, an awkward one. And one I usually relish. Nothing makes people run quicker than the fear of not knowing what to say.

'Ah…' She nods. 'Yes, I can see why you'd want to avoid *that* day.'

I wait for platitudes, cloying concern, even embarrassment. But Mia simply stares out of the window. Direct. Different. No bullshit.

In case curiosity gets the better of her, I steer us back to the transactional nature of this agreement, one that doesn't involve talking about my tattered psyche and shit personal life. 'Are you on birth control?'

She nods, eyeing me with her huge dark eyes, which are illuminated by the dash of my car, like I'm the wolf and she's Little Red Riding Hood. 'But I want to use condoms as well.'

'Me too.' Good, we're both into safe sex. And we're here.

I pull into the hotel's underground garage, park up and open her door. My manners give her pause—she glances at me like I've sprouted a second head. I can't blame her—I have been a little hit and miss. Time to pull my head out of my arse.

I put my hand in the small of her back, ignoring the unconscious jolt of surprise that jerks her body, and guide her to the lift. Perhaps she *is* nervous. Perhaps she's changed her mind and no longer wants anything to do with twisted, contradictory Kit Faulkner. Can't say I blame her—the guy pisses me off most days.

Once inside, with the doors closed, I resist the testosterone pounding through my body, resist the urge to touch her more than I already have and instead offer some reassurance. 'I know we made an... agreement, but I'm not a dickhead, despite turning up on your brother's doorstep and despite my behaviour Monday.'

She nods.

'I laid down some rules, but they are about us both having a good time—if there's something you don't like, or you don't want to do, just say and we'll stop. Okay?' I'm not into major kink, I just want sex the way I want it.

The one thing I can control.

And I want Mia.

'I will.' She lifts her chin, that flash of determination returning to her eyes, and I'm reminded not only does Mia consider me a challenge, but also that Little Red Riding Hood eventually triumphs over the wolf.

She's in the driving seat here. She suggested this mutually satisfying arrangement before I had time to suggest it first. I'd have at least bought her a glass of wine, dinner, spent the evening showing her my intentions before offering her a nightcap at a conveniently placed hotel on the way home.

My stare falls to her full mouth and sweeps lower to her pale neck. My fingers flex, impatient to have her naked. The glimpses of her body that the sexy dress revealed and the one spectacular breast I'd sampled in the car, the memory of the feel of her softness on my fingers left me hollow, unfulfilled. I want more of Mia. Everything she has to give me, and even then I'll wring a little more from her compliant body.

If she'll let me.

The lift reaches the foyer and we check in at the desk. Mia stands beside me, but not too close. She's clearly confident about her sexuality, but she's not remotely flirty or overly affectionate. Has she really never been in a relationship...? Why?

I shelve my curiosity, keen to get my hands on her, the self-denial torture now she's this close. There isn't much night left and a whole lot of pleasure to cram into it.

Another lift. The air seems thicker, warmer in this one, heavy with sexual tension when Mia glances sideways at me, her lips parted, thick enough to slice with a knife. And then we're in the suite I've booked, the bottle of wine I've ordered already chilling in a bucket of ice.

The door clicks closed behind us and some of the tension coiled in my muscles leaves me with my slowly exhaled breath.

I've barely uttered the word 'Drink?', barely made one step in the direction of the wine before she drops her bag on the floor and flies at me, taking what she wants with a rough tug around my neck and voracious kisses.

Thank fuck!

My patience snaps like overstretched wire. I'm right there with her. Her hands slide into my hair and her body mashes to my front. The release leaves me in a groan as I scoop my arm around her waist and haul her up from the floor and onto my mouth. Her hands twist, seeking anchorage, and her thighs cling to my waist as she kisses me, as if she too had been seconds from breaking point.

I kiss her back, slaking the need pounding through my veins, while I grapple with the urge to rush this. My body wants one thing, but my head demands control, and right now Mia's wildness matches the storm in me.

I slide the coat from her shoulders and slip my hand under her sweater to find her nipples hard and straining against her bra. I drag my mouth away from hers, loving her throaty gasp of outrage and the pink flush to her skin.

'Take off your clothes.' I want her naked. I want to fuck her all the ways I can.

She lifts her sweater over her head and I resist the urge to reach out and stroke her cheek, which is dotted with the same freckles that cover her shoulders. She shivers, wetting her lips with a swipe of her tongue, and lust pounds me but there's no time to enjoy the show because she's back, kissing me, intermittently clawing at my clothes and grappling with her own.

No need, darlin'. You had me at 'Good to meet you.'

I slow things down, taking hold of both her wrists in one hand and raise them overhead while I walk her backwards and press her against the wall. The longer I draw this out, the greater the reprieve from feeling. She'll be lucky to sleep before dawn.

With my free hand I unfasten her bra and push it down, tearing my mouth from her wild kisses to get my lips around the nipple that's haunted the few hours of sleep I've managed since Monday.

Her hips buck against mine and she gasps as I first tongue the nipple and then scrape my teeth over the bud.

I look up, revelling in the mixed emotions flitting through her beautiful stare while I press my erection into her belly. 'You know we're going to be good together.'

Her pupils dilate, a breathy little shudder leaving her as she offers a shaky nod.

I force my exhale through relaxed lips to stop the whoosh of air revealing the need pounding in my blood. Her body undulates against mine, unable to keep still, but this doesn't surprise me about Mia.

She holds my stare.

Good.

I want her eyes wide open, watching what I'm going to do to her. I step back, muscles punishing me for my change of pace. But Mia needs to be savoured, like the wine we're both too impatient to drink.

I lift the bra and cup her perfect breasts, one at a time, my thumb torturing the peaks while passion blazes across Mia's face. My dick throbs. Can she see the effect she has on me? But my excitement is laced with poison, yesterday's turmoil still fresh.

I need more. Need all of her.

She releases a small cry, half-moan, half-protest. Perhaps she senses the barely controlled beast in me. Perhaps it's too big for her to handle, like, some days, it's too big for me.

I finish opening the zip of her jeans and push the fabric over her hips. She wriggles, helping, her hands still trapped by one of mine. She's given me the control I need, but it costs her, lust and defiance warring for control of her stare. I reward her with my hand burrowing into her underwear, my fingers probing between her legs to find the slickness I expected.

I let go of her hands so I can crouch in front of her and help to peel the skin-tight denim from her long, slender legs.

When I lift my stare up her body, resisting the temptation to press my mouth to her flat belly and taste her silky skin, I catch sight of her fingers tapping against one thigh.

I capture the fluttering fingers and stand, pressing her hand to my erection through my jeans and holding it there until the tension seeps from her hand, her arm and finally her face.

Mia has an Achilles heel. The fidgeting, the need to prove herself, the fight. Does it go deeper than nerves?

She asked me in the car on Monday if I wanted to tame her—also not my kink. But now, the urge to unearth Mia's secret places calls to me, a curiosity, a hedonistic indulgence I'd believed long ago extinguished. I shouldn't care—it's not what this is about. But I'm beyond intrigued. And I'm selfish. When I push inside her, when those tight internal muscles of hers squeeze my dick, I want to know I'm the only thing she feels; that the only thought in her head is how good it feels.

The only thing Mia has to prove is that she's come, several times.

I release her hand. Her fingers linger, rubbing and gently squeezing for one beat, two. I press her back against the wall, the small gasp as her arse hits what is probably the cool paintwork filling my mouth.

Her wild kisses match the way she kissed me in the car, her breathy moans and whimpers loud enough to be heard in the room next door. My body is all but roaring, the adrenaline off the charts and my dick painfully engorged. This is what I've craved since I met her. The release. The all-consuming rush. The command of her pleasure.

Another surge of blood to my groin makes me wince, reminding me I'm still fully clothed. I pull my mouth away and push her shoulders back against the wall to break the kiss.

'Stay there. Don't move.'

She listens, panting as hard as I am, those glorious tits rising into my field of vision with every breath. I toss my shirt and pop the buttons on my fly, providing my dick with some relief. And then I press up against her, loving the way her eyelids droop over those sexy eyes, and her fingers reflexively clutch my forearms as if she'd fall over without me there to hold her up.

I kiss her again, revelling in the way her nails dig into my skin, and her eyes turn glassy, and then I slide my mouth to her ear, sucking in her essence—honeysuckle, warm woman and sex. My muscles scream with inertia. I want Mia undone, her façade cracked open, any detachment she's clinging to flying to the stars as she succumbs to pleasure at my hands.

'Stay against the wall, or I'll stop.' It's a low growl and a promise. While she's here, she's mine. My hand returns to between her legs, my fingers instantly coated in her arousal.

'Kit…'

My name on her lips slams fresh heat through me. I watch the lust bloom across her face as I push my finger inside her and twist my wrist. She cries out, her hips bucking against my hand. Euphoria thickens my blood—this is the control I seek, the brief interlude from punishing myself with *what if* and *it should have been me.*

I pull back and she collapses against the wall, fire in her eyes, as if she's forgotten this was her idea. 'Don't stop.'

I smile, nowhere near done with her. 'I have no intention, gorgeous.' I drop to my knees and her thighs tremble.

I hold my breath, the burn in my throat fiercer than it should be. I want to taste her more than I want my next heartbeat. More than I've wanted anything in a long, long time.

My hands bracket her narrow hips, my stare locked on the sight before me. Her breath hitches, her chest expanding as she too holds her breath.

'Open. I want to go down on you. I want you to come watching me.' Fuck, my voice is sandpaper-rough—this game with Mia is ten times as rewarding as my usual sexual encounters. Because her eyes tell me she wants everything I can give her, but something in her head holds her back.

She obeys, but when I look up the expected hint of rebellion is there in her eyes. We're similar, Mia and I, I suspect. Neither of us keen to perform to an expected societal role.

And here we don't have to. Just two people, enjoying pleasure. Free to walk away afterwards, expectations intact.

I lean in, pressing the flat of my tongue against her and locating her pouty clit.

'Oh…' Her hands re-find my hair and her hips shunt backwards, withdrawing. But I follow, and now she has nowhere else to go, trapped between my insistent mouth and the wall.

From between her legs I watch every reaction, every cry, every flush. Her hips jerk restlessly in my hands. She scrunches her eyes closed, her head falling back against the wall with a thud, and her hands cling to my hair as if I'm the only thing between her and the floor.

Fresh blood pounds in my groin and roars in my head. I smile as all the while my tongue alternately works her clit and plunges inside. I love that she's not afraid to watch me go down on her. The challenge sparking in her amber stare, as if she can take anything I can dish out, spurs me on. I delay my own need a while longer, desperate now to make her come like this, pressed against the wall, watching me work her to orgasm with my mouth.

I don't have to wait long. With a final whimper, some unintelligible curse, her face contorts, jaw slack as she comes. Her stare latches to mine until the last, blissful seconds when she loses some inner battle and her head once again falls back against the wall.

Perfect.

Blood pounding, temperature soaring and muscles twitching, I'm all action. I kiss her while I shrug off my jeans and heel off my shoes. If she needs recovery time, she's not going to get it. She can ball me out while she's coming again. I encourage her towards the bed, pausing to scoop off my socks and fish out the condoms from my jeans pocket.

I tear my mouth away from hers. 'Get on the bed. All fours.'

She follows my curt orders while I cover myself. My pulse pounds in my head at her position of relative vulnerability on the bed.

My hand traces the bumps of her spine and I caress both smooth cheeks while I stare at the place between them, a place I'm soon to get lost inside.

'Kit, hurry…' Her voice is a whimper.

My head swims and my knees practically buckle. I position myself at her entrance, the tip of my cock nestled in her heat. I grit my teeth, the pleasure so intense, the urge to rush this almost suffocating me. But Mia is worth savouring. I bite my lip, the metallic tang of blood helping me find the control I need.

With my hands once again encasing her rounded hips, I slide inside, just an inch.

Mia's fingers curl into the sheets. My brain overrides every muscle in my body as I hold myself perfectly still. 'Am I hurting you?' That's not my kink, either.

'No…no, don't stop.' Her chest works hard with the soft pants she's emitting.

Only a stampede of wild horses bursting into the room could stop me now. I ease myself inside the hot clasp of her until I'm buried to the hilt. My eyes roll, but not before she writhes her fantastic arse and rears her head up, the wildness of her dark hair flicking down her back towards me.

How did I get so lucky? Tomorrow I'll thank Reid and Drake.

While I give her a second to grow accustomed to me buried deep inside, and myself a second to will away the tingles shooting down my length, I reach out and stroke her hair, loving the contrast of its rich colour to the golden skin of her back. I want to grip the thick mass of it, to twist it around my wrist and hold firm while I pound into her.

I close my eyes, engulfed by her...her tight heat clamped around my cock, her feminine scent clinging to my skin, invading my nostrils, and her wild, silky hair flowing through my fingers. I slam my eyes open, shaking the stupid poetic shit from my head. But Mia is impatient. She shunts her hips back onto me with a small mewl.

I abandon her hair to caress her arse as I begin thrusting. She's perfect. She's given me everything I wanted, conceded to my whim and embraced the unexpected sexual tension raging between us.

Why was I worried? As long as she's as pragmatic when this ends, I'm home free.

As I pound her harder, guided by her cries and gasped encouragement, I clasp one of her shoulders for purchase. Her moans grow choppier with every thrust even as my brain shuts down to everything but the fire building at the base of my spine.

But I want more. Want her with me. This sexy, ballsy, beautiful woman. I bend over her, my free hand delving between her legs to locate her clit once more. She's drenched, coating my fingers. My cock swells and she cries out as I strum the swollen bundle of nerves back to life.

'No... I can't...' she says, but she grips my cock tighter. And I won't take no for an answer.

'You will.'

She braces her weight on one arm and her fingers join mine, each of us greedy for the slip and slide of pleasuring Mia.

But then it's just my fingers, because she's coming again, her hands clawing the bedclothes and her muscles clutching me so tight I let go and join her. With her wails still sounding in my head, fire shoots down my length and I come, pumping into her and collapsing my weight onto her back, finally spent.

We lie in a sweaty, panting, tangled heap for a few seconds until I slip from her and dispense with the condom.

My chest burns, but it's the good kind of burn, the endorphin-associated high of extreme exertion. I wait for the icy revulsion to return, to dampen the rush—the usual loathing that I've just cheated on Laura. It's there but distant enough to ignore after a few harsh swallows.

Mia stirs beside me. I throw my arm around her waist, stilling her escape. If she leaves now, it might return full force. I slide my hand to her arse, caressing the pale cheek as my still engorged cock flicks on my thigh.

'I'm not done. Give me five minutes.' Fuck, after that I might need ten.

She groans, burying her face in the bed linens, but I catch her hint of a smile, which fills my lungs with the freshest cool mountain air.

It's three a.m. by the time we're too exhausted to wring any more pleasure from each other. I'm in a semi-slumberous state, my body sated and mind blank, when she crawls from the bed and pads into the bathroom. Two minutes later the door clicking closed informs me not only isn't she coming back to bed, but she's left.

Without so much as a goodbye.

I prop myself up on my elbows and scan the room for confirmation. But no, her coat and bag are gone.

Well, that's a new one on me.

I wait for the flood of lightness in my head heralding relief, but instead I'm greeted with a gnawing sensation in the pit of my gut I don't want to examine too closely. I exhale, scrub at my haphazard hair and stretch, certain it will pass. I shower, dress and head home through quiet, darkened streets to my even quieter, darker home.

CHAPTER FIVE

Mia

A WET SNOUT and a doggy whine greet me as I open the door and peer gingerly inside Kit's darkened house. I'm not proud that I'm resorting to hunting him down at his swanky Chelsea address, but he has his side of the bargain to uphold.

I stroke the dog, a beautiful, sleek Weimaraner with soulful eyes and the happiest tail I've ever come across, my chuckle of delight banishing any reservations I might have had for inviting myself into Kit's domain.

Dogs are certainly Mia's best friends. I drop to a crouch, my throat hot and achy, and give rein to my homesickness, my mind back in New Zealand with my family's elderly Labrador, Bess, as I bury my face in his wriggling neck. A quick check of his collar and we're on first-name terms.

Aside from the clatter of Bob's claws on the hardwood flooring and my joyful sniffling, the house is silent and shrouded in relative darkness. I drop the key Reid gave me onto the hall table, lean my heavy backpack of equipment against the wall and move into the kitchen, relieved to see Bob has fresh water in his bowl.

Bob laps at the water as if showing me he's perfectly well cared for. I lean against the immaculate, clutter-free bench top, my muscles restless. It's midday. Like me, this dog has way too much energy to be cooped up inside. And it's London. Why does Kit need a dog like this in the city? I'm one misdemeanour from calling the RSPCA when I spy the framed photo on the wall in the living space.

The electrical signals to my heart short out as if the wiring is faulty.

A beaming Kit and a beautiful blonde woman sandwich a puppy version of Bob. It's Kit's smile that slays me the deepest, the knife sliding through my vital organs until I release the hushed gasp trapped in my chest. It's exactly as I suspected—his genuine, unrestrained smile changes his face completely, taking him from cruelly handsome to weep-worthy, dashing and a hundred other clichés. I stare, marvelling at the way happiness brightens his eyes, deepens the grooves that bracket his sensual mouth and lends his entire face a playfulness that makes me smile myself. But it's so alien I want to rush to find him and check I have the right address. I wonder how long it's been since he wore that smile. Perhaps this woman here, his dead wife, was the only one ever to inspire such dazzling happiness.

My eyes start to burn looking at the impossibly beautiful trio, their joy pouring from the photographic paper. I look away, acid in my throat and my shoulders around my ears.

Intruder.

I shouldn't have come here. If he'd wanted me in his home, he'd have brought me here in the early hours of this morning when he sought me out at four minutes past midnight.

For incredible sex.

I flush hot at the erotic memories—I was correct about the sheet-clawing ride of my life—reminding myself I don't have to belong here. I'm here because Kit and I have a deal.

But then I remember his expression while he filled my brother's doorstep—unmistakable fire in his eyes, yes. But something darker too. Some demon lurking. Pain…? Regret…?

Of course, his anniversary must have brought up difficult memories. So he had ghosts to banish—we all have motivating factors. The sex should be out of our systems so we can move on.

I kept my side of the bargain, despite being unprepared for the dark intensity of what we did last night. Yes, I'd been a willing accomplice to the best sex of my life. But, somehow, I'd expected less. Some rushed fumbling, a perfectly adequate orgasm and a lift home.

Something forgettable.

Liar.

You know we're going to be good together...

I knew. I wince, the niggle of jealousy at seeing Kit with his wife irrational but strong enough to linger. For the hundredth time I wonder what I'm doing here. A place I definitely don't belong...

Kit Faulkner, that's what—an unexpected man on multiple levels.

I hadn't expected the irresistible thrill at the bite of command in his gruff voice, or the searing eye contact as he pressed me against the wall and licked at me, or the ruthless way he dragged another climax from my over-stimulated, weaker-than-I-thought body.

But last night was simply really good sex. He'd needed it. I'd needed it. And now it's over.

My stare wanders to more informal snaps on the contemporary bookcase and then to one of Kit, Drake and Reid together. It's a few years old, each brother younger and alike enough in looks to show the family resemblance. Reid and Kit bracket Drake, who wears army dress uniform. All three point similar handsome smiles at the camera.

I swallow hard, hoping to ease the burn behind my sternum. I'm standing in Kit's beautiful home, looking at his family photos while I stroke his beautiful dog. Kit, his life, the trappings on display, scream roots. Family ties. The permanence of a pet to love.

A place to come back to, to belong. Just like Will has with Josh. Just like Kit must have had with his wife.

I fill the empty space in my chest with air, re-minding myself *I* have everything I need. Every-thing I want.

Bob nudges my hand and I suck in a calming breath in the here and now, refocused on my mis-sion—Kit had his way last night, and I'm determined to get mine today.

'Go on, then,' I say to my companion.

Bob understands me, clever dog. I follow him down the hallway. My hand finds the light switch as I push open the door to what I'm guessing is a bedroom.

I was fired up enough when I lugged my backpack of filming equipment here on the tube, even before I discovered poor, neglected Bob. Just because we shagged a four-race marathon last night, there's no excuse for Kit's lazy-arsed antics.

Bob sits obediently beside the occupied bed, whining, his tail swishing across the hardwood.

I know the feeling. The occupant has let us both down. I move to the floor-to-ceiling drapes, drag-ging them open to let in the gloriously sunny day, already half wasted. There's a groan from the bed and the mound under the duvet reconfigures itself. I plop down at the foot of the bed and scratch the top of Bob's silky head.

Another doggy whimper.

Kit's arm shoots out, patting the air as he searches, presumably for his hound.

An incoherent mumble.

More tossing and turning.

The duvet slips to his waist.

I freeze while my lady parts clench viciously. My mouth dries as I trace his back muscles with my greedy eyes. Part of me craves a repeat of last night, even though I still feel him between my legs when I walk. But, as good as the sex was, it's done. We've scratched that itch. Time to keep moving forward. Time for work.

Still, I indulge my stare, taking in the golden skin covering Kit's sculpted shoulders, the dimples at the top of what I know to be his superbly muscular arse and the dark hair covering the strong arm pillowing his head.

My fingers tap the bedclothes, restless to grab my camera and photograph his male beauty. I've been addicted to visually capturing the world around me since a sixteen-year-old Will saved up all his money from his summer job to buy me a camera for my fifteenth birthday. Even as a teen, my brother knew me better than I knew myself; saw something in me others had failed to pick up—that the reckless, rebellious girl was hurting and needed an outside focus beyond her own head, her own demons.

Bob whines again, and I clear my tight throat. 'Why would you name such a sleek and regal creature as this *Bob*?'

Kit leans up on his elbows, his back clenched to show me all those yummy muscles my artist's eye longs to immortalise in digital form, all disarrayed bed hair and sexy sleepiness. I press my thighs together, the resultant twinge reminding me of the multiple orgasms I received a mere eleven hours ago. Orgasms that should have cured me of this distraction.

Tearing my mind from the possibility of a repeat, I pre-empt his likely question. 'Reid gave me your key and your address. He said skipping work wasn't that unusual for you. But I know you're not lazing in bed because you're welching on our deal. I have my business to run, even if you don't care about yours.'

Bob rests his chin on my knee as if he senses the tension coiling between Kit and me.

'Fuck.' Kit plops back on the pillows and scrubs at his haphazard hair. 'What time is it?'

'Just before midday.' I focus on Bob, a distraction from thoughts of Kit naked under the duvet. 'Has this poor creature been out for a toilet stop?' First things first. I can berate Kit once Bob's needs are met.

He nods. 'Eight o'clock. I must have dozed back off.'

I'm not surprised. I assumed he would stay at the hotel after I'd left. His extreme stamina and short recovery time kept us both up until three a.m. We used all his condom stash *and* one of mine.

I dive right into the reason I'm here, keeping my own tricky libido on track. 'So, I've looked at the program Bounty Events provides through *Off the Guidebook*. I want to do a recon today, visit one of the venues, perhaps do a little filming if the light is good.' I stand, eager to start work. Bob wags his tail.

Yes, it is walk time.

To Kit I say, 'Up and at 'em.' My knee nudges his foot.

Kit mumbles something unintelligible and then throws off the duvet and strides bare-arse naked with a full morning glory to what I assume is an en-suite bathroom.

I roll my eyes at Bob. 'At least he had the class to close the door.'

With a flush and some running water he's back, drying his hands on a towel and staring from the doorway. My nipples chafe on my shirt—he does that so well. Brooding. Intense.

'You left. Last night.' Clipped. Pissy. And completely unapologetic for his nakedness.

I fight the urge to stare at his erection. I don't need to look. I remember his prowess in minute detail. He's waiting for my response, so I shrug. What did he expect? The sex was over…eventually. Did he think I'd want to snuggle, that I'd come over all clingy?

Instead of his being appeased, his jaw clenches. 'Women don't normally run from my bed.'

I bet they don't.

'Is that what's bothering you?' My eyes flick to his crotch—I can't help myself—to his magnificent, proud cock, and my internal muscles flutter, keen for more.

He tosses the towel and I drag my eyes from his cock. It's long and thick against his thigh and if I closed my eyes I could conjure how he felt moving inside me. 'I didn't run. We were done.'

His eyes narrow, brows pinched together. He looks like I stole his line, like the clichéd role reversal is freaking him out.

I stifle my smile. 'No one's ever got up and left you after sex before?' I ask, but I know the answer. Who in their right mind wouldn't want as much of Kit Faulkner as they could get?

But I'm different.

'I told you—I don't do relationships. Cuddling, sleepovers…that's for lovers, couples.' My last word tastes bulky in my mouth as if I'll never be able to swallow it down. I glance around the room for signs of his wife—more pictures, her perfume still on the dresser, clothes in the wardrobe—and then snap my eyes back to him when I realise what I'm doing.

I'm greeted with his silence and the hard stare. Why is he so offended? It's just sex.

'Why have you never had a relationship?'

Of course he would be that blunt. That direct. I shrug, ignoring the tension across my shoulders and at the back of my neck. 'It's just too time-consuming.' *Too permanent.* 'Work has me travelling a lot. Casual works best for me.'

My eyes burn with the force of holding his inscrutable stare. Our reasons for avoiding commitment may be different, but in practice we're the same.

'So you've never been tempted, not once?' He folds his arms across his chest, rubbing at his bottom lip with one thumb and forefinger.

I wish he'd put some clothes on... Do I? Really?

'I came close to something serious at uni. But it didn't work out. I'm too flighty, too…busy, I guess.' I look away from his penetrating eyes to Bob—my distraction and my escape plan.

'Anyway, I'm going to take Bob here for a walk. That should give you enough time to shower. We'll talk about a work schedule when I get back.'

With a lazy smile that hints he's seen through my flimsy excuses, Kit stretches his arms above his head, gripping the doorframe so his thick biceps bulge and his abs contract as his cock jerks back to life. 'Why don't you join me?' A sleepy smile. A sexy head-tilt.

Before I can answer, the smile slides from his face and that look of regret returns to his eyes. 'Still casual.'

He's serious.

The throb is back between my legs. I force myself immobile, breathing through the urge to do just that. My brain panics around inside my skull. He's looking at me as if mentally stripping me. Like I'd be looking at him if he weren't already naked.

No. No. And hell, no.

I laugh to fill the silence.

My throat is dry so I swallow the saliva pooled in my mouth. I assumed once the sex was behind us this pull would abate, but despite feeling like an intruder in his home, despite the shadows Kit hasn't quite chased away from his stare, my lady parts love the idea of mutual showering with sexy, no-strings Kit.

'You kind of cheated me, after all,' he adds, releasing the doorframe but still in no hurry to cover his fantastic body.

I waiver, the arguments becoming more obscure. 'I did?' No way does he need to coax and cajole women into morning-after sex—if they last that long. His photo-ready physique is enough temptation.

Plus, he delivers. Astoundingly. In multiples. Another slug of hormones weakens my resolve. But I conceded to him enough last night. And that cloud behind his stare… How long will I be able to ignore it before it blurs the lines? Before it drags me under? Already I'm burning with curiosity about Laura. How she died. What it did to him. Could he ever get over such a loss? Why I even care…?

'No way.' My fingers toy with Bob's silky ear— *flip-flap, flip-flap.* 'We had a deal. I kept my side of it. Time to pay up, Mr Faulkner.'

'Scared?' A derisive lip-curl—he's good at those too.

You bet. Way too tempting.

I lift my chin. 'Of what?'

He shrugs. 'I'm stark bollock naked, inviting you into my shower. Your nipples are practically breaking out of that top, your eyes are full of that excitement you love so much and yet you're fully clothed and about to run.'

I splutter, 'I am not. Your dog needs exercise, and I have work to do. No more bending me to your will until you've paid up with your co-operation.'

'Bending you to my will…?' His brows pinch and a playful smile dances on his sinful mouth. 'You didn't enjoy yourself last night?' He stalks closer, as self-assured as if he wore one of his immaculate suits. He folds his arms over his chest and plants his feet wide as if he's fully dressed while he manspreads.

I fight the urge to drop to my knees, swallow him the way he swallowed me last night and wipe the cocky smile from his face. I shrug, scratching at Bob's neck to combat the urge to fidget. 'I like sex. It's not a crime.'

His eyes narrow and he rubs his bottom lip, as if I'm a puzzling conundrum, one of those brain-twister 3D puzzles to be teased apart. 'You sure I can't persuade you to reconsider?'

I snort, shaking my head and looking away, because he's close enough I can see the sparks of blue flame in his eyes, the other darker emotions absent. His bed, the starkly white linens rumpled, inviting and probably still warm from the heat of his body, is two steps away.

My body starts to sway towards his, although my feet remain glued to the spot. And then the photos flash into my lust-fogged mind. Kit with his wife. Kit with his brothers. Kit with his dog.

A shiny, happy family life. He and his wife probably would have gone on to have shiny, happy children had she lived long enough. Would Kit's children bear the Faulkner resemblance he and his brothers share?

The skin-prickling restlessness I've had since my plane touched down at Heathrow returns. I try to think about my appearance as little as possible because thinking about my looks, so different from my adoptive family's, leads to wondering where they come from, and that rabbit hole is infinitely deep and dark and full of unknowns.

I hate to concede, but Kit is right. The violent chemistry hasn't gone away. The pretty constant buzz between my legs is fully on Kit's side. But it makes no difference. We had sex. Just sex. And now I have a job to do before I move on. End of the Kit and Mia story.

'What my body may or may not want right now is irrelevant.' I toss the statement at him and the dog whines. I drop my voice, soothing Bob with gentle strokes to his head, although I'm probably sucking up more comfort than I'm imparting. 'The point is, you're trying to get out of today, and that's not cool, Faulkner.'

He frowns, annoyance tightening his mouth. 'You know, that name really doesn't do it for me.'

'No?' I drag my eyes back to his, away from the

temptation of his lips. 'It's a Kiwi thing, I guess. Most men I know wouldn't bat an eyelid.'

He steps closer and my insides tremble. I should have left five minutes ago. I'm certain he's still hard. That his offer still stands. That it would be so easy to give in…

Don't look down. Don't look down.

'I'd prefer to hear something else when you address me.'

Pompous dick.

'Such as?'

Another step. My neck cranes back as I maintain the eye contact that's preventing me from touching him. Preventing me rolling around naked with him for the rest of the day.

Kit shrugs, his heated eyes only leaving mine to trace my parted lips before returning. '*Kit. Yes! More!* Or even *I'm coming* will do.'

I shake my head, beyond tempted to silence his conceited drivel with a kiss. But it wouldn't end there; my fizzing blood and galloping pulse tell me how close to danger I am. He's not distracting me from work today, not with his fantastic body or his sexual commands. Not even with his beautiful dog…

'Well, *Kit*,' I step back, away from his body heat. Away from temptation, 'as soon as I've walked your poor, under-exercised pet, I'm going to Bounty Events. With or without you.'

I stride from the bedroom, furious with my body's weakness. While I battle my hormones into submission, I retrace my footsteps down the hallway with an excited Bob at my heels, snatch up the brown leather lead I'd spied hanging from some hooks just inside the entranceway and grab the house key.

'Mia.'

I spin around.

He's still naked, but now he's wearing a wide, cocky grin, as if he knows he's rattled me. 'The dog-walker will be here in,' he looks down at his watch, 'ten minutes.'

It's beyond infantile but I give him the finger and storm out with my new four-legged friend to hit the bustling streets of Chelsea.

CHAPTER SIX

Kit

WHEN SHE RETURNS with Bob, I'm dressed and finishing a bowl of cereal. Her cheeks are a fetching shade of pink as if she's enjoyed herself. An urgent need kicks me below the belt—I want to be the one to show the intriguing Mia here a good time. To show her the sights of London. To impress her, because I already know it's no easy feat—convention won't cut it.

I snort—fucking jealous of my own dog. I'm clearly still hungover from the sex or something...

I remember my manners and raise the bowl in offering. 'Would you like some cereal?' I wince. What a moron; I should make her some lunch, but I've no idea what's in the cupboards. Ronnie, my long-suffering housekeeper, has given up trying to feed me, claiming it's wasteful to throw food away week after week.

Mia shakes her head. 'No, thank you.'

Perhaps she's already eaten lunch, still on New

Zealand time. Now I wish I'd dragged my unmotivated arse out of bed and accompanied Mia and Bob on their walk. We could have stopped at the bistro at the end of my street for brunch—they do an excellent eggs Florentine and I could have dug into the fascinating Mia while she tucked into the food. Perhaps that would have put some more colour into her flawless skin and sated my urge to continue fucking her.

I swallow, my breakfast souring. It's still there in the crackle in the air between us. Chit-chat, getting to know her, caring was not part of our arrangement. But she's in my home, working for my family business—I have an obligation to vet her and look out for her welfare.

Yeah, arsehole—that's what you're interested in...

At the thought of last night, my dick tingles. I should be over this need by now, moving into the phase of polite indifference. But I'm still sporting the semi she left me with, the disappointment that she turned me down an itch beneath my skin I can't shake. Of course her talk about casual sex didn't help—all that did was sharpen my vision every time I look at her, as if, if I'm patient enough, observant enough, I'll figure out her every nuance.

Who is this woman my brothers have forced into my nice, orderly, defunct life? And what the hell am I going to do with her, because the sex sure as shit isn't over.

Mia's still fidgeting, but this time it's with Bob's ear.

'A dog-lover, eh?'

She shrugs, looking down at Bob with something close to adoration, her face as serene as I've seen it. 'I prefer dogs to most people. They're always so genuine, so happy to see you.'

As if he senses she's talking about him, Bob looks up at her, wags his tail and then slinks off to his water bowl for a noisy drink before returning to Mia's side to sit at her feet with canine devotion.

Traitor.

One walk in the park and Bob's ready to swear undying loyalty. Of course, my still buzzed body tells me the intriguing Mia has had a similar effect on me, albeit a purely physical one. Because that is all I have to offer.

I can't blame Bob. He's Laura's dog. Puppy Bob was my wedding present to her and she was at home with him more. Of course, when we travelled together Bob came everywhere with us—canal boating, walking holidays in the Lake District, Christmas in Scotland. Even when Laura and I travelled abroad, Bob would visit Laura's parents' farm in Norfolk. No boarding kennels for Laura's pampered pooch.

But I don't do those things any more. Bob's life has shrunk too.

Remembering my wife, remembering what a home bird she was, how she loved nothing better than curling up on the sofa with Bob and me on a Sunday afternoon to watch some old movie, the sappier the better, my appetite deserts me completely.

I clatter my unfinished cereal into the sink.

Bob looks up at Mia as if she has all the answers. I will a calming breath into my lungs and feast on her instead of soggy cereal. I too find Ms Abbott fascinating. Today she's wearing a bungee T-shirt with the words *Life Without Risk* emblazoned across her breasts. She's heaped her hair up into one of those messy topknot things and escaped wisps kiss her high cheeks and pale, slender neck.

I turn to the sink, adjusting my cock. My libido, not satisfied with last night's ball-shrivelling session, would happily follow Mia anywhere, sniffing at her heels, just like Bob.

'Do you own a dog? Back in New Zealand?'

Looks like I'm going with the chit-chat after all.

I rinse the bowl clean and put it on the drainer then dry my hands.

She nods, wary. She probably thinks I'm still trying to stall on my side of the deal. But what do I care if she wants to film what we offer our clients? More importantly, if she's going to be around, if she's done screwing me, I'll have to come up with some strategy for keeping my hands off her. The itch intensifies and I rub at my lip for something else to do with my hands. Would Mia welcome the continuation of our temporary arrangement? I swallow down the thud that beats in my throat and focus on Mia's full mouth while I wait for her answer.

'She's getting old now—a Labrador. And my

brother—you met him last night—has a Maltese terrier.'

I nod, although her brother and I hardly met. I simply called to invite his sister out for sex.

Arsehole...

She stoops next to Bob and unclips the strange harness I've only just registered he's wearing.

'What's that?'

She stands up, folding the straps into a tight ball and fastening them with Velcro while a flush colours her face. 'I... I filmed our walk. Well, Bob filmed it. I hope you don't mind. It's just such a lovely day out and I... Sometimes the most unusual technique yields the best footage. A dog's eye view of Chelsea, if you like.'

The hairs on my body stand to attention, as if I have Spidey-sense and I'm about to face a baddie. But the baddie is me. Have I inadvertently neglected poor, ownerless Bob? Is there a gaping hole in his life?

My throat is tight but I manage a gruff croak. 'Can I see?'

She eyes me with hesitation. But then, perhaps remembering I'm in charge of the company and she's a contractor or that she just kidnapped my dog and used him to capture unique film footage, she fishes the small, handheld action camera from her back pocket.

I step close enough to see the small screen, the fresh-air, outdoorsy scent of her gusting my way. She fumbles with the buttons. Affected by my proximity, or afraid she's crossed a line by dog-napping Bob...?

Both her discomfort and her proximity wash over me, a cloud of heat that fans my libido higher while I watch the short film featuring familiar streets near my home—the high street with its trendy shops, bars and cafes, the park, my street—all viewed from Bob's level. At one point Bob lunges for a pigeon, his favourite sport, and I laugh at the close-up footage. It's charming and quirky—a different way of seeing the familiar—just like Mia.

I suck in a big breath laced with this unusual woman. My fingers curl into a fist mere centimetres from her waist. I could reach out. Pull her close. Remind her of our physical connection.

I grit my teeth, fighting the urge. What the hell am I going to do with her? I can't dismiss her with a polite *We had a good time, see you around* as I normally would, because she's the one who left my bed in the middle of the night. She's the one who turned down my offer of more sex this morning. And I'm the one who still wants her, the physical high we create between us as potent and addictive as it was when my knuckles were poised to knock on her brother's front door.

My stare settles on her serene face, which is wreathed in a dreamy smile as she watches the footage of Bob doing nothing more remarkable than walking and sniffing. Her nose and cheeks are dotted with caramel freckles, some of them coalescing into intriguing shapes, like clouds.

She must sense my shift in focus from the video to her, because she stiffens and looks up at me. Her tongue touches her top lip and her chest expands with the indrawn breath she's managed to keep silent.

I stay close, relishing the scent of her and the way her pupils dilate as she stares at me. 'We seem to have a problem.'

Her eyes flit to the screen of the camera, her brows pinched in confusion. 'I won't use the footage if you object. I can delete it.'

'I couldn't give a fuck about you recording my dog, Mia.' My eyes slide over her parted lips. 'I'm talking about us.'

She snorts. Actually snorts at me. But the pulse in her neck hammers double time. 'There is no *us*.' She steps back as if my proximity reminds her there is very much an us—a working us and a fucking fantastic sexual us.

'I disagree. You said we'd get it out of our systems… I'm certain one night hasn't achieved that. And as you said, it's just casual.' She can deny it all she likes. Her body, her stare, the breathy way her voice has changed in pitch, speak the truth.

But when I want something, I can be patient. I hand back the camera. 'Think on it today, while you're working. I suggest we continue our arrangement—but it's your call.'

The tension in my shoulders dissipates and I collect my watch from the counter and strap it in place. She's glaringly uninterested in anything beyond the deal we brokered, so I don't have to worry about her becoming unrealistically attached to what is just great sex. She played her part beautifully. And now I have to pay up. I move to the door and indicate she follow me. 'Shall we?'

She stares, clearly pondering my proposal, as if she expects me to strip again and invite her into my bed. Tempting. But she's already turned me down once this morning. I do have *some* ego.

And I'm a man of my word. It's work time.

Mia follows me downstairs, her gaze flicking around the spacious home that is too big for just Bob and me—one of the reasons I've converted the lower ground floor into offices for Bounty Events.

'It's massive.' She emits a breathy little sigh, one that reminds me of her coming last night.

I shrug. 'Four floors.' Prime Chelsea real estate. Worth millions.

The restlessness that only vanishes when I'm fucking, or thinking about fucking, returns with a vengeance, shunting my shoulders north. I should sell the place, live out my existence on a canal boat. Just me and Bob. But would the memories stay a fixture of these walls? Sold on to the highest bidder and left behind with the alarm system and the contemporary chandeliers? Or would they follow me wherever I went? My regret has a million triggers—I suspect I'd simply carry all my baggage with me.

As we descend, she says, 'Can I smell chlorine?' Her cute freckled nose wrinkles and her eyes widen.

'Yes, there's a pool.' My cock twitches, banishing unwanted reflections. 'Fancy a dip?' I can't help myself—Mia is hypnotising. Perhaps it's her boundless energy, her no-bullshit attitude. Perhaps it's her secrets which intrigue me, as if I'm a sick bastard who's glad he's not alone with his mistakes and shame, recognising a kindred spirit who, despite appearances, hasn't quite got their shit together.

My smile drops as a familiar heat creeps beneath my skin. I shouldn't care about unearthing her layers. Focus on the sex—that's all it can be.

She does a great *haughty* as she looks down at me on the stair below her but there are flickers of excitement in her stare. 'Not right now, thanks.'

Promising—I'd say she's giving my proposal some serious consideration.

We traverse the glass tunnel that overlooks the small rear garden, the persistent lure of last night's intimacies dogging our steps. The flush at the base of her throat tells me she's equally aware of the effect we have on each other.

Bet she's regretting not joining me in the shower now.

In the office, I make introductions. Sally, one of my loyal, hard-working team of two, hands me a tablet with the schedule for this week and I direct Mia through the French doors that lead to the immaculate, postage-stamp garden my gardener keeps trim and shipshape. Bob curls up on his bed in the sunniest corner of the patio and succumbs to a snooze.

When we're seated close, but not too close, I slide the schedule Mia's way. 'These are some of the things we offer Faulkner guests.' I lean back to appreciate the way the sun reveals glints of fire in her hair and renders her white T-shirt partly seethrough. Not that I need X-ray vision or any help from Mother Nature. Mia's perfect nipples are etched into my brain, along with other tasty images that provide an erotic film reel of last night's highlights. I run my index finger and thumb along my bottom lip while she scrolls through the screen, a small furrow between her brows.

Then her eyes light up, delivering another slug of potent blood to my groin. 'Can we do that?' She leans in. Her scent wafts over me, escaped strands of her hair brushing my arm, and I reach for the device, deliberately ensuring our fingers touch.

The thing that's caught her eye is one of our standard packages. A private helicopter tour of London's iconic landmarks that will set you back a few thousand pounds. It's one of our most popular experiences and a good place to start for the promotional video she's making.

I shrug. 'Sure. Drink?'

She smiles like I've handed her a two-carat diamond and nods. 'Some water would be good.'

I move to the small outdoor bar underneath the

awning and select two bottles of frigid mineral water and a glass for Mia.

'So tell me your vision for this project? I see your eyes light up at the thought of this,' I indicate the tablet screen she's still scrolling down, 'but Bounty is more than just exhilaration. It's all about the sell, the luxury, the lure of decadence.' And Mia Abbott is as down-to-earth, as unaffected by appearances and trappings as any woman I've ever met. What does think-outside-the-box Mia have planned for one of London's most exclusive, privately owned chains of boutique hotels?

She pours the water into the glass and takes a sip, eyes challenging me over the rim. 'I know what it is you do at Bounty, and I visited all the hotels this morning.'

'All of them?' She *has* been busy.

She tilts her head, watching me closely. 'Of course—I'm here to work, not laze around in bed.'

Her reference shunts my temperature higher, but it's the heat of arousal, the reminder she could have woken up with me, sleepy and well-fucked; joined me in the shower…

My shoulders tense at the feeling that we've been short-changed of morning sex.

'They're all very elegant, luxurious—I'm impressed.'

I grin. That the family business impresses her stirs something in my gut. A restlessness. And the urge to find other ways to impress this enigmatic woman.

'Thank you. You're well-travelled. I'm sure you see a lot of hotels.'

She nods, taking another sip of water. We're sitting side-on to each other, and so it's then that I notice the small tattoo on the back of her neck, just below her hairline. Forgoing the urge to ask about it, I drone on about work, although I'd rather get to know Mia.

I take a swig of my own drink, the cool liquid doing little to dampen either my ardour for this woman or my burning curiosity. I want to hear *her* ideas. I want to see the woman I've witnessed in her YouTube videos, albeit predominantly behind the camera. The one with a clear passion for travelling and exploring and capturing the world on film. The one who is always on the move, even if it's just her damned fidgeting fingers...

She nods. 'I've taken some stills of the exterior and the communal interior areas. And Reid sent me the company media pack, so I have a sense of where the Faulkner Group sits in the market.'

She's done her homework. Time for me to do mine. And I have the rest of the day to unearth Mia.

'Of course I want to focus on the luxury—the once-in-a-lifetime experiences you offer,' she points at the tablet, 'like this. But I've also read Bounty Events' company website and, correct me if I'm wrong, my impression is that anything goes for the clients, right?'

I nod. If you want it and can afford it, I'll make it happen. 'As long as it's legal.'

She smiles, torching those eyes once more. She clasps her hands together on the table in front of her. Even now, one index finger taps on the back of her hand. I want to pull those fidgety fingers into my hand, to still their constant fluttering. I curl my own hands on my thighs.

'So I really want to show that. Film as many locations and experiences as possible, perhaps including some of the more…obscure attractions London has to offer.'

She's warmed to her subject, her voice hitching slightly as it had last night, seconds before orgasm.

'Such as?' I know London like the back of my hand. I grew up at the Faulkner Hotel, Cromwell Road. I studied Luxury Brand Management at Goldsmiths and, until recently, I lived, breathed and relished the travel and adventure lifestyle at the heart of Bounty Events. Can this unconventional woman from a country on the other side of the world of only four million people add a fresh eye to what's long been a stale enterprise for me?

Mia leans her elbows on the table, her T-shirt stretching across her chest. 'I've done some research. There are all these cool, secret places most tourists never hear about. Yes, we can film at the London Eye et cetera, but wouldn't it be awesome to include one or two of these lesser-known places, to show that whatever you want, no matter how niche, the Faulkner can give it you?'

'Tell me.' Her eyes sparkle now, and it's not just the sunlight.

'Well, did you know you can spend the night at the Natural History Museum? And there's Europe's oldest surviving surgical theatre in Southwark—it's a museum now but they offer lectures on Victorian surgery and you can privately hire the venue.'

Her enthusiasm burrows through the ambivalence I've worn longer than I care to remember. We have a client's birthday party planned at the Faulkner tomorrow. I'll speak to the customer, check he's okay with an extra guest and a few discreet photos, although in my experience most of my clients relish any opportunity to advertise their wealth. And more pressing is, what does Mia want? What can the Faulkner and this Faulkner in particular offer?

For the first time in a long time, I'm enthused by something other than getting off.

I take another swallow of water, enjoying the way her eyes dip to my mouth. Then I lean forward, my forearms resting on the table between us. 'Did you keep the other dresses?' She leans back, her colour high. I'd love to see her in the red, the only dress I'd personally chosen because, even within minutes of meeting her, I knew it would complement her dark hair and cling to her sensational body in all the right places.

She sighs. 'I haven't had time to return them yet, but I plan to.'

'Keep them. As you can see, the events calendar is

full, and you'll need something other than jeans. Although you look sensational in and out of clothes…'
I slide my stare over her, enjoying the mini-glare she shoots me and the flush of colour screaming up her neck. Yes, I'm an inappropriate arsehole blurring the lines of professional and personal…

I brush my lip, remembering her taste. 'I told you we'd be good together.'

Her mouth tightens and her eyes narrow and then she smiles, a begrudging twist of that delicious mouth that's over before its effect—my lungs expanding in my chest—has time to register.

'You're a dick, you know that?'

I laugh and she stares me down, shaking her head. 'I do. But as we discussed this morning, "Kit" will do.'

Mia rolls her eyes. 'I think we should keep what's left of today about work. I'm on a deadline.'

The sun on my back intensifies, my neck prickling as if singed. 'You're leaving London after the three weeks?'

She nibbles her lip and nods, her fingers on the move once more. 'Maybe earlier if the weather's good.'

I glance at the sky, the haze of cloudless pale blue, and suck in a steady stream of air, telling myself that our temporary acquaintance couldn't be more perfect.

'Okay, I agree. Today we work. I'll introduce you at City Heli Rides and ensure they are at your disposal.'

But later, off the clock...

'Great. Let's get started.' She's on her feet in a second. Bob, sensing her enthusiasm, wakes from his nap and joins her side, tail keen as if he expects to be included on the fun.

Not this time, buddy.

I stand too, something about Mia's energy contagious. 'Make sure you're free tomorrow evening. There's a VIP event on at the Faulkner I'd like you to attend. You might find it useful, for the film.'

She nods, setting off for the house. 'I have my gear here so let's go.' Before I realise what I'm doing my feet have moved to follow her, my limbs now twitching with restless excitement. I text my driver and grab my sunglasses from the kitchen.

Inside the front door, she turns, one hand on Bob's head, scratching. 'Can Bob come?' For the first time since we met her voice holds a hint of uncertainty.

Two pairs of hopeful eyes stare up at me, the one-two jab perfectly aimed at my solar plexus. My automatic 'no' hovers on my tongue, blocking my throat, almost suffocating me.

This excitable, bubbly side of her infects Bob, whose tail thumps the wall in time with the jiggles of Mia's leg, as if she can't hold in the vibrating energy that transmits across the space to affect me too.

Two weeks; three tops. Temporary with a capital T.

I shrug, using the time Mia is distracted by cheering and dropping to her haunches to give Bob a good neck scrub in celebration to draw in a calming deep breath.

All I have to do is let her do her job and persuade her to extend our arrangement beyond last night.

Should be fairly straightforward.

Two weeks.

CHAPTER SEVEN

Mia

As we leave the house, Kit reaches for my backpack. I resist. Not only is it the reason my arms, shoulders and back are well-toned, it also contains my livelihood, my passion—I guard it with the ferocity of a mama bear protecting a cub.

'I won't drop it.' He's ridiculously handsome grinning at me, the sunnies hiding his intense eyes.

'I've got it, thanks.' I'm not some delicate female. My chosen field is dominated by men—I've never once needed help carrying my gear.

Kit relents and opens the car door, ushering Bob and me into the back seat. While he rounds the car I breathe and try to compose myself. I'm off balance, my thoughts veering between certainty and intrigue—not just a consequence of Kit's raw sex appeal, which still beckons me like I'm a moth who likes nothing better than the smell of her own singed wings. But the glimpses of family-man Kit, dog-owner Kit, relaxed-eating-breakfast-in-his-own-home Kit—it's too much. Not to mention chivalrous, bag-carrying, door-opening Kit…

Bob, between us on the seat, provides the perfect barrier, but it doesn't diminish the cloying sexual tension filling the car. We *were* good together. Better than good. One time, two…what difference does it make? I'm not interested in a relationship, and Kit's not offering one. I fiddle with the strap of my backpack and stare out of the window.

'So why film-making? Is it a *Hobbit* thing?'

I laugh, determined to fight our still potent chemistry and my unsettled emotions and make the most of today's filming. 'Tolkien adaptations aren't New Zealand's only exports.'

At his silent watchfulness and small smile, I cave with a sigh. Conversation is better than the way he silently observes me, and my trip to his house achieved the desired result. 'It began with photography. My brother, Will, bought me my first SLR for my fifteenth birthday.'

'That was generous.'

'Yes. Will is one of my life's gifts. And he knew me better than I knew myself back then.' I tap my fingers on the leather seat, only stopping when Bob nudges them with a wet nose and a lick.

'In what way?' His eyes narrow and I choose my next words carefully.

'I guess I went through something of a rebellious stage—skipping school, dying my hair blue, becoming a daredevil tomboy.' An ache settles under my ribs and I look away, the memories evoking the emotions as if it were yesterday. 'He…saw I needed something.'

The silence slides over me until all the hairs on my body stand to attention.

'What did you need?' Kit's question is hushed. He glances over at me, cool eyes searching.

I shrug, ignoring the gnawing feeling inside, so much a part of me it's coded in my DNA. 'A focus. A way to get lost, to get outside my own head.'

Perhaps he knows what that feels like… Perhaps that's what inspires his precious control…

He presses his lips together, as if holding back. My stare latches there—I know there's more to come. 'Don't worry, it's nothing bad. I had a great upbringing. My folks are fantastic, despite me probably contributing to their grey hair.'

'Are they still together?'

I nod, the set of Kit's mouth prompting the reciprocal question. 'Yours?'

'No.' He strokes the top of Bob's head, a faraway look on his face. 'So what was it? Boy trouble? Hormones?'

I laugh, debating giving Kit a full menstrual history just to see his reaction. 'Nah.' I force the next words out, challenging myself to speak them unaffectedly, just like the first time I confided them to my closest school friend. 'I'm adopted.'

The silence lasts a beat or two. 'For a while, as

a teen, I struggled with my identity.' I've no idea where my colouring comes from, which grandparent is responsible for my wavy-hair gene or who I follow height-wise. And that's without the whys…

'I see.' Kit shoots me another look, but I turn away and stare, unseeing, out of the window, my skin shrinking and compressing the rest of me as if I'm trapped in a vice. I've known I was adopted from the age of nine or ten, known that my biological mother moved to the UK shortly after my birth, but unlike my brother I've resolutely refused to pursue my past. I have a loving family. My work, my travels keep me busy.

It's enough.

The remainder of the journey to the heliport in Battersea passes in a heavy silence as if Kit has dissected me as easily as he turns me on. I should turn down his offer to enjoy our mutual and in no way lessened attraction, tell him I'm fine without his assistance, deliver the finished product to Reid and never see him again…

My abdominal muscles tense, my stomach hollow while that image filters through my thoughts. Whatever this is, neither of us is interested in anything more than the pretty great sex that went down last night. I'm overthinking. I look over at an equally pensive Kit. His raw masculinity, his still potent sex appeal, his high emotional barriers all form a perfectly packaged distraction.

Temptation personified.

At the heliport, I spring into action fuelled by the relief of switching off any thought unrelated to lighting, angles and resolutions. I'm keen to get my teeth stuck into more than elegant stills anyone could take with a decent phone.

Kit wanders inside the building with Bob to speak to the owner-operator, someone he tells me he knows well, while I set up my tripod to capture a few stills of our shiny white helicopter sitting against a backdrop of London's iconic skyline.

When I'm happy with the shots taken from various angles I speak to the pilot, who fires up the motor while I film some footage approaching the craft at differing walking speeds I hope will translate into the very real excitement bubbling inside me. I'd love to have booked some models, a glamorously dressed couple, him in a tux, her in a floaty dress, just to lend the footage more class and authenticity, but I can always return another day to film those sequences. The Kit distraction has rendered today's filming rather ad hoc.

I shake my head—I'm usually more organised. I should have turned him away from my brother's doorstep last night, kept things strictly business. But then, where's the fun in that?

As if he's heard me inwardly cursing his nocturnal proclivities, he appears and within minutes we're strapped into the chopper and up and away.

The afternoon weather conditions are perfect for filming. I'm up front with the pilot, the comforting weight of my shoulder-mounted camcorder capturing what has to be the best way to see London. I don't bother with the microphone, as the finished video will boast an elegant soundtrack suited to the contemporary opulence of the Faulkner hotels.

The helicopter is fitted with multiple external mounts, one of which fits my action camera, which I've gaffer-taped in place, just to ensure it doesn't end up at the bottom of the Thames. I can splice together the dual footage to give both the personal and bird's eye views of this thrilling scenic tour.

As our pilot points out the city's landmarks I scan the city beyond the landmarks lining the Thames. Filming is almost second nature, something I don't have to think about. This frees my mind to spin off in distracted circles. Does my biological mother live somewhere out there? In one of the sprawling suburbs, perhaps, under one of the thousands of chimney-sporting rooftops? How easy would it be to track her down? To see a picture of her as she is today—not just the faded, blurry one my parents have of a young woman with big scared eyes. Is my father still alive? Still in New Zealand? Were they together, or am I just the product of a casual hook-up?

Kit taps my shoulder and points out the Faulkner, the largest of the group's hotels.

'We grew up there.' His disembodied voice reaches me through my headset. 'I was always jealous of kids at school who lived in a regular house with a garden and a letterbox. Somehow having your birthday parties in the Faulkner ballroom couldn't compare with having a den in the garden shed. The first thing Reid, Drake and I did when we got our first jobs was buy a house. With stairs and a garden.'

I smile at the image of a young Kit and breathe through the band around my chest. The Faulkners, for all Kit's personal loss, are a unit. They have history. A family-run business. Identity. Roots.

The forty-minute flight is over too soon. Back at the heliport, while Kit talks to our pilot, I lead Bob down to the path lining the river and set off at a jog, knowing, like me, he probably has excess energy to expend and he'll bound alongside. Pretty soon we're on Battersea Bridge, the photo-worthy view east along the river of the white suspension cables of Chelsea Bridge in the foreground and the London Eye and the Shard in the distance. I tie up Bob to an obliging lamp post and climb onto the barrier, sitting up on it to shoot some selfies for my website and social-media feeds.

I'm halfway back to the City Heli Rides base when I spy Kit striding to intercept us, his scowl firmly back in place.

'What the hell was that?' He takes Bob's lead and walks back in the direction of the car.

My smile slides from my face. 'I wanted some photos—the views are spectacular.'

'The views are just as good from the pavement.' His voice is matter-of-fact, but his jaw is clenched. Is he annoyed? 'I didn't know where you'd gone.'

'I needed to blow off some adrenaline. And I figured Bob would appreciate the walk. He was perfectly safe.'

At the car park he opens the car door for a panting Bob. 'You could have fallen. People die in that river, every year.'

Is he serious? It was just some tourist snaps. 'Come on—it's not like I jumped from the chopper into the Thames or anything. Although I totally would.' He's not impressed so I switch tack. 'Look, I didn't mean to worry you. Bob was perfectly safe the whole time.'

Kit's mouth twitches and then he sighs, holding the door open for me.

'So where next?'

'Drinks. I'm checking out a new potential partner for Bounty.'

Great, he's forgotten his snit. He settles beside me and gives instructions to his driver. If we're still on the clock, I can ask another probing question I've been pondering.

'You downsized Bounty a couple of years back.' He nods. Bounty Events used to be international, Kit's brand of tailor-made luxury available anywhere your heart desired. Then he sold up, keeping only the London-based operation. 'Why?'

He stares for so long I wonder if he's still smarting. My fingers start fidgeting. I force myself not to blink while I wait for his answer. With a reluctant sigh, he looks away. 'I got sick of travelling.'

It's believable but insufficient. I want more. It's as if I'm determined to poke and prod until I satisfy myself he's still in love with his wife. The green light I need.

'Is that all? I love travelling. Seeing the world.'

I'm unaware it's still moving, so Kit's hand covering mine where it taps on the leather seat between us makes me inhale a small gasp. His fingers press, warm and insistent and stilling my own.

'You're never still, are you? Are you okay? Is it a nervous thing?'

My fingers tense. Heat climbs my neck. Of course Mr Observant, Mr Flay-You-Alive with the deeply penetrating stare would notice my worst habit. I don't need his permission—I can fidget as much as I like. 'I'm fine.' I bite the inside of my cheek, waiting for my temperature to return to normal. But his hand still covers mine, reminding me how his warm, slightly callused touch explored my body last night.

Why can't I pull away? This gesture feels way more intimate than everything we did in that hotel room. And if he's going to get personal…

'Was it because of Laura?' My voice cracks.

A hard gleam enters his eyes. Then he lifts his warm palm from the back of my hand, which, perversely, instantly misses his touch.

He stares, as if debating how much to say, while emotion filters through his dark eyes. I want to reach out, to touch his hand the way he's just touched mine, to let him know I see his pain, but I'm frozen, my stomach flipping through somersaults. I should have kept my mouth shut. He owes me no explanations. All we've done is share some pretty great sex.

And I shouldn't care, but...

'After Laura died, my job, the travelling... It all just seemed so...pointless.' He shrugs. 'Don't you get sick of roaming the world?' His beautiful mouth pulls into an unexpected smile, given the gravity of the conversation. 'If you lived in one place, you could get a whole heap of your own dogs...'

I smile at the image of canine bliss he depicts. He's hit the nail on the head—my lack of pet-ownership the only downside to the way I live. I stroke Bob, gorging myself while I can. But the last thing I want is Kit picking apart the reasons for my fancy-free lifestyle. 'I'm lucky. I love my work. There's always another view to capture, another adventure to film.'

'I used to feel that way.' His voice is low, his eyes pensive.

I sober. 'It must have been very hard for you.' I think of Will and Josh's domestic contentment, their plans for a family, a future together. My brother's happiness makes me smile, but an acidic burn settles behind my sternum.

Kit's hand joins mine on Bob's back. We set up a rhythm of alternate strokes, avoiding each other's hands. 'So where are you off to after London?'

I suck comfort from Bob's sleek fur, resisting the temptation to slow my stroke and allow Kit's hand time to catch up. 'I'm going to Rio. I have work lined up that will take about two weeks, and then I'm going to travel to Machu Picchu, then Bolivia and wherever else the wind takes me. Chile has great ski resorts—ever tried heli-skiing?'

'Once. In my single days.' His eyes cloud, perhaps with memories, but then he shakes it off, leaning forward, and says, 'We're here.'

The car slows outside an indistinguishable glass tower block. An unusual location for a bar. Kit informs me we won't be here long enough for me to capture any footage so I leave my equipment in the car with Bob and the driver. Kit guides me inside the building with a hand in the small of my back, the heat generated sliding down into the pit of my pelvis—a bubbling cauldron of lust in no way diminished.

'What is this place?' I watch his mouth, torn between prying about Laura and kissing him again, uncertain which urge is more unexpected. The dwindling adrenaline from the helicopter ride must have me worked up. Less than twenty-four hours ago, this man had wrung more orgasms from my body than I thought I could survive. How can I still want more? Especially the intensity of the brand of sex on offer.

'It's a champagne bar—the highest in London. You'll like the views.' His mouth twists, eyes alight, so certain, just as he was certain of the pleasure he could draw from me last night. The promise of that pleasure is back in full force now, the toe-curling throb between my legs. But I won't enslave myself. Determined to raise the subject of Laura again, I follow Kit as we disembark on the thirty-eighth floor. It's barely four p.m. The bar doesn't open for another hour. We have the place to ourselves.

The manager welcomes us and sits us at the best table in the house, although the entire place is a testament to class—a glass castle at the top of the world, every contemporary chandelier sparkling, every table, every glass gleaming as if doused with fairy dust.

A bottle of champagne sits in a bucket of ice at our table—the real thing, no imitations. We're handed menus so we can see what's on offer but the chef delivers a platter of delicious amuse-bouche that we're told complements the champagne.

My head spins a little and not in a good way. Being in a gravity-defying skyscraper viewing the city doesn't bother me. But this—the luxury, the extravagance, the hedonism—carries a date-like quality that shunts me out of my depth. Is this how he wined and dined Laura? Of course, Kit isn't even trying to impress—it's work.

I wriggle in my seat, left wondering what it would be like to live in his world. To attend his parties and work functions alongside family and then return home to Bob. I swallow hard, forcing ridiculous images from my mind.

Our flutes are filled with a flourish and I snatch

mine up, too fast, sloshing some of the bubbles onto my wrist in my haste to take a calming sip. Kit raises his glass, one eyebrow arched in puzzlement. 'Cheers.'

I touch my glassware to his, the clink adding to my discomfort. Like a scab I can't leave alone, I plough back into the conversation we began in the car. 'So…do you mind me asking? How did Laura die?' I wince, worried I've crossed a line, the hairs rising on my arms.

He's so young to have been married and widowed, I've assumed his wife must have died from cancer or a car accident. And although it really makes little difference to what we're doing—just sex—I want to know what's shaped Kit into this rarely smiling version who needs control and rules to function.

He shrugs as if neither my probing nor the answer bother him, but the truth is in his eyes. He clears his throat, staring at me over the rim of his glass. I squirm inside, wishing I'd kept my curiosity to myself. Wishing I didn't need to know. Wishing I could simply walk away, right here, right now, without a backward glance. No more sex and no more Kit.

'She died suddenly.' His words, when they emerge, are brisk, clipped, as if he's torn off the mental bandage. 'She was there one second, gone the next. A brain aneurysm.'

I can't envision the shock, the devastation. But then, I can't envisage the kind of matrimonial love that Kit and Laura had, that Will and Josh have, either.

Far from satisfying me, his candid response reveals further questions I have no place asking. His hand is right there on the table beside mine. It would be so easy to reach out. I hover on the edge of a decision, the air trapped in my lungs. But I'm not his girlfriend, or even his friend, comfort not mine to offer.

I swallow, disguising my tight throat with another glug of wine. 'Do you want to talk about it?'

He tilts his head, a *Don't be stupid* look on his face.

'What I want,' he places his barely touched glass on the table and steeples his fingers in front of his mouth, 'is to fuck you again. Have you considered my suggestion?'

And we're back to something he likes to control... I shake my head, onto him, but the tension coiled in my belly unwinds, replaced by the easier to handle simmer of lust. I understand why he wants to change the subject. He's right to steer this back to the sex. I should be relieved...

His lip curls, stare challenging. 'You know we're not done. Nowhere near.' He shoots me a grin I want to hurl back in his sure-of-himself face.

My pulse thrums in agreement with Kit. It's not over. *Yet*... 'Aren't we?' The fizz in my blood returns, a belly-flipping thrill akin to seeing London from the sky.

Kit shakes his head—slow, confident, daring.

'What do you say?' His thumb and forefinger toy with his lip, a hypnotic swipe as addictive as our verbal foreplay.

I groan inside. Why is he so addictive? Why is 'no' the last thing on my mind? I think back to his particular brand of bedroom bossiness and its abundant rewards. But can I do this? Hold myself distant enough to stay whole, stay me in Kit's crazy, hedonistic world of shiny people while steering clear of the emotional trap of caring too much about the pain in his eyes?

Laura's face slides back into my mind, a talisman. A safety net to catch me when I fall. I shrug. 'I'm up for anything.'

He raises one eyebrow, a calculating look in his eyes as if he's plotting filthy pastimes. Will he take me to another hotel when we leave here, or will we even make it that far?

'Good.' A bright flicker of heat lights his eyes, the earlier pain chased away. My heart pounds, pleased to have been instrumental in distracting him, even though I was the one to remind him of his loss in the first place.

Reminding myself it's just sex, I toss out my condition. 'And tomorrow, we start work bright and early at a venue of my choosing. No lazing half the day away.'

His eyes narrow and I tilt my chin even though the urge to cave and dive head first into a three-week-long Kit sex-fest is hard to ignore. 'Full creative direction,' I remind him.

I swallow the final mouthful, the fizz of bubbles on my tongue spreading throughout my body.

Kit takes the empty glass from my hand, places it on the table and stands. 'Let's go.'

CHAPTER EIGHT

Mia

KIT PLACES MY bag on a chair and rewards Bob for his good behaviour with some playful rough-housing that leaves my lungs shrunken to the size of raisins and blood zinging to all my erogenous zones. A glimpse of sexy, intense Kit Faulkner with his guard down...*wow*.

When he looks up at me the smile slides from his face, his eyes hot with the brooding look he does so well. My body sways towards that look, as if being burned alive is a tolerable way to go for another round of amazing sex.

With a small hand gesture he sends an obedient Bob back to his bed and lifts an eyebrow in my direction. 'Do you want another drink?'

I shake my head, desperate now to be equally obedient so I can have my reward: him.

He licks his bottom lip and jerks his chin at my backpack, his hooded stare midnight-black. 'Bring the gaffer tape.'

What the...?

I snort, the gust of incredulity leaving me with a blast. But he's deadly serious, his eyes molten with licentious intent.

The tape I carry in my work kit has a hundred uses, sometimes the only thing between my expensive, sensitive filming equipment and the ground. But I had no idea Kit had spied it earlier, or that he had some perverse plan in mind.

At our continued stare-off, my throat closes and heat engulfs me in delicious waves. I probe my feelings—excitement, euphoria, but no hint of fear. My hands tremble slightly as I locate the two-inch wide tape in one pocket of my backpack.

Kit presses up behind me, his mouth skating the back of my neck, warm lips grazing my skin, the accompanying scrape of his stubble speaking directly to my nipples. 'Remember the rules—all you have to do is say stop...'

I moan as his tongue licks my neck, sending tendrils of pleasure south. To show him I'm on board, I push my backside into his groin. His fingers clasp my hips while he grinds his erection between the cheeks of my arse, dry-humping me over the back of his beautiful leather Chesterfield sofa.

Laura's on the wall behind us. I'm past caring why he brought me here instead of to another hotel. And despite the fact he strips me bare with his stare alone, and he's already probed at the dark place in me, I want him. I want the physical distraction we create—a safety net, a parachute, a soft landing, perhaps for both of us.

Tearing away with a grunt, he takes my hand and marches us to the bedroom. Poor Bob, perhaps sensing the excitement tingeing the air, clacks down the hallway after us, only to have the door closed in his expectant doggy face.

I take in Kit's enormous white bed, the linens freshly straightened. My stare scans again for Laura's presence in this room—I can't help myself.

'Laura and I never shared this room.'

It's as if he's read my mind. The whoosh of air recoiling from my lungs hints at the answer I'd hoped to find in the stark, masculine space, devoid of feminine whimsy or even photographs.

The roll of tape cuts into my fingers. For a second I waver, my blood on fire with anticipation, but a trickle of fear, of vulnerability is hot on its tail. His reasons for bringing me here shouldn't matter. I've spent years forcing myself to avoid permanence and crave freedom. I don't belong here, but I don't have to.

The fact he didn't share this room with his wife confirms Kit's emotions are still housed in a fortress on lockdown.

I strum my fingers on the roll of tape, focussed on my own emotional boundaries to stop my brain's flights of fancy.

He steps behind me, his breath whispering in my

hair as his hand covers my fluttering fingers. 'Do you trust me?'

My heart thunders anew, the realisation I do trust him almost choking me. The new territory stretches in front of me, terrifying but tantalising. I sway. Not with the momentum of him grinding against my backside, but with the weakness in my legs as I nod my assent.

His fingers skirt my waist. I lean back against his chest as he lifts the hem of my shirt and raises it over my head, freeing the roll of tape from my hand so he can fully divest me of my shirt. He groans, his chin perched on my shoulder from behind to watch the passage of his hands over my breasts.

My eyes follow the same path, as if hypnotised by the soft, sure touch.

'Your skin…so many freckles.' His lips brush my shoulder and I shudder. Just like the hand-holding in the car, him looking at me, inspecting every inch of skin, every place his fingers glide is way more intimate than anything we did last night. I suck air through flared nostrils and focus on the sensation under those rough fingertips, forcing my thoughts to switch off before they drive me insane.

The roll of tape sits like a bangle on his wrist, its presence in my peripheral vision shunting hot pulses between my legs. I can guess what he's going to do with me. I'm not scared, physically. But the feeling I'll be at the mercy of the scrape of those eyes of his, which seem to see past my barriers… Another involuntary shudder rattles my bones, the emotional wobble tempered by the pleasure of his hands and lips on my skin.

Still behind me, he flicks open my bra, scraping it down my arms, and then unbuttons my fly. His big hands cup my breasts—they're warm, his fingers teasing. His mouth whispers a *shh* against the skin of my shoulder at my breathy moan. His thumbs graze my nipples, stroking them, sparking them to life.

'Keep still.' His lips feather my neck. His command is soft but insistent. My head wants to hurry this along; to end the sensual, drawn-out way he's touching me, as if he has all the time in the world. His attention, his stare seem fascinated with whatever his fingers are doing, only detouring to watch my reaction blaze across my face.

I'm falling again; the effect Kit has on me, his control over this is so intoxicating, so alluring, so dangerous. Only the ghost of Laura keeps me complicit, keeps my feet glued to the hardwood floor of Kit's bedroom, as if *my* usual rules do not apply. Without her presence, the fear of giving him too much control, too much of my trust, would send me hurtling from the room.

He stoops behind me, sliding my jeans and underwear down my legs, and then his hot breath blasts one cheek of my arse seconds before he places a hot, open-mouthed kiss there. It's not particularly sensual, but the fact he's moved to kiss a part of my body I've never given much thought to sends pulses through my core. There's no time to linger, or over-analyse his action, because he stands and guides me to the bed with his hand on my lower back.

As arousal boils over inside me, I'm done being passive. He's had his fun, taken his time. I want to strip his sublime body, to touch every slab, every hard plane. To suck his delicious skin-scent into my lungs. To make him squirm in retribution.

I turn to face him, tugging on the hem of his shirt to drag his mouth down to mine. He kisses me back, eyes open. But then he pushes me away, a knowing half-smirk on his lips.

'Wrists.' It's a low, seductive request.

I'm foggy. Lust-drunk. My mind slow.

When he takes the roll of tape from around his arm, light dawns. His intention is clear. Compliance mine to grant or deny.

He grabs my hips while he waits, crushing his erection into my belly and nibbling at my mouth with teasing little kisses.

My blood floods with adrenaline, with power—potent and addictive. It's amplified tenfold with the knowledge that I trust him. Perhaps this is what it's always like for people entering relationships.

Ever since my first rushed and fumbling sexual experience, I've perfected the technique of hit and run, leaving before they leave first. But Kit, the deal I made with him to relinquish control, and the all-encompassing way he savours every second like the ultimate connoisseur, pushes me into new territory.

I swallow past my tight throat and offer him my wrists. I'm just getting caught up in my own head. Better to focus on the sex and whatever challenge he tosses my way.

He makes one revolution with the tape around each of my wrists, slipping his index finger between it and my skin as he goes. He takes it slow, his eyes darting from the tape to my face, the agonising pace drawing out the anticipation, flooding every inch of my skin with the scalding heat of his stare.

Kit's finger traces my cheek, sliding back a strand of hair. 'Still with me?' His eyes glint with addictive excitement.

I nod. I can easily escape from the loose gaffer-tape shackles he's created. Escaping the way he makes me feel will be another matter entirely.

I look down at his handiwork. The dark green tape is stark against my skin. Heat pools low in my pelvis. When this is over, when I leave, I'll need to change brands, buy a different colour and width to banish the memory of Kit Faulkner and his penetrating eyes.

Within seconds I'm secured to his headboard by my wrists. Kit's eyes rake my nakedness from head to toe as if he's cataloguing every dip, every hair, every freckle.

'You're staring and I have nothing to look at.'

He smiles down at me, a feral smile. He's still fully clothed. 'I am.' His finger traces a path from the notch at the base of my throat to encircle first one nipple and then the other, sending skitters of sensation across my belly. 'These freckles are fascinating.' The fingertip returns to my chest, tracing an outline, a dot-to-dot only he can see, before gliding over one cheek and ending up on the tip of my nose.

I shudder—he can stare until his eyes explode as long as he keeps touching me in this way, keeps talking in that low, seductive drawl. And my own eyes aren't idle, flicking frequently to the bulge he's sporting behind the fly of his jeans while saliva coats my parched tongue.

'They make me want to kiss each one in turn.' His finger glides to my top lip. 'You even have them here.'

I nod, lifting my head from the pillow and sucking the pad of his finger, my reward a lurch of movement from behind his zip. I can't wait to get my hands on him, my mouth on him. To render him helpless, even for a few heady seconds. My revenge plot formulates in my head.

He shakes his head, eyes alight. His lips replace his finger against mine, delivering the promised kiss. Slow and sensual. The now wet fingertip retraces its path back between my breasts and continues to head south until it centres over my clit.

'I wonder where else they might be hiding,' he says.

I gasp as he presses down with barest hint of pressure. So good, but not enough. I swallow my whimper, battling the urge to hand over all the power to him and beg.

I claw back some dignity, glaring up at him while I kiss him back. I shift tactics, spreading my legs a fraction and lifting my hips to gain the pressure I need.

He pulls back and smiles, his eyes burning hot. He whips his hand away and stands to shrug out of his clothes with rapid jerks, as if he can't tease us a second longer.

He's warm when he lies beside me, his body heat scalding my skin where we touch. His stare is too close for comfort. The delicate intricacies of his blue irises are fathomless.

I hold my breath, glad now for the shackles that hold me to the bed so I can't get sucked into those eyes. So I can't get lost.

And then his fingers are back between my legs and he's alternately kissing my mouth and tonguing my nipple and capturing my every reaction with his bold, hooded stare. There's nowhere to hide. Every speck of me, every blemish on display for his lazy perusal.

He kisses me with his eyes wide open and I brazen out the eye contact, which magnifies every surge of pleasure, even though it leaves me completely exposed to him. But no matter how much I want to retreat from the intense intimacy, I can't close my eyes.

Just when I'm finding my rhythm, Kit's particular brand of magic drawing from me choppy breaths interspersed with whimpers, he jerks away. A cry escapes before I can clamp my lips down on it.

'Fuck, sorry. I have to taste you again,' he says in explanation as he shuffles down the bed and guides my thighs open wider.

My abdominal muscles clench in anticipation of his devastating mouth. 'And if I want to taste you too?'

He grins up at me, reminding me that, while I allow it, he's in charge. 'All in good time.'

I can't decide which I want more, his mouth on me, or mine on him. I want it all and then I forget how to think, let alone speak, because he cups his hands under my buttocks and raises me to his mouth. I'm silenced for long, torturous minutes while he licks and sucks at me, intermittently spearing his tongue inside so I gasp and writhe, at his mercy.

This time, sexy little grunts of encouragement come from his throat, vibrating through my sensitive flesh, through my clit. Every time I glance down, he's actually smiling up at me, only sliding his eyes away to glance at my breasts, before continuing to watch the reactions I'm powerless to hold back.

Just when I'm primed to breaking point by his intimate kiss, Kit's mouth leaves me. My body protests, clamouring for more exquisite attention as he reaches for a condom and covers himself.

'Please…' It slips out—I can't help myself.

He leans over, soothing me with the swipe of his fingers over my sensitised clit. 'Still with me?'

I nod, frantic.

'Good. Don't hold anything back, understood?'

'Yes,' I hiss, all but sobbing with relief as he
pushes my knees back. He's primed me so effectively; I'll give him anything in this moment, un-
ashamedly. I groan as he eases inside me, all the
while his beautiful face tenses with ecstasy.

I'm gripping the gaffer-tape shackles so tightly
now the glue sticks my fingers together. But I'm
glad, because the way he's looking down at me as
he stretches and fills me so deliciously, nodding his
encouragement to the moans escaping me... It's too
much.

When he's fully pushed inside he scrunches his
eyes shut for a second, perhaps staving off similar levels of pleasure to those wracking me from
head to toe. Creases fan out from the corners of his
closed eyes.

My fingers twitch. Pressure builds in my chest,
my head, behind my eyes, and I have the crazy urge
to touch those wrinkles. To smooth them, just like
I managed to smooth the pain from his eyes earlier.
To cup his beautiful face and tangle my fingers in
his decadent hair. To pull all his weight down on top
of me so I'm completely engulfed by Kit.

When he's composed he opens his eyes, a smile
tugging at his lips. 'We weren't done, were we?'

I shake my head, words locked in my throat by the
building pleasure as he moves inside me, his strong
arms braced either side of my head.

He grins then lowers his mouth to mine, and I
raise my lips to his and we meet in the middle to kiss.

It's as carnal as it was the first time—I'm shackled to his headboard, for fuck's sake—but face to face, nowhere to hide, all the blood drains from my head as I cling for dear life to the tape, the only thing holding me safe from a free-fall into unchartered territory.

The pleasure rising in me trickles away. I'm too exposed—thoughts, doubts and demons tumbling. I flounder, kissing Kit harder in an attempt to reclaim the only thing I can take from him. The only thing I can want from him—sex. Another astounding orgasm.

But he pulls away, his stare sweeping down my body to my jiggling breasts and lower, to the point where we're joined.

He rolls his eyes back. 'You still with me?'

I nod. If anything I'm too close.

He scoops one hand around the back of my neck, fingers digging in, and lifts my mouth to his in a searing kiss. 'Then let's come together, gorgeous.' He drops his head to the crook of my shoulder as he powers into me with renewed enthusiasm, his mouth and his hot breath moving over my skin. 'We're not done, Mia. I want more.'

His voice, thick with pleasure and heated promises, does the trick, along with his mouth back on mine. I come out of nowhere, loud and long, while Kit pounds on, kissing up my cries and moans and stealing my air.

He's seconds behind me, slamming into me for

the last time with a harsh yell and then collapsing on top of me and pressing me into the mattress, like I wanted.

I lie beneath him, heart thundering, chest tight, trapped by his big body, his Kit scent, the last few judders from his hips reminding me he's still inside me. I'm trapped in more ways than one.

I close my eyes and try not to suck in too much of the scent of his hair while I breathe through the battle raging between my pulse and my adrenal glands. It's just sex. Just phenomenal sex. I'm overreacting.

With Kit's sweat evaporating from my skin, leaving icy tingles behind, I lie still as he raises himself up and withdraws. I close my legs, wishing I could get up too. But as I've tugged on the tape, it's tightened around my wrists. I can still escape, but not without revealing the vibrating panic that courses through my nerve endings like mini lightning strikes.

'Hold on a sec.' His voice is softer than I've ever heard it, as if this is the real Kit, and the previous versions I've witnessed have been personality programs selected from a menu in one of those freaky, lifelike human robots.

The grieving-widower program.

The arsehole-alpha program.

The lover-of-all-your-wildest-fantasies program.

My lungs spasm with the burst of inappropriate laughter I suck back down. Inappropriate because

I've never felt less like laughing as my eyes burn and I blink repeatedly.

Kit steps into the en suite and returns just as quickly minus the condom, his glorious cock still impressively engorged. We're both still naked, but with my high dwindling, with my emotions all over the place, I'm vibrating with the urge to flee. The urge to be footloose Mia, not Mia who's willing to hand over too much of herself to a man who has nothing but sex to offer in return. Holding back is the only way I can hold myself together. The only way I can be free of needing anyone.

Kit's face is blank, but the hint of regret is back. He isn't looking at me as he undoes the tape, which is well and truly stuck to my skin where I writhed and pulled and tightened my own shackles.

I snatch my hand away, too exposed for his tender touch, too confused by the fact I care about his regret and what it means. I make short work of freeing my other hand, wincing through the tug as the tape yanks on the tiny hairs on the back of my wrist.

I welcome the sting—a timely reminder that this fuck-fantasy with Kit comes at a price. A price that seems affordable, but quickly drags me down into spiralling debt. And then I'm off the bed and tugging on my clothes, unsure of what happened here tonight, but certain I want no part in it.

Before I run for the door, I give myself a mental slap—I'm acting like a madwoman. It's sex. Great sex. But just sex. Kit feels the same. Kit would rather be making love to his wife. That should be enough to appease my heart rate. Forcing a chilly expression, I shoot Kit a small smile. 'I'll pick you up early tomorrow. Eight a.m.'

He hasn't asked me to spend the night, but then, I haven't given him chance. I'm fully dressed and fiddling with my hair, trying to tame it into something that doesn't resemble a just-fucked cloud.

Kit nods, his face blank, piercing eyes unfathomable. And I'm naked again.

He stands, tugs on his boxers and strides my way, opening the bedroom door for me with a flourish and heading down the hallway ahead of me to do the same at the entrance.

With a curt chin-lift from a silent Kit and a whine from Bob, now sitting at his master's feet, I make my escape. There's no other word for it.

CHAPTER NINE

Kit

'I'LL NEVER WALK straight again.' I close the door on the ridiculously compact car Mia borrowed from her brother and stretch out the cricks in my back.

She laughs and rolls her eyes. 'You spend too much time being chauffeured around.'

I press my lips together, hiding my smile and fighting the urge to kiss her. After the way she practically ran from my bed last night, I'd prepared myself for her bailing out today. But she showed up, early, as promised, and shoehorned me into her brother's car without a hint of what she had planned.

'What are we doing?'

'Rap jumping.' She grins and crosses the car park ahead of me, her steps all bouncy with her excitement.

Fuck, seriously?

I don't know whether to drag her back into the car or distract her with sex. My stomach twists, halving my options. This is why I like being in control.

'Mia.' I catch up in two strides, stalling her and spinning her around to face me. I eye the building—the signage and the excitement on her face confirm her statement.

'Are you serious?' My scalp writhes—it's a fucking uncomfortable feeling.

She smiles, fiddling with her hair, which she's pulled into some sort of messy ponytail. 'Have you done it before?'

I nod, my hand gripping the back of my neck while I seek divine patience. I grit my teeth, choosing my words carefully so I don't come across as a total nutjob. 'I don't like surprises.' It was bad enough yesterday when I spied her leaning on the rail of the bridge, just for a fucking photo.

Once upon a time I'd have shared Mia's enthusiasm for adventure. But I've been there, done that… watched my wife slip into unconsciousness on the side of a mountain in the middle of nowhere… I clench my fists, helplessness gnawing at my insides.

Mia misinterprets my hesitancy, not that I care about bullshit emasculation. 'Come on. It'll be fun. It's perfectly safe.'

I glance over at the brick tower that the signs tell me was once part of an old Victorian water-pumping station, while I rationalise the chances of anything bad happening. I need this like I need a root canal. But I heard from Reid this morning, informing me he's signed off on all of Mia's ideas and he and Drake are excited about the angle she's taking and the end product.

Instead of surrendering to the stomach-churning impotence, I level my attention on Mia. I can't stop her or forbid her. It *is* perfectly safe. Damn, I'll probably even enjoy it. And from the look on her face, trying to talk her out of it is pretty pointless. Exactly the kind of futility that makes my skin crawl. I release my hair from my fist, my scalp tingling.

'I just…would have liked some warning, that's all. I'm usually in charge. I'm not used to having things sprung on me.'

'Okay, boss. No more surprises. Come on.' She tugs my arm and I follow her inside, struggling to put my finger on what's really bothering me.

On the one hand, I'm in a dream situation—having fantastic sex with a beautiful woman who doesn't seem to want anything from me other than a couple of orgasms, which I'm more than happy to deliver, and freedom to do her job. But on the other hand, not a view I usually linger over, once the sex is over she's out of the door with the speed of an Olympic sprinter and it's pissing me off. I gnaw at my lip to prevent me asking why, like some needy jerk.

Because why doesn't matter. This is temporary. Temporary great sex. And nothing more, as evidenced by the way she flew out of the door last night.

And I'm here, holding up my side of the bargain, despite the surprise she's sprung on me. But she's holding back, and for some unfathomable reason this has me itching to crawl out of my skin—a feeling absent from my orderly life for three lonely but predictable years.

As we listen to the safety briefing I swallow my disgruntlement and lean close to whisper in her ear, just to enjoy the way her neck muscles judder under my breath, 'You sure you want to do this? I can think of ten other ways to give you the same high. Private, naked ways.'

She nods, her fingers stroking away the goose-bumps left by my breath as she shushes me. 'Stop. I might use the footage for the promo if it's up to scratch.'

She puts her index finger on her mouth and turns back to listen.

It's not until we're all trussed up and standing on a platform at the top of the tower that my unease solidifies into a ticking bomb in my chest. It's irrational. The staff are well-trained. Mia tells me she's done this a hundred times. I've even done it myself, back in the day, but the mass compressing my lungs persists.

It's not even fear. It's anger—a great concrete slab of pure rage. But the last thing I need is to come across like some unhinged crazy man to this woman I can't figure out. A woman I'm just fucking, because I can't even say we're sleeping together. Mia doesn't do sleepovers.

I rub my sternum, willing the burn away while Mia listens to last-minute instructions. She turns and grins at me, shooting me a thumbs-up. She has a camera strapped to her chest and one on the top of her safety helmet, which has tamed the usual cloud of hair, but given her an adorable case of hamster cheeks. Not that she'd give a shit.

Before the instructor has even finished speaking she gives him a nod, shoots me a wide beam of a smile that dissolves the last of the mass in my chest, and before I have chance to suck in a steadying breath she's gone. The whine of the ropes and Mia's victory cry echo around the tower as she speeds to the ground in a single, free-fall rappel.

And then she's two hundred feet below me, on solid ground, her fists pumping the air and her euphoric grin splitting her face.

My face is frozen, my pulse thunders and a white-hot burn coats my throat. Did she even listen to all the instructions? Has she no reservations whatsoever?

I can't begin to analyse the last few minutes of turmoil my body's been through and I don't care to. I step onto the platform, keen to get my turn over with so we can head back into London...perhaps stop somewhere nice for lunch when I've calmed down.

I'm numb, acting on auto as I sit on the edge of the platform and hurl myself forward. It's a passable high, made more so by Mia's welcoming smile when I touch down. She flies towards me, her hand raised for a high five as I unhook my harness from the ropes.

Some out-of-body possession grips me and I ignore the high five, snake my arm around her waist, haul her up close and kiss her. Firm, taking what I want. No preamble. It eases some of the thunder roaring in my head, but it's not enough. I scan the nearby buildings, scoping out a place to take her and fuck her until we've both had enough adrenaline for one day.

With a sigh I pull my mouth away from her return kiss, venting some of the emotion before the top of my head explodes. 'You were a bit bloody reckless.'

She freezes in my arms for a split second, and then she pushes me away.

'What do you mean? That was fantastic.' Her freckles are out in full force today. If I weren't wound so tightly I'd indulge my eyes, picking one of the fascinating myriad, which seems to change every time I look at her, to study.

But all I can see is red. I suck in air. I have no right to berate or even question her. I got myself in this stupid situation by agreeing to give her control of this project, despite my better judgement. My dick was clearly in charge that day.

'You just threw yourself off. Had you even finished listening to the instructor?'

She laughs, clearly still high. 'That was the best. I'm doing it again.' She's breathless, her face flushed, wisps of hair escaping her helmet. Oblivious to my inner meltdown, she loops her arm through mine and tugs me back towards the entrance to the base of the tower.

'I don't think so.' My heels dig into the grass. Fuck. What can I possibly say to make this better? I'm screwed, bent over a barrel, a victim to indulging both myself and Mia.

She turns, her smile slipping and her eyes narrowing. 'What? Are you telling me what to do?'

I scrub my face. I can't forbid her to do this. But I can't not watch, either. I swallow down the acid in my throat and smooth out my expression. What the fuck is wrong with me?

Avoiding her question, I say, 'Give me this.' I point to the chest camera. 'I'll film you from the ground this time.' If I can't put an end to this, I'll watch it unfold. Be there, on the ground, just in case. And some weird, twisted part of me wants to see the reaction on her face, the joy I heard the first time. The real, unguarded Mia, not the version who more often than not presents me with her back as she flees from my bed.

For a second she hesitates. 'But the footage is for the Faulkner promo.'

Perhaps she's still smarting from my proprietary outburst. Perhaps she thinks I'm too chicken to have another go. Perhaps she just prefers to be behind the lens rather than in front. 'And I'm a Faulkner. I want to film *you* for a change.'

I scoop my hand around her waist and kiss her forehead, indulging in the scent of her hair for a second, which calms me a fraction. I pull back and kiss her, pressing her up against the wall as she returns my kiss with her usual enthusiasm.

When we break apart she's staring at me, eyes searching. My scalp prickles and I'm grateful for the jumpsuit and crash helmet and the protection they grant. 'Go on.' I reach for the chest-mounted camera and jerk my head skywards. 'It's not like I'm asking you to make a sex tape.'

Yeah, joke your way out of it...

She grins but hesitates.

Then she winds her arms around my neck and kisses me. 'I totally would—I considered it the first day I met you.' She hands over the small, hand-held camera and walks backwards towards the doorway, excitement in her eyes, and then, at the last minute before she disappears into the stairwell, winks at me.

I capture every moment of her second jump, the twisted knot in my gut at her ginormous smile as big as the concrete block of earlier. Carefree, fun-loving Mia steals my breath more than any adrenaline thrill. More even than the idea of making a sex tape featuring her as the star.

Fuck. That's not a good thing.

CHAPTER TEN

Mia

THE LUNCH KIT insisted on was delicious, but not that informative for my raging curiosity. We mainly talked about other venues I have planned for the film and travel, Kit confessing New Zealand is one of only a handful of countries he'd yet to visit. But at least food seems to have cured him of whatever snit the rap jumping brought about.

I glance across at him bent double in the passenger seat of Will's car. Still ridiculously hot. 'Am I dropping you home?' My belly clenches at the idea— today has been fun, despite the hangover from my freak-out last night and Kit's initial reluctance. I can interpret the latter many ways, but I'm left with more questions than answers.

He glances across at me and I duck my head back to the view of London traffic through the windscreen so I don't have to register the flicker of what looks like disappointment in his eyes.

'You can. Or...' He pauses, as if wrestling with an internal decision. 'I have an engagement this afternoon—you could come with me.'

It's the first time I've heard him speak with anything other than extreme confidence. The first time he's *asked* for my company. The tension seeps from my fingers on the wheel and I smile.

'Sure.' I tell myself the relief is for the lure of more work—I like to keep busy. And whatever he's doing might be perfect for the promo video. 'What's on the agenda? All of my equipment is in the boot, so we're good to go.' Talking about work seems to be our safe place—and hopefully stops him from mentioning my weird behaviour last night. But then, perhaps he didn't notice. Perhaps he was thinking about Laura...

I swallow.

Last night's wake-up call hit me hard, requiring a good twenty-minute self-lecture in the shower when I returned to Will's. There's no reason I can't enjoy Kit's astounding bedroom skills, as long as my euphoria-addicted brain understands the high is simply physical.

And the urge to hold him, to comfort him, to give him more than control of the sex...? I'm simply confusing empathy and compassion with other feelings. Ones that have no place in our casual arrangement.

'It's not related to the Faulkner.' Kit snaps me back to the conversation. 'It's... I teach a class. You might find it useful to sit in. You might even enjoy it.' His mouth curls, dimple flashing, and my pulse skyrockets. I've enjoyed everything I've done with Kit so far, some things too much.

'Yeah, sure. I'm up for anything.' When I'm active, when I'm pushing myself, challenging myself, I feel like me. No time to wonder who that is and no time for errant feelings.

Kit snorts as he types the change of address into the GPS. 'Yes, I know. The way you hurled yourself off that tower…'

I'm about to laugh when I catch his expression. He's made light of it, but there's tension around his eyes. I nudge him with my elbow. 'It was fun—the bigger the risk, the bigger the rush. And that was nothing—the first time I tried bungee jumping was on a bridge over a gorge…' My voice trails off as I catch his expression. 'Did I freak you out?'

That would explain his reticence. He covered it up, but his bossy streak broke through. For a moment back there, I sensed an argument brewing. But not even Kit would issue commands beyond work and outside of the bedroom…right? I hold my breath, unease sliding over my skin.

He shrugs, but he looks sideways at the traffic. 'A bit… I saw lawsuits, damages payouts, bad publicity headed our way.'

Is that all he's worried about? 'Nah, I'm fully covered—insurance, indemnity, you name it.' The look he shoots me, hard and searching, throws up a dead end to that line of conversation.

I don't have to explain my choices to him. To anyone. I'm a free agent. End of story. 'So tell me, what's the class?'

'It's just for an hour; you don't have to stay for the whole session. I teach basic first aid and CPR.'

Shit. He's serious.

I forget how to breathe, how to speak, any comeback dying on my tongue. Urbane, sophisticated, professional Kit Faulkner teaching…? And CPR? I'm stunned into silence for so long, I've passed the point of polite surprise, so I go with honesty, giving free rein to the curiosity that's been an itch beneath my skin since I first met him.

'Is it something to do with Laura?' Was he alone with her? Did he try to revive her? That would explain his reluctance for rap jumping, his lecture about safety at the river yesterday.

He manages to keep his face neutral, his eyes seemingly focussed on the car in front, but his throat bobs as he swallows and one of his hands forms a loose fist.

'Yes. I had a vague inkling of what to do before. But after… I decided to learn properly. We should all know the basics—you never know when you might need to help someone.'

I nod, my head heavy, clunky, and my face hot. It's not something I've given much thought. But he's right. Just like the basic lifesaving skills we're taught alongside learning to swim, an understanding of how to perform CPR is extremely valuable.

No wonder he's out-of-sorts. Not that I'd have done anything differently today—we were both perfectly safe—but if I'd known I might have been a little more sensitive, a little more reassuring.

My throat is tight but I clear it and say, 'I'd love to come to your class.' My mind whirrs, questions about Laura's death trapped in my chest. 'I'll admit I've never had formal training.'

He keeps his eyes forwards as he nods, acknowledging my statement, a small frown squeezing his brows together. He's quiet, pensive. It's unnerving. I want bossy control-freak Kit back—at least I could butt horns with that guy with impunity.

He's lost one of the most significant people in his life. Suddenly, he said. I'd assumed Laura died in a hospital surrounded by professionals and in a safe and sanitised environment. I'm desperate for the details to fill in Kit's missing pieces, but too scared to ask. Because it blurs the lines, lines that are already as shaky as a seismograph trace, as my reaction to him last night proved.

On the back foot, my stomach in knots, I change the subject in a way that explains, without explaining. 'Do you remember the first time someone, a kid, dared you to do something?'

He nods, his stare sliding sideways to pin me, as usual.

I keep the conversation flowing in case I've inadvertently offended him or the memory of Laura. 'Me too. Most people wouldn't do the dare. But I did.'

'Why?'

My hands tighten on the wheel. 'Because I'd grown up knowing I was adopted. My parents are wonderful, but a part of me couldn't help feeling like I had to be constantly better to compensate. To prove myself.' Tension builds at my temples. I hadn't meant to confide quite so much and now the silence in the car pushes in on me from all sides.

'Anyway,' I brighten my tone, aiming for carefree, 'that was the first time I did something terrifying and came through the other side, triumphant. I've kind of been addicted to the rush ever since.'

The GPS tells me we've arrived and I pull off the road into the car park of a community centre. I busy myself with parking and turning off the engine to avoid looking at Kit.

As we make our way to the front entrance I only become aware of my left hand fidgeting when Kit wraps his long, warm fingers around mine without comment.

'You're perfect as you are, you know? You have nothing to prove.'

My breath freezes and I force my fingers to relax in his strong, sure grip as we both stare down at our connected hands. The contact, the intimacy feels as foreign as the first time he briefly held my hand, but my blood thrums through my veins, delivering adrenaline to every cell and lighting me up from the inside. This time he doesn't let go, nor does he expect any comment from me, simply tugging me by the hand through the door.

My reaction speaks volumes to my growing suspicions. The physical connection is a manifestation of the emotional connection. To stop the return of last night's panic, I tell myself it's the sex. In theory, when the sex ends, the foreign feeling should end. Perhaps we'll even stay friends.

So we actually talked about something real, so we actually confided in each other. No need to make a big deal out of. And my fidgeting habit must be irritating to someone so controlled.

That's why he's holding my hand.

Whatever the reason, I use the excuse of helping myself to a drink of frigid water from the water fountain to free my hand, only marginally appeased, because the contrast in temperature between the cold cup and my palm, still warm from Kit's body temperature, amplifies the loss of his touch.

At the desk the receptionist's face lights up. 'Kit, how are you? It's a full class today,' She's in her fifties and she smiles at Kit like he's the prime minister.

'Hi, Shelia. I'm sneaking in one more. This is Mia Abbott. She's come to observe.'

Shelia flicks me a cursory polite smile and then her beam returns to Kit. 'That's fine.' She issues me with a visitor sticker and I follow Kit down the hall.

There's so much turmoil in my belly I'm nauseous. I have no idea which piece of information I want first and I'm fully aware none of it is relevant.

Curiosity killed the cat.

'How often do you do this?' The idea of big, sexy billionaire Kit hanging out at the local community centre shakes the foundations of every assumption I've made. It's clearly important to him, not just to hone his own skills, but the motivation to teach others.

'Once a week.' He pauses outside an empty meeting room and looks at me, a small frown on his face. Perhaps he senses the dizzying spin of my thoughts, my emotions. He reaches once more for my hand and pulls me into the room, flicking on the lights.

After watching Kit teach the small group of adults for an hour in his confident, husky voice, I'm frayed ragged by the man he's shown me today. He even tossed in one or two jokes, his clear instructions and light-hearted teaching style so at odds with the controlled, uncompromising man I've witnessed so far, it hits me with the force of a sledgehammer. Here, under predictable scenarios, with only the well-being of a rubber-faced mannequin at stake, Kit is fully in control. Just as he likes to be in the bedroom.

I help him pack away the equipment in strained silence, not because I have nothing to say, but because I have so much running through my head, I need to filter my thoughts into coherent sentences. In the car park I spot Kit's car and driver, my stomach inexplicably hollowing.

At my questioning expression he says, 'I thought

it was easier…for you…if you don't have to drive me home. You need to get ready…for tonight.'

I nod, force a feeble smile.

'Great. I'll see you later.' I hover for a second, unsure how to leave. I want to kiss him but can't. Will he kiss me? After two awkward beats, I head for Will's car.

'Mia.'

I turn, heat welling in my throat, making speech unlikely.

'I'm required at the hotel early so I'll send a car for you. Be ready by six.'

And with that he leaves me in the car park, more dismantled than ever.

CHAPTER ELEVEN

Kit

MIA STRIDES INTO the ballroom, her made-up eyes hesitant, scanning the crowds, and the unsettled gnawing in the pit of my stomach that's been there all day dwindles away. She was so quiet and watchful during the class, I suspected she might cancel on this evening.

She's wearing the red beaded and feathered headpiece I selected to match the red dress I hoped she'd wear. Tonight's party has a nineteen-twenties theme, the hotel ballroom decorated to resemble a speakeasy—a stage and small round tables for two, each dimly lit with a small table lamp.

The dress isn't exactly in keeping with the period, but my imaginings of how stunning Mia would look in red were spot-on. The silky fabric slides over her tall, toned frame, accentuating the swell of her gorgeous breasts and pooling below the knees of her long, slender legs.

I shift, discreetly adjusting my cock as I excuse myself from our host and make my way to intercept a floundering Mia. I know I flummoxed her earlier with my confession, but it seemed the only way to still the hint of panic in my chest.

She spots me, her cheeks twitching on a smile, and some of the hesitancy slides from her face, just as the tension left those fidgeting fingers today when I held her hand. I exhale slowly and wind my way to her through the clusters of guests.

'Hi.' She accepts the kiss I place just shy of her mouth with the hint of a flush. I let it linger there for a second longer than is polite, her warm skin under my lips fuelling my fantasies of how I'll remove her from this dress. When I pull back, her eyes flash with the flickers of excitement I've come to learn.

'You look beautiful. I'm glad I chose this colour— I was right about it suiting you.' I dip close again, burying my nose in her hair so I can keep my next statement private. 'I want to take you somewhere right now and fuck you.' I soften my crudeness by reaching for her cool fingers and enclosing them in mine so she can't escape. That they feel right there is a thought I choose to gloss over.

She doesn't freeze this time. But she shoots me a look that contains enough censure for both of my presumptions. I tighten my grip. After the day we've spent together—her hesitant confessions over her need to prove herself, her obvious uncertainty about her past, perhaps even her need to fit somewhere—

I just want to get her alone. To communicate that to her in the way that seems to suit us best—physically.

I fight the urge to pull her close now, knowing even before the high dwindles she'll be out the door, just like she's probably dying to pull her hand from mine.

She hides any residual discomfort at the gesture with a change of subject. 'I left my equipment at Reception. Shall I get started?'

I dip close once more, the conversations buzzing around us my excuse if she needs one. 'Let's get you a drink, and I'll introduce you to David Barnett. It's his party.'

The courtesy my professionalism requires stabs me between the shoulder blades as I introduce my wealthy client to Mia. David, a still fit and virile businessman in his fifties, scrapes his keen eyes over her like she's caviar about to burst on his tongue.

Mia drops my hand so she can return David's handshake. I swallow my bile and endure their easy conversation, which begins with him relaying the details of his delightful trip to Mia's homeland. Within seconds he's made her laugh three times, pumped her for information on what she does for a living and is already handing her his business card and recommending colleagues in South America.

Fucker.

I look away, the sight of Mia's excitement, both for her departure from the UK and the businessman's nepotism, disruptive to my party mood. With impeccable timing, Reid and Drake join us and talk of Mia's looming departure continues.

'How are you getting on?' Reid asks Mia. 'Everything on schedule?'

Trust Reid to turn a social event into a fucking board meeting.

Mia smiles, fidgeting with the headpiece. 'Great, thanks. I have some awesome footage in the bag and I'm ahead of schedule, actually. I've booked some actors for tomorrow so I can shoot some scenes in the restaurant, gym and spa facilities.'

Ahead of schedule? Does that mean she'll be leaving sooner than planned?

The back of my neck tingles, making my collar tighten. I want to rip the tie from my throat and use it to gag my cheerful brothers, who look delighted their promised promotional film might be delivered ahead of deadline. 'Reid. Let the woman have a drink. It's a party.' I make a fist, itching to reach for her hand again.

Reid's jaw muscles pop as he slides me a curious look, and Mia turns away to watch the nearby entertainment—a woman clad only in a heavily beaded corset wallowing seductively in an enormous champagne glass as she fills the flutes of passers-by.

Drake, the easier-going of my two older brothers, engages her in conversation, offering her a tour of the Michelin-starred kitchen at the Faulkner. Mia laughs, her face lighting up, and I'm hit once more with the need to get her alone.

Reid steps closer and lowers his voice. 'If you don't want to be here, why didn't you ask Sally to attend?'

I shoot him a look I know he interprets correctly and take a swallow of my drink. 'I'd love nothing more than to leave. But I'll be taking Mia with me.' Barnett keeps sliding his eyes over her from across the room. Mia, quite rightly, seems keen to crack on with her job. And I... Fuck if I know how I feel or what I want. I just know I feel better when I'm with her.

Reid's eyes widen, correctly interpreting the situation. 'Fuck, Kit. Is that wise?'

I barely hear him, my stare returning to Mia as she speaks to Drake and then pulls her phone from her clutch. Has David, the randy old bastard, managed to get her number already?

Mia smiles down at the screen of her phone and then types a reply. My jaw clenches so hard my teeth ache. It's none of my concern who Mia fucks after me. But my stomach rolls at the idea of wily David Barnett anywhere near her.

'Mia can handle herself, no need to worry.' There's no chance of her heart being the slightest bit bruised when she walks away for the final time. She'll probably sprint. The uncomplicated end of an affair should lift my spirits, but I'm struggling to feel even a flicker of relief.

Reid interrupts my fantasy of discreetly informing David that Mia is taken, or gay or a nun, raising his voice to hiss above the nearby conversational din.

'She's practically an employee, for fuck's sake.' He rubs his eyebrow, mouth twisted.

My smile is brittle. 'None of your business.'

'You know, Kit, we all have our own shit to deal with, and on top of that, Drake and I are also organising the extended-family gathering for Dad's retirement bash—the least you could do is tune in occasionally.'

'What date is that?' Will Mia still be in town? She could come as my guest. Meet Faulkner Senior and all my overweight uncles. Of course, I'll have to keep my cousins away.

I glance at Mia, hoping to catch her eye and beckon her over so Reid can invite her formally—she's more likely to accept his invitation—but she's still typing, a small frown pinching her eyebrows together.

'Include Mia on the guest list,' I say to Reid, who shoots me a curious stare.

Drake is now occupied with a blonde I don't recognise and Mia returns to my side, sliding her wide smile to Reid. Lucky bastard.

'Is everything okay?' My fingers twitch to retake her hand. She's barely touched her champagne, and the text seems to have left her distracted.

'Fine. My brother was going to come and help me out with the filming. But he can't make it after all.'

A grin threatens. So it wasn't Barnett texting Mia.

Her mouth tightens, telling me there's more bothering her than inconvenience. I may not be able to whisk her away as I want to, but I can solve one of her problems, escape Reid and hog Mia for the rest of the evening.

'*I* can help you.'

She looks at me like I've just announced I'm selling my house to relocate Bob and me to a cardboard box.

She snorts. 'You?'

A shrug. 'Sure.' How hard can it be to carry a light stand? The harder part will be keeping my hands off Mia while she works.

Mia hands her untouched drink to a passing waiter and settles her stare back on mine, as if assessing my credentials to hold a tripod.

'But first, why don't we get the dancing started?' There are only two couples on the dance floor. I reach for her hand and she hesitates, shooting a *Rescue me* look at Reid.

I tilt my chin at Reid in farewell and grip Mia's elbow, guiding her through the crowds.

'You're here to film a party, Mia. Not a wake. If we dance, others will follow.' She can't argue with my logic, and this way I get to put my hands on her, something I've wanted to do all day.

On the dance floor I pull her close so her sensational body is flush with mine. I smile down at her, loving the flood of colour in her chest and the way her breath catches in her throat.

'Dancing was definitely *not* in my contract.' She's a little stiff at first. But I lead her deeper into the throng of those who've joined us, further from escape, as I manoeuvre her through the swaying steps, although the desired effect, of course, is pressing our bodies together.

'Neither was fucking the boss. Not that I'm in any way complaining.' Unless it's to question the penchant she has for fleeing even before I've caught my breath.

I tug her closer, the hairs on my scalp pricking. I've no right to question her, no right to expect anything. All I can offer her in return is what we have right now. Would she come home with me, if I asked her? Stay the night?

'You're an arsehole, you know that, right?'

I shrug, the flash in Mia's pretty amber eyes hitting me between the ribs. 'Sure.'

My hands flex, gripping her a fraction tighter. But why doesn't *she* want more? The sex is pretty astounding—I'm not blowing my own trumpet, but she can't hide her body's reactions.

I'm done fighting the urge, so I ask her, 'Will you come to a family party with me before you leave?'

She stills, the tension back.

'Reid's going to invite you formally,' I add. 'He's good at that.'

My smile evaporates with her next statement. 'Your brothers really care about you, you know.'

She's right, of course. But brothers can be dicks to

each other. And she has no idea what I put up with, being the youngest, growing up. Something shifts in me, that feeling when you wake from a dream and know with certainty you've forgotten something, but can't remember what it is. I've spent so long pushing people away that it's become second nature.

'You're clearly close to your brother. You can invite him—Josh too if you want.' I'm babbling now. What the actual fuck…?

Why is it so important to me that she come? That she be included in a family function? That she gives me more of herself than hit and run sex?

She nods. 'He's my best friend.'

I swallow, squeezing her hand tighter, preempting the flutter of her fingers. My stomach churns. Perhaps that's why she's always running, closed down to anything that gives her roots.

'Are you and Will biological siblings?'

She shakes her head, her shoulders drooping a fraction more.

'Have you ever thought about finding your biological parents?' I tighten my arm around her back, sensing, despite her earlier confession, she won't want to discuss this.

When she looks up at me, her luminous eyes are achingly vulnerable. I want to cut out my tongue.

'Not really. Life's been too busy. Will reunited with his birth family a few years back. They live in New Zealand, so he doesn't see them often.'

'So he's settled in London?'

She nods. 'He and Josh are trying to adopt. And our parents are planning to move over later this year.'

My heart accelerates, the warmth spreading out from my chest. Surely if all her family are here, in London, she'd be back from time to time…? But she doesn't look happy about the fact her family will be in one place. She looks a little lost.

Just as quickly my spirits slump and my senses are on high alert—the music is too loud, the flashing lights are too bright. 'Perhaps finding your parents would help you feel more settled, give you a sense of belonging…'

She nods, like she's had similar thoughts and already dismissed them.

'Yeah. Last I heard, my mother moved to London. She could be out there somewhere, a stranger on the tube and we wouldn't know each other.'

My pulse skyrockets. 'That must be a really hard decision. But if Will's done it, he could help you. And it's all the more reason to come back…' Of course, the benefits for me are pretty abundant too. We could catch up, continue this whenever she's in London. But I should let it go. It's not part of what we're doing, and it's none of my damned business. Nothing's changed—I shouldn't demand more from her because I can't make her any promises, even if she wanted them.

'Just like that, huh? Easy?' Her eyes flash me a warning.

'Well, it has to be easier than running, holding

people at arm's length all the time. Why should you miss out on your family, your nephew—?'

'You have to be kidding?' She slams to a halt. 'You are the master of keeping people at arm's length, especially your family, your brothers. Even your dog.'

My shoulders tense. She's right, of course.

I see red, then the mist clears. 'And you're a champion of leaving my bed quicker than an Olympian athlete.' I mash my runaway mouth closed, swearing under my breath. This won't help my cause. It's a dead end, just like our relationship.

There's a wide space between her body and mine now. We stare each other down. The dance floor beneath my feet shifts as if I'm balanced on the crumbling edge of a cliff. I've taken this way further than I normally would. 'Look, Mia, I don't need anyone's pity—'

'And I don't need anyone's approval for my choices.' She leaves off the 'especially yours', but it hangs there in the air between her parted lips and mine.

The crowd around us is still dancing. Mia glances around and deflates. 'Look, I need to work.' She lifts her chin, squaring up to the challenge once more, where other women I know would leave or cry or slap me in my conceited, hypocritical, interfering face. 'If you still want to help me, perhaps we should end this conversation here. This isn't what we're about, is it?'

I want to argue, to fight for the right to make her

see she has so much to give, so much love around her to enjoy. But I have no fucking right and no leg to stand on.

She looks away, her small smile one of brave inevitability rather than victory.

I bite my tongue and follow her from the dance floor.

CHAPTER TWELVE

Mia

I'M PACKING AWAY my equipment when Kit finds me.
The party rages on, but I have sufficient footage
and, after our disagreement, my whole skeleton aches
with a weariness that I fear is more than physical.
A weariness that makes the inside of my chest sore.

'You're leaving?' he says.

I nod, keeping my head down, focussed on the job
in hand. Away from his perceptive stare.

Kit waits silently beside me while I stuff cables
inside the last pocket and then he lifts the backpack,
tosses it over one shoulder and takes my hand. He
summons the concierge, instructing him to deliver
the bag to the car.

'I'm fine. It's not late. I'll take the tube.' My re-
sistance is snappier than usual, sharpened by my
growing unease in the wake of our earlier fight. At
least, I think it was a fight. I'd certainly had a whole
heap more I wanted to say before I realised there
was no point.

Kit's expression told me everything I needed to know. Couples fight and make up. I was right, although the victory tastes foul—that isn't what we're about.

I wanted so badly to be wrong. To have him deny it even while I formulated a lecture on how he didn't really know me, had no right to question my fuck-and-run tactics and should spend some time looking in the mirror.

Yep, definitely a fight.

Kit grips my hand, spreading the now familiar heat up my arm. 'I'm taking you home, Mia. Or my driver is.' His mouth is grim. Obstinate. Brooking no refusal.

'You don't get to tell me what to do, you know. That's not a part of this.' Oh, I'm all about what we aren't now, as if I need the reminder, even if he doesn't.

I understand Kit's need to control what he can. A similar urge currently pounds through my blood, the only antidote for the unsettling emotions I'm experiencing. Emotions I've always shut down in the past. And now, with everything I was certain of in my life questioned, I know why.

This is what happens when you let people in. Not only do they see you too clearly, they feel they have a right to tell you what to do.

I lift my chin. 'I'm a grown woman who's managed to live perfectly successfully without your assistance up to this point.' That he's reduced me to a cliché, just a woman who craves more than his phe-nomenal sexual prowess—those rare glimpses of his dazzling personality, the unguarded moments where he's warm and caring and funny—shunts my strung-out body close to the skin-crawling urge to run.

He can't get away with that unaffected. He can't have me all figured out while keeping his own guard unbreachable.

A gaggle of partygoers breezes past, heading for the exit, no doubt in search of a smoke. Kit turns on his heel and ushers me into an office accessed by a keypad.

Inside he flicks on the desk lamp and shrugs off his jacket. 'I'm not telling you what to do, I'm con-cerned for your safety.' He pulls the phone from his trouser pocket, his thumb flying over the screen. 'Just take a seat, Mia. Give me a second to text my driver…'

Have I overreacted, led down the wrong track by his insightful observations? What's the point of fighting? I can't have him, anyway. I chew on my lip, the same urge that overcame me the first day I met him in another office washing over me. The urge to defy…the urge to prove…and now the urge to outrun my feelings, just like I've always done, intensifies, as if this time there's more to run from. More at stake.

Because if Kit sees me that clearly, enough to see I'm incomplete, to see what I might need, then I've allowed him too close.

I've worn his clothes, answered his questions, put

up with his rudeness, and even tolerated his sexual dominance… Okay—that's a bit rich. I've revelled in the latter. But either way, I want Kit to suffer similar turmoil to what's eating away at me. How dare he do this? How dare he make me something I'm not? How dare he make me see a future I've spent my whole adult life avoiding? How dare he make me… care? For him? A man so closed-off, it's laughable. But the joke is on me.

No.

It's just sex. Sex is all it's ever been. While I don't mind giving him the control he needs over our sexual activities, he doesn't get to tell me what I need, or what to do. It's time the power balance shifted my way.

Clarity settles over me and I succumb to my needs with a sigh. 'Sit down.'

He spins to look at me, a small frown pinching his brow.

That's right, I can make demands too.

I point at the leather chair behind the desk.

'Mia, look, if this is about earlier—'

I rise up on my tiptoes and press my mouth to his, transferring the heat burning inside me to my kiss. I don't want him rational, consoling. I want to undo him as he's undone me. I want to push him to the edge of whatever this is between us, so he feels it too. The panic. The prickly heat. The stripped-bare vulnerability which slides over my skin like warm treacle—seductive but bordering on discomfort. That

I'm alone in this stiffens my resolve. If I'm going down, he's coming with me.

With my gentle shove, Kit stumbles back into the seat, his hands on my hips tugging me after him until I'm slotted between his strong thighs. For once I am in the driving seat.

He looks up. I look down, the dynamic forcing blood to my head in a rush.

'Fuck, you've been driving me crazy all night.' His hands slide under my dress and up the backs of my thighs to knead the bare cheeks of my arse. 'Are you wearing a thong?' He leans forward and groans into my belly.

My hands brace on his shoulders; the power trip is heady. 'I'm not wearing anything. This dress is ridiculously revealing.'

He lifts his head, a blue spark in his excited eyes. 'You've been walking around all night without underwear?'

I feel like a naughty schoolgirl called to the principal's office. Not how I want to feel. I scour my psyche for my inner seductress, scrapping the idea as soon as it forms. He's hard against his fly. Kit wants me. I am determined to be me. To be who I am.

His eyes flick to the door behind me and then he levels earnest eyes on mine. 'Come home with me.' It's a demand. Gruff with desire, but bearing enough bite to tell me he's still in control.

Yesterday, I'd have gone along with his demand. But today...today I'm different. He's made me different with his hand-holding and his confidences and the small glimpses of his genuine smile.

'I don't think so.' I reach for his belt and tug it open.

'Mia, I don't want to fuck you on a desk...' His eyes flick over my shoulder once more. I don't know if anyone else knows the entry code, but I don't care.

'Come home with me? Stay the night?' This time it's a question, but I shake my head. Why is he pushing so hard? Why is he still trying to nudge me out of my comfort zone without offering anything in return...?

My stomach twists. I want Kit vulnerable, confused, as rudderless as I've felt since the community centre—while he grapples with whatever this is flaring between us.

I drop to my knees on the carpet, loving the conflicted thrill of excitement in his hooded stare.

'It's late.' I shove his zipper down and free him from his boxers. 'I have to be back here early tomorrow for the shoot.'

'Mia...' he groans, so close to losing the battle he has going on in his head. I taste victory. He wants to control this chemistry. And I was happy to concede when I had nothing to lose. But now...

My hand pumps him. He's steel and velvet in my palm. His hips shift. Is he getting comfortable or recoiling...? But his fingers toy with my hair, his stare dropping to my mouth every few seconds, while his chest lifts and falls at an increased rate.

I lean in, my tongue sliding over the head of his cock while I look up at him. I channel my defiance into my stare, just as *he* did that first time we kissed in the car the day we met. We're both hiding. Both running. Time for Kit to feel the burn in his lungs and the lactic acid scream in his muscles…

I wrap my mouth around him.

He hisses, his head falling against the backrest and then snapping up to watch the show once more.

'Mia…' There's a hint of warning in his voice, a hint of danger. But he cups my cheek, fingers gentle in my hair as he shifts his hips once more.

I blank out his voice, blank out the sight of his male beauty, blank out his words from the dance floor, needing to keep him at arm's length. Because I'd known he was dangerous the day I met him… I just fooled myself I could handle the challenge, as usual. But the Kit effect is too strong. Overwhelming. He's already seen too much, seen me too clearly. Probed too close to an area of my life even I don't have figured out. If I'm not careful he'll dismantle me completely.

I suck him hard, hollowing my cheeks while I pump with my hand. Kit spreads his steely thighs, his grip tightening in my hair and surrender softening his features.

It's a heady feeling. I bob my head with renewed enthusiasm. I want him breathless. I want him reeling. I want this urbane man who wears his pain like a second skin at *my* mercy, just for a second.

His knuckles whiten on the arms of the chair, and my pulse thunders in my head. His breath seesaws in and out of his flared nostrils and his pupils are massive black pools, honed on the action.

For a few delirious seconds he's mine. Completely vulnerable. Undone.

The relief washes through me and I groan, the sound buzzing my lips where they're stretched around him.

'Stop.'

What?

My fingers release him and I rear back on my heels, allowing him to slip from my mouth.

His thumb wipes the saliva from my bottom lip, his eyes soft, searching. He finds his breath then says, 'Come home with me.'

He rises and pulls me to my feet, still hard and still wet from my mouth. He really wants this to go his way. He's not going to let me finish him. He can't give me even that.

I wipe my mouth with the back of my hand, smearing what's left of my lipstick, glad he's rumpled my stupid hairdo so much the sequinned headband is somewhere on the floor, the pins have fallen out and it's as wild as usual.

'Why? So you can tell me what I need?'

Disappointment flashes in his eyes. And then they harden, taking my resolve along for the ride. It would be so easy to cave, to lose another little sliver of myself to him. I shake my head. My slivers, as rootless and uncertain as they are, are precious. I can't give him more. I can't give him more than he's willing to give me.

I'm not relenting this time. '*I* know what I need— kiss me.' I know that look on his face, and I'm determined to pre-empt whatever comes next. To cling to a shred of the old me. The me who had her life figured out. The me who needed no one. The me who didn't belong, but didn't need to.

He wavers for a split second and then he scoops one arm around my waist and hoists me up onto the desk. I tunnel my hands in his hair, dragging his mouth down to my kisses, and he fumbles in his pocket for what I assume is a condom.

I spread my thighs to accommodate him, desperate now, as I am every time with him, to slake this fire. He breaks away to stare between my legs and groans. I was telling the truth about the underwear.

'Fuck!' He drops to his knees, his mouth covering me as his hands grip my thighs and he spreads me open on the desk. My mind shuts down as he pushes his tongue inside me, once, twice, three times and then he's back on his feet, tearing into the condom and shunting my backside to the edge of the furniture.

My legs curl around his, drawing him closer, and he notches himself at my entrance, teeth gritted as if he's holding back things he wants to say. But it's all there in his eyes. The same flicker of regret he's always harboured.

I close my eyes, blocking out what I'm not ready to see, not ready to admit. I yank on his neck, kissing him so those things stay unspoken as he pushes inside.

Our coupling is quick, but no less spectacular for that. We come together and for a few breathless minutes in the aftermath I think I've overreacted; made shit up in my head and everything is the same as it was a week ago.

When he shifts and withdraws, I push him away and stand, my jittery limbs covered in goosebumps as the surge of orgasmic adrenaline dwindles. His phone on the desk behind me buzzes, breaking the silent tension and gifting me an escape.

As if he senses my intention, Kit makes a grab for my fingers with one hand and tucks himself away with the other, before smoothing the wrinkles from my dress down over my hips. 'Come home with me.' It's quiet, almost a plea, but still a command. He's still angling.

I want to capitulate, to say 'yes, take me home'. To have him spend all night reminding me how good we are together. Sex is all I can want from him and all he can expect from me in return. If I go home with him, if I give him more, I might lose the identity I've clung to all these years.

I tug my hand free and smile, stepping backwards. 'I don't think so.' I shrug. 'I'll see you tomorrow, boss. Work to do.'

Kit shoves his hands in his pockets and some of

the tension leaves me. If he doesn't touch me again, I might find the strength to follow through.

I grab my clutch and make it to the door.

'Mia.'

I spin, shoulders back, carefree grin wobbling in place.

He's holding his phone, his clothing renewed so no one would know what has just transpired. Still beautiful, still in control. 'My car's waiting for you. Take it.'

I nod and leave, like Cinderella regretting that she's seduced Prince Charming hoping to find him a frog, only to discover he's the one hundred per cent authentic heir to the throne.

In the back of Kit's car, I collapse into the leather. Even now he surrounds me—his scent on my skin, his voice in my head, his stare tattooed on my retinas for ever. I watch the world whizz by, blind to everything but the weight sitting on my chest. There's a reason I've avoided relationships all these years. This feeling, right here, is the reason.

Vulnerability.

Making me question everything about myself. And there are enough questions in my life. Relationships, like mortgages and dog ownership, represent permanence. And for a woman who's scared to dig too deep, to look too hard beneath her surface for fear of the answers…

I fish a tissue from my clutch and dispense with what's left of the make-up, scrubbing too hard but welcoming the burn as I peel away Kit's uniform. He's changed me enough with his champagne and his family gatherings and his control.

I take some deep breaths, willing my heart rate into submission and telling myself that, underneath the £3,000 dress and out of the chauffer-driven pumpkin, I'm still me.

When I arrive back at Will's, every muscle in my body sags. He's still up.

I find him in the kitchen, a cup of cold tea at his fingertips, his laptop open and paperwork spread over the table.

I make fresh tea, snag his sweater from the back of a chair, don it over the dress and sit beside my brother. Fatigue rims his eyes. He rubs at his face and takes a grateful sip of the tea. 'Thanks. Sorry about bailing out tonight.'

'No problem. How are you doing?'

He sighs, but smiles. 'Good. It's all happened a bit quickly.'

Will and Josh applied to adopt a year ago. Today, this evening, they got the call. Josh is away on an overnight business trip.

'It's so exciting,' I whisper around my tight throat. 'What you're both doing will change someone's life.'

He nods. We both understand the importance of growing up in a loving home. Who knows where either of us would be without that stability?

'Have you told Mum and Dad?' They'll be beside themselves… Their first grandchild…

Will shakes his head, some of the fatigue leaving his face. 'I will. As soon as I'm sure it's really happening.'

I nod.

'You okay?' he asks, intelligent eyes probing over the rim of his steaming mug.

I try to nod, but it comes out half-shrug, half-collapse as I slump into the chair. At last I force the words out, barely a whisper. 'I don't know what to do.'

I'm not sure which of us is more startled by my confession. By the tone of my voice, which is clogged with the threat of tears. I'm always on the move. Always know what I'm doing next. But something here... London... Kit... Family has tripped me up.

He frowns. 'What do you mean?'

I chicken out, confessing only half the issue. 'I should be here for you. To help out.' I swallow hard so the next words emerge as no more than a croak. 'Aunt Mia...'

'There's nothing to stop you coming back. You have a room here anytime you want it. You know that.'

A part of me wants that so badly. And what *is* stopping me? I'm the only thing standing in the way. My need to outrun who I am. Because who exactly is that?

Perhaps Kit is right. Perhaps finding answers from my birth mother will help me feel like I belong. Somewhere...

I rub at my face, disgusted with the smear of mascara on my fingers. 'How did you do it?'

He knows what I mean.

Will tracked down his birth parents five years ago. His mother had been easy—she'd left the door open. But it had taken a year of soul-searching, a year of doubt and disappointment to find his biological father.

He shrugs, but he understands the portent of my question. 'I needed to know.'

I nod. 'I think I do too, but I'm scared of the whys.' It's easier to keep moving. To act like it doesn't define me. To exist without certainty in case certainty hurts like a bitch.

'Of course you are. But they may not be as bad as you're imagining. And if they are the worst-case scenario you still have love. You still have us and Mum and Dad.'

I smile at my brother, despite the turmoil swirling the tea in sickening circles in my stomach, because that, right there, is how I know he's going to be a superb parent.

'You've met someone, haven't you?'

I swallow, forcing my eyes to stare at the tea ring drying on the table and trying not to blink away the burn.

My silence tells my perceptive brother all he needs to know. Will reaches for my hand; his is warm, solid and undemanding. Just like Kit's hand.

'It's okay.' His voice is barely a soothing whisper

now, as if he understands the fight or flight building inside me. 'It had to happen some time.'

I shake my head—it's too full, too conflicted. 'I can't. I need to focus on me.'

To work out who I am and where I come from. To...try and stop running.

Without that, what do I have to give, even if I do meet someone who can give me everything in return?

When did beginning the search for my birth parents become the least scary of my problems?

I shudder in a breath, marginally appeased that my brother knows me so well that there's no need to vocalise the way I feel. Perhaps making that call isn't so terrifying...

And Kit?

I look up at Will, my watery smile earning me a hug. I close my eyes and succumb to my brother's big, bulky comfort offering. I'm overthinking this. Overcomplicating the issue. At the end of the day, all I have to do is let things with Kit unfold.

Kit loves Laura.

I'm leaving London.

A plus B equals simple.

CHAPTER THIRTEEN

Mia

THE MODELS, JAMES and Bryony, still wearing Faulkner-monogrammed robes, talk while I review the footage we've spent the morning shooting. It's been two days since the burlesque party and Kit has been notably absent. It's a good thing. I focussed on the photo shoot of the hotel's interior—simple stills of James and Bryony taking a champagne breakfast in the restaurant, drinking cocktails in the bar and enjoying the spa facilities.

But in between shots, my mind stubbornly refused to leave Kit. I hallucinated him striding through the hotel foyer in one of his sharp suits, the epitome of confident male swagger. Deservedly so.

'Okay, guys, that's a wrap. You can get dressed. Thanks for all your hard work today.'

The duo were so professional that we've finished a day ahead of schedule, a fact that should please me but leaves a nasty gnawing in my belly and my head full of dangerous ways to fill the time… Not physically dangerous. Emotional peril is far more terrifying.

Yesterday I researched websites that help you locate adoption records and missing family members. My fidgety fingers didn't quite press 'send' on the enquiry form, but I've taken what feels like a massive first step.

A clatter of claws on the tiles forces my already fluttering heart into my throat, alerting me to Bob's arrival, Kit by his side.

My pulse goes into overdrive for the sight of the owner decked out as I'd imagined him earlier in one of his suits. I channel my enthusiasm into greeting Bob, whose tail swings while I scratch at his neck and fight hard to keep my face from hiding against his sleek fur until the urge to kiss Kit abates, despite the way we left things.

Come home with me.

I've asked myself a thousand times if he was simply trying to stamp his need for control on me, on our sexual encounters, or if he meant the request that, as time went on, sounded less like a command and more like a plea.

Will I see the answers I'm searching for if I look at Kit's face? Will those answers even help? Or will I see what I always see when I search for a hint of more: regret?

I focus on Bob instead of risking confirmation either way. 'Are dogs allowed in here?' I don't care one way or the other, but my guarded question is better than the alternative—succumbing, kissing Kit and then demanding to know where his head is at and whether, if I returned to London, he'd want to see me again.

I stroke Bob, falling back into the no-man's-land of our non-relationship and my endless run-stay cycles.

Kit shrugs. 'The Faulkner is a pet-friendly hotel. And even if it weren't, I'm one of the owners.'

Duh…he can do what he likes. He's always done what he likes. He's always been in control of this. Of us. I'm the only loose cannon here.

Dragging myself away from Bob, I close down my laptop and continue packing away my filming equipment, keeping my hands busy and my vision occupied. 'Well, I've just finished. The models have gone home, so if you were hoping to add direction to the shoot, you're too late.' Although if he'd have been here any earlier there may not actually have been any footage worth having. He's a perfect, mouthwatering distraction and, despite all that's gone through my mind in the last forty-eight hours, I want him still.

Kit leans against a pillar, hands casually slung in his front pockets while his keen stare follows my every move. 'I'm not.'

A lens cap clatters to the tiles. I retrieve it with an internal curse. I need to get my shit together, before I make a fool of myself by reading too much into his words. By blurting out questions when I'm not ready to hear the answers. There are enough of those in my head.

'I've come to escort you to your next assignment.' Kit's lazy drawl grates over my eardrums and sparks every wrung-out cell in my body to vibrant life.

I need to withdraw, not succumb. To wean myself off his effortless lure. Reminding myself I'm the same person I was two weeks ago—and so is Kit—helps.

But it's poor protection.

'I'm kind of done for the day.' I have ample footage already. A couple of days of editing and I'll be out of his hair.

Kit smiles, self-assured and so tempting. 'Think of it as a field trip.'

I look away from his navy stare, deep and dark and full of promises.

The physical kind.

That's where *my* focus needs to be honed. On where we began, and the reasons why. Perhaps if I can get back there, the tumultuous feelings in me will disappear. But I suspect Kit's as dangerous as ever.

Zipping up my backpack and tossing it over one shoulder, I say, 'What's the assignment?' The sight of a spectacular Kit slouched casually against the wall with a regal Bob at his heels scrambles my already threadbare wit. Who needs models when Kit is around, all brooding, untouchable masculinity?

'*Off the Guidebook* offers a weekend trip to a winery on Jersey. Ever been?'

I shake my head, my mind tripping over itself with the timing. It's past noon. Will it be an overnighter? My chest tightens as the fizz of adrenaline builds, even as I tell myself it's not a good idea.

The hesitation must show all over my heated face, because Kit adds another layer of inducement, as if spending time alone with him isn't temptation enough. Even if our time is running out.

'We're taking Bob.'

I raise my brows, about to ask if dogs are allowed on planes. But they probably are on private aircraft and... Kit is all the permission required.

I'm still prevaricating, battling myself and the crazy flights of fancy my mind conjures. I give free rein to my fidgeting.

Come home with me.

When he steps up behind me I close my eyes, my body swaying. I stiffen my muscles, preventing me from leaning back into his solid chest.

He's close, his breath on my neck. My stomach clenches—close, but not close enough.

'It's work, Mia.'

My stomach drops like I'm on a roller coaster. I open my eyes, the room coming back into focus. Of course, he's right—it's part of my job. There's no question.

'Plus...' his voice drops and the fabric of his jacket brushes against my bare arms '...you'll soon be done. Your work for us completed...'

Yes. This is the reminder I needed. For Kit, I'm work. Temporary. A distraction. All he can be to me.

Liar.

I stare until my eyes burn at a peaceful watercolour on the wall at the far end of the spa reception area to stop myself from turning into his chest.

He can't be my comfort, my consolation. I'm a big girl. Self-reliant, same as always.

His next statement makes me smile and snaps me from the heavy turn of my thoughts.

'Bob's really looking forward to it.'

He doesn't need to coax me, he could simply wave my contract in my face and insist. I capitulate, clinging to the fact it's work, probably the last place I'll film before I leave.

'Did you just anthropomorphise your dog?'

He shrugs with a grin that flips my belly. Then he takes my elbow, hefts my backpack onto his shoulder, crumpling his immaculate suit, and whistles for Bob.

The flight takes an hour. Kit regales me with details of the winery we're to visit and the history of Jersey, the largest of the Channel Islands between England and France, and the beauty of the beaches.

Before we land Kit changes into jeans and a T-shirt so that when the car pulls into the gravel driveway of the boutique winery he lifts my backpack from the boot, instructs our driver to have the remaining luggage delivered to our rooms and, taking my hand, whistles for Bob and turns for the nearby cliffs.

'I thought you might be missing the beaches of home.' He keeps his stare focussed on the horizon, as if his thoughtful admission leaves a bad taste in his mouth. 'This one is private and quite stunning, and Bob needs a walk.'

'Great. Come on, Bob.' I slip my fingers from his—I'd been enjoying them there too much and need to wean myself off—and trot ahead down the winding, sandy cliff path behind the excited dog.

The bay, a secluded inlet, is exquisite, backdropped by the pink and orange tinges of the setting sun. Kit arrives at my side and hands me my backpack with a smile, before I've even had a chance to ask for it, as if he knows I'm itching to capture the views. Within seconds I've fitted the harness and camera to Bob and set up my digital SLR with a wide-angle lens.

Bob bounds into the gently lapping surf at one end of the bay in pursuit of the small pebbles Kit skims across the surface, while I take some photos of the view at the opposite end. But the beauty of the setting sun can't compete, and my focus is quickly drawn to the man and his dog frolicking at the water's edge.

My bare feet pivot in the damp sand as I grab my second camera, adjust the shutter speed and fire off shot after shot, unseen. The evening sun glints off the water, Bob's sleek coat is dark and soaked as he jumps and runs back and forth, but it's Kit who draws my eye, holds it captive and burns his image there for all of time. Because he's laughing. Joyous, delighted, head thrown back in laughter as he rough-houses with Bob, his jeans, even his T-shirt, getting splashed over and over again while he selects a new pebble to throw.

With every click of the camera, my heart beats faster until it feels like it's trying to climb out be-tween my ribs. I taste salt on my tongue and realise my mouth is open.

I return my cameras to my bag and stride towards him, my feet acting on instinct, as if Kit's a mag-net and I'm little more than a pile of iron filings, as fine as the sand and held together by unseen forces.

He turns at the last second, catching sight of me, his face split into the beatific beam he wore in his portrait with Laura and Bob—eyes alight from within, a deep groove on one side of his beautiful mouth and his hair lifted by the breeze. I expect the smile to slide from his handsome face as I place my bag on the dry sand, but it stays there, only morph-ing into something hotter, more licentious, when he guesses my intentions.

As I reach him, his arms come around my waist and I stretch up on tiptoe and grip his face between two palms. And then our mouths are lost to our kiss—smiling, talking, even breathing forgotten.

Before I'm even aware I've moved, he's hoisted me up and my legs are wrapped around Kit's waist while I kiss the life from him. Kit carries me, stumbling a few paces to the dry sand dune behind, before laying me on my back and following me down until his body covers mine.

I switch off my thoughts, my doubts, my fears and just feel. His hip bones dig into my thighs, sand trickles down the neck of my T-shirt and marram grass tickles my cheek. But I claw at Kit's T-shirt, my mouth never leaving his, desperate now to prolong this moment. Just us. This. Now. Kit and Mia. No past to regret and no future to fear.

Kit's ice-cold fingers snake under my shirt and I squeal. He laughs, his cool lips moving over mine while he mumbles an apology against my mouth. I've just released the fly of his jeans when a shower of salty spray leaves us both shrieking and breaking apart. Bob drips water over us as he wags his tail, and jumps up and down, keen for the game of fetch to continue.

I clamp my hand over my mouth, stifling hysterics at Kit's expression, which is one of frantic coitus interruptus. His eyes dart around the deserted beach as if problem-solving a way to continue what we've started, and then he braces himself over me, a defeated grin replacing the very turned-on man of seconds ago.

'I can't perform while he watches.' He kisses me again through my sniggering. 'And I don't want my arse licked during proceedings.' His hot stare, full of promise, the return of that smoulder he's so good at, ends my fit of mirth. 'To be continued.' His voice is gruff and I can barely speak, I want him so badly.

Playful, jovial Kit.

A man I've inadvertently fallen for.

Stupid, reckless Mia...

We right our clothing, throw a few more stones for Bob and head back up the coastal path. This time I let him have my fingers, luxuriating in his warm palm sliding against mine. Who knew hand-holding, an activity I've always associated with teenage crushes, could imbibe my entire body with gooey heat and leave me craving Kit's arms, his touch, his kiss? So this is what it feels like to...fall.

The surge inside me on the beach when I saw Kit's unguarded expression of joy hit me like a tidal wave. I want that for him. Every day. And I want to be the one to put that look on his face.

But some wants aren't meant to be...

Back at the hotel, with Bob handed over to the accommodate-anything staff, there's no question I'm following Kit to his suite, even though he's reserved me my own room. Within seconds of the door softly closing we're naked and plastered all over each other. My mouth is frantic on his, as if kissing him will silence those questions still filling my head and the dead-end feelings stealing my breath.

He never made me any promises. Not one. When I walk away, I can do so without regret. But for now, I'm still here.

I'm still kissing him like there's no tomorrow but

at every turn Kit slows things down, dictating the pace as if demanding more from every touch, every look, every whispered moan. By the time he finally pushes inside me, I can no longer hold in the sob that escapes me, hiding it inside a cry to prevent giving myself away.

This I *can* feel. The chemistry. The euphoria of us together, physically, all it can ever be between us—an unavailable man and a commitment-phobic woman.

With one hand braced on the pillow beside my head, he cups my cheek with the other, his fingers tangling in my hair as he leans low to kiss me before he rocks into me again and again. I come with his eyes on mine, his hand cupping my face and a searching look shining from his heated eyes. He finishes and collapses on top of me with a loud groan, his face buried in my neck while he pumps through the last of the tremors.

My heart rate should be settling but adrenaline kicks in, the usual urge to flee shunting it sky-high once more. Kit rolls onto his back, his arm pillowing his head as he stares at the ceiling and recaptures his breath.

I must have made some tiny movement, because his free hand jerks out and his palm settles, warm and detaining on my belly.

'Stay.'

A single word. A demand, but soft, heartfelt.

My throat burns, the only words I'll allow searing

nerve endings as they emerge. 'Why? We've talked about this. This isn't a relationship.'

Is it...? Tell me what this is...what it might be...

I hold my breath.

His fingertips trace a hypnotic path on my skin, the pleasure of his touch bordering on too close for comfort. Too intimate. Because he's silent still.

Then he presses his lips together, determined. 'This *is* a relationship, Mia.' His voice is low, a look in his eyes that makes breathing impossible.

'A...sexual one, but still a relationship. Stay.' Something beyond the simple request hovers in his navy stare—perhaps loneliness or doubt. Perhaps a hint of that vulnerability I wanted. Perhaps I'm full of shit and simply seeing what the primitive part of my brain wants to see.

And just like the first day I met him, I'm powerless against the pull of his force field.

Can I risk this? A one-off indulgence? A goodbye gift to myself? So when I walk away at least I'll know I gave my all, even if I couldn't tell him what I'm beginning to suspect.

Kit's lips skate over my temple, his soft sigh gusting through my hair. 'I wake up with your scent all over me, my pillow, my sheets, and no you.' He cups my face, his thumb gliding over my cheek. 'Please, just stay...'

I'm already too attached. To his country, his rare smile, even his damn dog. But I swallow down the tightness in my throat and nod, powerless to the Kit effect.

We shower together, soaping every inch of skin without conversation. Over a room-service dinner we watch an old movie, our hands entwined between us on the bed.

Later, with the room in darkness, I lie next to Kit, my breathing shallow and my heart racing, so far from sleep. Sharing Kit's bed is as bittersweet as I'd feared. I grew up wondering where I belong, but I know with certainty I can't *ever* belong here.

CHAPTER FOURTEEN

Kit

I WAKE WITH Mia's head on the pillow next to me, a hot kick of satisfaction delivering more than lust to my gut.

She stayed. All night.

I hold my breath, acclimatising to the ring of triumph roaring in my head. My stare traces the freckles across her nose, so many that I'm certain I've spied a handful of new ones I've never seen before. I follow the constellations past the dark crescents of her thick lashes to her cheeks, an ancient astrologer scanning the beauty of the cosmos.

She must sense me looking, because I've deliberately kept my body still and my breathing shallow but her eyes pop open and land on mine. Her cheeks flush and she clears her throat, as if she's embarrassed to be caught snoozing.

'Morning.' With her awake, my cock reminds me I've been staring at Mia for the last five minutes, noticing things about the woman in my bed. Like the fact her lips move while she sleeps, as if she's mumbling in her dreams. The honeysuckle scent of her is strongest in her hair, as if it comes from her shampoo, and I notice she has faint tan lines on her shoulders. My hand curls over her naked hip and I draw her closer.

'Hi.' Her voice croaks. She's warm and sleepy and I can't stop myself nuzzling her soft-skinned neck. 'How long have you been awake?' she asks on a small, sexy hum.

'Not long.' I brush my mouth over hers and she softens next to me, a small sigh escaping. 'I was trying to count your freckles.'

She covers her face with her hand, groaning. I tug her hand away and kiss the end of her nose. 'They're cute.'

'No woman wants to hear she's cute.'

'Doesn't she?' I touch the tip of my finger to her cheek, tracing a path one freckle at a time. 'Well, your freckles fascinate me. Like I could join the dots and discover something new about you.' Her fingers on the bed between us begin their habitual fluttering.

I lift her fidgeting hand to my mouth and press each overworked fingertip to my lips, kissing each one in turn until her hand falls completely slack in mine. She's wide-eyed when I'm finished, her irresistible lips parted.

Wordlessly I cup her face, press my mouth to hers and push her hair back. She kisses me, my mind blanking to everything but how good she feels and how glad I am that she spent the night. But I can't fully enjoy this until I make amends.

'I owe you an apology.' She moves to speak but I press a fingertip against her lips. 'At the party, I… I crossed a line, suggesting you search for your parents.'

She doesn't want to talk about this—I sense her withdrawing. I flex my fingers on her hip, trying to convey that there's more to come. 'It's just that I understand what it's like to feel…uncertain, helpless.'

Her eyes cling to mine, the tiny shake of her head her only movement. She's even holding her breath. Her hand strokes my back. Is she even aware she's doing that?

'When Laura collapsed, I was the only other person there. We were in the middle of nowhere, hiking the Banda Api volcano on one of Indonesia's Spice Islands.' I don't know why I'm telling her this, but I can't stop. 'One minute she was talking, laughing,' tension pounds at my temples, 'the next minute she was on the ground, unconscious.' My swallow burns my throat. 'She never woke up.'

'Kit, I'm so sorry.'

I plough on. I can't give Mia much, but I can give her answers, and perhaps the wisdom of my experience. 'A month later I signed the paperwork to switch off her life-support machine. I guess the reason I said what I did at the party, the reason I'm telling you this now, is that you already have so much love in your life, but there's room for more. You deserve more.'

This time when she kisses me it's different, her mouth slow, soft, hesitant. I kiss her back, my eyes on hers as I draw all I can from the melding of our mouths. It feels like the first time.

An exploration.

A lesson in the real Mia.

And, for the first time, a possibility.

Our kisses don't stay exploratory for long. Soon she's writhing against me, her nails digging into my shoulders.

'Kit...' I hear the silent plea in the catch of her voice.

I fumble for a condom while she slides kisses over my face, my throat and my chest.

When I push inside her she arches up to meet me, her head thrown back on the pillow and her neck exposed. My fingers link with hers, our stares locked as I rock into her, setting a rhythm that's slow and lazy—everything that's perfect about sleepy morning sex. The breakfast of champions. I'd forgotten.

But as I loom over Mia, lost in her stare and her tightly clamping heat and covered in her honeysuckle scent, growing unease creeps up my spine to settle between my shoulder blades like a crop of nettle rash.

I want to see her again. I'm not ready for goodbye and something in her eyes, in the way she trusts me with her body, conceding to my control, tells me she'd be open to the idea. If only she can get past some of her demons. Surely the fact she stayed last night is progress?

Her fingers squeeze mine, digging into the backs of my hands.

I ramp up my thrusts, lost to the pleasure. Mia's eyes widen, her moans growing in frequency and volume. I cover one nipple with my mouth, sucking hard, and she clamps around my length, tightening my balls, my belly, my thighs, and I wince, gritting my control back into submission.

She stares up at me, panting, flushed and so fucking beautiful that I forget how to breathe.

'Say you'll come back, one day...to London.'

The command comes from an unconscious corner of my mind, but I'm not sorry the words are out.

'Kit... I...'

I grind harder, adding a swivel to my thrusts that drags a cry from her and sees her wrapping her legs around my hips.

'Say it, Mia. Give me something, this one thing.' I'm a bossy, manipulative bastard, but she knows that about me. And all I want is words, a glimmer of hope that I might see her again.

Releasing one of her hands, I slide my fingers between us to press down on her clit. 'Give it to me, Mia, tell me what I want to hear.' I'll take nothing less than her orgasm and her promise.

She nods, whimpers, already there. 'Yes—I'll come back one day.' She grips my arm like she's on the top of a cliff and cries out, her muscles clamping down on me. Her words fill my chest, leaving no room for air. With my head oxygen-deprived and this beautiful, brave woman clinging to me, I join her and let go.

I'm not sure how long it goes on—years, it feels like. Eventually, my hips still and I lift my face from the crook of her neck, releasing the strands of her hair that have become trapped in my stubble, and slide my mouth over hers until our breathing settles.

Mia smiles up at me, a flicker of sadness in her eyes, and my pulse hits the roof again.

She's braver than me and smarter, because it's clear she knows before I've had a chance to realise that, if the request was reversed, I wouldn't be able to make her any promises.

I have no appetite, but we shower and I take Mia for breakfast while I battle the knowledge that I'm the biggest hypocrite on the planet.

After breakfast Mia forgoes a tour of the vineyard and the wine-tasting I've organised. It's a perfect Jersey morning and she's buzzed to do some filming. Mia sets up her tripod for some panoramic shots of the estate, which is surrounded by gently sloping hills adorned with parallel rows of vines, and I leave her to walk Bob on the beach again.

I'd hoped to find answers, solace, some kind of sign with the sound of the sea drowning out my doubts and turmoil. But nothing helpful materialises. Bob senses my distraction, bounding up to me time and time again until I resume our pebble-throwing game. Mia is right—dogs are always happy to see you, whether you deserve it or not.

And I most certainly don't. I kick at a half-buried pebble. I'm selfish. I haven't told Mia that Laura and I frequently came here. We never stayed at the hotel, preferring to rent a house near by, but we walked Bob on this beach.

The relentless rhythm of the tide kidnaps my stare, sucking me into a trance. Will I ever be free of regret? Intellectually, I know there was nothing I could have done to save Laura, aside from not selfishly dragging her to the middle of nowhere in search of…what? Another thrill, world domination of the luxury-travel industry? I didn't put the aneurysm in her head. But I did drag her all over the globe. And I couldn't save her, no matter how hard I tried. That feeling—that nothing you do, or have, or say, or promise makes one bit of difference—is a kick in the gut. And the reason I've successfully steered my life and my feelings away from risk these past three years.

Until now.

Until Mia.

I wince, thinking of our earlier conversation. I'm in no position to challenge her self-belief, to offer her anything beyond a continuation of what we have now, no matter what I might want.

Is that enough for her? A one-sided commitment, without a single guarantee…

Bob's smooth, damp muzzle finds my hand, nudging me back to the moment. 'Yes, time to go.'

Bob senses our direction and bounds ahead up the cliff path. He must catch the scent of a rabbit or something, because he pauses near the top to sniff at the grass, allowing me time to catch up. When we round the headland, the estate comes into view and I spot Mia. My renewed hope surges.

Perhaps, in time, we could have more.

She's walking backwards, a fair distance away from where I left her, a large remote control in her hands. I look where she's looking and spy the drone she's operating as it circles the estate.

Bob must see her too. He takes off at full pelt in her direction, clearly still buzzed from all the attention he's been getting lately.

I yell and wave, but she's concentrating and likely deaf to my call, which is whipped out to sea.

Oblivious to our approach, Mia focuses on the sky, still slowly backing up while she manipulates the drone. From my angle, she's straying perilously close to the cliff edge. Only two years ago someone fell just along the coast—a serious accident that left the tourist paralysed. There are warning signs posted at regular intervals along the cliff top—has she ignored them? Why didn't she wait for me to return, to help her out?

Icy fingers climb my spine.

Fuck. She's too independent, too…reckless. The bridge, the rap jump and now this…

I call again, my pace increasing, but then she turns, spots me and smiles.

'Be careful!' I point to the edge.

Mia returns her attention to the drone, shaking her head as if I'm overreacting. Is she blind? Oblivious? Or just tossing my concern back in my face as if this is some sort of game…? After I confided in her, told her about Laura…

The rage from the day of the rap jump returns, powering through me, stronger, more immediate and white-hot.

Mia's still ignoring me. Still ignoring her immediate surroundings.

My stomach rolls in a familiar lurch and I start to run.

Bob is ahead of me, bounding towards Mia. She spots him, but instead of stopping what she's doing she grins and adjusts the flight path of the drone, steering it our way to capture Bob running.

I call him to heel but I'm too far away.

Mia's still backing towards the cliff edge.

Bob skids up beside her, breaking her concentration. She sidesteps, losing her balance as she tries to avoid the excitable dog. The remote control hits the ground, she calls out and then disappears from view, over the edge of the cliff.

I'm sprinting before I've even registered the cry in my head, muscles tight with frustration because they won't work as quickly as I need them to. Bob's peering over the edge, his tail wagging, flooding my brain with hope, even as the adrenaline screaming through me sweeps all else aside.

As I reach Bob, I drop to my knees and crawl the last few feet to peer over the edge.

She's on her side turned away from me on a ledge about six feet below. The cliff in this area is stepped and gently sloping, not the sheer drop of other areas. The relief of seeing her paralyses me. 'Mia!' I yell, my throat on fire.

She moves, gingerly pushing herself into a sitting position. She holds up one hand in my direction, the other gripping her side. 'I'm fine.'

Her voice is strangled, hoarse, as if she can't draw in a full breath.

'Stay still, I'm coming to help you.' It's not as steep as I first feared. Hopefully she slid most of the way down. But it's far enough of a drop for her to have done some damage…a broken rib, a punctured lung, a ruptured spleen…

'I'm fine.' She turns to me, trying to laugh it off, but then winces and gasps as she holds her side.

'Don't move.' My heart pounds as nausea swirls in my gut. I slide down beside her, telling Bob to stay. She's covered in dust, her face pale with shock or perhaps pain. I cup her cheeks, demanding her eyes. 'Where does it hurt?'

Another gasp as she tries to sit up straight. 'My ribs.'

I lift her T-shirt. There's already a bruise forming the size of my hand.

'I'm okay—think they're just bruised. I slid over that rock.' She scrambles to her knees.

I slide my hands over her arms and shoulders. 'Did you hit your head?' Her hands are a bit scraped up, but there's no blood and she seems to be breathing fine, if a little shallowly.

She shakes her head, batting my hands away. 'I don't think so.' She looks around, presumably for her remote control.

By the time I've helped her to scramble back up to where Bob is waiting, my adrenaline has drained away to nothing and I can no longer hold in my rage.

'You could have been killed.' My voice is calm. How am I achieving that?

She laughs, wincing again. And then she spies her remote control, lying on the ground. 'Shit!' Her eyes scan the property, searching. 'My drone.'

I reach for the remote first to stop her bending. 'It's not funny. All you're worried about is your damned equipment.'

She laughs. 'I'm fine. It's just a few bruised ribs. Stop overreacting.'

Overreacting...?

I swallow down the worst of the impotence pounding through me, trying to rein in the sense of déjà vu. 'Overreacting…? I told you to be careful. To look at the signs.'

Her eyes flash my way. 'I'd seen the signs. It was an accident—my foot slipped.'

I grit my teeth and shake my head. I can't stop

my judgement, my chastisement. It's like pus in a
wound—it needs to be vented. 'So fucking reckless!
Filming near the edge of a cliff? Why didn't you
wait for me—I could have been here, helped you,
looked out for you?'

'I didn't need help and I'm perfectly fine.' She
sets off for the winery, her gait lopsided with a slight
limp, despite her assertions. When we get back to
the hotel I'll check her out more thoroughly, and ask
the staff to summon a local doctor.

I reach for her elbow and walk beside her, providing
a crutch. 'You need to see a doctor—you may have a
concussion.' She's still scanning the grounds in search
of her blasted drone, as if nothing else matters—her
safety, my concerns, the stuff I've told her about Laura.

'I don't need a doctor, Kit. I've been in worse
scrapes.'

No way. Concussion is notoriously sneaky. One
minute you're fine then next... I swallow hard, refus-
ing to allow my thoughts down that particular path.
'I'm not asking, Mia.'

She spins on me then, furious, and snatches her
arm from my grip. 'What are you going to do, Kit?
Be there every day? Follow me around the world, just
to ensure I stay safe?' Her eyes blaze, full of truth.

She's right. I taste acid.

If she trips next week or the week after, I won't be
there. By *my* choice. Because I can't do that again—I
can't care so much. I know how much that pain flays.
I barely survived last time.

I try to focus on the relief that she's safe, rather than lifeless on the jagged rocks below, pressing my lips together rather than answer her accusation, while my temper simmers.

Mia looks away and then tilts her chin up to say, 'I appreciate your concern, your help, but I'm a big girl. I can take care of myself and *I* can decide if and when I need medical attention.'

She looks away and swallows, as if she's deciding how much to say. When she turns back, her guard is up again. 'Look, I made some concessions for you, gave you the control you seemed to need, but that doesn't mean you get all of me. It doesn't mean you get to control my life, my choices, my—'

'I'm not trying to control you…'

Am I though…? I brought her here… I told her about Laura…

She fists her hands on her hips. 'You are. It's control, change, suggesting improvements… Ever since the day I met you, you've tried to intimidate me, trussed me up in your designer clothes, invited me to spend time with your family, coerced me into… hand-holding and spending the night and…' She breaks off and stomps away, picking up her drone from a flowerbed behind the hotel, one of its blades bent out of shape.

Then she spins back to face me. 'This is over, Kit.' She tilts her head, daring me to contradict. 'Isn't it? Despite what you said this morning. We're a dead end. Time to admit it.'

I don't want to do this now. I knew it was coming but…

I force some words out through my tight throat. 'I don't want to change you.' Fuck, that's the last thing I want. 'And it doesn't have to be over.' The acidic words burn, because I know she's right. I'm not free to always be there, I'm not free to make promises, even if I've selfishly dragged them from her.

Mia shakes her head. 'We had fun, but you have to admit we're too different.'

I start to speak—fuck knows what I'd been about to say. I don't get the chance because Mia ploughs on, as if she's had this speech ready prepared.

'I need to deal with my own issues. That's all I really have the energy for, right now. And so do you.'

She's right. We both have unresolved issues, but…

With a sad little smile, one she slides from me to Bob and back again, she spins and heads for the hotel.

Stop her. Give her something…some reason to return.

I swallow the razor blades in my throat and grip the remote control until it digs into my palm. I should chase her, convince her there's something to salvage. But what am I offering? Fuck buddies? Friends with benefits? A hook-up whenever she's in town?

I sigh, succumbing to the powerless feeling still rattling my skeleton, which is way too familiar and as uncomfortable as the fiery pits of hell.

CHAPTER FIFTEEN

Mia

I KNEW IT would happen the first day I met him. It was the eyes. I'm a stupid woman who broke her own rules, only to discover she'd been right all along. But the victory, the confirmation is far from triumphant. Because...*feelings.* Even the word sucks.

Kit began his tactical withdrawal before we even left Jersey. Yes, I'd laid down the gauntlet with my speech on our differences and all along I'd been expecting to be cast aside. I want to slap myself. Because although that suited me at the start, a tiny part of me thought, hoped, he might be ready to fight for me, for us.

Stupid woman.

Of course he was polite after our argument, dropping me home, accepting my excuse of needing a couple of days to get the editing done a little too readily.

With a bolstering sigh, I exit the elevator on the

Faulkner Group floor and try not to fidget with the new outfit I bought specially for my handover meeting with the Faulkner brothers—a simple trouser suit I'll never wear again.

It's pathetic. A cliché, I know. But the outfit protects me like a crash helmet or a safety harness and I need armour for this encounter. My old defence mechanisms were clearly as shoddy and friable as a sandcastle. And if I have to face Kit one last time, I need the power balance to sway my way a fraction.

Despite my walls and my battles, and my denials, in the end he achieved the one thing I've resisted all these years.

He made me care.

He made me fall.

I make a fist—I want to punch him and kiss him in equal measure. But neither is an option and I only have myself to blame.

'Mia. Lovely to see you again.' Reid shakes my hand. Drake smiles and offers me a seat.

Kit, busy at the bar, slides his closed-off stare my way and lifts his chin in greeting. 'Mia.'

Icy blood stills in my veins so I'm grateful for the suit jacket as I stare at those intense eyes I should have run from the first day we met in this very office. I'd known back then he was dangerous. Turns out I couldn't handle the challenge unscathed.

I refuse his offer of a drink and settle in the same white leather armchair.

'I've watched the video,' says Reid. 'It's exactly

what we wanted. Thank you.' He's all business, perhaps immune to the tension filling the room.

'You're welcome—you've been dream clients. Thank you for the testimonial.' I risk a look at Kit—I don't want him to think I'm avoiding looking at him, although my eyes burn at the sight.

I tell myself this is what I wanted all along—just sex, a fling we could walk away from. So why is it hard to draw breath…?

My fingers fidget, this time recalling the tactile memory of his silky hair, his abrasive scruff, his satin skin over the sculpted steel of his muscles.

Drake glances at Kit, who is perched on the front of his desk, his finger and thumb tracing his bottom lip as he observes the meeting from afar. I force myself to direct a question his way, just to prove I'm not distraught by his rejection, his return to cool indifference.

'Any questions for me in relation to the video? I've emailed the files, so the finished footage is all ready to upload onto the hotels' websites.'

At last he finds his voice. 'Thank you. I think we're perfectly happy.'

It might as well be a secret message, a hidden meaning, only for me.

We no longer need you. We never did.

I stand, restless legs propelling me upright. 'Great. If only all my clients were so accommodating.' I laugh for good measure, although it's hollow to my ears.

See, Mr Faulkner. I don't need you either.

Reid takes my hand again. 'What are your plans now, Mia?'

I clear my dry throat. 'I'm off to South America tonight.'

'You moved your trip up?' asks Drake.

I nod, searching for the flutter of excitement for the trip I planned months ago.

'Tonight?' This from Kit, who's managed to overcome his apathy, abandon his perch and join us at the threshold to his office.

I nod, focussed on Drake. 'Yes. I changed my flight. Your project ran so smoothly, I'm a few days ahead of schedule—I'll have time to catch Peru's Festival of the Sun.'

Reid smiles, his concerned eyes flicking in Kit's direction. 'Well. Safe travels, and come to see us next time you're in London. And if you ever need a place to stay, you'll always have a room available to you at the Faulkner.'

I swallow, his kindness touching, even though I can never make use of his offer. 'Thank you.'

I stick out my hand in Kit's direction, praying it stays tremble-free. Our shake is brief, polite, a perfect ending to our time together. I smile. It's genuine. He never duped me; he gave me all he could. And I believed it was enough.

'*Ka kite ano,*' I say. 'That's "see you" in Te Reo Maori.'

I slide my hand from his, trying not to miss its

warmth. My legs win, successfully carrying me away from him and keeping me upright. I'm waiting for the lift, searching for one tenth of the thrill I'm expecting for my next adventure, when I sense him behind me.

'So, no goodbye…?' His breath tickles the hairs at my nape, where I've scooped the rest into a messy topknot.

I turn, ensuring my face stays relaxed by digging my short nails into my palm. 'I thought we just did goodbye.'

'Technically "see you" implies "see you *again*".' His hands are in his trouser pockets, his shirt is immaculate and his spicy scent slaps me in the face. Beautiful, untouchable and firmly back in control.

Air gusts from his nose as he presses his lips together, as if frustrated with a mischievous child. 'Look, Mia…' He draws in a breath and I know the brush-off is coming. 'I'm sorry.'

Bam.

I feign confusion while my stomach turns inside out. 'Why?'

He peers down at me, shrewd eyes searching while the seconds stretch.

'For my rudeness, the clothes, prying into your personal stuff, overreacting in Jersey…' He hesitates. 'For…for making you promise to come back. For all of it—I had no right.'

Because you don't want the right. You don't want me.

My face feels like a rubber mask as I smile. 'No

worries. I hope I didn't give you too many grey hairs with my…antics.'

Look at us, being all adult…

Kit sighs, as if he doesn't believe a word I'm saying. Of course, it's what I'm *not* saying that carries more import. And Kit is right there with me. We're both cowards. Both skirting the unsaid.

'How are your ribs?'

'Good, thanks. No fractures.' I shrug. 'How's Bob?'

'Great—a bit of a diva, to be honest. He's started his own YouTube channel.' The humour doesn't quite reach his eyes, but I laugh. I can't help myself. I've always been helpless to the Kit effect.

Awkward silence settles.

Kit stares for long seconds. I employ every ounce of control my body possesses to keep myself from fidgeting.

He dips his chin, his voice, his stare earnest. 'I'm sorry I couldn't offer you more.' His voice breaks, genuine regret shining in his beautiful eyes. 'As you established, I'm a selfish, controlling fuck-up. You deserve more, Mia.'

I nod, a small, stupid smile stuck on my face while my head bobs, too heavy for my neck to support. There it is—his line in the sand. Right where I knew it would be.

Despite feeling like I've taken a second blow to the ribs, my chest aches for Kit. For his loss. For his unresolved emotions. For the timing. Would it be different had we met three years down the track?

But it is what it is—I'm leaving.

And I love him. The last thing he'll want to hear.

'I never wanted more, Kit.'

Coward.

I make a fist to stop myself reaching for his hand, a place that doesn't belong to me, no matter how comfortable.

I can't say everything I feel, but I can say something. 'Thanks for inviting me into your family for a while.'

I need to leave. Now.

I suck it up, fearless Mia once more. 'Don't punish yourself for ever. You did everything you could.'

The flash of pain in his eyes tells me he understands. Then he scowls. What did I expect? Kit's an expert at wall-building.

'Goodbye.' I turn away, my throat hot, terrified my mask might slip before I have a chance to flee.

'Mia.'

I spin, my smile wobbling on lips desperate to feel his kiss one last time.

'For what it's worth, I wish things could be different with me…with us.'

Just when he seems about to speak again, the lift arrives and my belly somersaults as if I'm already hurtling towards the ground.

I step inside and look anywhere but at Kit, who is framed in the doorway.

The cool metal square marked with a G is rubbery under my fingertip as I press the button that seals my fate. Just before the doors close, I look up into Kit's eyes, determined to brave it out, to prove something.

See. I'm not in love with you at all. I'm walking away, without a backward glance.

The words that come, a faint whisper scraped past my tight vocal cords, shock the hell out of me and deepen Kit's scowl.

'I'll miss Bob.'

The metal doors slide into place, separating us.

Fuck.

'You're sure you don't want me to wait with you?' Will's concern shines from his kind, intelligent and worried eyes. I can't speak so I shake my head, jump out and busy myself with retrieving my economical luggage from the boot.

Before we set off for Heathrow I hand-delivered the unworn dresses to Harvey Nichols, donated the worn, dry-cleaned ones to Will's local charity shop and used my fat fee from the Faulkner Group to buy a new drone and action camera. I realised, after I said his name, that the last time I saw the old one it was strapped to Bob. Kit must have it. Or it's still in Jersey. Either way, it's easier for my mental health to replace it rather than see Kit again.

As jobs go, it's been an expensive one in terms of damages and losses. But as I snuggle into my brother's hug, pressing my eyes into his chest to stem the tears, I know it could have been worse.

I'm free again. I'm me again.

I wait for the familiar buzz but it doesn't materialise. I tell myself it's a baby thing, leaving now, for work, when I could be decorating the nursery with Will and Josh…

But it's more.

It's the age-old trap—woman meets unavailable man, falls in love, then realises too late she doesn't possess the superpowers to change a single thing.

I'm so early for my flight. The check-in line is blessedly short, despite the number of people filling the busy terminal.

I'll be back in London—how can I not be? I'm going to be an auntie to a boy with special needs. Will and Josh will need support. And, when I get back from South America, I'm going to meet my biological mother—I have her name and address and contact number in my phone and I won't allow my past to hold me prisoner.

Thinking of fear reminds me of Kit—everything reminds me of Kit. His fear is understandable. Opening his heart again is a big risk for a man with his past. But who am I to judge—I've let my own fear hold me back for so long? Perhaps we can even be friends…in time.

Maybe.

I glance at the doors, the steady stream of people coming and going, none of them with the right face.

I swallow, looking away while I blink enough times for the burn to leave my eyes.

With time to kill, I wander into Harrods and get lost amongst the T-shirts, selecting one in ages one, two and three for my new nephew, to be on the safe side. I'll mail them to Will from South America.

I'm smiling to myself at my tiny purchases, my shiny green carrier bag swinging by my side as I emerge back into the hustle and bustle of the terminal, when I come to a complete standstill.

Standing on a chair, head and shoulders above the milling travellers, his head jerking to the left and then to the right as he frantically searches, is Kit.

The air leaves my chest in a whoosh to make space for my double-sized heart and its rapid thumping.

CHAPTER SIXTEEN

Kit

I'M ABOUT TO tear my hair from my scalp, impotence and rage at my own stupidity boiling up inside, when I scan the shopfronts for the third time. The air is knocked from my lungs as I spy her standing among the chaotic moving sea of bodies, a tranquil island in stormy waters.

My heart skips several beats until I fear I'll black out. *I haven't missed my chance.*

She's obviously seen me, because I'm standing on a chair like a pretentious arsehole, drawing attention to myself.

By the time I fight my way through the crowds, sustaining only minor calf injuries from the cases and trolleys in my way, she offers me the frosty reception I deserve.

'Why are you here?'

Straight to the point. No bullshit. Perfect. I fight a smile.

'What's in the bag?' I stall, uncharacteristic hesitation tripping me up. Reid and Drake's words ring in my ears… *'Don't let her leave without telling her how you feel…of course you deserve another chance…grab her before it's too late, dumb-arse.'*

My brothers can turn a pretty phrase when the circumstances warrant. But Mia was right. They have been there for me and I've been treating them, and anyone else around me, like shit in compensation for my own pain. But the only time it lessened was with her.

Mia made me want to smile again. She gave me everything—her trust, her joy, her bravery—and she gave me back Bob. But most importantly she gave me hope of a future.

'Baby clothes—well, toddler clothes. For Will and Josh.'

I nod, my head so light it could pop like a balloon. 'So you will be back, then…? To London…?'

She shrugs.

I deserve that.

Then she lifts her chin. 'Of course. I have family here.'

Not for me…?

I deserve that too.

I wince. I have lots of making up to do. The fidgeting catches my eye. As soon as I glance down she stops.

'You're nervous?' Her tell gives me hope. That she's not forming a fist and planting it in my stupid face gives me hope. That she hasn't run away, through Security and out of my reach, gives me hope.

She bristles, standing taller, her eyes wary. 'I do it a lot, but I don't like flying.'

I nod, my hand reaching for hers, sliding down her wrist until our fingers connect, slot together, meld. 'What you need,' I step closer, sucking in honeysuckle, 'is someone to hold your hand.' Until this moment I hadn't been certain what I intended to say, but calmness settles over me and the hustle of bodies, the stares, even the piped airport music drains away until everything shunts into sharp and brilliant focus. Everything becomes Mia.

The answer has been shadowing my life for the past two weeks, having marched in, uninvited by me, challenged the hell out of me and then effortlessly filled the unfillable void.

She frowns, still unconvinced. I increase the pressure on her hand—I'm not letting go this time. I'm doing this in front of an audience of strangers because I'm an idiot, but, like Reid and Drake, she probably knows that about me.

I swallow. 'I thought I wasn't ready. Thought I didn't deserve another shot.'

'At what?' A wrinkle settles between her brows even as her cheeks flush.

'At love. I love you, Mia. And I want a chance to start over, to see you again, to give you as much as you've given me.'

She frowns. I made her doubt.

With my free hand I cup her face, sliding my fingers into her hair, hold her eye contact so she sees my truth.

'You're fearless and funny and generous and so fucking beautiful.' I squeeze her hand. 'You never took my crap—you challenged me. I got caught up in regret…in guilt.' I wince, starting over. 'Look, I'm not asking you to stay—I know you have work to do. But *if* you come back—' *please come back* '—*when* you come back, I'll be here…ready to hold your hand if ever and whenever you need support, comfort, body heat…' I clamp my mouth shut before I do more damage than repair.

My chest is trapped in a vice.

She chews her lip, her eyes flicking between mine, as if searching.

Fuck this, I'm all in. Time to tell her.

I tug her closer, dip my head towards the mouth I'm dying to kiss. 'Look, I love *you*, just as you are, and you can still be you even if you love me back one day. I know I'll still fuck up, I'll still have triggers and bad days, but I'll wait. And whether it's while you search for your parents or simply tell the man who's in love with you to fuck off,' I look down at our joined hands, my fingers tightening on hers, 'my hand will always be here, ready and willing.'

I look up. If I've blown it, I can take it.

Don't let me have blown it…

And then she kisses me, the rustle of the monogrammed carrier bag clasped in her hand blocking out whatever she said before her mouth touched mine. But I'll take deafness, because Mia shows me all I need to know with her kiss and the way, when I lift her from the floor, she wraps her arms around my shoulders and her legs around my hips.

'What did you say?' I laugh when she lets me up for air.

'I called you a rude name.' She kisses me again, my jaw, my cheeks, my nose.

I grow serious. She still hasn't admitted any feelings for me, and I've fucked up, big time. I need to have the hope confirmed. 'Please…don't give up on me…on us.'

She pushes at my shoulders, and I relax my grip on her waist, allowing her to slide down my body, but not to escape entirely.

'I can't…'

'Can't what?' A breeze block settles in my gut.

'I can't fight the Kit effect.' She sighs. 'I think I love you too.' Her cute freckled nose wrinkles, as if she doesn't much care for the emotion. 'A new experience for me.'

'You do?' My grin actually makes my cheeks ache. I'll have to convince her again and again.

Fucking yeah, I will.

'And if you're going to be my first boyfriend, you'll have to hold my hand a lot, right…? It's part of the job description.'

I lift her hand to my mouth, sliding my lips over her knuckles while a low growl escapes me. 'We're going to have to come up with a manlier title than boyfriend, darling.' I press my hard-on into her belly. 'That's really not working for me.'

She laughs. 'Fair enough. I'll think of an alternative while I'm away. To be continued…?'

'To be continued.' And then I kiss her.

EPILOGUE

Mia

I'VE WATCHED THE footage three hundred and twenty-seven times in the three weeks I've spent in South America, the last fifty of those on the flight from Rio to Heathrow. Surely that's some sort of sappy, lovesick record… Surely no girlfriend in history has been more committed…

I have Bob to thank for my current obsession. Kit sent me the footage Bob's harness camera captured on the beach in Jersey. He'd had it edited. One short segment in particular he sent in a separate e-mail entitled 'We miss you, come home!'

It's a little jerky, Bob's enthusiastic bouncing rendering the film far from useable, but as he races across the beach, his claws flicking up wet sand and spray dripping from his sopping coat, he inadvertently films a kiss.

A Kit and Mia kiss.

It's the kiss following the first time I admitted to myself that I loved him. It's not Hollywood-worthy or particularly romantic—we're lying on the sand, yanking at each other's clothes like randy teens. But there's passion and heat in the way we're staring at each other, and the first glimmer of what I assume love looks like when Bob finally reaches us and sprays us with seawater and the passion turns to laughter.

That's the point where I pause the movie. The look on Kit's face as he grins down at me steals my breath.

Every time.

Three hundred and twenty-seven times.

My lungs are still struggling as I pass through the first-class arrivals lounge—my upgrade a surprise from my new *boyfriend*—and follow my escort to the exit.

Because I know he's waiting.

He's already texted me six times. Sexy, urbane Kit can be as impatient as a kid on Christmas morning when he wants something. And he still hates the boyfriend title, which I use all the more because every time I do he promises physical retribution—the belly-quivering kind. I have three weeks' worth of retribution waiting for me.

I can't wait.

I bite my lip, recalling all the filthy phone calls and video calls we've managed to squeeze into three weeks. And then there's no respite from the fizz in my blood because he's there, and I'm engulfed in his hug and swung in a circle while he kisses me senseless.

'Fuck, I missed you.' He cups my face, his hands big and warm and as real as the man himself, stealing my air with his kiss. His hair is longer, his handsome face partially obscured by scruff. But I wouldn't have him any other way.

I gasp, breaking away to stave off light-headedness. 'You need a haircut.'

He laughs. 'Straight to the point. How about *I missed you too, Kit? Take me home and make good on all those orgasms you owe me, Kit? You're the sexiest man on the planet, Kit, and I love you?*'

I look down, still too bewildered by the Kit effect to voice those things, although every word is true.

Kit tilts my chin with one index finger, his other hand reaching between us to capture my hand. He lifts my fingers to his mouth, his stare hot on mine as he presses each fingertip to his lips.

'I.' *Kiss.* 'Love.' *Kiss.* 'You.' *Kiss.* 'Mia.' *Kiss.* 'Abbott.' *Kiss.*

He's out of fingers and I'm out of oxygen, because my lungs are shrivelled husks.

'I love you too.'

He flashes his best grin, plus dimple. 'Good. Let's go home and celebrate. There's a surprise in the car.'

He tugs me towards the limo and opens the door to reveal Bob sitting on the back seat, his happy tail ecstatic.

After doggy hugs, watery laughter and more Kit kisses, I sober enough to see the gift-wrapped box beside Kit.

Kit explains as I tug at the ribbon. 'Bob bought you a new drone. He said he was very sorry for breaking your last one and he won't do it again.' He reaches into his trouser pocket and pulls out a smaller wrapped gift. 'And this one is from me. I wondered if you'd like to make a new arrangement?'

I take the small package and lift my eyebrows, waiting for his explanation.

'You move in with Bob and me, help us eat all the food we've bought especially for your return and we'll promise to love you every day. Just the way you are—perfect.'

I gasp, squeezing the package which, in light of his proposal, feels like a key. 'I can't. We've only known each other six weeks.' When the fuck did I become so sensible and conventional?

Kit takes the gift, lifting it to face level between us while he slowly, assuredly unwraps it. His intense eyes hold mine captive. 'You can, Mia. You can live with me, while you're in London, if that's what you want. Every day is precious. Let's enjoy them all together—the best adventure.'

I kiss him then, fighting him for air without letting him go. Because he's right. With our lips still locked I pull my phone from my pocket, stretch out my arm and fire off a burst of kiss selfies for later perusal, although with the real thing close at hand I may not get around to watching the footage as many times as I'd like.

Mia's going to be very busy.

* * * * *

FIRST CLASS SIN

CARA LOCKWOOD

MILLS & BOON

For Peej—my amazing husband.
Thank you for giving me wings.

PROLOGUE

THE SEAT BELT LIGHT blinked on in the bathroom of
the A380 Airbus, but Juliana failed to notice. The
man's lips had claimed hers, and his hands ran the
length of her oversize cashmere sweater tunic, finding her hips beneath the fabric. His big hands felt hot
and heavy, and she leaned into them as she caught a
glimpse of herself in the small mirror above the tiny
steel sink. Her dark hair mussed, cheeks flushed, pupils dilated so her normally light brown eyes looked
nearly black. The man, so tall, so fit, the muscles in
his back and shoulders moved beneath his thin T-
shirt as he claimed her neck with his mouth.

Was she going to do this? Was she *really* going to
have sex in the bathroom? A planeful of passengers
just on the other side of the thin, plastic door could
no doubt hear everything, if they weren't tucked in to
their devices, noise-canceling earphones plugged in,
the flicker of their screens in the darkened cabin the
only light on the red-eye flight. The man—a complete stranger to her just two hours ago—laid a trail

of kisses up the side of her neck. She moaned, unable to help herself as his tongue flicked out, tickling the lobe of her ear, his teeth nibbling there with the slightest hint of pressure. It had been too long since she'd gotten out of her brain, indulged in her body's demands. She'd forgotten how good this could feel. Her body screamed for this release, burned for it. Juliana had never in her life done this—sex with a stranger? Sex on a plane?

Yet she wanted to feel him deep inside her; she wanted him to fill her in the way only a man could. This was what she wanted: this man, on *her* terms. She started this, and she was going to finish it.

She realized with a jolt that she didn't even know this man's last name, didn't even know where he lived and yet here she was, kissing the life out of him, feeling him pressed against her in the cramped space, his need for her growing firm against her belly. Yes, this is what she wanted. Right here. Right now. Quick, dirty, practically anonymous. Two animals doing what animals do best. For once in her hectic life, she could switch off her anxious brain, focus on this, on this one thing, the man's mouth on hers, his body strong, muscled, in front of her.

He broke free of their kiss, panting, and then whirled her around, and hoisted her up on the tiny edge of the bathroom sink as if she weighed nothing, and suddenly she realized how strong he really was, how compact and powerful his muscles must be. She met his blue-eyed gaze and felt desire pool between her legs. She'd wanted him the moment she'd seen him, and now she'd have him. *I'm an animal in heat, running on pure instincts, pure need.* He found the waistband of her stretchy leggings, pulling them downward to reveal her secret: she wore no underwear.

His hands slinked up her leg, finding her bareness. He grinned, eyebrow risen in a question. Normally, she went commando for comfort, but now she realized he put a different meaning on this altogether. "Well, well," he murmured, surprised, as his fingers roved deeper, gently caressing the bundle of nerves sitting taut there, sending her heart racing as they slipped across her slick center. "Did you come here ready for this?"

She wanted to tell him she'd never done this before, not ever, but her throat closed up, and she couldn't manage words. Not here, not with his lips so close to hers. The hard truth was she'd never done anything close to this: sex with a stranger, on an airplane or anywhere public, for that matter. *Mile High Club*? It was never a membership she'd ever sought, or ever thought she'd gain.

His finger slipped inside her then, and she gasped as he penetrated her, his touch driving her wild as she realized he now understood just how much she wanted him, how wet he'd made her.

"Yes, you came ready," he murmured and she realized the truth in his statement. She felt like she'd always been ready for this. For him.

Her heart hammered in her chest. She'd never had a man like this—hot, heavy, urgent. The fear of being caught rippling through every moment, the naughtiness of breaking the rules turning every caress into white-hot desire. She'd always been the girl who insisted on dinner first, on a whole host of hurdles a man would have to clear before she'd ever let him even see her underwear. But now, here, on this plane, with this stranger, she was going to give him everything, right here. Right now. No strings. No obligations.

Maybe this was what she needed all along. Dirty, quick sex with a stranger, where she didn't have to be the prim and proper consultant, the suit-wearing professional she played all day. Here, she could be who she wanted to be: a woman who would take a man where and when she pleased; a woman who was sitting on a bathroom basin counter, legs spread and half-naked, a hard pulse thrumming inside her.

Any minute the flight attendant could knock on the door. Or another passenger. They were doing this *here*, in a place they could easily get caught. At any time. Yet she felt strangely…free. She felt alive, for the first time in a long time. She was doing something wrong, but it felt so right. This was *her* choice. And it was delicious.

He worked his fingers inside her and she laid her head back, cracking against the mirror near the sink as she let out a low groan of appreciation, her hips moving in time with his hand. It felt so good. No, scratch that, amazing. He might just make her come right here. She groaned, louder, her need taking over.

Did anyone hear that? she wondered. Was someone, right now, listening against the door? Did she even care?

He inched back in the tight space and she lunged for his fly, eager to free him, eager to do this. He claimed her mouth again and she moaned once more, the rush of need, a tsunami of desire, flooding all her senses. She freed him then, heavy, hard and smooth in her hands. Yes, this was what she wanted. Him, all of him, inside her. To hell with consequences. Because chances were, they'd never meet again. Hell, she didn't even know his full name and she held him, his most intimate part, in her hands. Impressive, too. Wide. On the north side of average, and oh, so very, very ready for her.

He groaned as she wrapped her hands around him, as she felt the proof of his need. He wanted her as much as she wanted him. She felt giddy suddenly, powerful, as she clutched him in her hands.

This was going to happen. She could barely believe it. She'd only just met this man, a random stranger who'd sat next to her on the emergency exit row, and now she was about to take him inside her, a place only a handful of men had ever gone in her whole life. She glanced at his blue eyes, that sexy, squared-off chin. Yes, she wanted him. So badly. No regrets. Not for this.

He nudged against her, his bulging tip pressing

against her most tender of places, the promise of pleasure, of pure animal lust, of precious, sweet release. She'd held the reins so tightly in her life, so taut, and now she'd let go. She'd let everything go, as she clutched his shoulders, her core aching for this, to be filled, to be stretched, to be taken to new heights as this tin bird glided through the clouds, the ground thousands of feet below them.

"You ready?" he asked her, rubbing the tip of him against her once more, sending a wave of urgent want thrumming down her legs to her knees.

"Yes," she whispered, hoarse, her nails digging into his shoulders. She'd never been more ready in her life.

CHAPTER ONE

Two hours earlier

JULIANA HATED BEING LATE. She jogged through the terminal at JFK Airport, past the dads pushing strollers and the sunburned college kids headed home from spring break and prayed she made it to her gate before they shut the doors. She *had* to make this flight, the last flight home to Chicago. She promised her sister she'd be there for her birthday dinner tomorrow, but with her never-ending consulting work for the Blue Sky project, she'd been AWOL for weeks, crisscrossing the country to evaluate the nation's biggest airline. She would've been on time, except traffic had been monstrous, even more so than usual around JFK. And then her smart watch dinged with an incoming text. She glanced down at it.

Garrison had texted.

We need to talk.

Juliana groaned. She didn't have time for her boss right now. He could wait. She rushed through the airport, her trim, rolling carry-on spinning behind her, her dark hair, normally up in a tight bun, begging to spring loose as she bounded through the terminal. If she didn't make that flight…she'd have to wait a whole day for the next one, and she badly needed that day to write her report—which she couldn't start until she'd evaluated the airline's service on this route.

She headed to the gate and saw a worker in a Blue Sky uniform—blue-and-white scarf, and dark navy pantsuit—standing at the gate. Thank goodness!

She arrived, panting, and held out her ticket. "Just…made it," she said, gasping.

"I'm sorry, miss," the airline worker said, "but we're loading standby passengers now, and we've already given away your seat."

"But…the gate is open, and I've got my ticket." Juliana held it up, as if the business class ticket ought to speak for her. "Has the standby passenger boarded yet?"

The airline worker—whose tag read "Bette"—reluctantly looked down at the computer screen in the counter. She typed on the keyboard, clearly out of sorts at having to do a little extra work. "No, not yet." Her voice sounded clipped, annoyed. *This is why you're in a social media marketing mess*, Juliana thought. *Where your clients keep saying your philosophy is the customer is always wrong.*

"Then please let me on." She was the paying customer, the original customer, and standby was just that—a person who didn't have a ticket for this flight but hoped to get one. Mentally, she noted the airline employee's sullen attitude, her lack of willingness to help. Kicking off paying customers from flights had gotten Blue Sky in trouble in a series of damning viral videos of late, and here was yet another unhelpful employee seeming oblivious to the poor optics of this situation. This would most certainly go into her mergers and acquisitions report to AM Airlines.

"But the standby passenger is airline staff and I'm afraid…"

"Can I help?" The deep baritone of another passenger behind Juliana caused her to jump. She whirled to see a tall, forty-something man with the most amazing clear blue eyes she'd ever seen. He wore dark jeans and a fitted Polo across his broad chest, looking more like the lead in some movie that hadn't been made yet, than a random passenger on a flight. Juliana usually didn't register attractiveness, really, when mingling with strangers, but something about the man made him impossible to ignore. She could almost feel his magnetism, a force demanding her full attention, like a Viking marauding on a foreign shore.

"Sir…" The employee's surly attitude seemed to get worse.

"I'm a standby passenger," he offered, his deep voice seeming to reverberate in her bones. It felt like pure power. "I'll give up my seat if that helps." He handed her his ticket, so she could read his name.

Juliana glanced at the man, surprised. She'd always thought chivalry was dead, especially at airports. It was fend for yourself or die trying, it seemed at gates, on planes and at the baggage claim. The offer took her by surprise. The man looked at Juliana and smiled, a bright-white, dazzling smile. Was he famous? He seemed to have that easy air of someone who'd done well for himself. She noted his Bruno Mali suede loafers. Yes, clearly, his bank account must be full. Still, Juliana hesitated. Did she want this help from a stranger? She was no damsel in distress. She could handle herself. She never asked for help, because doing that was a sign of weakness, and she wasn't weak.

Another Blue Sky employee glanced up from the nearby counter. "Bette, a word?" she said, calling the employee over. The two women put their heads together and conversed and in seconds, Bette looked ashen. What happened? What had the other employee told her? Was her cover somehow blown? She didn't think rank and file knew about her being a consultant or about her covert flights to take notes about customer service.

"I am so sorry," Bette babbled as she returned to her post. "We can get you both on this flight, not a problem." She glanced at Juliana's ticket. Bette nodded quickly, typing even faster on her keyboard, her fingers clacking on the keys. The small printer at the counter spit out two new tickets. "I hope you don't mind new seats. They're both in coach, but…"

"I don't mind," her rescuer quickly said. "Unless you do?"

She glanced at the intriguing man next to her, craning her neck to look at him, he was so tall. Juliana wondered if she'd be able to concentrate on the work at hand with this man sitting next to her. She also wondered if he *was* a celebrity. If the employees were fawning all over him for a reason she didn't understand. Then again, maybe it was just that smile, with the hint of mischief.

"No, I don't mind," she said.

"So glad to hear it. So sorry, again, for the inconvenience, Ms. Hart," the employee gushed to Juliana again, apologetic. Maybe someone told them Juliana was there to evaluate their performance. But who? If someone had leaked her route, then all evaluation of the flight would be moot. The whole point was she needed to be anonymous on this flight, just another regular customer. She glanced at the man behind her. "Yes, sorry, let me apologize again." Bette scanned both tickets and handed them back, eyes lingering longer on her rescuer's face. No, Juliana thought, this wasn't about her at all. This was about him. He was the reason she was getting on this flight.

"Not a problem," he said, waving a hand as he stepped back. His voice carried the vaguest hint of an accent. British? She couldn't quite tell.

He glanced at Juliana, stretching his hand out to

show her she ought to go first. Chivalry, again. Part of her bristled at the prospect. She had always been strong enough to get her own doors and chairs, and yet another part found it oddly…refreshing. She was so used to elbowing her largely male coworkers for space at the conference room table that she'd forgotten what it was like for a man not to be vying to go first.

She rolled her compact carry-on through the open door of the gate as they both walked down the jet bridge. She could feel the heavy weight of the man's steps behind her in the aluminum hallway with the thin carpet. The man was tall and solid, a wall of muscle, clearly. Who was this man who got things done with a snap of his fingers? A flight attendant greeted them with a curt nod of her head as she read their tickets and directed them upstairs to the two-level airbus, the airplane equivalent of a double-wide trailer, Juliana thought. The big plane was headed to Chicago, but after that, Honolulu. She knew the itinerary by heart, part of her Blue Sky project knowledge. Still, she felt a ripple of unease in her stomach as she boarded the plane. It was nothing, really. She flew all the time and never got nervous, so why did she suddenly feel like the walls of the plane seemed too tight? She gave herself a mental shake. *Get it together.* She glanced at her ticket and then realized they were at the very back of the plane, last row. Well, that was what they got for being late, she figured. She hoped being so close to the bathroom didn't turn out to be unpleasant during the long flight.

"Window seat or aisle?" Juliana asked him.

"What would you prefer?" he demurred, cocking his head slightly, clear blue eyes never leaving her face. He gave no hint about whether or not he cared about where he sat. His broad shoulders blocked the aisle as he waited for her answer.

"Window," Juliana said. "If that's okay." She hated when the flight attendants rushed the cart down the aisle. Sometimes they'd hit her laptop or smack her elbow if she wasn't careful.

"Absolutely." He smiled, flashing his bright-white, toothpaste-ad smile once more. Wow, but his clear blue eyes looked like the clearest, purest water, almost the ice-blue of a wolf's. Something about him screamed danger, too, the delicious kind that promised breathless fun, like riding helmetless on the back of a motorcycle. Confidence radiated off his shoulders, and she could tell by the way he carried himself he was put together, worldly, sophisticated. She worked on collapsing the handle of her bag, and Law stepped in.

"Let me help," he said, his voice leaving no room for argument as he whisked her bag up to the overhead compartment as if it weighed less than a pillow. *I could've gotten that*, she wanted to tell him. *I'm not helpless.* She scooted into the window seat and he took his place at the aisle. Blue Sky was like many other airlines, where coach seating was tight.

The space was so close, and Juliana realized she'd be taking note of every slight shift from the man next to her. He'd absolutely be a distraction this flight, as she felt his elbow graze hers on the arm rest.

"Uh, so…" Juliana flashed him a smile as she set about fastening her seat belt to give her hands something to do.

"Call me Law. Short for Lawrence." Law, as in *lawless*, she thought. His broad shoulders seemed better suited for leather and steel, rather than the domesticated Polo he wore.

"Law. Nice to meet you. I'm Juliana."

Law took her hand and shook it. She liked the feel of his palm across hers, big, protective, strong. Made for wielding an ax or sword, not a briefcase. "You…have an accent," she pointed out. "Are you… British?"

"Australian, actually." He flashed a perfectly white smile. Now she imagined the Viking wrestling crocodiles. Just when she thought he couldn't get more masculine, he somehow managed it. Then she mentally shook herself. What was wrong with her? "But I've lived in the States since I was twelve, so lost most of the accent. But it creeps in now and again. Usually after a drink or two at dinner."

She loved how he sounded, how *dinner* almost became *dinnah*. It was decidedly faint, though, just the hint. "So, how did you manage that magic trick back there? Do airline employees always fall for your charms?" Juliana meant it to sound flirty, but it almost sounded…envious. Juliana wasn't the type of woman who usually got what she wanted from charm. She usually got what she wanted by working hard and having all the facts at her disposal, by relentlessly pounding away until her opponents gave in. When she was younger, she'd been a nerdy bookworm, for the most part, an all-honors, all-A student. It didn't help things that she'd been a late bloomer, not actually growing curves until her sophomore year in college. Until then, she'd been rail-thin.

"Well, I'm a frequent flier," he explained, thick elbow resting dangerously close to hers on their short armrest.

Juliana swiveled, surprised. "So am I, but I don't think I've ever gotten that level of service."

"Yes, but I've got eleven million miles, give or take."

Juliana barely prevented her mouth from dropping open. "Eleven *million*?" She did a rough calculation in her head. "That means if you traveled fifteen years, you'd need 733,333 miles a year."

His mouth quirked up in an amused smile. She was relieved he didn't act surprised, or say, *Wow, you're really good with numbers*, like some men who seemed genuinely shocked that a woman could do math in her head.

"Yes, give or take that. I've been traveling regularly for twenty years, though, so really it's just about 550,000 miles a year."

"Still… That's…mind-boggling." Juliana struggled to process the staggering reality. "I thought I travel a lot, and I just hit 200,000 miles last year. What do you do? Are you a pilot?"

He chuckled, voice low. "No, but I wanted to be. I have a special kind of color-blindness. I mix up blues and greens, so I can't fly." His stark blue eyes never left hers. It was hard to imagine anything being wrong with them. "I wanted to fly fighter jets but couldn't, back when I was twenty." He shrugged one fit shoulder. She got a whiff of his cologne. Something subtle but earthy. She liked it. She found herself leaning in a bit more. "So instead of going to the Air Force Academy, I went to Wharton. And... here I am."

"So what do you do?"

"What do I *do* for a living or what am I passionate about?"

Juliana considered this. She knew many folks who might not be so focused on their careers as their passion. She understood that. It wasn't like consulting was what she wanted to do for the rest of her life. She'd much rather someday run her own company, call her own shots. That was what she'd like to do. Be the boss.

"What are you passionate about?"

"Charity and innovation." Law's eyes grew a brighter shade of blue. This really was his passion. She couldn't help but be surprised. Something about his take-no-prisoners attitude didn't seem to fit with a nonprofit. "I just started a charity. It helps encourage entrepreneurs from all over the world. I think we need more innovation, and sometimes big companies can hinder competition."

"So what does the charity do?"

"We give out grants to small business owners, but from all over the world, whether that's Uganda or New Jersey."

"That's great."

He grinned, a blinding flash of white. She met his amused stare and found herself forgetting everything she wanted to say. Those *eyes.* So blue. So amazingly clear. Those firm, muscled arms on display through the thin cotton shirt. Juliana mentally shook herself. What was she doing? Drooling all over the passenger in 34H? Seriously? She wasn't some teenager crushing all over the new boy in class; she was a professional woman with responsibilities. Besides, he was probably married. Her attention wandered to his left hand. *No ring.* Not that that meant anything. He could still be attached. Probably was. With that strong chin and accent? No doubt.

Law gently nudged her elbow and all thought of the past fled her mind. His arm was warm and solid and strong. She wondered what it would feel like wrapped around her. "What do *you* do?"

Juliana swallowed, her mouth suddenly dry. *Focus on something other than his lips, Juliana. Geez.*

"Business consultant. Mergers and acquisitions."

"That can't be easy." He looked impressed.

"I don't like easy. There's no challenge in it." She

grinned as she delivered her signature line, the thing she said to strangers on planes, in hotels and at conferences. With all her travel, she'd become very good at summarizing her life in a few easy-to-digest lines.

Law chuckled a little. Juliana liked making him laugh. She wanted to do it again. But here was the part of the trip, no doubt, where he'd pull out his book or magazine or e-reader. He'd tuck his nose into his distractions and she'd answer her email on her phone and they'd become strangers again.

Juliana waited for it. After all, a man like this wouldn't talk to her the whole flight. It just didn't happen.

Her mother always thought she'd meet someone on her travels, a likely prospect for a husband, or heck, even a boyfriend, but it just didn't happen. Maybe Juliana was too focused on her work, too eager to pull out her laptop and block everything else out. But she also wanted to tell her mother that it was next to impossible to make real connections with people as she crisscrossed the country, spending her time in tin birds and hotels that all looked the same.

"So, what do you like to do for fun?" Law was still looking at her. He made no move to pull out his phone to check his messages one last time, or reach for the onboard magazine. He still seemed interested. Odd.

"Oh, fun is usually work," she said. "I like to run 5Ks when I can find a spare Saturday but normally, I'm working. Pretty boring life, I guess."

Here's the time he grows bored. Looks away. Finds something else to do. Men always get bored with her, especially good-looking men. She waited. But his attention didn't waver.

"I know what you mean," he said. "I spend most of my time working, too."

Juliana's smart watch dinged. She glanced down and frowned. Garrison again.

When you get back, let's meet. I want to explain.

She ignored it. Garrison needed to get over himself. She mentally rolled her eyes. Couldn't the man take a hint?

The flight attendants walked the aisles, shutting overhead compartments. They were getting close to takeoff. Juliana felt her blood pressure rise as sweat broke out on the small of her back. *What was going on?* She'd spent her entire life as a fearless flier, so what was up with her sudden nerves?

She took a deep breath and exhaled. Juliana didn't know if it was because she'd researched airline crashes so much during her recent project or what. She sucked in a breath. *Stop being silly,* she warned herself. *This is one of the safest planes in the fleet.* Still, her heart thudded harder. *Just get through takeoff.* She knew most accidents happened during takeoff or landing. More things could go wrong, because the plane was closer to the ground and moving slower... And... Deep breath, she told herself.

Take a deep breath. Think of something nice. Like your favorite glass of wine. Like lying on your favorite beach…like…

"Nervous flier?" Law asked, his sharp eyes missing nothing.

"Not usually." Juliana laughed weakly. What was wrong with her? Was she coming down with something? Food poisoning, maybe? "Actually, never. I don't know why, but suddenly—" she shrugged "—I just feel a little weird about it." Light-headed, scared, even. This was so embarrassing…an airline consultant…*afraid* of flying. She'd spent countless hours on flights this *month* and didn't blink an eye. "I don't know what's wrong with me. Maybe I'm coming down with something."

Maybe it's the stress. Blue Sky was a tough project, no doubt, but she'd had worse.

Her phone pinged again. Garrison one more time.

You take off yet?

She silenced her phone. No wonder she had a case of the nerves. Garrison wouldn't leave her alone.

Take the hint, she mentally begged him. *Just seriously, take it. Not interested. Never will be. Don't make me spell it all out. Let's just pretend none of it happened and move on.*

Garrison was a heavyset, barrel-chested married man in his early 50s. Just thinking about Garrison's stout body made her wince. Garrison might find her attractive, but the feeling was *not* mutual. And he was married, she reminded herself. He had a wife and two kids in the 'burbs. But then again, it was usually the married men who pursued her. She didn't know why. Did she give off some kind of vibe that told men she was desperate enough to consider someone already taken? She wasn't sure, but it happened more than she liked to admit.

She focused on the passenger next to her. She wanted a distraction, badly, and he provided the perfect one. Look at those blue, blue eyes. Yes, something about his face made her think he'd understand her. What was she thinking? This man cared? He was a stranger. And he'd grow bored with her soon enough.

"No reason to be embarrassed. Everybody's scared of something." She doubted the Aussie next to her was afraid of anything.

"Thanks. I really don't know what's wrong." She fanned her face and gave herself a mental shake.

Law cocked his head. "Well, you're flying on the world's safest airline. Blue Sky has the lowest accident rate of any airline in the world. That's why…" Law paused. "That's why I fly so much with them."

Juliana knew about Blue Sky's lack of accidents, of course, but hearing it again and from one of the airline's most frequent customers, made her feel a bit more comfortable as some of the tension left her shoulders. She liked talking to this stranger. It felt oddly freeing somehow.

"I'm glad of that," she said, and grinned.

The flight attendant announced the plane would be leaving the gate, and just as she clicked off the PA system, the plane rattled to life beneath them, slowly backing out. Juliana saw the ramp agents far below on the ground, walking with orange-capped flashlights, leading the plane away from the jet bridge. She thought about how they would soon be off the ground, and felt more sweat pool between her lower back and shirt. She looked about the cabin for a distraction and saw a woman wearing a "just married" sweatshirt, cuddling up to her new husband. So sickly sweet, so…silly. She frowned at the happy couple. She wondered if that husband would be Garrison in a few years, sending inappropriate texts to his staff member.

Law followed her gaze. "You don't like newlyweds?"

"I just think love is a waste of time." She waved her hand, feeling the futility of it all. Garrison was hardly the first man she'd met who believed monogamy applied to other people. When Juliana was just fourteen, her own father ran off with a younger woman. Her mother had spent most of her adult life hammering home the fact that career was more important than family. *Families break up, but a good résumé never does*, her mom would always say. Her mom had spent fifteen years as a housewife, and when their father ran off with a younger woman, she found herself having to go back to school, learn new skills, as she was woefully underprepared for the workforce.

"You think *falling in love* is a waste of time?" Now Law looked incredulous.

"It's a distraction," Juliana said as the plane rolled out to the runway. She tried not to think about the fact that in a few scant minutes, they'd be airborne. She still didn't understand why she felt so uneasy out of the blue. She'd flown thousands of times. Why should this time be any different?

"People think it's this wonderful thing, this great thing, and yet most of the time it doesn't work out. It causes pain and heartbreak. Who needs it?"

Juliana thought of Garrison. Just one more reason *not* to waste time running after a happily-ever-after. Save those fairy tales for her three-year-old niece, Evie.

"What about love making the world go around? What about all the songwriters and poets?"

"They're wrong." Juliana shrugged. "Give me a glass of wine and a cat. I'll be fine."

Law laughed, his eyes, blue like the ocean, crinkling with merriment. "I don't see you as a crazy cat lady."

"Oh, I could get into the role. Believe me." She grinned and he chuckled again.

"Seriously?"

"Why not? I don't need a man to be happy."

Law laughed again. "Well, of course not. Usually, we're more trouble than we're worth."

The hint of the Aussie accent hit her ears and felt rich and layered, like a European espresso. Now it was her turn to laugh. She loved a man confident enough to poke fun at himself.

"That's what my mom always said. She put career first and taught me to do the same." Juliana was unapologetic about that.

"You don't want kids?" Law asked.

Juliana shrugged. "I practically raised my younger sister, so I feel like I've already had one. Kids, marriage…they're a waste of time."

Law's blond eyebrows arched so high on his face she thought they might leap off. He clearly didn't agree with her assessment. Well, this was why some of the men in her office secretly called her an ice queen or ballbuster behind her back. It was why many of them kept their distance. She made it perfectly clear she didn't need a man. Didn't want one.

"Well, take the emotion out of it, and look at the facts. Half of them end in divorce. More than half of men and almost half of women cheat." Juliana shrugged and folded her arms across her torso, trying not to look out the plane's window as they taxied down the runway. Her stomach leaped. They'd take off soon. The plane rumbled down the tarmac, and then, suddenly, took off. She gripped the hand rests, her knuckles turning white. *What's wrong with you?*

"What about dating? Relationships, then?" Law asked her. The cabin shook a bit as the plane fought the earth's gravity. She was suddenly glad for the distraction of his deep voice. "So you don't want the legal entanglements, then wouldn't you want... companionship?"

The way he said it implied he might have more than a passing interest in the answer to this question. Law's elbow grazed hers as his shoulders seemed to take up all the oxygen in the cabin. He shifted his long legs, stretching them out beneath the seat in front of him.

"It's not my top priority," Juliana admitted. The shuttering of the cabin finally eased. Thank goodness. She loosened her grip on the armrests. "Men can be needy. And they don't understand my work schedule." She shrugged, thinking about the last time she'd tried a relationship. She'd dated the man eight months, but she'd been traveling at least half of that time. She returned after a particularly hard project in California, only to discover he'd put up his profile on dating websites without telling her. When she confronted him with all the Facebook photos she'd found of him hanging with other women, he'd told her it was all *her* fault. She needed to pay attention to him more, as if he were a toddler in need of supervision. "Even when I do, I don't have time for needy men. My work comes first. What about you? Do you want to get married?"

"Oh, yes. I definitely want to get married someday," Law declared. "And have a gaggle of kids. And find my soul mate."

"Oh, no. You believe in soul mates?" Now Juliana

forgot entirely about her unease about being thousands of feet above the ground. "Like one person in a million, just for you, that kind of soul mate?"

"One in four billion, actually," he said.

Juliana couldn't believe it. This man, this smart, successful man, believed in the kind of fairy tales usually reserved for children. Did he arrange tea parties for his stuffed animals, too?

"You think there's just *one* person. *One*, for each of us?" The plane rumbled up its ascent, barreling up to cruising altitude. But she was so intent on their conversation, she barely noticed.

Law shrugged. "Maybe." This man, this reasonable, successful man, was a romantic. Juliana couldn't believe it. He might as well have told her he believed in unicorns.

He shifted a little and his elbow touched hers. She didn't move her own arm. She let the contact stand. He shifted again so his whole forearm touched hers. She felt the warm press of his arm against her, every hair on her forearm standing at attention. She might not be a romantic, but she certainly understood physical attraction. That seemed a much more reasonable idea: two people wanting to mate, barely different than animals, really, except that people liked to pretend it was something else. *Like romance.*

"I think it's very possible we're on this planet to find the person who's made for us," Law said, sounding like a cheesy Valentine's Day card.

"Oh, geez. I think that's a cop-out. It kind of implies you don't need to do the hard work of getting to know someone. A person just shows up on your doorstep and—*bam!*—instant love."

"It might work like that." Law grinned. "It could be fate. Do you believe in fate?"

"Fate implies we don't get a say in our own lives." She shook her head. "I bet you buy a woman flowers on the first date. And insist on paying." Juliana rolled her eyes. She felt the plane beneath them level out a bit. Cruising altitude almost reached.

"What's wrong with flowers?" Law asked, puzzled.

"They're pretty for a half second and then they die," she said. "A waste of money."

Law barked a laugh. "Well, then, I'll make a mental note *not* to buy you flowers when I pick you up on our first date." He pretended to scribble on an invisible notepad.

Juliana laughed. "Who said *we're* going out?"

"We're not?" Law challenged, eyes fixed on her. Did he feel the little snaps of electricity running back and forth between them? A small smile tugged at the corner of his mouth, and she knew then he definitely felt it. And the way he was looking at her now told her he had no plans to ignore that electric current. "Are you sure about that?"

CHAPTER TWO

LAW KNEW HE was playing with fire. What was he doing, flirting with Juliana Hart? He'd had one goal, and one goal only, to evaluate the independent consultant working for AM Air, trying to figure out if she knew her stuff or if her work could jeopardize the sale of Blue Sky to AM Air next month. Law, the reclusive majority shareholder at Blue Sky, and acting CEO, wanted very badly for that sale to go through. He'd spent nearly fifteen years in the airline business, and he was done. He was ready to focus on his charity, and spend the rest of his forties enjoying life a little, maybe even starting a family. He'd spent his whole adult life up until this point working seventy hours a week, and that had to change.

That all started with the sale of Blue Sky, and the only thing potentially standing in the way was this little independent report, commissioned by the board of AM Air, to prove the merger would be beneficial. That report would be written by *this* troublemaker sitting in 34G.

She smiled at him, pink lips inviting as they broke to show him the hint of her perfect smile. Nobody told him the woman would be drop-dead gorgeous. That little detail had been left out of all the meetings when his senior VPs had cried into their beers and wrung their hands about the hard-charging consultant who didn't take no for an answer. She even had a nickname: the ice queen. Distant, hardworking, demanding. He could see why so many of his colleagues were intimidated by her. Though, looking at her now, he couldn't for the life of him understand why anyone would think she was cold. He'd known she was whip-smart, because she'd run circles around his entire management team. She intrigued him, and he was here to find out more about her.

"Give me one reason I shouldn't ask you out right now." He couldn't help himself, actually. Apparently, he liked flirting with danger.

"Because I'd say no." She grinned, softening the blow.

"Ouch," he said, splaying his fingers across his chest. "That hurt." He faked a cough. *She's tough and doesn't need every man's approval then*, he thought. *I like that.*

"Come on. I'm sure you get turned down all the time." Juliana's smile grew bigger, her light brown eyes teasing. He was so intrigued by her. He suddenly wanted to know everything about her. The nearly three-hour flight seemed too short suddenly.

How was he really supposed to get to know her during such a short time?

"Hey! Are you trying to make me feel better... or worse?"

"Worse," she admitted. He had to laugh. She was surprisingly quick, and she kept him guessing. Few people managed to surprise him, but Juliana did.

Above their heads the seat belt light flicked off. They'd reached cruising altitude. She looked far more relaxed than when they'd begun takeoff. His mission to distract her from the ascending plane had worked, clearly. He'd been worried there for a minute. She'd been wound so tight, he thought she might burst. That little chink in her armor took him by surprise. She was afraid of flying but had taken on the report from AM Air, anyway, knowing that she'd have to crisscross the country on Blue Sky flights for months. He admired her more in that moment. That took nerve.

"Besides, I don't date random strangers I meet on planes. Especially ones who believe in *soul mates.*" She rolled her eyes again. He had to laugh at her disdain for all things romantic. Still, what was her beef with true love? He'd never met a woman so insistent that it didn't exist. It made him want to figure out just *why* she was not a fan of love. Broken heart in her past, maybe? Or was it a defense mechanism? Lord knew he'd spent a lot of his professional life not wanting any personal entanglements. He thought they got in the way, until he realized one day that he had an entire airline empire but no one to go home to at night. He wanted that now for the first time. But he realized that to get it, he'd need to scale back his work, make room for a woman in his life.

"You are the least romantic woman I've ever met," he managed, not quite keeping the surprise from his voice. He actually didn't know they existed. The women he'd dated were always clamoring for commitment, to settle down. Maybe that was because they knew how much he was worth, he thought sourly. Juliana didn't know who he was. As far as she was concerned, he was just another business traveler, a stranger. She didn't know how many zeroes he had in his bank account. Too many, really, when he thought about it. Growing up middle class, he'd never imagined he'd have this much wealth at his disposal, that he'd own one of the world's biggest airlines. Yet here he was.

"I'll take that as a compliment." She flipped her dark hair over her shoulder and he admired the slimness of her neck. He loved how quick she was, how smart. He admired that she had strong opinions and stuck to them. He found himself wanting to ask her personal questions: does she have a family? Does she ever want kids? But those questions weren't the ones he was supposed to ask. He ought to be focusing on her consulting work for AM Air. *This is business. Just business. Don't make it personal.*

He doubted Juliana would ever guess she was sitting next to the man who ran the company she was evaluating. Law didn't like the spotlight, and shunned social media, so few outside Blue Sky even knew what he looked like. He knew it was unfair to keep Juliana in the dark, but he'd been tasked with evaluating how competent she was, and that was what he'd do. He'd never had a problem keeping his professional life separate from his personal one before. He wasn't about to start now.

Then, out of nowhere, the plane hit a serious and unexpected patch of turbulence. He clutched his armrest as the nose dipped. Without warning, they seemed to fall ten feet and Law felt his stomach leap to his throat.

Whoa, what was that?

Law knew turbulence could pop up unexpectedly but there was barely a cloud in the sky, and weather forecasts had been clear almost all the way to Chicago. His mind instantly clicked into survival mode: assess the danger, form a plan, act. But of course, there was nothing he could do. He was wearing his seat belt, and Juliana had on hers, and someone else was flying this bucket of bolts, and all they could do was wait and hope for the best. He glanced at Juliana, who'd lost all the blood in her face, looking a shade paler than the tray table stowed in front of her. He reached out and clasped her hand. She let him, glancing at him with fear in her eyes. How he wanted to tell her everything would be okay, that she shouldn't be afraid, but the hairs standing up on the back of his neck told him maybe that was a promise he couldn't make.

The plane jostled again, one overhead bin flying open and a backpack falling out into the aisle with a hard thud. Gasps and one shout went up from nearby passengers as Law held Juliana's hand, pulling her arm closer to his, worried that all his bragging about Blue Sky's accident record might have cursed them. He glanced around the cabin, looking at the panicked faces around them, many with eyes squeezed shut in prayer, and saw he wasn't the only one who thought this contraption might fall from the sky. Goodness, the irony: *Blue Sky President and Majority Shareholder Dies in Own Plane Crash.* He was pretty sure all his shares would be worthless after that. Although, who cared if he was dead?

He realized in that moment the stark truth: no one. He had no one to leave his fortune to other than a couple of distant cousins he rarely saw, and his alma mater, the University of Pennsylvania. The Ivy League school would be getting a substantial portion of his estate. If he went down with this plane, he'd be a tiny blip in history, one soon forgotten.

He looked at Juliana, who had pressed her lips into a grim line.

"We're going to be fine," he told her, glad he sounded authoritative, and hoped it wasn't a lie.

The cabin rattled once more, hard, the nose of the plane dipping down. Another round of shocked gasps pierced the air, and this time one high-pitched scream. She squeezed his hand hard, holding on with all her might, her grip surprisingly strong. Not a sound left her clenched jaw, but Law could tell she was using all her strength to keep the panic in check. Law found himself running through all manner of different scenarios—none of them good. He heard the ceiling rattle and prayed the cabin stayed in one piece. Once bits started flying off, the cabin pressure would be done for. He tried to think of ways he could protect Juliana, but he knew if the plane really did go down, his options would be limited.

The plane dipped twice more as the cabin rattled and his armrest vibrated. Now a man shouted from somewhere behind him. Much more of this, and none of the passengers would be able to hold it together. He could feel the pilots struggle to get control of the nose once more. Then, after another harrowing few seconds, the plane righted itself. Sheesh. What the hell had that all been about?

The pilot came on the intercom seconds later. She sounded calm, and completely collected. "Sorry about that, folks. We hit an unexpected patch of turbulence, but we're all okay now."

Law made a mental note to find out the pilot's name and send her his own personal commendation. Not only had she gotten the plane back on track, but she'd made it look easy, too.

Applause rippled through the cabin as collectively everyone let out a sigh of relief. "We'll be keeping the seat belt sign on for just a little bit to make sure we're out of it."

He damn well wasn't taking his seat belt off this whole flight at this point. He glanced over at Juliana, and he could tell by the look on her face she wouldn't, either.

"Are you okay?" he asked her, realizing her breathing came in rapid, staccato breaths. She kept a viselike grip on his hand, nearly cutting off his circulation.

"I think so." Her voice sounded shaky. He wanted to pull her into his arms and hug her until she stopped shaking. A flight attendant darted down the aisle and grabbed the backpack that had fallen onto the carpeted floor. She grabbed it and tucked it back up into the open overhead bin and then shut the door.

"Well, I don't know about you, but I think I need a drink."

Juliana laughed a little, still holding his hand tightly. "Yeah, for sure," she said. "But now? We're at the back of coach, and there's no beverage service."

"Actually, sitting at the back of the plane is the best place to be," Law said, sharing a little-known secret. "Flight attendants are more likely to give you special treatment, because the other passengers can't really see."

"Really?" Juliana seemed skeptical. No matter, Law would show her. CEO or not, passengers at the back of the plane did get a few perks. The studies at his airlines showed flight attendants were twice as likely to respond to a call button at the back of the plane than the middle. This was part convenience, but also practicality. There only existed so many blankets and extra drinks on a plane. If staff gave them out where everyone could see, there'd be more demand. Besides, if he needed to, he'd pull rank.

"Trust me. What's your poison?" he asked.

"Wine, normally, but I'd say this deserves a vodka soda," she murmured, taking a deep breath.

"Coming right up." He signaled the flight attendant sitting in the jump seat behind them, realizing he knew her. He'd met Sari on her first day a few years ago when she'd accidentally spilled soda on his pants. She'd spent the rest of the flight profusely apologizing and near tears after another flight attendant told her who he was. He'd told her that as long as she treated every customer as if they were the president of the airline, then she'd do just fine.

Her face broke out into a smile when she saw him.

"Law! So nice to see you," she said. "What can I do for you?"

"You and the crew okay? Anyone banged up after that little bit?" he asked, concerned. After all, these were *his* people and he wanted to make sure they were all right.

Sari shook her head. "We're fine." She flashed him a brave smile. Juliana still held his hand and he was almost afraid to move it for fear she'd realize they were still touching. He liked the feel of her hand on his, her long, delicate fingers wrapped around his.

"Good." He nodded. "Could you do me a huge favor? Would you mind grabbing us two vodka sodas?"

"Right away, sir," Sari said, not missing a beat as she turned around and disappeared into the plane's galley.

"How do you *do* that?" Juliana exclaimed, watching the flight attendant shuffle off. "Normal, non-first-class passengers don't get to order up drinks whenever they want."

Law shrugged. "Well, it's the magic of the back of the plane," he improvised. Juliana shook her head, clearly still skeptical. "Plus, I'll admit, Sari owes me a favor," he said. "She spilled soda all over me on her first day a few years ago."

"Do you know everyone on this airline?"

"Almost," he said.

Juliana seemed to realize that she was still clutching his hand, because she glanced down as an "Oh!" escaped her lips. "I'm sorry... I..." She hurriedly withdrew her hand, and his felt cold suddenly, empty. He'd liked comforting her. "I didn't mean to..."

"Comfort me? I thought I was going to chuck a piss."

"Chuck a...?"

"Pee my pants," he added and grinned. Law flashed Juliana a smile and she laughed a little.

"Thanks, but I think I was the one about to panic. I almost thought I was going to hyperventilate there for a minute."

Sari reappeared almost instantly then with two bubbling plastic cups, tiny slices of lime floating in each one. "Here you go, sir," she said, handing one to Law and the other to Juliana. Law reached into his pocket for his wallet, but Sari held up a hand in protest.

"No, no. On the house, sir." She bustled away, leaving Juliana with another perplexed look on her face.

"Apparently, I should make a note always to travel with you," she joked.

"You're welcome anytime." Law realized he meant this. It wasn't just formality as he held up his plastic glass in a toast. "To not dying."

"Yet," Juliana breathed as she touched her cup to his and took a big sip. "We still have...how much time to go?"

"I think one patch of bad luck is probably all we're allotted this trip," he said, swallowing the crisp, but potent, vodka down.

"I hope you're right." Juliana sounded rueful. She took another long drink, her hand still shaking slightly. He wanted to comfort her but wasn't sure how. Crack a joke? "I was supposed to do work on this flight." She nodded toward the laptop stowed under the seat in front of her. "But..."

"Work can wait," Law said, voice firm. "We almost *died*. So, work can wait." He clinked his plastic cup against hers. Before he knew it, they'd both downed their drinks, though it still hadn't taken an edge off his nerves. Even when the pilot turned off the fasten seat belt sign, he still felt a tad uneasy.

"My life just flashed before my eyes and, I'll be honest with you, I didn't like what I saw," Law admitted.

"Why?"

"All work. No play. Hardly anything *real* about my life. Find the person I'm supposed to spend my life with," he said, taking another deep dreg of vodka. *That's why I need to sell Blue Sky. Get on with my life, my real life. Make something real. Preferably with a woman who hates corporate spreadsheets.* "Somehow, feels like a wasted life."

"You think love is the answer?" Her light brown eyes showed skepticism.

"What's the point of life, if not love? To make real connections with people." The cabin around them darkened as the pilot dimmed the lights for those wanting to sleep the evening flight away. Juliana glanced around and so did Law. He saw all the people staring at the screens of their small devices, now seemingly back to normal after the plane nearly fell from the sky. It amazed him that something so profound could happen, and then normality snapped back; people acted as if nothing important had happened.

"You know... I..." Juliana shook her head. "I think I need to go to the bathroom. Do you mind?" She nodded toward the aisle. Law stood so she could shuffle by. As she did, he got a whiff of her perfume, something crisp and sweet. Grapefruit, maybe? Whatever it was, he liked it. As she brushed by him, her hip slid by his groin, making all his senses come to life. *Down, boy*, he told himself. *Down. This is business, remember? Not play.*

He watched as she slipped into the empty bathroom behind his seat, noticing how her hand shook as she turned the latch. He knew then something was wrong.

Juliana was not okay as she shut the bathroom door behind her and slid the lock into place. Her whole body felt like jelly, like it might melt into a puddle, and she was too addled to even notice this bathroom was extra-roomy, a detail she would have normally jotted down in her head for the future report. She'd never experienced turbulence that bad before and she'd been convinced she was going to die. The stress of it, added to everything else that happened this week, hit her like a falling concrete slab. She'd worked so hard to pretend everything was okay, that she could handle anything life and work threw at her, that she didn't realize her body was trying to tell her she couldn't, actually, do it all.

The panic that settled in her throat burst forth now as tears streamed down her face. She couldn't control the sobs anymore as they racked her small frame. *I almost died. This tin bird almost became my coffin.* The thought choked her and she was powerless. Juliana felt like she couldn't breathe. She clawed at the neckline of her tunic, trying to get some air to her collarbone. She prided herself on being in control of her emotions, cool and calm, and now they flooded her like a tidal wave. What would some of her co-workers say about her now? *The ice queen has lost it.* She cried now and felt like she might keep on crying.

I nearly died. She couldn't get the horrible thought out of her mind. *I nearly died, and the last man to touch me was Garrison.* That thought made her sick, suddenly. Because Garrison had touched her without her permission. Without her invitation. It had been entirely on his terms. Everything was always on his terms. Her projects. Her promotions. And now her body? The unfairness of it ripped through her like a blade. The thought made her want to hyperventilate. Suddenly, she felt like she couldn't get enough air.

Why was she panicking? The plane didn't fall out of the sky. She's fine. *You're fine,* she silently told herself, staring at her reflection in the mirror as she swiped at the tears glistening on her cheeks. *Garrison is a thousand miles away. Besides, he didn't rape you. He just grabbed you and tried to kiss you. What's the big deal?*

Yet it had shaken her to her core. She didn't know why.

Maybe it was she felt so out of control; everything seemed to be spiraling away from her. It was probably just lack of sleep, stress of the Blue Sky project. Maybe Garrison didn't even have anything to do with it. She'd dealt with men like Garrison before. She could do it again.

Then she heard a soft knock on the door.

"Juliana? It's me. Law. Are you okay?"

"Y-yes," she sniffed, grabbing a wad of tissues from the bathroom dispenser and crushing them to her face.

"Can I come in?" he offered.

She felt white-hot panic. He'd see her like this—a mess. Her mascara was running down her face; her cheeks were blotchy and red. All she needed now was for the sexy Aussie to see her at her worst.

"Look, you don't know me. But I know you're upset. Let me help."

His voice sounded strangely soothing, even through the door. She bit her lower lip, considering. When would she ever see the man again? Who cared if he saw her crying? The comfort he offered beckoned like the warm beacon of a lighthouse. She carefully slid the lock open. He stepped inside, shutting the door behind him. He opened his arms and she leaned into them, feeling his warm embrace, instantly feeling stronger, better, more whole. This human connection, as much as she wanted to deny it, meant something. She'd spent the past many months without anything more than polite social banter, or work-focused conversation, but nothing deep. Nothing meaningful.

He squeezed her tight, and she felt all the muscles in his chest, his strong arms around her offering the promise of comfort and security. She felt so small in his arms, so protected. Instantly, her tears dried as she hugged him back, thankful for the human contact. This was on *her* terms. She wanted this: Law's arms around her. Suddenly, she very much wanted something for herself. Something on *her* terms. She realized, with a shock, she wanted Law.

Right here. Right now.

Her terms.

Her body screamed for something tangible, for a connection that went beyond just a hug.

She tilted her head up then. He glanced down at her and swiped a tear from her cheek. The gesture was so gentle, so inviting, that she wanted to show him how much she appreciated it. And she wanted… more. Juliana glanced at his lips, full, sensual, and suddenly felt consumed with the idea that she wanted to feel them. Taste them. Know them. She was doing this because she wanted to.

She stood on tiptoes and pressed her lips against his.

CHAPTER THREE

THE KISS SEEMED to take him by surprise, because he froze at first. She almost panicked. Was he going to reject her? Was she…not pretty enough for him? She wasn't used to coming on to a man like this. She'd never kissed a man first in her life and wondered if she'd just made a huge mistake. He was the kind of man who probably got any woman he wanted, so what made her think he'd ever want her? Part of her would always be that awkward beanpole. Despite the fact she'd long since developed, she still carried around the insecure fourteen-year-old inside her. The girl who'd been flat-chested until age seventeen.

But just as she feared her kiss would be rejected, he softened and his lips parted for her. He was kissing her back! This amazing man, fit, handsome and clearly smart, was kissing her back. But of course he was. This was how men worked, she thought. They couldn't resist the physical, right? Why would Law be any different? She deepened this kiss, her passion rising in her, her need growing. He tasted so very good. This was what it felt like to *want* to kiss a man. The hint of lime and something dark and inviting hit her as the kiss deepened, and their tongues met. It felt as if a thousand volts of electricity shot through her nerves from the tip of her head to the bottom of her toes, hot, insistent. The kiss turned savage, needy, as she ran her fingernails through the back of his hair, clutching at his thick, dark waves. Her fear and her panic transformed into want, the need for release. She pressed her body against him, knee itching upward as if she wanted to climb him. He grabbed her leg, pulling her in even closer so she could feel the need hardening in him.

He wanted her as much as she wanted him. That thought thrilled her. Yes, she thought. Yes. She'd never imagined wanting someone so fiercely. Was it a reaction to Garrison? Was it her taking back her own body? Maybe. Because here she was, devouring this man. She'd never planned this, not here in the bathroom of a plane. She'd never in a million years believed she'd do something like this, but her reptile brain had taken over. She'd nearly died, nearly dropped thousands of feet to the hard earth below, and this connection, this defiant act of sex, was all about survival. Now she was all animal, all base instincts, all need. Every bit of force and ambition she usually poured into her work now came out as pure want, as she slammed Law against the bathroom door with a thump, her tongue finding his. She wanted this. She wanted him. Now.

Suddenly, it didn't matter that she barely knew the man. That made it all the better. She could do this, scratch this itch, fill this need, desperately knit a connection out of nothing. Her lips broke free of his.

"I want you," she murmured, voice low, hoarse. She couldn't believe her own boldness. Had she said those words out loud? Yes, she had. And she'd say them again. "I want you here. Now."

"I want you, too," he admitted, his pupils so big, they'd turned his blue eyes nearly black. She reached for his crotch, feeling the impressive swell of his want, proving that he spoke the truth. He groaned at her touch, leaning into her and claimed her mouth once more. The man could kiss.

She thought of the other passengers and the flight attendant on the other side of the thin bathroom door. Could they hear them? She almost didn't care. Let them. She needed this man. Needed him now. She'd denied herself this for far too long. Who cared about consequences? For once she'd live in the moment, in the now, drawing on her basest desires. This wasn't just about pleasure; it was about survival. She clutched at him as if he were a life raft. She needed this. For her body, for her sanity. For once she'd put away the logic and the calculations and let thousands of years of pure animal instinct take over.

Yet she wanted to feel him deep inside her; she wanted him to fill her in the way only a man could. He broke free of their kiss, panting, and then he hoisted her up on the tiny edge of the bathroom sink as if she weighed nothing, and suddenly she realized how strong he really was, how compact and powerful his muscles must be. She met his blue-eyed gaze and felt slick desire pool between her legs. She'd wanted him the moment she'd seen him, and now she'd have him. *I'm an animal in heat, running on pure instincts, pure need.* He found the waistband of her stretchy leggings, pulling them downward to reveal her secret: she wore no underwear, not beneath the comfy leggings, not for a long, red-eye flight.

His hands slinked up her leg, finding her bareness. He grinned, eyebrow risen in a question. Normally, she went commando for comfort, but now she realized he put a different meaning on this altogether. "Well, well," he murmured, surprised, as his fingers roved deeper, gently caressing the bundle of nerves sitting taut there, sending her heart racing as they slipped across her slick center. "Did you come here ready for this?"

No, she wanted to tell him. *Never done anything like this.*

I also never thought I'd nearly die on a plane, either.

But she wanted him. Badly.

His finger slipped inside her then, and she gasped as he penetrated her, his touch driving her wild as she realized he now understood just how much she wanted him, how wet he'd made her.

"Yes, you came ready," he murmured and she realized the truth in his statement. She felt like she'd always been ready for this. For him.

And then she knew she would. She knew she would like it, hot, heavy, urgent. The fear of being caught rippling through every moment, the naughtiness of breaking the rules turning every caress into white-hot desire. She'd always been the girl who insisted on dinner first, on a whole host of hurdles a man would have to clear before she'd ever let him even see her underwear. But now, here, on this plane, with this stranger, she was going to give him everything, right here. Right now. No strings. No obligations, just pure animal need.

He inched back in the tight space and she lunged for his fly, eager to free him, eager to do this. He claimed her mouth again and she moaned once more, the rush of want a tsunami of desire flooding all her senses. She freed him then, heavy, hard and smooth in her hands. Yes, this was what she wanted. Him, all of him, inside her. To hell with consequences. Because chances were, they'd never meet again. Impressive, too. Wide. On the north side of average, and oh so very, very ready for her. She'd never seen a man so hard, so ready. He groaned as she wrapped her hands around him, as she felt the proof of his need. He wanted her as much as she wanted him. She felt giddy suddenly, powerful, as she clutched him in her hands.

This was going to happen. She could barely believe it. She'd only just met this man, a random stranger who'd sat next to her on the emergency exit row, and now she was about to take him inside her, a place only a handful of men had ever gone in her whole life. Had ever *wanted* to go, a sharp, insecure voice in her head told her. The voice belonging to her insecure fourteen-year-old self.

She glanced at his blue eyes, that sexy, squared-off chin. Yes, she wanted him. So badly. No regrets. Not for this. He nudged against her, his bulging tip pressing against her, the promise of pleasure, of pure animal lust, of precious, sweet release. She'd held the reins so tightly in her life, so taut, and now she'd let go. She'd let everything go as she clutched his shoulders, her core aching for this, to be taken to new heights as this tin bird glided through the clouds, the ground thousands of feet below them.

"You ready?" he asked her, rubbing the tip of him against her once more, sending a wave of urgent want thrumming down her legs to her knees. They shook with anticipation.

"Yes," she whispered, hoarse, her nails digging into his shoulders.

Then he reached into his back pocket and pulled out his wallet, condom sleeve inside. It took seconds, but he'd ripped it open. She wondered how often he replaced that condom, how often women took him into plane lavatories and offered up their secrets to him. Dozens of times probably. Maybe even hundreds. He unraveled the latex across himself and then she drew him in before she lost her nerve. He went, plunging deep inside her, filling her, stretching her, as they both became animals in the basest sense. He took her again and again in the small space, and she spread her legs wider, taking him ever deeper inside, each thrust bringing her closer to the edge. She felt as if she could come at any moment as she teetered on the edge. So close. So very close. Any second now. He slowed then a bit, sliding the soft pad of his finger between them, rubbing her, bringing her even closer as he slipped in and out of her.

"You have to come first," he demanded. "I can't come until you do."

The declaration sent shivers down her spine. A true gentleman, she thought, before she realized that what he was doing to her was not gentlemanly at all.

"Come for me," he demanded, voice a low growl, blue eyes commanding. "Come hard."

She could hardly refuse him. Oh, she was going to come. Going to come so very hard. Her whole body tensed, anticipating the climax. She held for a second, at the very peak, and then, in a tumble of pure pleasure, the climax hit her, wave after wave of shuddering ecstasy as she plunged over the edge, feeling as if she was plummeting out of the sky. She clutched his shoulders blindly. He fell into her then, his forehead resting on her shoulder as they both breathed hard in the small space. She couldn't believe what they'd just done. She'd taken a man, practically a stranger, right here where everyone could hear. Had she lost her mind? Reckless. It was the only word to describe it. What if they'd been caught? Could a person go to jail for having sex in a bathroom? She was an airline consultant and even she didn't know.

Yet she couldn't regret it. She'd needed that, needed it in a way she'd never imagined.

"That was…amazing," Law sputtered, voice just below a whisper. He withdrew slowly, delicately, but still making them both shudder at the loss of contact. She felt so empty suddenly, so barren. He unraveled the condom and slipped it into the bathroom's trash. How many times had he done that before? she wondered. He moved to zip himself up. "You are… amazing."

"So are you," she breathed, still reeling from her climax, still amazed at the depth of her want for this man, about how she'd thrown every bit of caution out the window for him. He moved back so she could slide down from the sink. She pulled up her leggings, feeling the slickness from her climax between her legs. She didn't even smoke, but she felt she needed a cigarette. Or a drink. Of course, now she was fully aware that they both had to somehow get out of the bathroom without someone noticing. Did the people outside hear them? Was a flight attendant waiting to scold them? She'd never done this before. She didn't know how this worked.

"I'll go out first, okay? Then you follow in a second?" Law offered. "I'll knock once on the door if it's clear, but twice if it's not."

Had Law done this before? The thought darted

into her brain. *Maybe he did this all the time.* Still, she was relieved he offered to go first. Bits of her logical brain began to come online. What would she do if a flight attendant stopped her? Questioned her? What would she do if one of the passengers laughed as she exited? She hadn't thought this through, she realized. She hadn't been thinking at all.

Law slipped out then into the darkened cabin, and shut the door behind him. One single knock came and Juliana exhaled. The coast was clear. No flight attendant waiting for them. She counted to twenty and then she opened the bathroom, too. Guiltily, she glanced at the rows of passengers ahead of them, rows and rows of the backs of heads that stayed focused on their screens, earbuds tucked into their ears. Thank goodness no one seemed to hear them. A beverage cart down the aisle made its way slowly to them. She felt triumphant then as Law stood, letting her slip back into her seat, no one else the wiser that she'd just had passionate sex with a man she'd just met.

Why did doing bad things feel so very…good?

This wasn't her, she reminded herself. *I don't do things like this.*

You just did, sweetheart, an inner voice told her.

Of course, now she had to sit next to the man she'd just ravished for the next hour and a half. Would it be awkward? She settled in next to Law, their elbows touching. She still couldn't get over the fact that a second before, she'd seen him half-naked. That he'd made her come harder than she'd come, maybe in her whole life.

"Look…uh… I mean, I'm sure you do that all the time, but…"

"I don't, actually," Law admitted.

Juliana wanted to believe him, but with that smile? Those eyes? Could that be true?

"Just once, and that was a steady girlfriend. I… usually don't do…this."

"Do what?"

"Anything like this. With a stranger, on a plane, you name it."

The idea buoyed her. Was he not a man who went looking for casual hookups? She wanted to tell him that she, too, had never done anything close to this, and yet part of her felt a little bit like pretending she did. After all, she'd never done anything close to this reckless before, but the idea of her being a woman who took sexy men into lavatories kind of appealed. No one at her office would believe it, and she kind of liked that. *I'm not who you think I am, either*, she wanted to shout at her coworkers.

"I hope I wasn't too aggressive. I feel like I attacked you," she admitted, voice low. She remembered how she'd dug her fingernails into his shoulders, how she'd insisted he take her, how her need overwhelmed her good sense.

"You can't attack someone who's a willing participant," Law pointed out. "Besides, you're…so gorgeous. I am not complaining."

She laughed out loud. Gorgeous? Her inner bean-pole beamed. "No, I'm not."

"Yes, you are." Law shook his head. "Come on." He hesitated, realizing she was serious. It wasn't just a transparent attempt to illicit a compliment. "You can't be serious. You don't think you're beautiful?"

Juliana remembered senior year of high school. Not a single boy asked her to prom. "I don't get asked out very often," she said. She thought about Garrison and cringed. Though he'd not technically asked her out.

"That's because you're too pretty. You intimidate men."

"I do not!" Juliana laughed. She glanced at her reflection in the open window of the plane. She was all right, she supposed. Button nose, oversize brown eyes that sort of looked like a rogue anime character. But her skin was pale, too pale, and she still felt lanky, despite finally growing into her long legs, and filling out a bra. Sure, she'd noticed the attention of some men, especially the higher she rose in the company and the fewer women that were there. Most recently—Garrison. But she'd never taken it seriously. Always assumed boys would just be boys—hitting on whatever was available.

"Are you kidding me?" Law looked genuinely surprised. "You're gorgeous, love. Gorgeous." The bit of Aussie accent came through once more. He sounded so confident. *I could start to believe him.*

"You know, you don't have to compliment me. You already got in my pants," she teased.

"I know," he said, gently taking her hand in his. "That's how you know it's the truth."

She laughed a little, deep in her throat. She loved flirting with this man. She didn't even care if he was lying. The lies felt good. She couldn't remember the last time she'd even fantasized about a man, and then—*boom*—Law lands in the seat next to her and she'd gotten naked for him within an hour. That must be a new land speed record. No, scratch that, air speed record, since they were a mile up in the sky.

Law entwined his fingers in hers. He glanced at the beverage cart near to them. "Want another vodka soda?"

"Hell, yes," she said and he laughed.

Juliana fell asleep against his shoulder sometime after their second drink, and Law kept very still, not wanting to wake her, but also taking the opportunity to study the woman's beautiful face. Her skin seemed flawless, not a hint of a blemish anywhere, and asleep she looked a tad vulnerable, her thick, dark lashes lowered. He still couldn't believe the burst of passion. The way she'd demanded his participation, the way she'd taken control. It was sexy... beyond sexy. World-changing, really. He'd never met a woman with an appetite as big as his, with the courage to take what she wanted, and now here she was, asleep on his shoulder. He loved that she demanded what she wanted, that she didn't try to hide her desire. Yet a small part of his brain wondered if she did this all the time. Not that he'd ask her, of course. *Do you jump men on every flight you take?*

Did he even care if she did? Shouldn't he be grateful she'd jumped on him? Even now, as she drew deep breaths through her just-parted pink lips, he wanted to feel her once more, take her again.

What was he doing?

This was supposed to be business. Yet he'd made it about as personal as it could get. *What happens when she finds out I'm no accidental stranger? That I own Blue Sky? Or even worse, what happens when I tell Omar? He'll go through the roof.*

For a man who planned his every move, he sure was winging it. He never did anything this rash. What was it about this woman that had made him throw all his good sense out the window?

Snap out of it.

Then he glanced down at her soft, dark hair cascading down her shoulder. The electricity, the raw animal magnetism between them—it was something that couldn't be faked. But he couldn't let base want, no matter how strong, sideline his mission. He had to find out more about the report. About how she worked. Just because they'd had amazing sex didn't mean he would sideline his plans.

Keep on point, he told himself, even as he studied her button nose as she slept, remembering how her pink lips felt against his, the taste of her tongue in his mouth.

It's just business, he told himself, though even he wasn't sure he believed it.

CHAPTER FOUR

JULIANA CAME AWAKE just before landing to the sound of the pilot announcing the plane's incoming approach. The cabin lights blinked on, the sun not yet above the horizon to the east. She realized she'd rested her head on Law's shoulder and quickly straightened, blinking and feeling disoriented.

"Did I sleep that long?" she murmured, swiping at her mouth and hoping she hadn't been drooling.

"Just a half hour or so," he said and grinned.

"I didn't snore, did I?" She almost dreaded hearing the answer. Her hand flew to her hair, which she could feel was forming a rat's nest in the back. Juliana smacked her dry lips together. Her tongue tasted like sandpaper, and she probably reeked of morning breath.

"Nope," he said and shook his head. "Quiet as a mouse."

Feeling relieved, she bent over to retrieve her purse and dug through it to find a packet of gum. Juliana offered Law some and he took it. She popped her own small piece in her mouth, the mint flavor exploding on her tongue. That felt better; more civilized, at least. Then she dug out a mirror from her purse and saw the mascara raccoon rings under her eyes. Oh, geez. She looked terrible. Juliana swiped beneath her eyes, trying to make herself presentable, all the while conscious of the fact that Law looked magazine-shoot ready, ever the muscled Aussie, the hint of blond stubble on his squared-off chin only making him look…more manly. Just all testosterone.

As the rest of the passengers shifted, stowing tray tables and adjusting stored carry-ons, the captain dimmed the lights once more. Juliana tried not to think about the fact that he dimmed them in case of emergency. If the plane went down, if passengers needed to act, their eyes would already be adjusted to the dim light—when the power of the plane went out. She shelved that dark thought and found herself surprised it stayed there. She wondered why.

Hmmm. Maybe the cure for her sudden fear of flying is sex, she thought and nearly giggled. That would make one hell of a self-help book. *Get over your phobias with quick, anonymous sex.* This was the most relaxed she'd ever been on a descent. Law glanced at her, assessing her state of mind, worried about her, she assumed. She smiled back. *Nothing to worry about*, she wanted to tell him. *I feel fine.* She took his hand and squeezed it, the gesture conveying all of that and more. Law smiled at her, relieved. For a one-night stand, he sure was sweet, she thought. Maybe…

Maybe what? They'd call each other? Text? Be Facebook friends? Maybe go on a date sometime? That was crazy. Nobody would ever be interested in a serious relationship after a quickie in a plane's bathroom.

No, no, no. Keep it simple. One time. No attachments.

Besides, she had no idea what came over her in the bathroom. She wasn't usually so…bold. What happened when Law realized that it had been a fluke? That she was really a buttoned-up library type who liked watching reruns of *Downton Abbey*?

Besides, getting attached brought nothing but trouble. She thought of Garrison and sighed. Even when she tried to keep her life simple, somehow it always managed to get complicated.

The plane touched down with a nearly whisper-soft landing, to a splattering of applause. Apparently, some passengers remembered the bumpy start to the flight. Next to her, Law turned on his phone, scrolling through his messages. Juliana took her watch off airplane mode, and instantly three more texts came through. Two from Emma, more pictures of her and Xavier, and then one more from Garrison.

Please. Call me. I need to talk to you.

She ignored him.

Law cleared his throat. "Maybe we could grab a drink? I'm in Chicago for two days." She glanced up to see that Law was staring. Had he seen the message on her watch? She dropped her wrist by her side.

She was tempted, sorely tempted, but she also knew this quick trip home—for just three days—was just about refueling, getting her dry cleaning done, seeing her sister and then getting back out there. She had the board presentation in Seattle in a week, after all.

"I...probably won't have time." She avoided eye contact. *Just keep this simple, Juliana. The more time he spends with you, the more he'll find out you're nothing like this wild woman he met.* And it would be best if she did the dumping first, instead of waiting around to have him get bored. "I'm flying out to Honolulu for a consulting gig in two days, and then to Seattle for a meeting, so..."

Law whistled. "That sounds gruesome. You're going to actually put in more miles than me this week."

"All in a week's work." Juliana shrugged.

"Maybe we could get dinner tomorrow?" The offer was genuine, the desire real. As she looked at his star-quality cheekbones, she hesitated. Every fiber in her being wanted to scream yes, but was that wise? There were so many reasons to say no. She had a to-do list a mile long while she was at home, and the last thing she needed was more distractions, and if she spent more time with Law, she might grow fond of him. More than fond. As much as she pooh-poohed emotional attachment, she knew herself well enough to know that she could fall in love. Sometimes, too easily. Law was a million levels out of her league. He'd see that eventually.

"My sister's birthday. Sorry." Having the built-in excuse should've made things easy, but somehow, Juliana didn't feel so easy about it. She felt disappointment.

"Tell you what," he said, not at all the least bit fazed, and not taking the easy out she gave him. "Why don't I give you my number and if you find yourself with free time you can call me?"

He was really trying, but there was no point.

"Look, you are really amazing," Juliana began, watching his blue eyes never leave hers. "But I'm busy…and you're busy, I'm sure, and…" She was botching this. It was because she never had one-night stands, she realized. She didn't know how to get out of one gracefully. "I like you, but I don't have time to date right now."

She saw frustration on his face. He was a man used to getting what he wanted. She wondered how often women told him no.

"Who said anything about dating?" he said. "If you want this to be…like this—" he glanced at the bathroom "—I can do that, too."

Juliana considered this a moment. Was he offering a casual, sex-only relationship? She thought of him inside her, his hands on her backside. Her belly grew warm and she realized that idea secretly thrilled her.

"That sounds like it could get messy," she said.

"Only if you let it."

She shook her head slowly. No, it wouldn't work. Couldn't work. Best to end it now, keep things simple. One time, and done.

"I don't know."

"Think about it," he said.

As Law grabbed Juliana's bag from the carousel in baggage claim and slid it to the floor, wheels down and handle up, he saw her hesitate. She flicked her dark hair, now worn loose, off one shoulder. She'd shed the sweater tunic from the plane, now that they'd landed. She wore a simple tank top, revealing her smooth, bare shoulders for the warm, late-spring day outside. He didn't see how she didn't honestly know she was drop-dead gorgeous. She could be a model, if she wanted, with those high cheekbones, those amazing, big brown eyes, framed by lashes that looked so thick they seemed almost fake. Yet her humbleness seemed real, which boggled his mind. Women he knew who looked like her, knew exactly how much power they could wield over men, but Juliana seemed oblivious to the fact that if she raised her hand right now, in this baggage claim, probably about a half dozen men would fall over themselves to help her. Even now, the men around them were casting glances in her direction, noticing her. Did she not know the power she had, or was she good at faking ignorance?

"It was really great getting to know you…" She hesitated and a blush crept up her pale skin. The woman was gorgeous, and he felt his stomach tighten. He tried to focus on business, but when he looked at her soft brown eyes, he couldn't keep his mind on anything else but how good her lips felt on his.

"Don't say goodbye." It came out sounding more like a command than a request. "We'll see each other again."

He knew this to be true, even if she didn't. He'd be at the Blue Sky board meeting at minimum, but after their encounter tonight, he planned to see her again. He told himself it was just business, but even he wasn't buying it.

Her face broke into a warm smile.

"Nice to meet you, too."

God, those eyes. Look at them, so very perfect. He wanted to pull her into his arms and kiss her once more. She was shy and aggressive all at once, a bundle of contradictions that he wanted to unravel.

"Call me," he said, hopeful.

She hesitated. "I don't know."

There it was again: the rejection. He hated to admit that it stung. Why was she so determined to keep them apart? Did she not have fun?

Maybe she hadn't had as good a time as you did, mate. That thought unnerved him. He prided himself on being an attentive lover, making sure women had the pleasure they deserved. In fact, he had a hard time coming himself if he knew a woman wasn't satisfied.

Or maybe she had a big, strapping boyfriend at home.

He liked that thought even less. Then again, a gorgeous woman like that had to be taken, or spend all her time turning men down.

"Well, how about this. Don't make any rash decisions now," he said. "You know, throw my ego a bone. I'm really a delicate creature," he joked. "Just tell me maybe, or we'll see?"

She hesitated, then a small smile played on her lips. "Okay, then. Maybe."

"Good." Relief flooded him. "Let's hug it out?" he offered, opening up his arms. She glanced up at him and then opened her arms for a hug. He embraced her, feeling her small frame enveloped by his. She was so delicate, so thin. He wanted to take care of her, make sure she came to no harm. She lingered in his arms a minute and he inhaled the scent of her faded perfume. She withdrew and he watched her go. She didn't glance back once.

Wow, maybe she really wasn't into him at all.

Then again, maybe this is just what she does. Ravishes strangers on planes, discards them when she lands. After all, how much do I really know about this woman?

Maybe she was the cold and calculating consultant all his vice presidents feared.

Then he remembered her tears, how she'd clung to him in the bathroom. No, she was no ice queen. She'd been vulnerable with him. She might have a hard shell, but he knew the softness beneath.

His phone came to life then, and he saw Omar's number. He was one of his oldest friends and happened to be on the AM Air board of directors. He also wanted this deal to go through as much as Law did. Omar was the CEO of his biggest rival, but the two men—both ambitious, both self-made men—became fast friends after meeting on a Palm Beach golf resort. It was actually over a round of golf that Law suggested Omar buy Blue Sky. At first, his old friend thought it was a joke. It took some time convincing Omar he was serious. He really wanted to step down. It had been Omar's idea to hire Wickham Consulting, and his idea to request Juliana. Omar had heard she was the best. Of course, he'd been the one who'd asked Law to keep an eye on her.

"Law! You ignoring me, man? I've been calling you," Omar complained, and that was when Law realized he probably had unchecked messages since he'd deplaned. He'd been captivated by Juliana all the way to baggage claim. The woman was a serious distraction.

"I was on the flight to Chicago," he said.

"Oh, right. How is our little consultant?" Law felt his face grow warm. *Amazing*, he wanted to say. *She's got my head spinning.*

"Well…"

"Uh-oh. I know that tone. What happened?" Omar sounded on high alert now.

"I might have crossed a line."

"Did you piss her off? Is she going to tank the merger?" Omar had nearly as much to gain from this sale as Law did. Omar and his team had big plans for growing AM Air to the preeminent airline company in the world.

"No, at least not yet." She might feel differently once she realized who Law really was. "I might have made it personal." Law stopped there. He wasn't about to tell Omar about how delicious the woman's body had been, how much he'd enjoyed exploring it, even in the confines of a plane's bathroom. How even at that moment, he wanted to be with her again. Take his time. Try about a thousand different positions all over his hotel suite.

Omar let out a low chuckle. "I told you to *see what you thought* of her. As a consultant. I didn't think you'd treat it like Tinder time."

"I hadn't intended to," he protested. "It wasn't my idea." This much was true. She'd practically ripped his clothes off. He'd never been with a woman so single-minded before. Law saw his black rolling bag slide out onto the conveyer belt. He walked the few paces toward it and grabbed it.

"You're saying she held a gun to your head?"

Law thought about her amazing curves and her hungry mouth. "No, not a gun." *An amazingly soft mouth, though, and perfectly perky nipples in breasts that seemed to defy gravity. Those were weapons enough.*

"Seriously?" Law could hear Omar's eye-roll. "How is our plan going to work if you end up in bed with the consultant?"

"Technically, there wasn't a bed."

"Geez. Seriously? If I could, I'd fire you." Omar sighed.

"You can't. I'll resign first."

"But how are you going to be objective now?" Omar sounded perturbed. Law guessed he understood why.

"Come on. Since when did I ever let feelings get in the way of business?" Law asked.

"Never," Omar admitted. He knew as well as anyone that Law wasn't a man to be easily swayed by his feelings. He built his business based on cold, hard logic.

"Why not just cut your losses? Just tell me your first impressions. That's all we really need."

Why did Law not like that idea? He wanted to get to know Juliana better. He told himself it had nothing to do with the firm slope of her bottom, either.

"What about the report?"

"What about it?" Omar seemed unfazed. "You know if we both push this merger through it's happening, report or no."

That was mostly true.

"Let me spend a little more time with her." Law realized he was on the verge of asking Omar's permission. He never asked anyone's permission. Except Juliana's. Her permission was the only one he needed.

"Sure, but I don't think I'm the reason you want to spend time with her."

"This is just business," Law said.

"Is it, though?" Omar sounded doubtful. "Wait— has she become too attached? Like…what was her name?"

"Amber."

"Yes, Amber. The semi-stalker."

Law shook his head at the memory of the last girl he dated. She'd wanted to marry him before they'd finished dessert on their second date. He'd had to break it to her softly: she wasn't his type. She didn't take the breakup well. She'd even threatened to slash his tires. She hadn't, though, thank goodness.

"Actually, she seems fine with one and done." Law wheeled his bag to the exit, walking past the over-size Chicago flag, emblazoned with the four stars. He glanced around and found a cluster of limo drivers, most of whom were in black ties and white shirts. One held up a sign with his true last name on it: Mason.

Omar cackled a laugh. "Are you serious? She's *not* interested? What? Did you have performance issues?"

"No," Law snapped, feeling defensive. "She seemed very satisfied to me."

"Some women are very good at faking it. Just ask my wife."

Law couldn't help but laugh. Omar's wife was a

gorgeous physician, and they happened to be one of the most perfect couples Law knew. It was the one area where he was jealous of his friend. Law wanted that kind of stability, that kind of love.

"Don't even joke about that. Hailey is *in love* with you. You both kind of make me sick, actually, with all your gooey Facebook posts."

Omar laughed. "You're welcome. You can repay me by leaving our consultant alone. Let her go on to her next in-flight conquest."

Law felt a little morose as he thought of her loving the next man she met on a plane. Why did he care? he wondered.

"Maybe I should call her."

"No. *No.*" Omar sounded forceful on the phone, and Law could almost imagine him vigorously shaking his head. "Your ego is just bruised because she isn't falling all over you. Let sleeping dogs lie, my friend."

"Why?"

"Because she's an independent consultant. Key word: independent." Omar let out a frustrated-sounding breath. "And because if you tick her off, she could throw a wrench in the merger. Promise me you're not going to mess this up?"

"I'm going to hang up now, Omar. Don't worry. I've got a plan."

"That's what I'm afraid of," Omar said grimly.

CHAPTER FIVE

JULIANA CLUTCHED HER phone to her ear as she rode the elevator up to Wickham Consulting, juggling her laptop bag, a latte and her phone. It was just after eleven in the morning. She hadn't even planned to come into the office today—preferring to work from home—but her Wi-Fi had gone out and it was either head to the office or lose an entire day of work. She couldn't afford to fall further behind, not with the big presentation at Blue Sky looming. She pressed the phone to her ear and listened to yet another excuse from yet another Blue Sky accountant about why she didn't have the reports she needed for the employee retirement funds.

"What do you mean *those numbers aren't available*?" She tried to keep her voice calm, but her heart thudded in her chest. She needed those Blue Sky pension and 401K expenditures to finish her own report. They were not just important, they were also *essential* to her work even making sense. How could she recommend that AM Air buy Blue Sky if she couldn't provide debt numbers?

"We're waiting on a few line items and the quarter only just ended," said Jim, the not-so-helpful Blue Sky accountant on the other end of the line.

"The quarter ended more than a week ago, and those numbers should be ready to go. I don't need final numbers. I just need estimates."

"We're doing the best we can," Jim said, though his tone suggested he wasn't actually trying that hard. Juliana suspected, not for the first time, that the numbers people at Blue Sky were stalling. "I'm sorry, but Mr. Mason was fairly clear that we had to check and double-check these numbers before giving them to you."

Robert L. Mason, the mysterious Blue Sky CEO that she'd never met. He seemed always to be out of the office, traveling to satellite offices, never available when she sat in with some of the other top executives at Blue Sky. Juliana almost thought the man was a ghost, or a figment of the other executives' imaginations.

"You tell *Mr. Mason* that I need those numbers *by Monday.*"

"I will, but he's traveling and—" the assistant began.

"And tell him that I'm still waiting to get that one-on-one interview I was promised. I have some questions for him about Blue Sky pension plans." They were held over from the company's first stab at employee retirement. Pensions in general were hard to fund, which was why companies usually opted for 401Ks. Mason had bucked that trend for years, but eventually came to the understanding that he couldn't fund the pensions, just like dozens of other companies. But the company still had obligations to old flight attendants, mechanics and pilots.

"I've put in the request multiple times, Ms. Hart, but I can promise I'll put in another request today. Mr. Mason is a very busy man."

The elevator doors dinged open, revealing the open-cube, sleek offices of Wickham Consulting. The large open floor plan was dotted with glass and metal desks; most of the offices were walled in by glass, so everyone was visible. The floor's big windows looked directly into another high-rise in downtown Chicago, though sunlight did occasionally squeeze in between the two glass behemoths. The idea for the open floor plan was supposed to mean more collaboration, but now the office, as usual, just looked empty. Most of the consultants were doing what they did best: work on site with clients around the world. Juliana nodded at Keisha, the front office receptionist, and went to her corner cube with a tiny sliver view of Lake Michigan. Bright spring sunlight sparkled on the water, making it seem much warmer than it probably was. From the fiftieth floor, cars far down below rushed along Lake Shore Drive, looking like little toy Matchbox versions.

"I'm sure he is, but it's *very* important I speak with him."

A few people nodded at her as she walked in, but

as usual, there were no big smiles. She'd made a
point of keeping her distance. She walked down the
long line of cubes to her desk and noticed some of
the men in a nearby office huddled together, sharing some private joke.

"I'm not sure if I can manage that this week…"

"Manage it," she bit off, barely restraining her
anger. "Or this report will not be done in time for
the board meeting, and then you'll have to tell Mr.
Mason that."

She hung up, frustrated. Did Blue Sky *want* this
merger to go through or not? She'd heard Mason was
100 percent on board with selling the company he'd
built from scratch, but he certainly wasn't acting like
it. Maybe the successful CEO was having cold feet.
It wouldn't be the first time. Juliana glanced over at
her coworkers who'd stopped talking and were staring at her. Caught looking, they abruptly disbanded,
making Juliana think whatever joke they'd been sharing had been about her.

I'm probably just being paranoid, she thought.
They gave her curt nods. She'd made it more than
clear she wasn't the kind of colleague who had time
for idle chitchat. She was here to get work done—period. She slid her laptop bag onto her desk, realizing
she hadn't been here except for the brief pit stop last
week, when Garrison had taken the opportunity to
corner her in the conference room. She hadn't seen
or talked to him since then. She shook herself. She
needed to focus on work, not Garrison.

Juliana strategized about whom to hit next. She needed answers only Mason could give her, and yet he was stalling. But why? Was he hiding something? Maybe Blue Sky wasn't as sound an investment as everyone thought. Of course, her job was to find out. She fired off about a dozen emails, though if the CEO was dodging her, then how could she expect anybody else to answer her requests? She'd just have to keep asking for a meeting. She'd fly to Seattle if she had to. She needed to get those numbers.

She booted up her laptop, scanning the office. Out of the corner of her eye, she saw Garrison engrossed in some meeting in his glass office. She made a mental note to keep tabs on him. The last thing she needed was to find herself alone with him. Juliana's plan was to evade and avoid, do her work, then get the hell out and go to her sister's for dinner.

Then Garrison saw her and made a beeline for Juliana's desk. She tensed and realized how sad that she used to actually look forward to talking with him. Since he'd been one of the few people in the office who didn't seem to care about her "distant and cold" labels. Then again, he was her boss and he had to talk to her, but they'd developed a rapport that she'd thought was friendlier, until Garrison mistook it for far too friendly.

"I wasn't expecting you in today," he said. He looked older. The wrinkles under his eyes more pronounced. And he had dark circles there, as well. Had he had trouble sleeping?

"I hadn't planned on coming in," Juliana said, voice flat. *Take the hint, buddy. I'm not interested.* He hovered over her desk, too close.

"Well, I'd love to hear where you are with Blue Sky. Maybe a quick meeting to go over the details in the conference room?"

Juliana felt bile rise in her throat. The windowless conference room. No, she wasn't going in there. Not today.

"No." Juliana's voice came out sounding too forceful. "I mean, I've got a conference call shortly and then…meetings." Nice one, Juliana. Even her excuses sounded lame. "But I'll email you an update."

Garrison didn't look pleased, but he could damn well be unhappy. Juliana was going to do everything in her power never to be alone with that man again.

Juliana had always thought of herself as self-sufficient, independent, able to tackle any problem. The last role she ever wanted to play was victim, and she wasn't going to start now. Besides, he'd made a play; she rejected him. Now he just needed to *get the hint.*

"I'd love an update when you get a chance and then we can strategize on next steps." Garrison's tone made it clear he wasn't going to be fully happy with an email.

She squeezed her eyes shut and found herself back in the conference room. When he'd cornered her, closed his eyes and tried to kiss her. Why did it shake her up so much? He hadn't actually kissed her. And it wasn't like it was the first time a man at work had expressed interest. But usually they got the hint and left her alone. Garrison seemed determined not to give up.

She'd not led Garrison on intentionally. She searched her memories, trying to figure out if she'd sent him signals that he'd misread. Sure, she'd laughed at his off-color jokes and turned a blind eye when he'd made comments about what she might be wearing. She hadn't told him that when he said she looked good in a new skirt the comment made her a tad uncomfortable. But she'd given him the benefit of the doubt. Assumed that he hadn't meant anything by it. Hell, he was married with two kids in the suburbs. She'd suspected he might be interested, but she'd told herself it was mostly in her head, or it was just a harmless crush. Part of her, especially her awkward inner fourteen-year-old, would always doubt men's attraction to her, anyway. And it had been nice to have an ally in the office, somebody who didn't snicker about her behind her back. She'd never imagined he'd misread the situation so badly.

Garrison moved away from her desk, and Juliana desperately tried to focus once more. Her watch pinged with an incoming text from Law.

How's my frequent flier doing this morning?

Thankful for the distraction, she studied the message a moment. Sure, she'd told him she wanted to keep things simple, but seeing his missive on her phone made her smile, despite herself. She felt isolated and alone in her own office and wanted a real connection with someone. She knew she ought to ignore him. An entanglement would just be messy. And yet she figured, what harm could a little text do?

Wishing I was with you in a bathroom.

That much was true. Juliana remembered Law's strong hands, the urgency, the blissful release. That was what she needed right now. She didn't want to think about Garrison or what she ought to do next. She wanted Law's strong hands to distract her.

That could be arranged.

Juliana barked a laugh, feeling a blush spread across her face.

You could come to my hotel tonight.

Juliana suddenly felt tempted. A night of pure bliss, with a stranger, no strings, no attachments, no complications. She thought about what it would be like to explore Law's perfect body, to distract herself from the mess her work and personal life had become for one night. Then she remembered the promise she made to her sister. It was her birthday, and she'd be driving out to the 'burbs tonight to celebrate with her and her husband. Ugh. She couldn't cancel on her, not when she'd been AWOL for weeks.

Can't. Sister's birthday dinner. The 'burbs.

Come after?

Law didn't give up; she'd give him that much. But was that really a good thing? Garrison didn't seem to give up, either.

Won't be back tonight. Spending the night there.

It was the routine. Her sister plied her with wine and then offered up the guest room. She knew how much Juliana hated to trek back to the city late at night. And she also knew that men gave up easily. A few hurdles, and they backed down, almost to the one.

Law didn't respond. For a minute Juliana thought he was turning out to be like every other man she'd ever dated, easily derailed. It wouldn't be the first time a man had gotten frustrated trying to compete with her hectic schedule.

Then came another message.

How long are you in town?

The man wasn't giving up, after all.

Till Thursday. Have a 5 p.m. trip to Honolulu.

Okay.

Then that was it. She stared at her phone for several minutes, but no new message popped up. No push for another meeting, no suggestion for a dinner date tomorrow night. Nothing. Hmm. Maybe she'd read him wrong. Maybe he had given up. Easily chased away just like all the others. It was why these kinds of distractions were a waste of time. She'd been right, then. But why did she feel a tiny tinge of disappointment in her chest?

Juliana tucked her phone away and tried to focus on the work at hand. Work would save her as it always did from thinking too hard about her personal life. That was the beauty of work. It was difficult, challenging and sometimes frustrating, but work was something she could do something about. Her personal life? How men felt about her? That was entirely out of her control.

She was so far behind and had so much to do before her big presentation in Seattle in less than two weeks. Then she'd have to find time at some point to run out to Michigan Avenue and buy a birthday gift for her sister. No matter how hard she worked, her to-do list never seemed to shrink.

Juliana stood on the doorstep of the quaint three-bedroom Colonial her sister and brother-in-law bought last year in the western suburbs. They'd been city dwellers for years, but had decided they wanted a yard for their dog, Roscoe, and were probably going to start a family soon. It was the worst-kept secret in the family, and her mother called regularly to ask if Juliana had any hint about whether or not Heather and Jason had "news." Juliana felt it was a little unfair and put a lot of pressure on the couple, especially since everyone in the family seemed to want a blow-by-blow update of their sex lives. It was one more reason Juliana was glad she'd focused on her career and didn't have to worry about their mother nosing into her sex life. Nobody wanted to know where *she* was in her cycle.

The big oak panel door swung open and her sister stood there, dark hair up in a sleek ponytail, wearing her suburban casual uniform of yoga pants and half zip pullover.

"Jules! You made it!" Heather gathered her younger sister up in her arms and Juliana went, feeling a little guilty for not seeing her for so long. Work just came first. But her older sister knew that. She looked good—a bit flushed in the cheeks a little and like she might have gained a little weight since the last time she'd seen her—was it longer than a month?

"Of course I did! Happy birthday!" Juliana pulled away from the hug and handed her sister a boutique store bag. She hadn't had time to get a card—or wrap the gift—but the clerk had tied a nice pink ribbon around the handles and she hoped her sister would like the scarf and earrings inside.

"Oh, thank you. You're a sweetie," Heather said, smiling.

"There's the long-lost sister." Juliana's brother-in-law emerged from the kitchen in socked feet, grinning. He pulled her in for a bear hug. Juliana liked Jason. He was sturdy and strong, and wore a big bushy beard, making him look more like a lumberjack and less like a social media consultant. But he owned his own firm, and his clients mostly included local bands and bars, and national motorcycle companies. He often said one of the perks of owning his own company was setting his own dress code. Now he wore a thick red flannel shirt. He looked like he ought to be chopping wood in Canada, not posting messages on Twitter.

"How are you liking the 'burbs?" Juliana asked him. Jason had lived most of his life in the city limits, so being out with the strip malls and grocery stores just didn't seem to fit the independent thinker, but Jason just shrugged.

"I was skeptical at first, but, man, parking is great. And have you seen those gas prices? I mean, seriously. Plus, they opened up a microbrewery down the way, so I can't complain." He held up a bottle with a label Juliana didn't recognize. Normally, she didn't, given that he and Heather were into small craft batch beer. They were always finding something *amazing* named something outlandish. But Juliana loved that her sister had found someone as playful as she was, as young at heart. Heather took Juliana's coat and they hustled inside. The warm spring weather had turned unexpectedly cold, as happened in Chicagoland this time of year.

In the kitchen Juliana instantly inhaled the scent of some amazing homemade pasta sauce, and her stomach grumbled. Heather knew how to cook. Juliana's mom was there, too, busy stirring a pot. Between her mother and her sister, it was hard to know who was the better cook. Both vied to be the Rachael Ray of the family.

"There's my long-lost daughter!" Mom pulled Juliana into her arms and gave her a quick peck on the cheek. "You've been gone *forever*."

"Four weeks, actually, barely a month," Juliana murmured into her mom's hair.

"You mean *eight weeks*, actually," her mom corrected, releasing her from the hug.

Had it been that long? Perhaps it had. She'd made the one stop in the office last week, but when had she last made it out to the 'burbs to see her family? Maybe it had been two months.

"Valentine's Day was the last time I saw you," her mom said. Juliana realized she was right. It had been twice as long as she'd thought. Two months? Eek. Ugh. She was a terrible daughter and sister.

"This Blue Sky project has just been crazy, and…"

"They're all crazy." Mom picked up the spoon and began stirring again. "I worry about your work-life balance, Jules. You need to make sure to take care of yourself, or you'll get sick."

"I'm not sick, Mom." This was a familiar refrain from her mom, who was always concerned about whether or not she got her flu shot every year. She guessed motherly instincts didn't wane, even when a mother's charges were long grown.

"All that travel on those dirty planes? I saw on TV they don't clean those blankets. Don't use those blankets."

"I don't." Juliana sighed. This was nothing new with her germ-phobic, pro-Purell mother. "So what's new with you two?" Juliana glanced at her sister, desperately hoping for a change of conversation.

Jason glanced at Heather, and they both burst into laughter. Uh-oh. Something was up.

"We're pregnant!" Heather exclaimed, excited. Instantly, it all made sense: the flush in her cheeks, the extra weight. The fact that she saw how her sister was drinking water, not the craft beer she adored.

"Oh, congratulations!" Juliana hugged her sister once more, knowing how much this meant to her. She'd been wanting to be a mom since they were both little girls and changing dolls' pretend diapers. Well, Heather changed the diapers. Juliana had been far less interested in playing house. More interested in dressing Barbie up in suits and having her run board meetings at the dream house. But still.

"You are! How far…?" Juliana asked, feeling a little overwhelmed. She just thought…she might have more time before she was an aunt.

"Sixteen weeks!" Both Heather and Jason exclaimed at the same time.

"That far…!" That seemed like a long time. "Mom, did you know?"

"Oh, they told me three weeks ago. I was dying to tell you, but you know, was sworn to secrecy!"

"I told her not to tell you," Heather explained. "I wanted to tell you in person, but…"

"But I haven't been in town in a month… I mean, *two* months," Juliana finished. The fact that her job was interfering in her personal life hit her like a ton of bricks. Her own sister had to wait three weeks to tell her pressing news. Sure, she could've just called or texted, but news like this was meant to be delivered in person. She wondered what else she might be missing out on. And what more she might miss: the next six weeks would be equally packed with travel. Hell, she might even spend most of her sister's pregnancy on the road.

"I'm really happy for you guys," Juliana said, plastering a smile on her face. Mom looked over the moon, and for that, Juliana was glad. Her mother had made it clear how much becoming a grandmother meant to her. Now her dreams would come true.

She watched Jason gently kiss Heather on the forehead, wrapping her into a side hug, and wondered what that would be like: being in a committed relationship, maybe even have a baby. Why did she suddenly feel like the world was moving on without her? That she was stuck in the same place, while everyone else got on with their lives?

She wondered if she'd ever have a serious relationship, much less a baby. She wasn't completely against the idea of a baby. She certainly liked the idea of having a daughter. Someone she could give advice to, maybe suggest careers. A daughter? What on earth was she thinking? She didn't have the time to care for a plant, much less a baby. A flash of Law's confident smile crossed her mind. He'd have beautiful children. What was she doing? Fantasizing about some stranger's gene pool? She shook her head. No. That was crazy. Besides, she had her career to think about.

"How about you, Jules? Dating anybody new?" Mom asked. Heather immediately rolled her eyes.

"Come on, Mom. Leave her alone. You know Juliana doesn't have time to date."

Mom frowned a little, a worry line appearing between her eyebrows. "Yes, but…"

"Come on, give her a break. There's more to life than men. Want to help me make a salad?" Heather asked. Her sister was just being nice, but somehow it just underlined how lopsided her life was. Even her own sister couldn't imagine her in a relationship. She was all work and no play. She thought about Law once more. Well, *a little* bit of play. She almost had the urge to talk about him, but stopped herself cold. What would she tell her family? *You're right. I don't have time to date. But I did have a naughty*

*tryst with a gorgeous man in a tiny little airplane
bathroom Tuesday night.*

Yeah, she didn't think that would go over so well.
Besides, what were the chances she'd ever see him
again?

Juliana packed up her to-go bag the next morning at
her place and got ready to hit the airport again. She
had been thinking about how life changes, about how
much happier her sister looked, about how her mom
had been over the moon about being a grandmother.
She turned down the thermostat in her brownstone
and rushed out onto the street to the taxi waiting
there to take her to O'Hare International Airport. She
zoned out as the taxi driver drove, musing about her
personal life, watching much of Chicago pass by her
window. Her phone dinged with an incoming message from Law.

I'm at the airport today, too. Flying to Seattle. Meet
at the Blue Sky First-Class lobby? I hear they have a
roomy bathroom...

Juliana barked a laugh. Well, maybe she *would*
see him again, after all. He was full of surprises.

Are you coming on to me? she wrote back, fig-
uring flirt mode wouldn't hurt. And besides, what
she really needed was a little distraction. From becoming an aunt, from her insane work schedule...
from everything.

I hope so. Meet me there in an hour?

Juliana was almost to the airport. Make it forty-five minutes, she texted, grinning from ear to ear.

Half an hour later Juliana stood uncertainly outside the sliding glass doors of the first-class lounge for Blue Sky Airlines. Was she really going to go in there? Meet a near stranger and hook up with him in the bathroom? Sweat broke out on her palms. Sure, there'd been the tryst in the bathroom of the plane, but she hadn't *planned* that. She'd not gone into the bathroom with the intent of having sex. This was premeditated public sex. With a virtual stranger, she reminded herself. This was not what she did. She was straight-laced, by the book, strictly no kissing until the third date—usually. Yet now, here she was, doing something out of her comfort zone. So far out of her zone, she might as well be on another planet. She thought about what her coworkers might think if they even knew she was considering doing this. Her moniker of Ice Queen would be melted in a heartbeat.

How much did she even know about the man? Not much. She didn't even know his *last name.* He could be a felon. Hell, he could be…married. Plenty of men traveled without their wedding rings. She'd personally seen Garrison "forget" to wear his at the hotel bar when they traveled sometimes.

But somehow she thought Law was single.

Not that she could find out by Googling him.

"Lawrence" and "Australian" weren't bound to come up with much.

But somehow the *not knowing* made it all the more exciting. She liked the idea of a covert meeting—her, the most straight-laced person she knew, the most uptight, if some of her sorority sisters were to be believed—here about to have sex with a man she barely knew for a second time. Then she caught a glimpse of Law's broad shoulders through the glass sliding doors. He was half standing, half leaning against the front counter, talking to the receptionist behind it. God, the man was a specimen. Blond hair swept back behind his ears, stark blue eyes, broad shoulders and trim waist. He had that ageless quality about him. Oh, she wanted to do this. To hell with consequences. She *needed* this. She needed to be a little bit bad. Who needed a baby and the 'burbs? She could have *this*.

She walked through the automated doors, her suitcase rolling behind her.

"Ah, here she is." Law's accent hit her ears like the throbbing beat of a love song. He turned and smiled and she felt her insides turn warm and gooey. "She's with me," he told the clerk, who nodded quickly as Law reached out to hug her. In his embrace, Juliana remembered how strong his arms were, how good he smelled: like something sweet and savory. Could anyone so good-looking really want to be with her? She couldn't imagine it. Not really. So she'd take what she could. Here. Now.

"Hey," Juliana said, her stomach already tight. How quickly could she get this man into that bathroom?

"Want a drink?"

I want to jump you, she almost blurted, but glanced at the front desk clerk within earshot and changed her mind.

"Sure," she said instead as Law led her into the second set of doors and into the first-class lounge. Juliana hadn't been here before. As a business class traveler she didn't often spend time in the first-class lounge, a place where only the premier Blue Sky customers waited. The lounge itself was beautiful: tasteful, leather furniture, orchids on the small glass tables, small little nooks for working or taking naps and a small bar in the corner offering cocktails and small eats. All of it was far different from the fast food court and the gates crammed with discontented passengers.

Juliana heard piano music, too, and realized the lounge had its own piano player in the corner near the bar, playing relaxing tunes.

"So, this is how the other one percent lives?" Juliana said.

"I suppose." Law flashed her a smile. So white and perfect. She so wanted to kiss those full lips. Her phone dinged.

Where are you? Thought you'd be at work today.

From Garrison. Ugh. She ignored it, but not before Law noticed. "Trouble?" he asked.

"Just a boss that doesn't check his calendar." *Or take a hint.* Why wasn't he understanding the cold shoulder she'd been giving him? Just *leave it*, she wanted to shout.

Call me when you land.

Like hell I will, she thought.

"Then you deserve a double," he said, and led her to the bar, but she grabbed his elbow.

"What about the bathroom?" She stared at his blue eyes, so dark, so fiercely blue, and remembered how they'd look at her when he was deep inside her.

"Don't you want a drink first?" No, she didn't want a drink. She wanted his hands on her body. She wanted to forget all her problems, and she knew, for a few seconds, he'd make them all disappear. Plus, what if they talked and…he realized she was a policy wonk, a serious business nerd, and then want nothing to do with her? He wouldn't be the first man to be scared off by her intelligence. It had happened more times than she'd like to admit.

"Don't know if I have time. Boarding soon." She almost didn't want to look at her watch. It would tell how little time she actually had with Law. He'd soon be back on a flight to Seattle and who knows when they'd ever see each other again?

"But I want to get to know you. I'm not just that easy," he told her and grinned.

"You're not?" Juliana laughed. "Oh, really?"

"No. I mean, you need to take me to dinner first," he joked.

"How about we go to the bathroom now…and I take you to dinner some other time we're in the same city." The words popped out of Juliana's mouth before she thought about the consequences. What was she doing? Setting up a *date* with the gorgeous Aussie who at any time might wake up and realize he could land women much more beautiful than she was. That seemed like a bad idea. Of course, when would they ever meet again? She realized she didn't even know where he lived. It might be Melbourne, for all she knew.

"Deal," he said, grinning. Too late to take back the invite now, she thought. But soon, she didn't care as he led her to the back, where a series of doors hid single-stall bathrooms. He led her into the farthest one, which happened to be the biggest, complete with a shower, a bench and a hair dryer on the wall. The place was bigger than her gym's bathroom, and nicer, with slate tile on the floor and sea glass accents on the wall. He'd barely clicked the lock behind him before she had her mouth on his, eager for the feel of his tongue on hers. He tasted just as amazing as he had on the plane, and she felt her inner thighs warm as she ran her hands through his thick hair. She was untucking his shirt and then unzipping his pants so quickly, she amazed even herself. He had his hands down the back of her stretchy leggings, cupping her bare cheeks in his big hands. Just outside the door, dozens of people sat reading newspapers or their phones, waiting for their flight, oblivious to what was happening between them in this roomy stall. The thought thrilled her. She was being bad, so very bad, and she loved it.

Yes, she thought. Yes, this is what I want. She yanked at her own waistband and stepped out of the tights—her wool tunic now the only thing between them. Then he produced a condom from his pocket, ripping off the wrapper.

"I figured we might need this," he murmured and grinned as he rolled the latex down the length of him. He lifted her and she wrapped her legs around his waist. Soon he was inside her, deep inside, so big for her, and she gasped as he held her up against the cool tile wall. This was it: what she wanted. Mindless animal sex. She didn't even care if she came; all she wanted was to lose her mind, her reason, for a few minutes. To let go of everything. Before she knew it, he came in a hard thrust and then it was all over.

"I'm sorry," he murmured in her ear. "Couldn't hold it. You're…amazing." He let out a breath that she felt on her neck. She almost didn't care that she hadn't come. The sex was so intense, so amazing, she didn't care. She knew it would fuel fantasies of alone time for many nights to come. He withdrew, but then he touched her…there. He rubbed her swollen lips.

"Your turn to come now, my little wildcat," he murmured in her ear.

Wildcat. She liked that. No one had ever called her a wildcat her whole life.

"But...my flight," she whispered. She really didn't have much time. They'd be boarding in fifteen minutes.

"You have time. You always have time for this." He moved the pad of his finger faster and all her nerve endings came alive. Oh, yes, she'd make time for this. His touch felt a little hard, a little rough.

"Softer," she instructed him. "Tease me," she murmured, and he did. He could take direction. She liked that. Suddenly, she liked the idea of teaching him about her body, how it worked, what she liked. His touch lightened, as he barely grazed her swollen nerves. He kept up the light touch, stroking her insistently. The cold air of the bathroom caressed her bare thighs. Yes, this was what she needed. A release, to put her brain on hold for a second. Beneath his sure touch, she suddenly climaxed, her whole body tensing as every muscle contracted, and then released, endorphins flooding her brain, relaxing even the stubborn knot of stress in her shoulder.

"You needed that," he told her.

She nodded as he dipped down to kiss her. Oh, yes, she did.

For most of the flight to Honolulu she worked, and though she was sitting in the plush and a bit roomier business class seat, she found she missed Law. Stupid, really. She'd known him just a couple of days, but the grandmotherly woman with the oversize headphones in the seat next to her just was no substitute. She ought to have been grateful to have the extra time to herself on the flight to work, and yet all she could do was think of Law's intense blue eyes, and the hint of his just-barely-there Australian accent. Imagine how many times they could've gone to the bathroom on this nine-and-a-half-hour flight, she thought: four times? Five? Six? She could test Law's limits; that was for sure. Maybe even her own.

She giggled to herself at the prospect and then wondered what on earth was happening to her. Was she turning into a sex-crazed maniac? Then again, with a body like Law's, it was no wonder she'd become a raving lunatic. His abs were enough to drive any woman wild. She tried to focus once more on work, and was glad to see she could use the plane's Wi-Fi to download new emails so she could keep track of what Blue Sky was sending her—and what it wasn't. Looked like her latest round of calls to the accountant hadn't gotten her the results she wanted. She was still waiting on the numbers she needed to make the presentation in three days. The trip to Honolulu was really the last bit of research she needed to do about customer satisfaction and service. So far, the flight had run smoothly—no delays, impeccable service and a friendly captain who gave regular updates over the intercom.

For the most part, it looked like Blue Sky would pass her review. She just needed the pension reports and the final quarter numbers. Those were the only missing pieces for Blue Sky's financial health and without those, she might as well be flying blind. She became so wrapped up in work that when they landed in Honolulu, it almost took her by surprise.

"That sure went fast," she murmured to the older woman next to her, who'd finally taken off her headphones.

"You think so?" the woman asked, surprised. She clearly hadn't had the benefit of being distracted by pages of spreadsheets. After grabbing her bags from baggage claim she walked out of the open airport to her waiting cab, just as her phone pinged, announcing a new message from Law.

How's my wildcat?

She grinned.

Good. Just landed.

She almost typed *miss you*, but stopped herself. What was she doing? Missing a perfect stranger and then *admitting* it to him? Ugh. This was not a thing she ever did. Yet she had to admit, seeing his name on her phone put a smile on her face. Still, she reminded herself, she was just playing a role. This wasn't really *her*. She was pretending to be the fearless woman who took men when she wanted them. But what would a little text-flirting hurt? She was probably not going to see him again for a long time, if ever.

Headed to her hotel. :)

Which one?

The Hibiscus. Why? You plan on stopping by?

Maybe.

Well, by all means. If you're in the neighborhood.

She giggled to herself. What would he do? Jump on a plane? She'd be on her way back to the main-land by the time he arrived. Maybe she could be bolder with a stranger. He didn't know that she compulsively alphabetized her cereal boxes in the cup-boards back home, that she kept her tidy little condo pristine, though she was never in it, so it was easy to keep neat. She tucked her phone in her bag and jumped into the first cab, which took her to her hotel downtown. She'd never been to Hawaii before, and couldn't help but think how odd it was to have high-rises so close to the ocean. Honolulu was a bustling city, complete with traffic jams and skyscrapers. Juliana wondered how the other islands were. She'd heard amazing things about Maui. Not that she'd get a chance to explore that island this trip.

After a slow cab ride, she finally got to her destination, the gleaming upscale Hibiscus Hotel, which sat nearly on top of the ocean. She checked in and headed up to her floor, where she discovered her hotel suite had a glorious view of the beach and the beautiful, sapphire-blue ocean. She dropped her suitcase on the carpet and glanced at the rolling waves in the distance, the crystal-blue ocean water lapping at the pristine beach lined with palm trees. Her job had perks, she thought. She'd have to work while she was here, sure, but maybe she could do so on her balcony, absorbing that wonderful ocean breeze.

"Wow," she murmured. She looked at the black ledge of lava rocks ringing the sand, and from her vantage point on the tenth floor, the beautiful blue sky stretched out for miles. The Pacific loomed so clear and relatively calm, she could see the reefs lining the bottom of the beach. Vacationing tourists paddle-boarded in the calm water and sunbathers lay on chairs and towels near the beach. She inhaled and the scent of sweet tropical flowers lingered in her nose. The air even smelled beautiful here.

Too bad she was here alone. Too bad Law wasn't here.

What was she doing? Thinking about Law? She ought to be thinking about getting to work. He was already becoming the distraction she feared: this was why she didn't get involved with men. Her work came first. Always.

She yawned, realizing it was nearly 10:00 p.m. Chicago time, but here, the afternoon was in full swing. She'd have to stay up if she wanted to shake the jetlag. She unfolded her laptop and began answering the dozens of new emails that sprouted up in her inbox. Her repeated requests to see the CEO of Blue Sky, Robert L. Mason, had come back with vague and evasive responses. *He's traveling. He's got a full schedule this week. He might be able to do a call at some point.*

They all sounded like weak excuses. Why was Mason avoiding her? Probably because he didn't want to give her the pension numbers.

Her phone rang. She glanced at it, almost hoping for Law's number, but instead saw Garrison's name flash across her screen. She sent him to voice mail. And then he called again. Would he keep calling unless she answered? She sent him to voice mail a second time. Then she watched her phone, but no more calls. She let out a sigh of relief.

It was just a near kiss, not like she was going to report him to HR. Unless he kept hounding her, and she had no choice.

She really just wanted to pretend none of it happened.

Just let it lie, Garrison.

Suddenly, she felt as if she'd been doused in a slick of oil. She wanted a shower…or to get out of this small hotel room that suddenly felt airless. She glanced out once more at the beach. Juliana had never been one to feel comfortable lounging around and drinking fruity drinks at a beach bar, but she could do with a walk down the beach.

She slathered on sunscreen to protect her fair skin and then grabbed her phone and hotel key and headed to the elevator. Once outside, she inhaled the sweet smell of some tropical flower as she walked through the open lobby of the hotel and followed the sound of the sea as she headed to the water.

"Juliana!" Baffled by someone knowing her name, here on an island in the middle of the Pacific, she turned to see Law standing up from a lounge chair by the pool. He wore khaki shorts and a Polo, and wore a pair of aviator sunglasses and flip-flops. She stopped in her tracks, surprised.

"What are you doing here?"

"Surprise." He nodded back at the white hotel looming behind them. "You told me I should drop by if I'm in the neighborhood."

She still couldn't believe it. "You're…here? But… how? Were you headed here?"

"No. Changed my flight from Seattle to here. Had a couple of vacation days I needed to use, and I've got so many miles I go anywhere for free." He flashed her a smile. "I actually just got in. Just unloaded my bag in my room and then came down here."

He flashed a white smile and Juliana felt a tingle at the back of her legs. She was glad to see him, she realized and yet terrified all at once. What happened when he discovered she wasn't the bold, confident woman he thought she was? Maybe she could just fake it. Yet now, here they were on land. No escape in sight—no plane to rush to for a quick getaway.

"So it seems." *I actually don't even know your last name*, she thought, but how could she ask him that? Now? Here? *After I've seen him practically naked. Twice.*

Still, despite all that, in a world that seemed off-kilter, Law somehow seemed grounded and safe. She didn't know if it was because of his old-fashioned notion of soul mates, or his steady blue eyes, but she just felt like she could do anything with him and not be ashamed. After all, with him, she'd been a different person. A more confident person, a woman she wanted to see more of. Law tucked his smartphone into his pocket. She noticed his firm chest, remembered what his muscles had felt like beneath her palms in the bathroom at the first-class lounge. Just hours ago he'd been touching her, making her come. Juliana felt her face grow warm at the memory. Why did she feel like a slave to her own body? Why did this man bring out such need in her?

"Do you want to get a drink?" There, she thought, that wasn't so bad. She almost sounded…sultry. *Maybe I'm getting into this role-playing a little too much.* Then she had another shocking thought: *maybe it's not role-play anymore.*

He smiled. "Actually, I believe you owe me dinner."

They went to a sushi restaurant not too far from the hotel, where Juliana had some of the most amazing spicy tuna rolls she'd ever eaten, along with some of the most flavorful saki. Law seemed intrigued with her, asking her endless questions about where she grew up, what she liked to do, how she'd gotten into consulting. Where she wanted to be in five years' time, and what about her job interested her. She couldn't talk about specific projects, bound by confidentiality agreements, but she did talk generally about how she enjoyed her work, how it changed every day and challenged her. She stopped just shy of admitting that when she wasn't in the professional zone, she felt far less sure of herself. When she had a PowerPoint presentation nearby, she was darn near unstoppable, but put her at a table with a first date and she became like a meek mouse.

"You like the travel?" He dipped a roll in soy sauce and popped it into his mouth.

"I like the challenge," she admitted. "And if I keep moving, it's better. I just…like to be on the move." She picked up her tiny saki cup and took a little sip of the rice wine.

"Me, too." Law studied her. "I think it was because I didn't like the person I was at home very much." He shrugged. "When I moved to the States for middle school, I got picked on a lot."

"You?" Juliana couldn't believe it. This gorgeous, fit man got picked on?

"I was four feet tall when I started high school."

"But you're six feet, easily."

"Now I am." He shrugged one beefy shoulder. "But I was four feet when I was fourteen and I had this Australian accent. Kids used to call me 'little shrimp on the barbie.' It was embarrassing. Once, they hung a smelly raw shrimp and a Barbie doll from my locker. I was too scrawny to really fight back."

"I'm sorry," she said, knowing exactly what that was like. She'd found out the hard way that some boys had nicknamed her "flat top" because she hadn't developed.

"I was five foot one when I graduated, and then grew another foot while I was in college, but those early taunts… I don't know, they still live in here." He tapped his head.

She felt a sudden connection with Law, one she hadn't expected.

"Kids can be cruel. They'd make fun of me all the time, too. I…was a late bloomer." She glanced down at the sushi on her plate. "I didn't even develop until senior year of high school. But by then the wounds are already made."

"I bet you were still beautiful."

She barked a laugh as she dug out her phone and

searched for her old high school photo, one that a friend had recently posted on a throwback Thursday on Facebook. When she looked at the picture she saw the ugly duckling that she was: glasses, braces, no curves. "See?" She showed him the picture and his eyes bugged a bit.

"This is not you."

"It is."

"No *way* this is you." He peered at the old yearbook photo. And then at her. "Wow. You've... changed."

"Not that much." She shrugged. She still had that inner braces-and-glasses-wearing, triple-A-cup girl inside her.

Law quirked a skeptical eyebrow. Then he focused on the photo. "You're pretty cute here, actually, in a teenage, way-too-young-for-me way."

Juliana barked a laugh. "There's no way you're attracted to *that* girl."

"I don't know. I might ask you to wear glasses later."

She giggled a bit, feeling strangely at home with the handsome Aussie across the table. She'd never in a million years showed anyone she ever worked with that photo. She'd die before she'd let a single client know what she looked like in high school. Yet somehow Law seemed different. After all, he'd seen her in a more vulnerable position, naked in the bathroom of a first-class lounge. She realized she'd never directly asked if he was married or not. She realized there was so much about him she didn't know.

"So I know we just met, and I also know that… well, I just wanted to ask, are you…in a relationship?"

Law shook his head. "No, work doesn't allow for it."

"Really?"

"I know it sounds dumb. Like I can't squeeze in a date here or there, but my work life is really busy."

Juliana nodded her head quickly. He might actually understand, she thought. "I get it. I'm the same. My mother is making peace with the fact I might never get married."

"But you don't want to be married, right?" Law asked her as the two walked down the sidewalk to their hotel.

"That's right." Juliana lifted her chin. "I love my work."

And she did, didn't she? She wouldn't want to ease up on her career to find time to date. The two arrived at the hotel, walking up to the open lobby, past giant planters filled with the most colorful flowers Juliana had ever seen. The air was thick with the sweet smell of the tropics.

"Want to get a drink at the bar?" he asked her, but Juliana had other activities in mind. As they walked through the lobby of the hotel, she saw the elevator bank, and her heart thudded harder.

Why bother with formalities? she thought. A

drink wasn't really what she wanted and she was tired of being nice, tired of the formalities of social graces. She'd been the polite, demure good girl her whole life, and it only got her stuck in a conference room with Garrison. Maybe being uncertain of herself, of her own needs, was part of the problem. She liked the throw-caution-to-the-wind version of herself she was with Law.

"Want to go to my room for that...drink?" she asked, feeling suddenly bold as she bit her lip. She was going to ask for what she needed. She was going to get it.

"You know I do." Law's blue eyes turned nearly black, his voice low. An elevator dinged then, announcing its arrival in the lobby. Rashly, Juliana reached out and took Law's big hand. Without a word, he followed her into the elevator as Juliana's heart raced.

She felt like a different person, almost as if she wasn't in control of herself anymore. She knew when she got to her room, she planned to do bad things. Very, very bad things.

Law barely made it inside the elevator before Juliana grabbed his shirt and pulled him to her, their lips meeting in a rush of animal heat. He'd never been with a woman so determined to get what she wanted. Her hands seemed to be all over him, her tongue entwined with his. Boy, the woman could kiss. She drove him wild with the tiny flicks of her tongue, the way she seemed to want to devour him whole. Could he have met a woman with as much passion as he had? He thought she didn't exist, and yet here she was: the woman who'd demanded him on the plane, and the first-class lounge, and now here, at the hotel. She was a ball of barely restrained want.

Not good, mate. He hadn't intended for this to go on so long. He really had wanted to find out about her management style, pick her brain about corporate structure and generally get a feel of her areas of competence, all things that Omar wanted to know. Yet so far, what he was discovering was that she was the best kisser he'd ever met. *Not exactly the professional information Omar needed.*

Something about this woman made his brain shut off. He'd never experienced this before, being so reckless for a woman. He'd always been the kind of person who neatly put all the areas of his life in clearly defined silos, with never any two connecting. That fact hit him hard as the elevator door opened on her floor and she led him by the hand down the hallway. He could feel his ruffled hair where her hands had been. Warning bells sounded in his head: *this is supposed to be about business, but there's nothing businesslike in how you're feeling, you dumb bloke. You're falling for this girl. She's wrapping you around her little finger. Show some self-control.*

He watched the amazing curves of her hips as she walked in front of him, hands rummaging in her small crossbody bag for her keycard. She stopped at a door at the end of the hall and it clicked open. As soon as she walked through the door, she began to shed clothes as if she was fighting a fever, and he realized as she turned to look at him, she burned for him. Soon her clothes pooled in fabric puddles at her feet and she stood naked before him. He lost all ability to speak. Their quickie in the first-class lounge hadn't allowed him the luxury of taking in her amazing curves, the slope of her hip, the flatness of her stomach. He gazed at her in the Hawaiian moonlight filtering in through her open curtains. She walked to him and tugged on his shirt, and he, powerless to stop her, raised his hands as she pulled it off him. She laid kisses down his chest, and he groaned, amazed at the way she aroused every nerve ending in his body. His groin tightened with need as if she magically knew exactly how to bring him to life.

She kissed him as his hands followed the slope of her hips. Her skin was amazingly soft, and she smelled just faintly of something citrus-like and sweet. She found his mouth once more and then all other sensations vanished as he tasted her once more. He was pointedly aware he had a beautiful, naked and willing woman in his arms and the thought made him dizzy. Every woman was a gift, but Juliana was something special. Smart, fierce and uncompromising, she intrigued him. He wanted to know every inch of her. He may have just met her, and yet the way their lips fit together seemed like they had known each other for years. Suddenly, she broke free, tugging him to the made bed behind her, the dim light of the bedside lamp making her hair look like spun gold.

She paused at the edge of the bed and sat down, working his fly. She unzipped him and set him free, and he quivered in her hands as she expertly worked him, the shiny, thick drop of his anticipation beading on his tip. God, was he ready for her. So very ready. But he knew he'd wait. He wanted to explore her body, to worship every inch of her. Having her in the bathroom only felt like a distant dream, and it had been so cramped, so rushed. He was determined not to make the mistake of rushing this. He knelt, moving over her so she lay back on the bed, their naked bodies together, her tiny frame beneath him. She groaned in his mouth, and he broke free of the kiss, worshipping her neck and moving down to her collarbone. Her back arched as her nipples rose to attention against him. He found one and then the other, gently flicking their pink tips with his tongue, watching her breath catch in her throat. Blood rushed to her face, and she grabbed the coverlet, fisting the fabric between her fingers. But he wasn't done yet. Not by a long shot. He suckled her, one side and then the other, and she gasped, arching her back. He moved even lower then, pressing his lips gently against the flat, soft skin of her stomach. She smelled so good. Like some fresh citrus scent, pushing him downward. He found her bare mound, and gently nuzzled her as he slowly slid her knees open. She propped herself up on her elbows, a question on her face. But he already knew the answer. Yes, he wanted to go there. He wanted to make her thrash with pleasure, and this was where that started. He dipped down, slipping his tongue into her and she groaned aloud, her head falling back on the bed. Her knees spread wider as he worked her with his tongue, not too hard, a gentle, teasing motion he hoped would drive her wild. Her knuckles turned white as she gripped the covers even stronger, her breathing coming in sharp staccato bursts. He felt her whole body tense and knew she was close. So very close.

Her whole body went tense then, back arched, fingers clenched as she moaned, and then, as she hit the peak of her climax, she let out a high-pitched cry as her body went limp back against the bed. He'd never seen a woman look so beautiful before at that moment of release. He kissed the inside of her thigh and she quivered, like an instrument he knew exactly how to play. She sat up, eyes never leaving his.

"Your turn," she commanded, and rolled over him as they switched places, he lying on the bed, and she straddling him. He loved how she took charge, how she knew what she wanted and demanded it. She slunk down the length of his body then, and he felt his stomach lurch as she took him into her mouth. This woman was fearless, in control. He loved that.

Oh, God. She felt so warm and wet as she worked his tip, and he worried he might not be able to hold it. She was so very good at that. Surprisingly good. He leaned back, closed his eyes and let her do her marvelous work as he grew rock-hard against her tongue. More of this and he wouldn't be able to last long enough to be inside her, where he desperately wanted to be. He put a hand on her shoulder, and she released him, meeting his eyes and nodding. It was time.

She grabbed a condom from the bag at her bedside, her turn to come prepared. All he wanted was to be inside her once more, to feel her depths, to make her head drop back in ecstasy a second time. She rolled it down him as he trembled in her deft hands and then straddled him, bold, in control. She rode him, grinding into him, squeezing him as he lay pinned, wonderfully helpless beneath her. He watched as she took what she needed, riding him until she came a second time in a hoarse shout. Her terms, he thought. She came on her terms. She leaned down to kiss him and gently bit his lip. He growled and flipped her. Now it was his turn. He pinned her to the bed, pushing deeper into her, straining for more, each hard thrust faster, exactly the way he liked it. She wrapped her legs around him, inviting him in and he went, each push more urgent than the last. He came, like a molten river overflowing its banks, unable to contain himself any longer.

Sweaty and spent, he collapsed on her bare chest. She, like he, was breathing hard, sweat trickling down her temple. He ran five miles a day, but damn if he felt like fifteen minutes with her was like a marathon.

"Forget the drink," he murmured as his breathing slowed. "I need a cigarette."

She laughed in her throat as he felt the laugh rumble her stomach.

"By the way, I'm normally not this…easy," he murmured.

Juliana shifted beneath him. "Well, I did buy you dinner this time," she joked. "The least you could do was put out."

Now it was his turn to laugh. She joined him, and he loved the clear sound of her laughter, like a bell. Here, with her in his arms, he felt…whole. This was what his life needed. Amazing sex—and a real connection. All he wanted to do was rest a little and then do it again. Her phone dinged, then, breaking the moment. She reached out for it, but was too far from the nightstand to reach it. Reluctantly, he rolled off her, setting her free. He moved next to her on the bed, slipping off the condom.

He saw two words on her screen:

Call me.

She instantly became brisk as she reached for her clothes. Now she was all business. Who was demanding her attention on her phone? He couldn't see the name and she quickly hid the screen. Another conquest? he wondered. Another stranger?

Jealousy flared in his chest as he watched her. She rose, tugging on her tunic. Was she all done? He certainly wasn't. In another couple of minutes he'd be ready for round two. Maybe even round three after that.

"Where are you going?" he asked, almost scared of the answer.

"Sorry, got to run," she said, all business. Juliana looked distracted as she searched the floor for her leggings. She ran a hand through her hair as she lifted the comforter and checked beneath the bed. She retrieved the leggings and began pulling them on.

"So soon? But I thought we could…" *Talk. Share things. Bond. Then try a few more positions in the Kama Sutra.*

"Oh…" Juliana seemed like she'd woken up from a dream, as if looking at him for the first time. "Oh, you know… I've got a lot of work and…"

And someone's asking you to call them. Another lover?

Her phone dinged again. Same man, he wondered. Or different one?

"Come on. Stay." He sat, bare naked on her bed. It's not like she could make him put clothes on.

"No, I should go to bed early and…" He noticed there was no invite for him to stay. She flashed him an uneasy smile.

"I get it," he said. "You're trying to get rid of me." She shifted on one foot. "You had your fun and now you're done."

She didn't contradict him, which told him he'd hit on the truth. He crossed his arms in front of his bare chest. She wouldn't look at him. Wow, but she really *was* all about the casual sex, and forget everything else. He'd thought they'd had such a connection at dinner. Surely, she'd felt it, too? For him, this wasn't just about the sex. But she clearly felt differently.

"Okay, then. I'll leave, but I want to ask you a question first."

"What is it?" Juliana glanced up, unsure.

"How many other men are you seeing right now?"

CHAPTER SIX

JULIANA FELT LIKE she'd been punched in the gut.

"What do you mean?"

"I'm surely not the only man you've picked up on a flight."

Juliana felt blindsided. Was he saying she was… easy? "I never do that."

"No? It seems like you sure know what you're doing. If you don't want a real relationship, then that's fine. I just want to know how many others there are."

She felt hurt by the accusation. "Who do you think I am?"

"I think you're a woman who jumped me in an airplane bathroom. I loved it, but I'm also not stupid, either."

"What's that supposed to mean? You think I do that all the time?"

"I don't know if you do or not."

"It's none of your damn business." She glared at him. If she chose to sleep with every single man on a 747, it was *still* none of his damn business. What was this? 1880? Did he suddenly care how many notches she had in her bedpost? Even though, she had to admit, she had precious few.

"So there are others."

"No others." Juliana clenched her teeth. Why did this suddenly have to become a referendum on how many men she slept with? After all, she could sleep with as many as she wanted. Also, she really didn't want him to know that it had been nearly two years since she'd slept with anyone at all. And much longer than that since she'd had someone who slept with her and called her the next day. Her track record with men was beyond abysmal. She didn't want him to know that.

"Then who was asking you to call him?"

Juliana flinched. "You read my phone?"

"I tend to do that when a woman tries to run out on me," Law said, blue eyes sharp, not missing a thing.

"It's not like that."

"Then what's it like?" Law pressed. He wanted to know, and the urgency in his need to know rubbed Juliana the wrong way. Why did he care so much? She felt on the spot and exposed, and she didn't like the feeling. What did he want her to say? *No one wants me. No one but my pudgy old boss.*

"I think you should go now," Juliana said, suddenly keenly aware she wore no bra beneath her tunic. How could she have been so rash? Inviting this stranger into her room.

"Are you in love with someone else?"

"No." That was the truth. She pressed her lips in a firm line as if to prove her point. "I told you, I don't believe in love."

"You've never been in love?"

Juliana didn't want to talk about her dreadful love life, about her one serious college boyfriend who dumped her because she'd been his first and he wanted other experiences, or her string of no-go relationships since then. She spent all her time at work, and yet she was determined *not* to start a relationship there. She'd seen too many other colleagues get burned by office romance gone wrong. Not that she had many workplace offers. She had a habit of telling coworkers when they were wrong, not exactly the way to attract men in her experience.

"Love is a fairy tale. For kids."

Law frowned, displeased. She was afraid he would argue with her, but then suddenly, he seemed resigned to letting her have her way. "All right." He reached for his shorts and stabbed one leg in them. "I'm going."

His demeanor suddenly seemed cold. She felt a thick disappointment in her throat. He wasn't going to argue; he was going to do as she asked. But was being alone what she really wanted? She felt torn as she watched him tug on his shirt.

"I'm going down to the bar for a drink," he told her. "Join me if you want to talk."

He ran a hand through his thick blond hair and

stood. She almost wanted to tell him to stay, yet part of her knew that would be a mistake. He was gorgeous, model-gorgeous, and she was a seven on her best day. How could he really want her once he got to know her?

She watched him slip out of her hotel room, shutting the door with a faint click. She let him go, all the while feeling a gnawing sensation in her stomach. Was the man actually jealous? She didn't understand. He could have any woman he wanted, so why did he care who she slept with?

Then her phone rang. She glanced at the face of it. Garrison was calling. She felt like a fight, so she picked up.

"Jules." He sounded almost like a scolding father. "We need to talk."

No, we didn't. Just...leave it, Juliana wanted to shout. *Just let's pretend none of it ever happened, and make sure that it never, ever happened ever again.* But Juliana didn't say a word. She was almost afraid if she opened her mouth, she'd start yelling and not be able to stop.

"No, we don't." Her voice sounded clipped, annoyed. Her patience with Garrison had dwindled to nothing.

"You landed okay?"

Why do you care? "Yes," she said instead. *Garrison is still my boss. He could still fire me.*

"Good. Why did you change your flight? I thought

we were going to head to Honolulu together tomorrow. Check out the flight together."

Garrison had floated that idea *before* the conference room. Afterward, Juliana had changed her flight by a day. No way was she going to sit next to Garrison for nine and a half hours.

"I don't want to talk about it." And she didn't. Was he really going to make her spell it out?

"Listen, Juliana, come on. Don't be like this."

"Look, you don't have to worry about me telling anyone, okay? I get it—you made a mistake. You were under stress, whatever, okay? Let's just forget it ever happened, and make sure it doesn't happen again, and we'll all be fine. You don't have to worry about it."

"Is that why you think I'm calling? You think I'm worried you'll tell someone?"

"Of course you are! I mean, look, I get it. It was a mistake. Things happen. We're human, right? But let's just stop it now, and go back to how things were and nobody gets in trouble. You can start from here on out being a good husband to your wife, and then it's all water under the bridge. We'll just avoid each other and everything will be okay."

A long pause met her on the other line. Was he finally getting the message? Would he finally leave her alone now? Please, she thought. Please.

Then Garrison spoke. "But what if I don't want to avoid you?"

What was he saying?

"I know I shouldn't have tried to kiss you, but you do crazy things to me. You drive me crazy."

He seemed to be implying that *his* lack of control was all *her* fault somehow.

"Look, Juliana, don't put on that ice queen act with me." Juliana ground her teeth. "There's something between us. Don't fight it," he said, his voice a little off, his wording slow.

"Have you been drinking?" she asked him.

"Maybe."

"Look, I'll cut you a break. You've been drinking. But when you sober up, just remember. There's nothing between us. Won't ever be anything between us. Also, you're married."

"Things between my wife and me are complicated, you know that. You know we haven't had sex since our daughter was born…" Juliana wanted to hang up right now. She felt complicit instantly. She'd listened to him rattle on about his cold wife, hadn't she? About how horrible she was to him? She thought she'd just been being sympathetic, but now she realized he took that to mean she was interested in him in a way she'd never intended.

"Garrison, keep things professional, okay? No more…" Flirting. Stupid sex jokes. Trying to steal kisses. "Just…leave it alone."

"Juliana. There's something between us. Sh-stop fighting it."

God, he was drunk. Her boss had drunk-dialed her! This nightmare was just getting worse.

"No." Her voice was low and soft. But she doubted he'd hear her even if she screamed. "Don't do this." *Don't make me call HR. I don't want to do that but I will.* "You need to keep our relationship about business. Nothing more. I told you that already. I don't want to have to report you."

"You wouldn't do that."

"Don't try me, Garrison."

"But…you drive me wild." His voice suddenly became gruff. Where was he? Where was his wife? "I know this can't just all be in my head."

But it is.

"You're married," Juliana said, pinching the bridge of her nose, suddenly feeling a headache coming on. "Garrison, I don't want to talk about this anymore. Please, just don't, okay? If it's not about work, don't bring it up. And go sober up, okay?"

Then she hung up. Hung up on her boss who was almost old enough to be her *dad*. Her hands shook as she dropped the smartphone down on the comforter of the bed. She waited, frozen, fearing he'd call her right back. But he didn't. Juliana's heart thudded in her chest and she felt like she was back on the plane, when she'd felt like she was about to have a panic attack. *Get a hold of yourself.*

Why didn't he take the hint? Why was he going to make her call human resources? Why wouldn't he just leave it alone? Now he was drunk, too, and might just claim he never remembered any of it. She thought about how he'd spin her complaint, and did she have any real proof? Even if she did, she hated reporting him to HR. She was a big girl, and she could handle her own problems. She was nobody's victim.

Not to mention, a part of her feared what they'd ask her. *Why did he think you'd be interested? Did you flirt with him? Laugh at his inappropriate jokes?*

She knew she'd been friendly. Laughed at jokes she should've told him were wrong. But frankly, some of them were funny. It didn't mean she'd green-light an invitation to touch her. She glanced at her phone. She should call HR. Her finger hovered over the call button. But if she did, would she be labeled a troublemaker? Somebody no one wanted to hire? Besides, she realized as she glanced at the clock, the business day in Chicago was long done. Still. She knew Jennifer in HR. She'd email her. Just a quick message.

Call me tomorrow if you can, she wrote out on her phone and hit Send.

She sat back, looking at her email inbox on her phone screen.

She should find a new job. But then again, she'd never been paid nearly as much as she was paid at Wickham Consulting. Was she ready to walk away from six figures? What if she couldn't find another job like this one? Her last gig paid a third less.

Not to mention, bonus checks would be cut in six weeks. If she could hang on until then at least, she'd have enough to pay off her credit card bill and buy herself a nice, toasty vacation to the Bahamas. If she left now, she could kiss twenty percent of her salary goodbye. That was the cold fact of the matter. Six weeks? Surely she could hold on till then.

So she'd give him *one* last chance. That was all. Maybe when he sobered up in the morning, he'd realize he made a horrible mistake, and he'd leave her alone, and things could go back to where they were.

One more chance, she thought. And if he's not gotten his act together in six weeks, she'd walk.

It sounded like a plan. A good one.

Yet why did she feel hollow inside? She slumped down on the bed feeling very much alone. There was one person, however, who'd offered to help, or at least offered to listen. She thought of Law sitting at the bar. Then again, he'd also implied she slept around. Then again, could she blame him for drawing that conclusion since she'd gotten naked an hour after meeting him?

At any rate, she needed a drink. A stiff one.

Law ordered his second Old Fashioned, keenly aware he was the only tourist in the poolside bar who didn't have an umbrella in his drink, but his sour mood didn't exactly welcome a mai tai or piña colada. He knew he'd pushed Juliana too hard, but he also knew that he'd made a mistake letting her drag him into her hotel room without slowing down the pace. What could he expect from her? He'd been a willing participant in casual, no-strings sex, and then he expected her to be open to a more serious relationship? And since when did he *even want* a serious relationship with a hard-driving, corporate-ladder climber?

Juliana went against everything he had planned for. What about the pretty model or actress he wanted to marry? Someone as far away from the corporate world as he could get. He was tired of spreadsheets and payroll and board of directors meetings, and falling for Juliana would be a mistake. He'd dated women executives and consultants before. In his experience, they weren't very good a work-life balance, and he, more than anything, wanted a *balance.* He'd slogged away on the work half of his life for far too long.

Maybe Omar had been right, though. Maybe this was all about bruised ego. When was the last time a woman had told him no? Maybe he'd just be satisfied if she stopped running away from him.

This is supposed to be about business. How did I lose my perspective so fast?

He knew how. Juliana Hart and her light brown eyes, that was how.

He rattled the single oversize whiskey ice ball in the middle of his glass and took another sip of his cocktail, the warmth of the whiskey coating his throat on the way down. He glanced at the bright blue pool in front of him, ringed with tourists lying in the sun. Beyond that lay a stretch of pristine beach outlined with the dark lava rocks that made these islands so special. He watched the waves roll gently up the sand and wished he could appreciate the beauty of this place more. Law knew on some level he was being a hypocrite, too, asking Juliana to open up to him when he was keeping a pretty damning secret of his own. How would she react if he told her who he really was? *I'm the CEO of the company you're evaluating. Just FYI.*

What was he *doing*? He prided himself on being a smart man, yet he'd made a number of really dumb decisions. How did he *think* this was going to end with Juliana? When she found out he lied to her?

Law shook his head. He took another deep dreg of his drink. Then, out of the corner of his eye, he caught movement. He glanced over to the hotel lobby and saw Juliana, stunning in a fresh cornflower-blue sundress, her dark hair up in a messy bun. She sent him a faint smile, tentative, even as his heart sped up in his chest. How did that woman get prettier every time he saw her?

"Do you mind if I join you?" she asked, hesitantly standing next to the bar stool near him. Law jumped from his seat.

"Of course, please." He pulled out the stool near him and she slid on top of it, the light fabric of her dress settling around her knees. Such gorgeous knees, he thought. They matched the rest of her. But what he really wanted was to get to know her beautiful brain. Was she willing to talk? Open up to him? "What can I get you?"

"I don't know." She hesitated. "Maybe a mai tai?"

"Sure thing." He signaled the bartender and ordered. Shortly after that, Juliana sat sipping a rum cocktail in a tiki-shaped glass.

"Listen, I'm sorry for what I said before," Law began. "I didn't mean to imply…"

"That I'm a slut?"

Law cringed. "I'm sorry. I just… I hate the idea of you being with another man." He swallowed hard. "It's me being stupid. I'm sorry. I just… I care about you."

Juliana glanced at him, sharply. "You do?"

"You intrigue me, and I want to get to know you," he said. "I have no right to tell you who to sleep with or not, and I don't care how many partners you had… or have." He shook his head. "I just want to be with you. Whatever way that works for you."

"There are no other men," she said. "Only the fat, old ones are interested."

"That's not true." Law studied Juliana's face. Could this sexy woman really think she had no worth? "Unless you only work with fat, old men."

Juliana laughed a little. "No," she said. "Not all of them are fat or old. It's just, at work I have a reputation for being a bit cold, I guess."

He remembered her hot, wet mouth on his. She was anything but cold.

"They call me the ice queen."

Law laughed, even though he'd already heard that bit of gossip. "You're the opposite of that."

"Am I?" she challenged him. "Or maybe I'm just pretending with you."

"You can't be faking it, love," Law said. "I'd know." He felt certain about this. She was red-hot, and that level of passion couldn't be faked. She was the furthest thing from an ice queen.

"It's been a long time since I even slept with anyone," Juliana admitted. "More than a year, actually."

Law nearly choked on his drink. "That long? W-why?" She'd have to be fighting men off every day.

"I'm focused on work." She nodded once, staring at her drink. "Work used to be easier to understand than men."

"What about the text message?" Law asked, hating that he sounded like a jealous teenage girl. But he couldn't help himself.

"That...well, that's...complicated."

Law sucked in a breath. *Here goes*, he thought. *Here's where she tells me she's in love with someone else.* His stomach tightened at the thought. She took another long drink.

"You're involved with someone," he began, hoping to rip the Band-Aid right off. If she was taken, if his growing feelings for her were a waste of time, he wanted to know it right now.

"No, I'm not." She took a long drink of her mai tai, the ice rattling against the side of her glass. He released a breath. She wasn't taken; that was good news.

She took a deep breath.

"Garrison, my boss, tried to kiss me. Last week."

Law struggled to register what she was saying. "Wait…are you seeing him?"

"No! God, no." Juliana shook her head. She glanced at her drink, studying the liquid in the glass.

"Do you want to be?"

"No, I don't. I'm not even attracted to the man. He's too old for me and…" She squeezed her eyes shut. "It's partly my fault. I was being extra nice. You know, he's my boss. But he took that to mean I like him, too."

"So? What did you tell him?"

She took another deep dreg of her drink. "I told him to stop it. I didn't like him like that. But he drunk-dialed me just now."

Law whistled low. "The man has it bad for you." That he understood. He couldn't imagine how every man might at some stage fall in love with Juliana. The woman was gorgeous, smart and fierce. No wonder her boss was mooning over her.

"I shouldn't even be telling you any of this," she muttered, shaking her head.

"You've got to tell someone," he said, not bothering to fight the fact that he wanted to know more. "Keeping things bottled up inside… It's not healthy."

She nodded, her anxious blue eyes flicking to him, and then back to her drink.

"What happened?"

Juliana bit her lip, a stray dark wisp coming free

from her bun and falling across her forehead. She angrily swept it away. "He…he grabbed my arm and pulled me toward him. I was sure he tried to kiss me. In the conference room."

"What did you do?"

"I just got out of there. I don't think I even said anything right then. I should have."

"You were in shock."

"Yeah, but still. I told Garrison over the phone not to do that again, but he doesn't seem to be taking no for an answer." She shrugged one small shoulder. She looked so vulnerable then, so in need of protecting. Law wanted to tell her she'd have nothing to worry about ever again. He'd make sure of that.

"That's not okay. None of that is okay."

Law felt the stewing anger boil up in him. The man clearly crossed a line with Juliana—a confident, assured woman who would damn well *let* you know if she was interested. Imagining a man pushing himself on her made Law want to punch him in the nose.

"Are *you* okay?"

Juliana hesitated, which told Law all he needed to know. Law put one arm around her and she leaned into him against the bar.

"I don't know why it's affecting me so much. He didn't even kiss me, just tried. I feel… I don't know, like I shouldn't let it get to me. It's not that big of a deal, really. Other women have had way worse."

"It's not the near kiss that's bothering you. It's

that he's not taking no for an answer. You're worried about what he might do next and I don't blame you. What if it's worse the next time?"

Juliana gave a swift nod. "What if he keeps drunk-dialing me? What do I do?"

"I'd report him." At Blue Sky, Law made sure the company kept a zero tolerance policy on sexual harassment. That just had no place in the workforce as far as Law was concerned, whether that was among plane mechanics or CFOs. He'd fired his CFO last year after he'd badgered an intern at the holiday party, trying to pressure her to meet him in the coat closet. He didn't care if the man had had too much to drink. He was a grown man, with a wife and two kids at home. He should've known better.

"But what if he claims he doesn't remember any of that? What if he says it never happened and they believe him? You know people who are blackballed. They're labeled complainers and then they can't ever get another job."

Law wished he could solve this problem for her, but knew he couldn't. "What do you want to do?"

"I don't know. It's complicated."

She finished her drink and glanced out at the ocean. "Want to go for a walk?" she said, nodding to the beach and deftly changing the subject.

"Sure," he said as he signed the bill the bartender had left near them with his room number and followed her out to the beach, where a brilliant moon hung in the sky.

* * *

Juliana was already regretting telling Law anything about her situation. What was she doing baring her soul to a virtual stranger? Juliana knew why she'd told Law, though. He seemed safe, despite the fact that they'd only just met. The way their bodies seemed to fit together, the gentle, loving feel of his caress, she knew he'd take good care of her somehow. She trusted him. She knew she had no reason to do so—they'd only just met—yet, part of her felt like they'd known each other longer. Maybe it was the shared bullying in high school. Who knew?

Juliana shook the thought away. She just needed a release, that was all. Law was nothing more than a distraction, a way of avoiding her problems with Garrison. It had been her way of trying to take back a little bit of control in her life that Garrison had taken from her—nothing more. Law gently held her hand in his as they walked down the beach, now bathed in moonlight. The wind whipped the waves up in the distance, creating small white foam caps on the water flowing onto the secluded white-sand beach. As he walked beside her, she was hyper-aware of every move he made, the slightest swing of his arm near hers, the length of his stride as their feet sank into the sand. Juliana paused, kicked off her flip-flops and dug her bare toes into the cool sand. The sensation felt good and she reached down and picked up her sandals, swinging them from her left hand as they both walked to the water. His had felt warm on hers, strong and safe. Her troubles with Garrison seemed miles away. He walked her to the edge of the open beach and they climbed up on an outcropping of black lava rock, the tide splashing against the hard peaks.

The silver moon bobbed above the ocean, reflected in its waves. Juliana took in a deep breath and exhaled, happy to live in the moment, happy not to worry about what might happen next. Just breathe, she told herself and inhaled once more. Law studied her profile, and Juliana could feel the weight of his blue gaze.

"I care about you, Juliana."

She scoffed. "You just met me."

"I know what I like." He squeezed her hand and the hairs on her forearm stood up, her body reacting to him instantly.

Are you sure you even know me? Juliana wanted to say, but didn't. *I've just been playing a role with you. One where I'm fearless, but I'm really not.*

"Are you seriously talking about a relationship? I don't even know where you live."

"Seattle," he answered quickly.

Juliana barked a laugh. "Seattle! I'm in Chicago. How could we possibly even think about having a relationship? You're hundreds of miles away."

"I fly all the time and so do you. We could meet up."

"In bathrooms and hotels?" She couldn't keep the skepticism out of her voice.

"Maybe." A smile tugged at the corners of Law's mouth. Juliana had to admit that sounded like fun.

"That's crazy." She tugged her hand away and turned from him, hopping off the lava rocks and back onto the beach, as her toes sank in the wet sand. "Even if I did believe in love, which I don't, I don't even know your last name."

He laughed a little. "We could change that right now."

"Only if I plan to see you again."

"I want to see you again, Juliana. But I think there's something I should tell you," he said, and it sounded serious, too serious for this moment.

"Is it going to ruin this view?" she asked him, suddenly worried he planned to tell her something awful: like he was married, after all.

"It might," he said, hesitating.

"Then don't." She squeezed his hand hard.

"Juliana…"

"Look, let's just keep it simple, okay?" Juliana glanced at him quickly once and then looked at the dark waves before them. "What happens in Honolulu stays in Honolulu."

"You know I want more than that."

"I don't know if that's a good idea."

"Give me one reason why having the best sex of your life *isn't* a good idea." A slow smile spread across Law's face and Juliana had to admit, he did have a point there.

"You don't know me. Not really."

"I know what I need to know."

Juliana shook her head.

"I'm a big boy. I know what I want." His stark blue eyes flashed in the sunlight, and she had to admit, his chiseled good looks were pretty persuasive.

"I'll think about it," she managed.

"Juliana." The seriousness of his tone made her take note. "I have to tell you something. I'm not who you think I am."

"Is this where you tell me you have a secret identity as a crime-fighting superhero?" Juliana laughed anxiously. "Or that you're a felon?"

"No. Neither." Law pulled away from her. "I'm not a random stranger."

Juliana felt the hairs on the back of her neck stand up. What was he talking about? They'd only met days ago. He was definitely a stranger. He glanced at her, the moonlight making his blue eyes look even bluer.

"I'm Lawrence Mason."

Juliana blinked fast. Was she supposed to know that name?

"Robert Lawrence Mason."

Then it clicked. Robert Mason. The president and owner of Blue Sky.

CHAPTER SEVEN

JULIANA FELT HOT and cold all at once. *Robert Mason?* The man she'd been trying to get a one-on-one meeting with since her consulting gig with Blue Sky started and she'd fucked his brains out in her hotel room hours earlier.

"That can't be." Juliana's heart raced. She jumped to her feet, feeling vulnerable, exposed…and betrayed. The harsh sound of the waves crashing on the shore sounded angry and loud.

"It is. I wanted to tell you earlier, but…"

The wheels in Juliana's mind clicked forward as she raced to understand this new bit of information. "And if you told me then I wouldn't tell you what you wanted to know about the Blue Sky report."

Law hung his head. "I don't even care about the report anymore."

"Anymore." That implied that at one time he had cared about the report. Deeply.

"Was it an accident we even met at the gate in Chicago?"

"I was there on purpose," Law said. "Waiting for you. I had asked the gate attendant to sit us together before you even arrived."

Juliana felt like she couldn't breathe. She'd allowed herself fun with a stranger and now she realized she'd been played. She thought of all the awful ramifications: if Garrison found out, he could have her fired, for one. Fraternizing with clients or client associates was strictly against company rules. Not to mention, the objectivity of her report could be called into question by AM Air, which could jeopardize the entire account. AM Air could cry foul, fire them and then demand a full refund for their trouble. Juliana felt a tension headache coming on, pressing at her temples. Her ice queen reputation would be melted overnight. She dreaded to think about what people in the office would call her now.

"You lied to me." She still couldn't believe it. The one time in her life she did something risky, something just for *her*, something…naughty…and it turns out to be the very thing that could trash her career forever. Oh, the irony.

"I didn't exactly lie," Law said. "I just omitted a few important details. And you didn't ask what I did. You asked me what I was passionate about."

Well, that much was true. Why had she not asked him more questions about his job? Maybe on some level, she just didn't want to know. She hadn't wanted to get to know him, and now…this.

Law stood, moving toward her. "Let's go back to the hotel. Let's talk about this."

"No." She shook her head as she began move away from him, putting distance between herself and him and the ocean. "Do you understand how bad this is for me? I could lose my job."

"You won't lose your job. I won't tell anyone."

She flashed him a doubtful look. "You won't tell anyone as long as I make sure to write a favorable report for Blue Sky? As long as I don't do anything to risk the merger?" She jabbed a hand on her hip.

Law looked taken aback. "No. I wouldn't ask you to compromise your work. That's not the kind of man I am."

"No, you'd just sleep with analysts for what...? Insider information?"

And he had it, she realized. *He knew her boss sexually harassed her.* Her head spun. How could he use that? Would he use it to discredit her? Her consulting firm? The very report she was working on? She felt sick to her stomach.

He sighed. "No. I really just wanted to know *you.* I'd heard about you from reputation, but I wanted to see for myself."

"Then why not just *schedule* a meeting with me? I'd been trying for weeks."

"People put on fronts in meetings," he said. "I wanted to know the real you. But trust me when I tell you that I never thought it would get personal. I never planned this." He spread out his hands. "And *you* came on to *me*."

Juliana blinked fast. This much was true. She'd practically attacked him in the bathroom of the plane and then it had been her idea to drag him to her hotel room yesterday. Ugh. This was her fault at least in part. The night breeze off the ocean turned cooler suddenly.

"Maybe I wouldn't have done that if I'd known who you really were." She clasped her arms across her chest. Why with men was everything a deception? She'd thought Garrison was a friendly ally, but then he betrayed that trust. And now here, Law was betraying her, too.

"You didn't exactly give me time to explain if I remember right." Law cocked his head. "Please. Juliana. What we have here is more than any stupid report or merger. I never intended for it to get personal, but when it did… I didn't want it to stop."

Juliana felt herself being drawn in again; the man's gaze was hard to break. He looked so earnest there, standing barefoot on the beach, the stars bright in the sky above them. Could he be telling the truth? Had he not intended for it to go so far? Did he really care about her? Or was he just after information and…leverage? She didn't know, couldn't know, and she had no time to figure it out right now. She had to get her head back in the game, and get back to work. She still had a report to write, and a board meeting in less than a week now. She had more work than she could possible do, and she couldn't let trying to figure out Law's true feelings about her become the distraction that derailed her. Even though she could lose her job, anyway, she had to try to finish. This was why she hated personal entanglements. They never went according to plan and they always took her eyes off the prize. If she hadn't been so attracted to Law, so blinded by lust, she might've made a more rational choice. She'd let her feelings, her desires, get in the way of her work. She vowed never to let that happen again.

"I need to go," she said.

"Juliana," Law pleaded. He took a step toward her and she tried not to take in his impressive physique and remembered how well their bodies fit together just hours before. But did they have more than just a physical connection? How could they after this kind of betrayal? How could she even trust him? He reached out and touched her arm. "Please, don't go."

"I have to." She couldn't look him in the eye. "Please don't say anything about this to anyone. I'll lose my job if you do."

"I won't," Law promised, though she wasn't sure how well she could trust his word. "But we need to talk about this."

"Not now." Maybe not ever, Juliana thought.

Juliana's plane touched down at Chicago O'Hare International Airport Monday morning and she still felt numb. The entire flight she'd barely gotten any work done as she'd gone over every last conversation she'd had with Law. She still couldn't get over the feeling of betrayal. *He'd used me*, ran in a loop through her head. Should she have guessed who he was? What had he asked her about her work? Barely anything, she realized. Plus, if his motives were entirely business, then why did he admit to her who he was? It would've been easier for him to play her if she didn't know who he was.

Still, he used her. He'd deliberately "bumped" into her so he could figure out what she planned to say about Blue Sky. The fact she'd literally jumped him in the bathroom only made her face burn with embarrassment. She'd played right into his hands! She'd practically given him everything he wanted and more.

She felt like that awkward girl in high school again, the easy target.

Then again, hadn't she used *him*, too? Hadn't he been the distraction she'd needed to take her mind off Garrison? Inwardly, she groaned as the plane pulled into the gate and the flight attendants turned off the fasten seat belt sign and everyone began gathering their belongings, preparing to leave the oversize plane. Juliana felt half in a daze, realizing she hadn't even powered on her phone yet. She turned it on, and messages began popping up on her screen. But all she saw was the one from Law:

I'm sorry. I care about you. Let's talk about this.

She sighed and dumped her phone in the side compartment of her carry-on bag. She didn't respond, not sure what to say. Juliana felt a pity party creeping up. Why did this kind of bad luck always happen to her? Of course her only pick for an anonymous one-night stand turns out to be the furthest thing from anonymous.

Her phone rang and she dug it out of her bag. Garrison was calling. She let it go to voice mail.

She needed a new job, she decided. No job's really worth this. The bonus wasn't, either. She wouldn't wait for the six weeks. Hell, now she had to worry about Garrison *and* compromising her consulting project by sleeping with the very man she was supposed to evaluate. She thought about what it would be like to explain to Garrison or anyone else at Wickham Consulting that it had all been some innocent mistake. *I didn't know he was the CEO!* And they'd say, *what kind of consultant are you if you didn't?*

Quitting was the best option. Sure, she'd take heat for leaving in the middle of a job, and she'd burn her references. No way Garrison would give her a good reference, but would he, anyway? She'd reach out to a few contacts on LinkedIn, see if she could find any leads. It would be hard since she'd only been at Wickham Consulting for less than a year. She'd have to figure out a way to spin it somehow. It would be tricky.

But what if I'm not the only woman Garrison hit on?

The thought hit her suddenly. If she quit, and

didn't say anything, then he'd be free to do it again. And again. Who'd stop him if she didn't? It would be easy to quit, but then Garrison could hurt someone else. No, she'd need to report him to HR. She ground her teeth together. The second she got into the office, she'd file a formal complaint. Then right after that, she decided, she'd recuse herself from the Blue Sky report. That way, her relationship with Law couldn't be held against her. Not if she voluntarily stepped away and no one found out about it. After this, if she'd need to, she'd outright quit her job. If the HR complaint and recusing herself from Blue Sky didn't solve her problems, she'd quit. Yes, she thought, she could handle all of this. She'd take back control of her life once more.

Her phone rang again and she was ready to send it to voice mail when she saw it was Jennifer Bates from her company's human resources office. Her email! She'd nearly forgotten.

She answered Jennifer's call. They'd known each other for years, but it was six in the morning. "Hello?" she said.

"Hi, Jules. I got your message, but wanted to call you back before I got into the office because things are going to be crazy today." Jennifer's voice sounded strained. "We've got so many cases right now, you wouldn't believe. Just had a few minutes and wanted to ask you about your email."

Juliana took a deep breath. "Yes, it's about Garrison. There's something I need to tell you."

* * *

Juliana felt light-headed as she walked into the office, afraid she'd see Garrison and panic. She didn't know why she felt so shaken, but somehow it all seemed like she'd tattled on the playground in elementary school on a bully and now she was waiting to see how that kid would retaliate. Didn't all bullies retaliate?

Juliana knew she'd done the right thing. She'd outlined to Jennifer everything that had happened, asking for a formal complaint, but she still felt uncertain. What if HR didn't believe her? What if Garrison was able to spin this the way he wanted? What if she lost her job for being a troublemaker?

Jennifer had listened to her without judgment, but then that was her job. What if, in the end, HR just gave Garrison a slap on the wrist? Made him watch a few sexual harassment prevention videos? Or, what if they went the other way and fired him? He did have a wife and two kids at home. Jennifer had told her Garrison would not be her supervisor during the investigation period, and that she'd report to Garrison's boss. Now she'd need to tell him that she planned to step away from the Blue Sky project.

This and a ton of other distractions filtered through her mind. She walked by the row of cubicles and past the men normally with their heads together sharing some joke, but today they were all busy clacking away at their keyboards, eyes averted from her. Had word gotten out already? she wondered as she took her seat at her desk. She sat, smoothing out her steel-gray wool pants. She slipped out of her matching blazer and hung it on the back of her chair as she unsheathed her laptop from its neoprene case, plugging it into the monitor on her desk. Garrison's office lay dark and empty, and she wondered if he'd been asked to leave by HR or if he'd voluntarily stayed away. She figured she'd find out soon enough.

Right now she'd need to recuse herself from Blue Sky. The sooner, the better.

Sure, consultants didn't take Hippocratic oaths, but there was still a code of conduct implicit to her job, and even if she didn't know who Law was, she might not be able to be objective about her work. This was all the Aussie's fault.

He'd betrayed her. He'd been using her to get access to her report, to influence it maybe, to put Blue Sky in the best light. She was tired of men taking advantage of her. She felt like she was once more on that elementary school playground, a boy tripping her so she fell into the woodchips.

He was just using her, she decided.

Then why did he tell you? That little voice popped up in her head. *If he really wanted to take advantage, why admit who he was? He could've played you until the end, but he didn't.*

She gnawed on the end of her pen, swiveling in her desk and wondering about this bothersome little detail. She remembered the shock in his blue eyes when she'd accused him of trying to influence the report. He'd been so adamant that wasn't who he was. And on some level, she knew that was true. He'd made his reputation being a savvy CEO, but his reputation didn't include dirty tricks. She could feel herself wanting to believe him.

And that's why I need to recuse myself from the Blue Sky project.

But how? Consultants didn't usually quit less than a week before their job was done unless they were in the hospital. She'd have to come up with a good excuse.

As much as she hated to do it, it was the only right thing to do. Juliana felt a little pang as she realized this meant that she'd see far less of Law, maybe not see him at all. *He betrayed me, so why do I even care?* she asked herself, though found no answer. *It's not like he'd even want to see me again once he realizes I'm off the project. I'd have no information to give him.*

She pulled up an email and addressed it to Garrison's boss. Best to get this over with before she lost her nerve.

CHAPTER EIGHT

"YOU'RE PLAYING WITH FIRE," Omar warned Law as the two sat in his expansive office at Blue Sky headquarters in Seattle the next day. Law sat behind his glass desk, feeling pensive as he stared out at the beautiful crystal-blue waters of Puget Sound. A rare day of sunshine made the water glint and sparkle, and as he looked at the waves he was reminded of Honolulu and Juliana. She'd been resolutely ignoring his messages, but he had other plans up his sleeve. He didn't build one of the world's largest airlines because he gave up easily.

"I know."

"This isn't like you."

Law glanced at him. "I know that, too."

"Your priorities are all out of whack. You're thinking with your…uh, *well*, not your brain."

Law sighed. He knew all this was true. It infuriated him, actually. He'd had his plan: retire from Blue Sky, launch his charity project, maybe find some little actress to settle down with and have a few adorable babies. He'd wanted *out* of the rat race, not to fall in love with a woman who lived and breathed corporate mergers.

Omar shook his head. He sat on the chair in front of Law's desk, legs stretched out in front of him, dark hands pressed into a steeple beneath this chin. "No woman is worth losing a company you've spent your life building. *Or* taking mine while you're at it."

"You know the merger's going through. We can make the report just a technicality."

Omar sighed. "I *know* that. But I was hoping Juliana might help *lead* the transition. But if you mess it all up and we lose her…"

"I'm not going to lose her." Law glared at Omar. He felt determination rise in him. Fate brought Juliana into his life. He'd just need to forget about her. Of course, with Omar sitting in a chair on the other side of his desk, he realized that may be easier said than done. Law thought of her smooth skin, her radiant smile. The way she bantered and teased him, challenging him in a way few women in his life ever had.

"What are you going to do about this? What's your *plan*?"

Law looked up, feeling guilty. "I don't have one."

Omar looked so shocked Law could've knocked him over with a breath. "You? Not have a plan? You always have a plan. Are you *feeling* okay?"

Law shrugged. "Something about Juliana makes me want to *stop* planning, and yet start planning a whole new life at the same time. What does that mean?"

Omar shook his head and stood. "It means maybe we should look into buying State Airlines instead of Blue Sky."

"They have a hundred fewer planes, and their pilots just went on strike. Good luck."

Law checked his phone once more as he rocked back in his chair. Not a single message from Juliana. Not one. He'd messaged her multiple times a day for several days, and she'd not responded to any of them. Had she blocked him? He knew she was angry, and understood why. But he'd been hoping for...*something*. He knew he'd have to make this mistake up to her. But how?

"So you decide to fall in love with the woman who could drag down our bottom line?" Omar shook his head slowly. "You're not the only one with a stake in this sale."

"It'll go through, regardless of the report." Law sounded more confident than he felt.

"It better," Omar said, shaking his head. "So this was your big plan? Sleep with the consultant but instead of gleaning information, you fall for her? Then spend a weekend in Honolulu doing God knows what and then now you're hovering over your smartphone like some adolescent."

He glanced at the black brick in his hand. "She hasn't responded to any of my messages."

"You just proved my point. Look at you." Omar

clicked his tongue in disapproval. "Like a lovesick puppy."

"Why isn't she replying to me, though?" He knew she was upset, but if she just let him explain, he knew he could convince her they were meant to be together.

"Because she's mad."

"That's not helpful."

"You lied to her," Omar pointed out. "I can get why she's pissed at you."

"You're not helping me." But Law laughed a little as he said this.

"Before we started this whole thing, you should've told me you were this lousy at corporate espionage."

"That's why I'm getting out of the corporate rat race," Law said.

Law's desk phone rang then, his assistant in the adjacent room calling.

"Yes, Sylvia?"

"Uh, Mr. Mason, Juliana Hart is waiting for you in the lobby. She's fairly insistent she talk to you. I told her you were in a meeting but she…"

Law's heart sped up. Juliana? Here? He glanced at Omar, who looked equally surprised.

"Buzz her up immediately. Cancel all my other appointments."

"Oh…uh, yes, sir." Sylvia clicked off the line and Law felt a little giddy. Juliana had come to see him. Maybe she'd realized he wasn't the bad guy, after all. Maybe she'd forgiven him for not being completely honest with her. Maybe she cared about him, too. His mind swam with possibilities.

"You need to go," he told Omar.

"I think maybe I should stay," Omar said.

"I'll give you one minute and then I'm kicking you out."

He heard the click of her heels on the marble tile outside his office as he stood, sweeping lint off the front of his flat-front wool pants, hoping he looked presentable. He grabbed a mint from the small crystal candy dish on his desk. Juliana walked in, looking even more radiant than he remembered: dark hair flowing past her shoulders, her light brown eyes almost hazel in the sunlight. She wore a silk blouse, a long silver necklace and a flowing skirt that hit just above the knee. He also noticed her sleek black pumps. She looked stunning, actually. In his memory she was beautiful, but somehow reality managed to dwarf his recollection.

She froze when she saw Omar. "Oh, Mr. Khan. I wasn't expecting you here."

She glanced from Law to Omar and back again. "Sorry, Miss Hart," Omar said smoothly. "Law and I are old friends. We just had lunch."

"Well, actually, it's probably good I have you both here, because I'm going to be stepping down from the Blue Sky project," she said. "Effective tomorrow."

Law felt waves of shock run through him. She was quitting? He glanced at Omar, who also raised his eyebrows in surprise. He knew his friend would have a *lot* to say about that later.

"Miss Hart, we've been so happy with your work, and the board meeting is *this Friday.* Can't we just keep you on for this week?"

"I'm sorry, Mr. Khan, but…"

"Omar, can I have a minute with Miss Hart. Alone?"

Reluctantly, Omar left.

"What's this all about?" Law watched as Juliana frantically paced his office.

"You compromised me. I can't be objective, and this way, we can both go our separate ways. I can't provide you with any information so you can stop pretending to like me."

Law crossed the room and shut his office door with a decided click behind her. What they needed to discuss, no one ought to hear. "But the presentation to the board is in just a couple of days!"

"Someone else can take over for me," Juliana declared.

"You shouldn't step down because of me." He studied her. Juliana crossed her arms in front of her chest and glanced out his window at Puget Sound, looking determined.

"You'll have to find someone else to sell you secrets."

"I never cared about the report." Law only cared about seeing Juliana. He didn't want her quitting the project if that meant he didn't see her again.

"Really? So why didn't you tell me who you were from the start?" She turned, eyes burning with betrayal. He hated that he'd caused her this pain.

"Just because I might have been curious about you, and I didn't want you to know who I was, doesn't mean anything. I started out feeling one way about you, but my feelings have changed."

"When did they change? Before or after sex in the bathroom?"

Law slowly shook his head. "This isn't about the sex."

Juliana hugged herself tighter. "How can it *not* be about the sex?"

"Maybe it's about something more." A current of truth passing between them, their mutual attraction like an unwritten law of physics.

"Why did you *really* come here?" Law asked. He'd been wanting to ask this since she'd walked through his office door. They both stood near the big floor-to-ceiling windows overlooking Puget Sound, but for now he didn't care about the ocean.

She tensed, her guard clearly up. "What do you mean?"

"I mean you could've called me. Or texted. Why fly all this way to tell me you plan to quit this report?" Law leaned forward, into her personal space. He got a whiff of her perfume, sweet citrus.

"I just…thought it was the right thing to do. To do it face-to-face." Her tone was clipped, defensive.

"You could've come up with other reasons other

than getting on a plane." Law hadn't made it this far in his career, making a fortune out of nothing, without being a good read of people. He knew Juliana wasn't telling him the whole truth, even if she herself didn't want to admit it.

She shifted uncomfortably in her seat. "I don't know what you mean."

"I think you do." Law reached out and touched her elbow. She didn't move away. Her arm felt warm beneath his palm, and he remembered what she'd been like naked in bed: her appetite voracious, her need nearly insatiable. She glanced up at him, light brown eyes wary. "Maybe you came here to see me."

She shook her head. "That's not why I'm here."

"It's not?" Law knew she wasn't being honest—with him or herself. If she didn't trust him, why was she here in his office? It didn't make sense.

She didn't answer. Instead, she bit her bottom lip, worrying it as she seemed to think through her own tangled web of justifications.

"You'll see it clearly, just as I do, Juliana." Law watched the color spread across her cheeks. The blush told him all he needed to know. He was right. He knew it. "But until then, how about you use my office for the afternoon?"

"I told you, I'm off the report. I'm not consulting AM Air or Blue Sky anymore."

"We both know you quitting isn't the real reason you came here." Juliana's gaze shifted away from him.

"What do you mean?"

"The real reason you came is because you want me as much as I want you."

Juliana's lips parted, her eyes widening.

Law chuckled low in his throat. "You're not so hard to read as you think, ice queen."

Juliana's heart hammered in her chest like the beat of some long-forgotten '80s pop song. What on earth had just happened? Law's stark blue eyes seemed to see *right* through her. She hadn't even realized how much she'd wanted to be close to Law until she'd walked into his office. The man had been right. She'd come with an alternative purpose: to see him again.

Of course, now she knew Law was dangerous, and not in the way she'd thought. Not in a way that meant sharing company secrets. The way he made her feel when he looked at her told her she was in unfamiliar territory. His very presence rattled her, made her lose her train of thought. It was a bad idea to come, probably. How was she supposed to think clearly about what she should do next when Law was right here in the same office? The same man who'd lied about who he was to get the dirt on her report? *The same man who got your clothes off in 1.2 seconds.*

Yet, despite knowing that, why did she still want to kiss the life out of him? She was beginning to wonder if she was using sex as a way of avoiding her problems. Some people went for alcohol. She apparently went for the front of Law's pants.

"That's not why I came," she managed, even though her own voice sounded weak in her ears. Juliana glanced at Law—his blond hair perfectly swept back from his face, the hint of laugh lines just forming near his eyes. His broad shoulders didn't seem like they belonged in a business setting, somehow. He should be out wrestling crocodiles or whatever manly Aussie men did.

"Tell me right now if I invited you into my private conference room, right there, that you wouldn't go."

He was standing so close now she could smell his aftershave: something woodsy and the hint of mint.

Juliana's throat went dry. She glanced beside her, at the wooden paneled conference room door, the small meeting room with the only windows staring out to Puget Sound. Would he take her there? Across the small round steel-legged table, back against the cold glass? She swallowed. Even after he lied, even after everything…part of her was tempted to go into that meeting room, consequences be damned.

"We can't. You're the rival of a client."

Law's sensual mouth quirked up in a sly smile. "Not anymore. You quit the project."

He let the words linger between them, not breaking eye contact as she sat, spellbound, in his gaze. Why hadn't she thought about what would happen if she quit? She found herself leaning against his big, sleek, gray desk, her hands finding the hard corner behind her as he took one more step in her direction. She craned her neck up to meet his gaze.

"You're telling me you flew all this way to tell me you'd removed the conflict of interest...between us." His smile grew bigger.

Why did he look so happy about it? She thought he'd be disappointed or even angry. He'd worked so hard to play her, hadn't he? Now he'd be back to square one, no influence on a new consultant; no way of manipulating the results.

"You're not upset by this?" She'd thought he'd beg and plead for her to stay on, that he'd desperately want to keep his finger on the project. After all, that's why he slept with her, wasn't it?

He reached out, slid a single finger down her sleeve. "It's the best thing that's happened to me all day. The best if you don't head to that meeting room with me, that is." He nodded behind her. "What's stopping us?"

She realized the crazy truth: there *was* nothing stopping them. Her mind blinked off, and her instincts took over. Her body grew hotter the closer he came, and suddenly all she wanted to do was press herself against him, feel the smooth hardness of his chest beneath her fingers. Had this been her own secret plan all along? Had her own subconscious been working against her this whole time?

"We can't...it's your office... And you should be mad."

"Why would I be mad? I told you, Juliana, I want you. I don't care about the report."

Juliana sucked in a breath. Could this be true?

Or was he just playing her still? But for what angle? She racked her brain, but couldn't find out an angle. Not unless he really just wanted sex. She felt a giggle rise up in her throat. She'd never been so relieved a man might just be after her body. She'd felt so betrayed, so used, when she thought he'd just been after her report.

"So you just want sex?"

"You know I want more than that. I want you, Juliana. Not just your body. All of you. And for the record, you're not the only one giving up something here. I am, too. I'm risking you telling me to bug off."

Juliana couldn't believe her ears. *He* was worried about *her* rejecting him?

"That's unlikely."

"Really? Because ever since we met on that flight, you've worked on a dozen ways to reject me. You didn't even want to take my number in the baggage claim, but I convinced you to take it."

Juliana replayed their brief history, this time from Law's perspective. She realized he might be right. Had she been playing hard-to-get?

Law reached out, touched the back of her hand, stroked it just a little. Every nerve ending in her arm came alive at his touch. She was suddenly aware of how close he was standing to her, and how the wall of windows on the other side of his office faced out to the rows of open-desk seating at Blue Sky headquarters. How many people were right now looking at them?

"We shouldn't talk about this here," Juliana said, flicking a look to the open desks on the office floor. One or two workers glanced curiously at Law's office. "Maybe I should even catch a flight back to Chicago."

"There you go again. Trying to run away," Law said. "Look, if I don't have a chance at all with you, tell me right now. I'll absolutely respect your wishes and leave you alone. But if I do…"

Juliana felt her breath catch in her throat. All she wanted to do was stand on her tiptoes and kiss his mouth. "You have a chance. You know you do." Her voice was low, barely audible. But she'd said it. She'd admitted it, and felt vulnerable, exposed.

Law's face brightened, and he looked like she'd just delivered the best news he could imagine. "Good. Then maybe we can talk more tonight? Over dinner?"

Juliana nodded. "But I need to work first…"

"You can use my office."

"What?" She suddenly had an image of working shoulder to shoulder with him for an afternoon, being unable to concentrate on anything but his broad shoulders and stark blue eyes.

"Don't worry. I'll let you have your space." He smiled and she felt the heat in her toes. He snapped his laptop closed and pulled it from his desktop, tucking it under his arm. "You need a place to work, and this office has the best view." He nodded to the window. "I'll work in the conference room." He grabbed his smartphone and tucked it into his pocket.

Before Juliana could argue, he was gone.

She wasn't sure if she felt relieved or disappointed.

Despite Law's keeping his distance the rest of the afternoon, Juliana still failed to really get the rest of her work done. She plowed through emails, noting that Garrison failed to respond at all to her email about quitting the Blue Sky project. Garrison's boss, however, had written a one-line response:

You sure you want to do this?

She hated quitting. She'd been the perfect consultant, and the project had been meant for her. She knew she'd take a career hit by stepping down: consultants don't get promoted by quitting midway through the good jobs. Juliana also knew a dozen other coworkers would happily take her place. Some would probably say the stress got to her, no doubt. That she couldn't handle the big leagues.

She wondered if Garrison's boss believed her slightly twisted truth. She said one of her old mentors worked at Blue Sky, and she worried about her objectivity. In some ways, Law was a mentor...a *sex* mentor. The man had taught her things about herself she'd never known. Introduced her to her inner wildcat.

Even working in the conference room, he seemed

in command, as underlings hustled in and out, handing him papers, chatting. She noticed his assistant; a bubbly brunette in stiletto heels took her time getting him coffee, lingering near the door of the conference room, seemingly looking for a reason to stay. She felt jealousy burn in her chest, a bright-white flare, an unfamiliar sensation. How could she be territorial about a man she'd only just met? Especially when she told him she had no interest in pursuing a serious relationship?

Law glanced up as if feeling her gaze, and she quickly looked down at her laptop, feeling a blush creep up her cheek. Damn the man. How was she supposed to concentrate with his solid blue gaze on her? She began typing an email, typo after typo, hardly able to concentrate. At this rate, she'd get no work done.

Suddenly, she longed for Law's arms around her once more. She realized she'd come for that comfort as much as anything. She could still imagine his big, muscled arms around her, making her feel safe, secure. Yet how could she trust him? He'd lied to her.

And then there was Garrison. Being investigated for the allegations she leveled against him. *What if no one believes me?*

Sure, Jennifer had taken down her notes with quiet reverence, not commenting on any of them, but how could she? She was HR: trained to be objective.

Maybe I should just quit now. Sure, she'd lose her bonus and she didn't have a job lined up, but she could manage. Live on savings and then, if necessary, credit cards until she found a new job.

Forget all that and focus, she told herself. Somehow she managed to dig into her work, even though Law's many trips crisscrossing the office floor proved a major distraction. She tracked his long strides out of the corner of her eye, taking note of every purposeful step. The man moved gracefully, like an athlete who knew his own body. Anytime the man popped up in her peripheral vision she became distracted from the task at hand. Still, she got through some of the reports, moved further along on her report and even put together a few more slides for her PowerPoint presentation. She was so wrapped up in her work, she didn't notice the sun outside had set, the fluorescent lights blinking on overhead. Juliana was so wrapped up in her work that she didn't even notice Law standing in the open office doorway until he knocked softly.

Her head shot up, and she was surprised to see him standing there. "You haven't taken a break nearly all day," he said, but there was something else in his voice. Admiration?

"Sometimes I can get in the zone," she admitted. "I forget to eat, even."

"Well, you have to eat." He grinned, flashing a brilliant, movie-star smile. "Let me take you to dinner."

Juliana wanted to jump at the chance, but the logical side of her mind told her to be cautious. She didn't want a relationship, and going out to dinner seemed like a relationship thing to do.

"I really need to finish this," she said. "But... thank you."

"You realize we're the only two left in the office right now." He nodded back to the main floor, which Juliana noticed was completely empty, except for the janitor who wheeled a big trash can across the main floor.

"I know. I just need to finish this write-up."

"Are you always this industrious for projects you quit?" Law chuckled a little at his own joke.

"I take pride in my work," Juliana said. "And it's not finished until it's finished."

"Suit yourself."

Law left her and Juliana returned her focus to her laptop, furiously typing up three more slides for her presentation. She noticed a few more workers passing by her door, but figured they were cleaning staff. She didn't see Law again for another hour. Then he knocked again on his office door.

"About that dinner..."

She glanced up, her neck now stiff from the full day's work. Her fingers and wrist also felt sore from the constant typing. Her stomach, too, rumbled its discontent with her decision not to go to dinner with Law earlier.

"I don't know if that's a good idea." Dinner seemed too much like a date. While technically there was nothing wrong with them dating after tomorrow, she wanted to try to keep things simple. Besides, she was still a little angry at Law's deception, she realized. How could he have put her in this position? Jeopardized her job?

"We're not really supposed to…" She looked for the right word. "Fraternize."

"Too late for that," Law quipped. And suddenly she remembered him naked—the smooth feel of his chest beneath her fingers. So strong, so solid. "Besides, there's no real conflict anymore since you quit."

Juliana tried to think of an excuse good enough to avoid Law. Though, in fact, she didn't want to avoid him. She wanted to sit and relax with dinner and wine. But she needed to fight that urge. The more dependent she became on Law's companionship, the more dangerous the relationship became. Besides, she couldn't trust him. He'd pretended to like her to get information. And he could still be doing that.

"Come on," Law said. "I've got something to show you." He gestured for her to follow him, and she went, curious, as he led her to a conference room down a more secluded hallway. He opened the door for her and she walked through, amazed to find the conference room table transformed into a candlelit dinner for two, complete with red wine, some delicious-smelling pasta, salad and fresh-baked rolls.

"You said you were too busy to eat, so I brought the restaurant to you," he said, bowing at the waist. "Your seat, my lady."

Law touched her elbow and Juliana felt herself shiver. Juliana couldn't believe this. He'd transformed a work conference room into the most intimate, romantic dinner for two. The candles, the food, the wine. Her eyes took it all in, unable to believe it.

"How did you…" she managed.

"I ordered from my favorite Italian restaurant. I know the owner." He smiled. "He owes me a hundred dollars from the last time we played poker."

The table was even covered in a fine linen tablecloth, and the candlelight flickered, reflecting off the fine silverware.

"Wow," Juliana said, inhaling the amazing scent of food as her stomach grumbled in protest.

Law hurried over and pulled out a rolling office chair for her with a flourish. Juliana sat as he delicately laid a napkin on her lap.

"Wine?" He offered a bottle of Pinot Noir.

"Wait. Are you just doing this to ply me for information? I quit, remember?"

"This has nothing to do with the report."

She glanced around the corners of the conference room. "Are there cameras? Are you going to video this and show it to my boss?"

Now Law looked offended. "Just what kind of ass, do you think I am?"

"One that pretends to be someone else on a plane and doesn't mention he's the CEO of the company I'm evaluating."

"I never pretended to be anyone but me. I just

didn't *tell* you I owned Blue Sky." He flashed a brilliant smile. "Besides, if I wanted to play you, why would I tell you who I really was?"

"Maybe that's a genius-level manipulator move."

"Or maybe I just like you." He held up the bottle. "Wine?"

"Is it drugged?"

"The cork is in it, so doubtful." He went about opening it in front of her. "And if you keep at me like this, I'm going to drink this whole bottle by myself."

Juliana laughed a little.

"Fine. You win. I'll have some wine."

He poured a healthy glass and did so for himself, as well. He sat catty-corner from her at the massive table. She was keenly aware of the proximity of his elbow to hers near the edge of the table.

"To working hard," he said and offered up his glass in a toast.

"To working hard," she echoed and they clinked glasses. She took a sip of the amazing wine, notes of black currant and cherry in the mix as she swallowed. Unable to stop herself, she dug into her red-sauced pasta, amazed at how simple, yet how delicious, the food was. Much better than the pizza or hamburger she'd planned to grab on the way to her hotel later.

"This is…amazing," she mumbled, mouth full, as Law watched her eat.

"Good," he said. His blue eyes looked darker beneath the candlelight, and he ate with restraint as she devoured the food on her plate.

"Do you always spy on your consultants, then treat them to fancy dinners?" she asked him, hoping to keep her voice light, the mood playful.

"Only the ones I'm falling in love with."

CHAPTER NINE

JULIANA NEARLY SPIT out her wine. *Falling in love?* She felt her throat go suddenly dry.

"You can't really mean that." She carefully put down her glass of wine. Of course, when she looked into Law's blue eyes, she saw he was deadly serious. "You know if you lie about loving me, I'm still not going to let you see the notes I'm passing to my colleagues."

"I'm not lying." He reached over and took her hand in his. "I don't care about the report. This isn't about business at all. This has gotten very, very personal, and I'm not afraid to ask for what I want."

Of course he wasn't. That was how he built an airline empire. Sitting in the dimmed conference room, Juliana was acutely aware of his strength, the way his shoulders seemed to hold barely restrained power. He had a gravitational pull all on his own, and she felt herself being drawn in. She knew logically she ought to fight the connection between them, but something in her didn't want to fight.

"You don't have to fall in love with me. But I know you will." He flashed her a confident smile and she had to laugh.

"Oh, really? You're that sure of yourself?"

He nodded. "I am. Believe me, I'm impossible to resist." He wiggled his eyebrows and Juliana barked a laugh. "But I know how hard you're trying. Running away from me at every turn."

"Right, and then after tomorrow, when I no longer work on the Blue Sky project? Then what?" She took another bite of delicious pasta.

"Then we can finally stop sneaking around, and you can be officially my girlfriend."

Girlfriend. No one had called her that in a very long time.

"Is that so?" She swallowed her bite with one gulp.

"You're not going to be able to resist my charms." He shifted a bit, leaning into her space. "I have a particular set of skills." Law's voice was low, a grumble she felt in her abdomen. His eyes sparkled in the candlelight, and she felt transfixed by them. She glanced at his lips, full, sensual and inches from her own.

He gently reached out, his fingers lingering on the back of her neck. And then, ever so slowly, he drew her in for a kiss. Her brain told her to resist, but her body had different ideas. Their lips met, and their barely restrained desire exploded in an urgent need, the soft kiss quickly turning more passionate. Suddenly, all she wanted to do was have him for dinner *and* dessert. She forgot about his lie, forgot about the dangers of being with a man who could cost her her job. Maybe the fact he was forbidden spurred on her passion, made it burn even hotter. Her brain shut off, and hungrily, Juliana devoured his mouth, and feeling frustrated by the space between their two chairs, moved on top of him, lifting her flouncy silk skirt to midthigh, showing him a hint of her lacy thong beneath as she straddled him in his own chair. Then his hands moved down her back, across her hips, as his mouth found her neck, laying delicate kisses there. She groaned and arched her back, naturally pressing into his lap, feeling his need for her growing there. Juliana felt herself grow white-hot, her own want taking over, just as it had on the plane, when she'd thrown every caution to the wind. Here she was, in the Blue Sky conference room, with the president of the company, but all she could think of was how quickly she wanted to free him of his pants. Law shifted beneath her, gently moving her to the floor, and then he stood, walking to the conference room door where he shut it with a distinctive click.

Then her brain turned on again. Outside, distantly, Juliana heard the whirl of the vacuum; janitorial staff, she figured.

"We can't. Someone will find us. Or…cameras."

"There are no cameras here. Look around."

Juliana glanced at the corners of the room and saw none. Yet that didn't mean there weren't. "Maybe you want us to be caught."

"Why would I care? It's midnight. You don't technically work for AM Air anymore," he said, voice a low growl. "And I don't care about any report."

He pulled her to him and kissed her once more, his hands, gentle but firm as they squeezed her hips. Yes, this was what she wanted: this man, this way. A distant flash of memory suddenly disrupted her moment: Garrison, his meaty hands on her shoulders. As soon as the ugly memory came to her, she shelved it. No. Garrison was the man she didn't want.

Law was the man she wanted. That was what made this moment different. That, in fact, made all the difference. She pulled away from him and then reached beneath her skirt. She looped her finger into the waist of her lacy thong and pulled it downward, so it dropped to her ankles, never letting her eyes leave his. Juliana stepped out of it, still in her heels. She knew what she was doing was wrong, stupid, even, reckless. He could be playing her, but what was his angle now? She couldn't come up with one.

And without the project, this could be her last time to have this man. Maybe that was why she was willing to ignore the warning bells in her head. Maybe that was what made her so willing to do this now. Besides, she was already in too deep, wasn't she?

Law watched her deliberate movements, desire growing on his face, his body stiffening. Juliana turned then and put her palms down on the conference room table. Her invitation would be impossible to miss.

He moved forward, sliding his hands up her skirt, caressing her bare hip.

"Juliana," he murmured, barely a groan as she heard him unzip his pants.

"Take me," she commanded, her own voice hoarse with want. She felt her wet want, slick between her legs, the thrum of her pulse there, beating with need. Juliana loved the anticipation, her knees quaking as he lifted her skirt, the cool conference room air brushing against her bare thighs. *Yes, this is what I want. God, I want it so bad.*

She felt him then as he rubbed against her, thick knob ready and willing as he found her slick center. He filled her from behind with all of him, grasping her hips tightly with his hands and she nearly cried out. This deliciously full feeling. That was what she wanted. He began moving slowly at first, and then with more deliberate thrusts.

"Yes," she murmured, voice low as she kept her palms on the table, letting him dominate her, letting him take her in the basest way possible. Her skirt above her waist, here in the conference room where she'd later no doubt have to have a serious meeting. She wondered if she'd think of this then, of him inside her, filling her, making her his.

It was all so wrong. So very wrong. But why did it feel so right?

At any moment someone from the cleaning staff could find them. Law could be playing her for a fool, but Juliana didn't care. She wanted Law, and hated to admit how much she liked that he wanted her. That he was hard for her. He reached around, gently massaging her as he slowed his thrusts.

"I want us to come together," he whispered in her ear. She almost laughed at the idea. That never happened. Hardly ever. Usually she had to finish before…or after. "I'm not going to come until you come," he murmured, a challenge.

"But…" They were in the conference room. They could be found out at any moment. How could they take their time?

"Relax," he murmured, working her, building her want. She let herself focus on his gentle touch, on the way he filled her, his hard chest pressed in her back. He rubbed her front, gently, with his finger, the way she'd told him to. All she had to do was let herself go, let him drive this. Could she do that? It went against every instinct she had.

"I'm—" Juliana sucked in a breath "—close." She couldn't believe it. She was going to come, here, like this, Law's hands on her. Law inside her.

"Yes. I feel you." He moved inside her, driving her wild as he worked on deep, slow strokes. She felt the tension building, felt the inevitable coming.

"I'm going to…" She barely finished her sentence before the first wave of pleasure took her and she felt her entire body tense. Law joined her, thrusting hard and deep, letting out a hiss of pleasure in her ear as they both hit their climax and then tumbled down the convulsions of pleasure together. Then he hugged her from behind, in no hurry to disentangle himself. Juliana sucked in a breath, winded, wondering how she ended up half-naked in a conference room so fast.

"You are the sexiest woman I've ever met," Law told her. "God, I want to marry you."

Juliana stiffened. *Marry me?*

But Law withdrew then, grabbing a nearby napkin to clean himself. In seconds he was zipped up once more, looking professional, normal, the only indication they'd been bad was the slight flush of red on his cheeks.

Juliana decided to ignore the hint about marriage as she found her underwear on the floor and wiggled into it, feeling the thrum of the good sex chemicals flowing through her brain. They definitely had chemistry. Juliana couldn't argue with that. No man made her *want* him so badly. No man made her come so hard, either. No man ever made her abandon her good sense like this before.

"Do you have a place to stay tonight?"

"Yes. A hotel. Downtown. My suitcase is there."

"Why not come stay with me?"

Juliana knew she shouldn't. But part of her couldn't resist. She wanted to see where Law lived. She wanted to imagine him there…when she was in Chicago. She also wanted to sleep in his arms tonight. Did that mean she was developing feelings for the man? Or that she just needed human contact?

"All right," she said, agreeing, noticing Law's face light up.

"Good." He flashed her a white smile.

Law drove her in his Maserati up the winding streets of the Harvard-Belmont Historic Landmark District. Framed by old oaks, the homes dotting the hillside looked classic and stately. They pulled into the huge concrete half-circle drive in front of a massive Manhattan brownstone, three stories with a deck lined with trees on the roof that Juliana could see from the home's stately stairs.

"Wow," Juliana murmured, impressed. Such real estate, with such a magnificent view of both Puget Sound and the Olympic Mountains in the distance, must have cost a small fortune.

"This way," Law said, swinging her rolling suitcase out of his trunk and heading up the stairs. She followed him, feeling more than a little overwhelmed as they walked through the wrought iron gate and to his massive oak front door. He swung it open and she found herself standing in an immense marble foyer, the staircase ahead of them, abstract original paintings on the wall. Law's home managed to look both traditional and modern. He took her hand and pulled her up the stairs. They walked past an immense kitchen with an island bigger than her Chicago condo. Before she had time to gape, he walked her up more stairs, until she found herself on a modern addition to the old early twentieth-century mansion, a glassed-in room looking out onto a huge, modern fire pit ringed with expensive chairs and a pristine view of Puget Sound.

"Oh, my goodness." Juliana could barely breathe even though the air was crisp and clean up here. "It's beautiful."

"It's my little retreat up here. Maybe later we could try this out?" Law nodded toward the corner of the huge rooftop patio, where a square Jacuzzi sat, complete with one clear wall of glass.

"I didn't bring my swimsuit," Juliana said.

"You don't need one." He pulled Juliana into his arms and kissed her softly. He pulled away from her.

"I love you, Juliana."

Juliana's heart sped up. She searched her feelings. Was it love that made her so helpless in his arms? So unable to tell him no? Was it love that made her do the crazy things she did with him? It had to be. But could she say it? Was she ready to say it?

"You don't have to tell me about your feelings now," Law said. "I'm not looking for you to say 'I love you, too' if you don't mean it. I want you to wait until you're sure."

For that, she was grateful. Love? Could she love him?

Law dipped down and kissed her again, this time more sensually, more reverently. She kissed him back. He pulled away.

"I want to talk to you about…this. Between us." He gestured around the space between them as if feelings lived there. "I think you should quit your job at Wickham Consulting."

"What? Why?"

"There are other jobs, and I don't think the management team appreciates you. I don't like that Garrison still works there. What if he hurts you?"

"He won't."

"I just worry about that toxic environment at work. You don't deserve to suffer and you deserve to work for a company that appreciates you and values you."

"So I quit and then I'd have to find a new job. I'd already been thinking of this, actually. There are a few opportunities out there."

"Why wait? Just come live with me." Law's gaze never left her face. "I've got more money than I know what to do with. Let me take care of you."

She felt floored. She might have been thinking of quitting, but it was another thing for Law to suggest becoming her sugar daddy. He was rich, she knew that, but she loved her work. "You're asking me to give up work? Forever?"

Law's eyes sparkled with excitement.

"Think about it. We could travel," he offered. "We could see the world. You could help me with my charity work."

"But that's *your* work. Not mine. I..." How could she explain? She needed her own independence, her own work. It had never really been about the money to her; it had always been about the challenge, about tackling tough problems. On her own. "I could never just live with you. Have you pay the bills."

"Why not?" Now Law looked surprised.

"I have to be my own person. I can't just get *absorbed* into your life." Did he want a girlfriend or an accessory? She was always going to be her own person. She wasn't a sidekick. "Besides, you have a demanding job, too. What about that?"

"I'm not asking you to do anything I'm not willing to do myself," Law pointed out. "I'll soon be quitting my own job. I'm leaving the company."

She felt momentarily dizzy. "What do you mean? You built this company."

"I'm tired, Juliana. I've done what I can do in this space. I want to put my energies somewhere else. Charity work, making a difference that really matters. Helping to launch young entrepreneurs so we continue to innovate."

"You're really stepping aside?" Juliana still couldn't quite believe it. He might be a reclusive CEO, but he was still legendary. He couldn't stop people from talking about how he'd managed to be one of the very few successful airline companies in a time when many had already declared bankruptcy or restructured.

"The merger isn't about the money for you," Juliana said, realizing this stark truth.

"No, it isn't," he said. "It's about freedom." He glanced up at the starry night above them. "A lot of good people sit on the board, good people who've invested in the company and believed in it. I want to take care of them so I can feel better moving on to my next venture." He glanced down at her face. "Now do you believe that what we have isn't about any silly report?"

She was beginning to believe it, and that scared the life out of her. Could this be true? Could he be serious about her?

"You intrigue me, Juliana. I think we could be something together. Something special."

"Law…" Juliana sucked in a breath. She was ready to protest, ready to tell him all the million reasons they wouldn't work out: he was rich and gorgeous, and she was lanky and…not so rich. How could she possibly compete against all the women who'd vie for his attention? And could she really give up the thing that drove her? Her work? She couldn't imagine being a lady of leisure. It just didn't fit.

"Law, about this…"

"Don't give me an answer now," he said. "Just think about it, okay?"

She shivered, and he hugged her to him. "Are you cold?" he asked, rubbing her arms.

Not cold, she wanted to tell him, more like petrified.

He glanced at the hot tub behind her. "I know a way you can warm up," he said as he pulled her toward the tub and hit a button, the jets coming to life and the blue light at the base turning on.

He tugged off his shirt and slipped out of his

pants, too, and then he hopped naked into the hot tub, his muscular chest in full view. She'd never get tired of looking at his amazing body, all sculpted muscle, like a work of art.

"If I get in there, it's going to be trouble," she said.

"I like trouble." He splashed a bit of water in her direction and then they both laughed.

"You came to my house. You must have had it in your mind to seduce me. Again." He made a ripple in the hot water with his thick arms. "I think *you're* using *me*, Miss Hart."

I can't give up my job. There's no way.

She pushed the thought aside. Maybe he'd change his mind. Maybe she could change his mind.

"Oh, really?" She undid the buttons of her blouse and slipped out of the silk. "Why would I use you?"

"For the sex," he murmured as his gaze flicked from her head to her toes and back again. She slipped out of her bra and then her thong, as well. Then she climbed up the side of the spa and slipped in next to him.

"That's my plan, is it?"

"I can think of a better one," he said as he pulled her naked body closer to his.

"What's that?"

"This." Soon his mouth was on hers, and she thought it might be a pretty good plan, after all.

Juliana woke in Law's arms in the early-morning hours to the sound of her phone binging with incoming texts from a blocked number.

Did you do this to me?

Groggy, she reached for her phone and glanced at the face of it.

They called my wife!

Juliana swallowed hard. Was this Garrison?

Who is this?

You know who this is.

She should forward these texts to HR. Then again, they were from a blocked number. Could she prove it was him?

You shouldn't have done this.

Was that a threat? Juliana didn't know, but it sure felt like a threat.

Law shifted next to her and hugged her close.

"Everything okay?" he asked.

"Fine," she said quickly and tried to hide her phone. Then she felt Law shift beside her. He was awake.

"What's that?" he asked her.

"What?"

"The texts?" He blinked, eyes a bit bleary, but he was awake, and he'd seen.

"It's nothing."

Law sat up in bed. "Let me see."

"Why aren't you willing to share with me what's going on with you?"

"Look, I just…" *Don't want to get into it.* "What does it matter?"

Law slid out of bed then, standing on bare feet. "I asked you to live with me, so yes, it does matter."

"I didn't agree to live with you."

"I'm serious about you. I thought you knew that." He was so gorgeous there, standing in the moonlight, his bare chest inviting her to touch it. "But how can we be a couple if you aren't willing to let me in?"

Juliana's head spun. She just…wasn't sure she could trust Law yet. Hadn't he lied to her the moment they met? She wanted to forgive him. But she wasn't sure she had yet.

"I'm not ready for this."

"Because you still don't trust me."

"You *lied* to me. About who you were."

Law dipped his head. "I know, and I'm sorry about that. And I get it, I do. I should never have pretended to be someone else. I'll keep apologizing for that for as long as it takes. What can I do to make it up to you?"

Juliana put her head in her hands, feeling suddenly frustrated. Yes, Law was saying all the right things now, but it was true that she hated lies, hated the fact they'd started their relationship on a lie. He'd been pretending to be a stranger, and she had been pretending to be a fearless woman who took risks and never got hurt. But the fact was, Juliana knew she cared about Law. More than she wanted to admit. And that scared her. Especially now that he wanted her to quit her job.

"This isn't going to work." She'd known it from the start.

Juliana stood and grabbed her clothes from the floor, pulling her shirt over her head. "We started this—" she gestured to the air between them "—on a lie."

"I'm sorry. I never meant to hurt you." Law reached out to grab her arm, but she shirked it off. "I'm sorry I lied."

"But you weren't the only one who lied. I'm not the woman you think I am."

"What do you mean?" Law looked genuinely puzzled.

"I don't just do this... I don't have crazy affairs or go to men's houses I barely know, or have sex on planes or hook up with clients. You believed it, but it was all an act. I'm a mouse, most of the time, not even an ice queen."

Law frowned. "That's not true."

"It is true. I'm not who you think I am. I'm not this person. If you fell in love, then you fell in love with someone I was just pretending to be."

"I know you," he said.

"If you know me, then why are you asking me to give up what I love? Why would you ask me to quit my job, quit my career, forever? That just proves you really don't know me at all."

CHAPTER TEN

Law did his best to convince Juliana to stay, but she was determined to leave, to head back to her hotel and sleep there. No matter how he tried to convince her he wasn't asking her to give up herself, she was determined to leave. Law felt his head spin. Of course he wasn't asking her to give up everything. He thought he was offering her the chance of a lifetime: freedom. They could travel, have adventures. Hell, start up a new company if she really wanted. All he wanted to do was to live his life with her. He thought she'd be *glad* to have a way out of Wickham Consulting. But what if she didn't want to leave?

He understood her wanting to keep her independence, but at what cost? Why wasn't she willing to give him a chance? *And why wouldn't she talk to him?*

He'd lain awake most of the night and then when he couldn't take it anymore, he'd dragged himself from bed and taken an early morning jog to clear his mind. He'd texted Juliana, but she didn't respond, and now he began to worry he'd pushed her too hard.

Was he being too possessive? Too jealous? Demanding too much from her?

Or maybe she just doesn't feel the same way about you, mate. In his experience, the simplest answer was often the right one.

A few hours later Juliana walked into the Blue Sky offices and saw Law sitting behind his desk, looking pensive. Her phone rang then, a general number from Wickham Consulting. Could it be HR? She answered the call.

"Hi, Juliana, it's Ed Henderson." Garrison's boss. Juliana held her breath. "I'd like you to stay on with the Blue Sky report. It's a little late in the game to hand off the ball to someone else."

"But, sir..." *I'm completely compromised and can't be objective about this...*

"With Garrison...uh, *on leave*, there's no one who can take it over."

Juliana felt a lump in her throat. So Garrison was suspended. That was good, she guessed. But why didn't she feel relieved? *I need to quit this job.* Maybe Law was right. Maybe she ought to just quit. Go live with him in his mansion, forget about work, her career. Everything.

But first, she had to finish the Blue Sky report.

"Can I count on you to make the presentation Friday?" Ed was saying on the phone.

"Yes, sir," Juliana said, feeling a twinge of guilt. She had to finish the report now. She glanced up at

Law. Now she'd need to interview him. For real. Get the pension numbers she needed.

Juliana took a deep breath and then headed to Law's office. Law glanced at her with sharp blue eyes. After the argument they had last night, this was going to be anything but easy.

"I'm back on Blue Sky," Juliana said. "Garrison's boss has no one else to finish the report."

Law leaned back in his chair. "Well, then. Looks like we'll be spending more time together."

"Just business," she said. "I need numbers. And I need…"

Law gestured to the seats in front of his desk. "Please, have a seat, then." She sat, laptop in hand. "I'll happily give you all the information you'd like, but you have to answer a few questions for me."

"Like what?" Juliana felt wary. What was this? An office meeting or a teenage game of truth or dare?

"You ask your first question."

"I need your pension numbers."

Law swiveled to his laptop, clicked away on a few keys and then turned back to her. "Done. They're in your inbox." Why was he so cold? He seemed frigid. Was this still about their argument?

Juliana pulled up her email, and sure enough, there were the pension numbers, all of them. She'd just need to run a few metrics and then she'd know about retirement liabilities for the company. It looked, actually, at first glance, as if the company was even in healthier shape than she'd hoped.

"Why did you sit on these numbers? They *help* your chase with AM Air." Now Juliana just felt confusion. Why stonewall her if these numbers were so good?

"I wanted to meet you first. You had all my executive vice presidents running scared," he said. "And my friend, Omar, sits on the AM Air board. He wanted me to find out if you were as good as you say."

"Did you find out?"

He nodded and then put his elbows on his desk, pressing his fingers together in a steeple. "Now I get to ask you a question."

Juliana swallowed. "Okay."

"Are you going to move in with me?"

"I don't know."

"It doesn't have to be forever, just until you find a different job, maybe sooner than you think. I'm just thinking of you. Of your future. You don't have to stay at a place that's so awful. You don't have to do this."

Juliana felt sorely tempted. Why wouldn't she just take his offer? Why couldn't she just *say yes*? She was being stubborn, she knew, but it was because she was afraid. She didn't like the idea of relying on anyone.

"I know, but it's my life. My work. I have to do this my way."

"Is it that you don't want to give up your job,

or is this your way of telling me I have no place in your life?"

"No." She shook her head. "That's not what I mean."

"I told you if you tell me to go away, if you don't want—" he swallowed "—me, then tell me so."

"It's not that I don't want you." *I want you too much, actually.*

"Then will you tell me at least who's texting you in the middle of the night?" He met her gaze. "I have a feeling they weren't nice messages. I can't help you if you don't let me in."

Juliana sighed and then handed Law her phone. He scrolled through the texts, his cheeks flushed as he clenched his jaw.

"I am going to kill him," he declared, anger simmering beneath the unnatural calmness of his voice.

"No," Juliana said. "I'll handle it. Besides, he's suspended, pending the HR review, so you don't have to worry about him."

"He's all but threatening you." Law held up her phone. "This alone should get him fired."

"He sent it from a blocked number. There's no way to prove it's him, and he'll just deny it."

Law jumped to his feet and paced like a tiger in a cage. "You could always quit. Just quit. You don't need this job."

Juliana shook her head. She *did* need this job, and it wasn't just about the job; it was about her career. She wasn't going to throw that all away. She'd figure out what to do—in her own time.

Law stared at her a beat. "I don't understand why you won't let me help you." He took a deep breath. "Why you'd rather suffer *this* than let me in."

"I…" Juliana didn't have a good answer. Why was being dependent on Law so bad? But she couldn't. It just made her feel…weak.

"You don't understand."

"Then explain it to me." Law put both hands on his desk and leaned toward her, blue eyes sharp. How could she explain to him, when she could barely explain it to herself?

When she took too long to respond, Law sank into his chair and glared at his feet.

"I don't understand you," he said. "I just…don't."

She felt tears prick the backs of her eyes. Why couldn't she just accept his help? But she just couldn't. She knew that. "I have a report to finish." She shut her laptop and stood. "I have the numbers I need. And when I finish this report tomorrow, I'll fly home."

Law stood. "Maybe that's best."

Was he giving up on her? It felt like a punch in the throat. Tears threatened to spill as she choked them back.

"I need to work on this presentation, anyway," she said briskly, swallowing back emotion as she tried to convince herself more than him. "And it's about time we stopped pretending that our relationship is anything but a distraction."

CHAPTER ELEVEN

LAW FELT LIKE she'd punched him in the stomach. A distraction, that was all he was to her. He watched her stalk to the restaurant door and fought with himself: should he run after her? But what was the point? She didn't want what he wanted; she'd made that abundantly clear. He was a distraction, nothing more.

What do you expect, mate? She's just not into you. She's been pushing you away from the start. It was just about the sex for her.

He texted and called Juliana to apologize, but she wasn't answering either missive. Not that he could blame her. He spent the rest of the day and evening considering what had happened, and the more he thought about it from her perspective, the more he realized what a mistake he'd made. He sure had mucked it up this time, Law thought. For a man who prided himself on running a business like a well-oiled machine, his own personal life sure was a wreck. But what was he supposed to do? Beg her to quit her job? He had already. He was trying to *help*, but she'd made it clear she didn't want his help.

This was what happened when he let personal feelings get in the way of business.

He picked up his phone and dialed Omar.

"I think it's time," he told him.

"You sure about this? Once we do it, you can't go back."

"I know. I'm ready."

Omar sucked in a deep breath. "Okay. Sign the forms and send them to me. We'll have this all done before the meeting on Friday."

Juliana spent the next two days in her hotel room, finishing up the Blue Sky report for the board meeting the next morning. Normally, work acted as a salve for all wounds, but this time, even work couldn't lift her from her deep funk. She hated that Law hadn't believed her about Garrison. Sure, he'd texted her with his apologies, and yet, her hurt ran deeper than a text could treat.

I love him, that's why, an inner voice told her.

It was why she was so upset that he'd implied she'd been having an affair with Garrison. If Law didn't know her, then who did?

You've been playing a part with him, so what does he really know?

But had she been playing a part? Or had she just been exploring a part of herself that she never let loose? She thought about all their meetings, how alive she felt when she was in Law's arms, how much *herself* it felt to be a little reckless, court a little danger. She stayed so buttoned up in her professional life that letting go appealed on many levels, and so did taking charges of her wants and needs. As a consultant she spent so much of her time catering to clients, to her own boss, to her coworkers, and with Law, she could demand what she wanted, and he delivered.

Maybe they did have a future.

Used to have a future, she corrected herself.

How could she be with a man who didn't trust her, a man whom she didn't trust, either? And how could she possibly give him what he wanted? He needed her to quit her career, to be his sidekick, and that just wasn't in her blood. It wasn't *her.* She couldn't just give up everything she worked so hard for and let him pay all her bills. She knew she wouldn't be happy with that. And she knew eventually, she'd grow to resent him.

Juliana took a cab to the AM Air headquarters that morning, ready to present to the board what she'd found. She knew Law was likely to be there, and yet when she arrived, a quick scan of the glass-cubed office found no sign of him.

Omar greeted her near the elevators.

"I was so glad to hear that you're back on the job," he said. "I can't wait to hear your presentation, Ms. Hart. The entire board is looking forward to it. I hope we don't have any unpleasant surprises."

"None that I'm planning," she answered truthfully. "I think you're making a very good invest-ment. No need to worry."

Omar smiled. "That's a relief," he said. He led her to the large, glass conference room where she'd be giving the presentation before about twenty mem-bers of the board and twenty more executives from each organization.

Juliana felt confident she knew exactly what she'd say: the merger would benefit both companies, but AM Air slightly more. She thought, based on her analysis, the merger would likely make two already strong airline carriers even stronger. She felt good about her work, and ye, all she wanted to do was see Law. She kept glancing up at the office for him, but he never appeared.

What was she hoping for? An apology? He'd left one of those on her voice mail. Was she going to tell him that she finally, now, when it was all too late, realized she loved him? The thought made her laugh out loud. Her? The woman who hated fairy-tale endings, who thought love was for toddlers. She was suddenly going to admit to Law that he'd been right? She'd fallen in love with him?

Juliana focused on her laptop as she stood at the front of the empty conference room. She had looked for Law in the office, but hadn't seen him. An elec-tric current of nerves zapped her stomach. What would she do when she did see him? How would he be?

She focused on her laptop in the empty room. She

needed to prepare for her presentation. She almost missed the tall figure who came into the room, but then she glanced up and saw Law, dressed in a crisp, expensive dark gray suit and blue tie that made his eyes sparkle. The man was a living god; there simply was no other way to describe him. Would he take her breath away every time she saw him?

But then again, when, after today, would she see him again?

She felt a physical pang. But it was for the best. Theirs was a relationship that could never work, not as long as neither trusted the other.

Juliana glanced up, frozen momentarily by his striking good looks.

"Do you…have everything you need?" Law asked, almost too politely. He was done with her. She knew that now.

She nodded. Juliana felt her temples constrict. It all seemed so hopeless suddenly.

As the board members took their seats, Omar sauntered in looking like a corporate shark in his dark suit and tie. He took one look at Juliana at the head of the room and then raised his eyebrows in appreciation.

"You look like someone kicked your puppy," he murmured to Law as he slid into the open seat next to Law. "Is the report that bad?"

"The report is fine," Law said. "My personal life is another story."

Omar glanced at Juliana at the podium. "If it

makes you feel any better, she looks as miserable as you."

"She's the one who did the breaking up," Law said.

"Well, doesn't look like she's too happy about it."

Law didn't want to think about that. She'd been conflicted about them from the moment they met, and now he was beginning to see it was because she really, truly wasn't sure how she felt about him. *Can't live with me, can't live without me.* He hated the seesaw. He wanted to get off.

Board members from both Blue Sky and AM Air filed in, taking their seats all eager to hear the report Juliana would give. AM Air opted for the joint session, which gave some relief to Law. He could address some of the pension issues head-on. Not that he was too worried about those. He was more worried about Juliana and her state of mind, and what her boss might do next.

The presentation began as Juliana took the main podium, introducing herself with ease. If she was nervous, she didn't show it. Law couldn't help but be impressed. He knew the stress she was under, but she performed impeccably. Her professionalism just made her sexier. He shifted in his seat, wishing he could push aside his own raging emotions as easily as she did up at that podium. She was on her tenth slide when the door to the conference room opened and a man stood there, clearing his throat.

"Garrison!" Juliana exclaimed, and Law was on his feet. "You're not supposed to be here."

"Ladies and gentlemen, I'm sorry to interrupt this presentation," Garrison said, "but before we continue any further, I'm under the ethical obligation to inform the board of some troubling facts concerning Ms. Hart."

"This man has been suspended from Wickham Consulting," Juliana said. "I think we should ask him to leave." She made eye contact with Law.

"Yes, and I believe you need to leave the premises." Law was on his feet and ready to back her up. Law was on his feet then to back her up.

"Well, unfortunately, Mr. Mason, my allegations include you, as well."

"I don't believe you're in any position to talk about ethical standings," Law quipped. He looked at Omar and gave him a swift nod. Omar stood, as well.

"Sir, I'm going to have to ask you to leave."

"I've had confirmation that Mr. Mason and Ms. Hart have been seeing each other."

Law laughed. "We went out to dinner. Eating a steak hardly constitutes a breach of ethics."

Some of the board members laughed.

"Now it's time for you to leave," Law said, and moved toward Garrison. He backed up.

"It was more than dinner!" he called, but he was already out the door. "And once the brass at Wickham Consulting finds out, she's unlikely to have a job for long."

CHAPTER TWELVE

Juliana felt her head spin. Garrison had told the entire room she'd essentially slept with Law, and now she was being scolded and blackballed—in front of everyone. This never would have happened if Law didn't lie. She never would've gotten involved with him if he'd told her who he was. Then again, would she have been able to resist the magnetic pull between them even if she had known? There was no way to be certain. But what she knew was that her career as a consultant was likely over for good. Who would hire her now? She'd been so careful about her personal reputation and now it was blown. This little boardroom stunt by Garrison would follow her to every single job interview she ever did, most likely. She'd have to go into some completely unrelated field. Maybe consulting for theme parks? Chopping wood in Alaska?

"I'm sorry, ladies and gentlemen," she managed. "That was a disgruntled employee at my company. Shall we return to the report?"

Omar gave her a nod of satisfaction and she continued her report, even as she saw security escorting Garrison to the elevators, and Law straightening his tie as he walked back into the conference room. Somehow she managed to finish the report on autopilot.

After the report Juliana felt numb. Even if Garrison was suspended, and even if he got fired, the news he had could also get her let go.

"That was grace under pressure," Omar said, approaching her at the podium. "That was a wonderful save."

"Was it? I hope my...colleague's behavior hasn't jeopardized anything."

"No, not at all," Omar said, giving a single shrug. "The merger already went through."

Juliana froze. "What do you mean, it already went through?"

"Law already signed the papers, so really the report was just a formality."

Juliana felt blindsided. The report she'd worked so hard to compile was just a formality? Not to mention the public embarrassment of Garrison showing up. That was all for nothing?

"The merger's done?" Juliana still couldn't believe her ears. She turned to face Law, who'd broken free of another conversation with board members and was now walking to her. "Is this true?" she asked him. "Is the merger already done?"

Law nodded.

"When were you going to tell me?" Juliana's voice dropped.

"I…well…"

Juliana felt overwhelmed. Law had lied to her—again. Just when she thought she could trust him, just when she thought she could start to depend on him, she discovered another secret he'd been keeping from her. The man was a walking file cabinet full of them.

Juliana swung her bag over her shoulder. He glanced at Omar, who shrugged, just as bewildered as he was. She pushed her way out the door. Law followed, leaving Omar to deal with the questions in the boardroom. He caught up to her at the elevators. "Please, wait."

She felt her throat constrict. She didn't want to do this, not now. She had to go home, pick up the pieces of whatever was left of her career and find a way forward.

Tears streaked her face. "What is it?"

"Just…let's talk about this."

"Talk about what? About how you lied to me again? About how you wasted my time? Why did I even do that report if it had nothing to do with the merger?" She swiped at her eyes. "I've never been so blindsided."

"Juliana, it's not as bad as you think. Trust me, it's not."

"First, you lie to me about being the CEO and then you fail to tell me you already sold the company. Don't you think I would've liked to know that?" She balled her hands into fists at her sides, her nails digging into her palms.

"Yes, but Juliana, I couldn't tell you. Omar needed the secrecy to push the deal through. It's been done for days."

She didn't want to hear it. She moved away from him.

"Juliana...wait..."

"I have to go home and find another job," she said as she walked into the elevator and jammed a button angrily with one finger.

Law shook his head. "No, you don't. If you'll just calm down, I'll explain everything. There's something you don't know." He reached out and caught the elevator.

"I don't want to hear it. I'm going home." The elevator doors slid shut and Law let out a long, frustrated sigh.

The Chicago airport seemed strangely empty as Juliana arrived with her small rolling suitcase and laptop bag. Then again, it was ten at night, so not many people were taking this late a flight back to her hometown. She'd called to change her flight, and she'd gone ahead and put the charge on her corporate card. The thought of lying in her hotel room alone made her feel sick. She just wanted out of Seattle, and away from Law. Hadn't she pushed hard for the whole relationship to be casual? So why did the idea of leaving him hurt so much?

Because I love him.

The unwelcome thought popped into her mind as she watched a janitor push a rolling trash can down the concourse by her gate. That was why it hurt so much. She'd gone and fallen in love with the man. Even though he lied to her. Twice. Her stomach twisted into a knot. Did that make her a masochist?

Boy, she needed a drink. She glanced at her watch, noticing she had forty-five minutes to her flight, the last flight of the day. She felt strangely empty. It was likely that there'd be no job waiting for her when she returned. Not when Garrison reported what he knew. And how did he find out, anyway? She racked her brain, but couldn't figure it out.

She had no idea what she was going to do next. For the woman who planned out every little turn in her career, she felt aimless, afloat. She glanced at the airport bar across the way. She had just under an hour before her flight took off. She needed a glass of wine.

Juliana wandered over to the mostly empty bar and sat at the corner. She ordered a glass of white wine and sipped it slowly. How had everything in her life been turned upside down in a matter of weeks?

Her phone dinged then. A text from Law.

Please, call me.

She stared at her wine, now half-empty.

Gonna get on a flight soon. Can't.

Her heart ached even as she typed those words.

Suddenly, she felt a heavy hand on her shoulder.

"Well, look who it issh," slurred a man as he surprised her from behind. She whirled, nearly toppling her wineglass as she dropped her phone abruptly on the bar.

"Garrison? What the hell are you doing here?"

"Looks like we're on the same flight." He grinned, bleary-eyed, reeking of whiskey. He must've ordered a few of those long before Juliana got here. Where had he been sitting? Some dark corner she'd failed to notice, apparently.

"Please leave me alone. I'll have to call HR and..."

"Go ahead. Who cares? They fired me already."

This came as a shock to Juliana. "When did that happen?"

"This afternoon." He swayed unsteadily on his feet, his bloodshot eyes never leaving her face. "You and those other bitches got me *fired*."

"Others?" There were others? Garrison took a big swig of his drink. Juliana's phone dinged with an incoming message, but she kept her focus on Garrison, worried that if she took her eyes off him he might... what? Try to kiss her again? Despite the fact they were in a public airport bar, she still felt he could be dangerous. And the fact that he no longer had his job to worry about made him seem even more...unhinged.

"You think you were the only piece of ass in the office?" Garrison cackled at his own joke. Juliana wondered who else he'd harassed.

"Garrison, you need to leave." She stared at him, not willing to cede any ground.

"You can't tell me what to do." He grinned, but the smile didn't reach his eyes, which were watery and bloodshot. "Where's your boyfriend? Did I scare him off?" He laughed at his own joke. "My spies at Blue Sky. They told me…things about you two."

"Spies?"

"Sure. I've got them everywhere."

So that was how he knew about their relationship, Juliana thought. She wondered who fed him the information. Law's assistant? Someone else in the office?

"Garrison, this is the last time I'm going to ask nicely for you to go."

Garrison frowned. "Come on, don't be like that. I heard you like it in conference rooms. I heard you… *really* like it in conference rooms."

Juliana felt her face flame red. She remembered the romantic dinner Law had laid out for her in the Blue Sky conference room…and what they did afterward. "I don't know why you wanted to do that with him and not me."

Garrison sounded like a petulant little boy now. How was she supposed to explain the basics of consent to a man foolish enough to think any woman he was attracted to must like him back.

"You need to leave now."

"Why? Come on. I'm going to go back to my

boring wife in a few hours. Let's have a little fun before then."

Juliana got the bartender's attention with a flick of her wrist.

"Excuse me," she said to the bartender as soon as he was in earshot. "This man is bothering me."

The bartender saw him and frowned.

"Hey, buddy, I told you no more," he said. "You're overserved, and we asked you to leave."

"I'm just talking to this pretty lady," he murmured, swaying on his feet.

"I don't want to talk to this man," she said, meeting the bartender's gaze.

Then Garrison grabbed her arm—hard. Before the bartender could act, she cried out and tugged, wrenching it free of his grasp. The momentum sent her backward and she stumbled into someone— broad and tall. Strong hands came around to hold her.

"Are you okay?" came the words slightly tinged with an Australian accent. Law! She craned her neck, unable to believe it. Where had he come from?

"This isn't any of your business," Garrison snapped, and swiped at Law. He sidestepped the drunk man easily, and then he nodded at the bartender. "Sir, please call airport security." He moved Juliana behind him so he'd be between her and the belligerent drunk.

Garrison tried to take a swing at Law, but missed.

"Fighting isn't going to help anyone," Law tried to reason with Garrison, who was beyond all logic. "She doesn't want you, mate. Stop being so pathetic."

"I'll sh-low you pathetic," he slurred and lunged once more, this time, falling on his face. Juliana let out a little shriek as one of his hands reached for her shoe. She jumped back, even as she saw two uniformed Seattle police officers headed toward them. Garrison lumbered to his feet just in time to take one more swipe at Law, in full view of the officers, as Law backed away and the man stumbled forward, nearly losing his balance.

The officers arrived. "That's enough, buddy," one of them said, even as Garrison whirled and managed to land a punch square in the chest of one of the officers. Everyone froze.

"All right, gonna have to take you in," said the second officer, who reached around and easily subdued the angry, but out-of-shape man. The two officers had cuffs on Garrison in seconds. Law moved to put his arm around Juliana, who leaned into his bulky comfort. She wrapped an arm around his back and felt safe. The officers quickly took their statements about what happened, and asked if they'd be willing to press charges.

"Yes, I would," Juliana said without question.

"Me, too," Law added and nodded as he gave the officers his contact information.

After the officers had taken Garrison away, Juliana hugged Law.

"Thank you," she said.

"You're welcome."

She glanced up at him. "Why are you even here?"

"I heard he'd changed his flight to coincide with yours. So I asked for a ticket, and here I am." He held up a ticket from his coat pocket. "I tried to text you— to warn you, but it looks like he got to you first."

Juliana reached for the phone still sitting on the bar. She saw the text she'd failed to finish reading had been a warning: Law trying to tell her to watch out for Garrison, who'd be at the airport.

Looking at his earnest blue eyes, Juliana realized how much Law cared for her. He'd come to the airport to help her. He hadn't wanted her to be alone.

In that instant she realized she'd been a fool for keeping him at arm's length.

"I'm sorry for pressuring you to move in, but I just want you to be happy with your job. I want you to work for a company who truly appreciates you." Law handed her a folded note from his pocket. "Omar wants to hire you. To oversee the transition. This is your offer."

Juliana read the little piece of paper and thought she saw too many zeroes.

"President of operations? This can't be." Juliana blinked fast. "He wants to offer me a job, and not just any job, the *top* job?"

"Omar asked me weeks ago to evaluate you personally, which is why I met you that day in the Chicago airport. I'd been charged to figure out how well you'd fit in to the AM Air culture," he said. "The merger was always a done deal, and your report was simply a formality, but he wanted to see if your reputation was true. If you were as smart as people say."

"Why not just interview me?"

"Omar doesn't do things that way. He's a bit un-conventional. And he trusts me." Law flashed her a grin.

"So you never were trying to pry information out of me?"

Law shook his head. "Nope. I told you it was never about the report."

Could she believe him?

"Why didn't you tell me about the merger being a done deal? Why didn't you let me know?"

"I wanted to, but... Omar thought seeing you present your report would be the best way to convince the board that you were the best person for the job."

"And if I knew it was an interview, I might have done the report differently," she said.

"You might have. Omar wanted the authentic you."

Juliana nodded. She felt tears sting her eyes. He didn't want her to give up her career, after all. He'd been trying to help her advance it. "Law, I love you."

"I love you, too."

Law pulled her into his arms and they kissed, knees touching, at the bar. When he finally broke the kiss she felt light-headed.

"You asked me if I'd quit my career. Live with you." Juliana still felt confusion swirling in her brain. She had really thought Law wanted her to be dependent on him, give up everything for him.

"That was before I realized how much your career meant to you," he said. "I love you for *you*, Juliana. And I'd never stand in the way of your dreams. If you want to work, then work. I think together we can strike a balance, somehow. All I want is some time with you, any way I can get it."

Law wasn't asking her to give up her job. Could she have him and work? Could she learn how to balance it all?

"What if I work all the time? What if you never see me?" She thought of all the other men who couldn't handle that, how she thought Law had been one more in a long line of them.

"I understand what it takes to do a job like this," Law said. "We'll figure it out. We'll work on striking a balance—together."

Juliana nodded, still reeling. Could this truly work? Could they be together?

"Could we really do this?"

Just then the worker at the gate began to call for preboarding of her flight.

"Only if you stop running away from me." Law said.

"You mean, stay?" she asked. She could, she realized. She could stay indefinitely. Why would she even think of going back to Wickham Consulting? Omar's letter had her starting immediately.

"Come back with me, to my house. Stay with me, Juliana. And I don't mean you have to be dependent on me. Pay me rent if you want. If that will make you feel better."

Juliana laughed at that. Maybe she would. "You have to promise me that you'll never lie to me. Not about anything."

Law held up three fingers. "Scout's honor," he promised. "I'm sorry… I kept things from you. I promise, never again. I'd never risk losing you again."

As Juliana stared into his earnest blue eyes, she believed him.

"Can we really work?" she mused aloud, her heart thudding in her chest with excitement at the prospect.

"There's only one way to find out." Law pulled her into his arms and kissed her. She kissed him back, long, sweet and tender.

"Before we go, though, there might be one thing we need to do first."

Law glanced at her, puzzled. "What's that?"

Juliana nodded toward the sign for the first-class lounge about twenty feet away.

Law threw back his head and laughed. "You're incorrigible, Ms. Hart."

"You're not really protesting that hard, Mr. Mason."

She took his hand and pulled him off the bar stool, and he followed her. Yes, she thought, maybe this could work, indeed.

* * * * *

COMING SOON!

We really hope you enjoyed reading this book. If you're looking for more romance, be sure to head to the shops when new books are available on

Thursday 24th January

To see which titles are coming soon, please visit
millsandboon.co.uk/nextmonth

LET'S TALK
Romance

For exclusive extracts, competitions and special offers, find us online:

f facebook.com/millsandboon

🐦 @MillsandBoon

📷 @MillsandBoonUK

Get in touch on 01413 063232